MARK TANNER

Mark Tanner was born in Bristol in 1963. He is a well known concert pianist whose performing and academic career has taken him all over the world. He has a number of CD releases to his credit, achieving high critical acclaim, and has commissioned, premièred, recorded, edited and broadcast works by prominent contemporary composers. He is music critic for the leading music press, having contributed over 100 reviews and articles to *International Record Review, Classical Music, International Piano, Musical Opinion* and *Piano Professional.* He has published scholarly articles in the UK and USA, edited four contemporary works for Edition Peters and Europa Edition, and his new eight–volume series of piano pieces *Eye–Tunes* is published by Spartan Press. His PhD focused on the formidable Hungarian composer Franz Liszt, whose music he has performed in many of the country's top concert venues, including London's Wigmore Hall, Purcell Room at the Royal Festival Hall, St John's Smith Square and many of the UK's foremost universities.

Mark has given close to 300 recitals on cruise liners, has performed in West End shows and backed top cabaret artistes. He is an international examiner for ABRSM and an adjudicator for the British and International Federation of Festivals. For 16 years Mark was Assistant Director of Music at Taunton School, Somerset. Among his more famous keyboard pupils is rock band Coldplay's front man, Chris Martin, who acknowledged him robustly in the Band's latest biography. Mark is a Fellow of the Royal Society of Arts, an Hon. BC and a member of Mensa. He divides his time unevenly between Somerset, Cornwall and the rest of the world. Hobbies have included conjuring, paragliding, microlighting and sleeping. This is his first novel. Much of it was written while imbibing overpriced coffee in the Far–East, New Zealand and USA.

www.marktanner.info

LIFE ON MARS?
A CATINEL'S CHANCE

❖

MARK TANNER

www.llamapress.co.uk

A Llama Press book.
The moral right of Mark Tanner to be identified as the author
of this work has been asserted in accordance with the Copyright,
Designs and Patents Act of 1988.

First published in Great Britain in 2009 by Llama Press,
Waterford, Somerset TA3 5QQ

Copyright © 2009 Mark Tanner

A CIP catalogue record for this book is available
from the British Library.
ISBN (Hardback) 978–0–9560051–0–6
ISBN (Trade Paperback) 978–0–9560051–1–3
Typeset in Garamond and Curlz

Printed in Great Britain & USA and distributed globally
by Lightning Source UK Ltd,
Chapter House, Pitfield, Kiln Farm, Milton Keynes, MK11 3LW.
www.lightningsource.co.uk

Cover designed by Martin Davey
www.martindaveyillustration.co.uk
Author photograph: John Knee

www.llamapress.co.uk

For Gily

Contents

AUTHOR'S NOTE & ACKNOWLEDGENTS

It seems customary for writers to distance their characters from real persons. While I have changed a few names to protect identities I'll not claim that all the characters are figments of my imagination, for this would be nonsensical (besides, anyone able to read a little of him/herself into the script is evidently highly thought of). The completion of this book will come as some surprise to my good friend Carl Bowen, from whom the inspiration for at least one chapter derives more than a little sustenance. Somewhere out there, bobbing about harmlessly, is a canal boat by the name of Wagtail, onboard which Carl and I shared many a candlelit evening together putting the world to rights.

My condolences go to Somerset Microlights (currently the UK's largest microlight school, I'm told) whose misfortune it once was to teach me to fly, not to mention a litany of paragliding schools in Wiltshire, Dorset and Southern Spain, which, despite stalwart efforts, never fully dispelled my fear of heights. My gratitude goes to Gillian Poznansky for her calm forbearance (and wise censorship over matters as abstruse as glucose–sated molluscs and poison–dart frogs), and to illustrator Martin Davey for coming to terms with the bizarreness of his brief so unflinchingly. A sideways acknowledgement goes to Augustus, whose august presence lingers even in his absence. Occasionally, and without a crumb of apology, geographical, entomological, biological and other details have been tinkered with to smooth the progress of my dastardly plot.

The Snail: William Cowper: (1731–1800)

…Thus hermit–like, his life he leads,
Nor partner of his banquet needs,
And if he meets one only feeds
The faster
Who seeks him must be worse than blind,
(He and his house are so combined)
If, finding it, he fails to find
Its master

Prologue

Singapore, January 2009

GIDEON PEE comes round with a jolt, carps two syllables into the fetid haze and strides off purposefully down Serangoon Road, the flamboyance of his trouser–adjustment betraying just a frisson of smugness. The bill he's left poking out from the leather pouch is for only four dollars, but in any case the indolent waiter doesn't notice him slip away. He's cut it fine, again. By 6:00 PM he'll be in make–up, and by 7:00 he'll be in the greenroom batting off a vapid seventeen year–old Entertainment Officer called Kylie, whose IQ barely aspires to the number of glitter–studs circumnavigating her left ear. He's clutching a stack of laminated paper; several others still await his retrieval, for he won't be returning here for some months.

1

LIFE ON MARS? A CATINEL'S CHANCE

He waits a mercifully brief two minutes at Doby Ghaut
MRT Interchange and a couple of stops later alights at
Orchard Road. Better grab a taxi, quick. He's practically
running now, and as he staggers past Istana Park he
speculates how many dilapidated Toyota Crowns will have
heaped up in gameness for the early evening carousers. Six,
he decides confidently. But, at the frenzied intersection with
Buyong Road, there are only two; one's pulling away, its rear
doors still yawning open, an acute psychosis of Cantonese
jangling in its wake.

The other one's got his name on it. First stop, the
shuttle bus shelter on Stamford Road. Thirty seconds later
they're moving again, now in the direction of the Raffles
Hotel, damned with faint praise by the bogus abstinence of
its dappled concourse. Unassumingly he lifts away two A5
fliers from inside a proscenium archway and ducks back
into the car, sweating like a Landrace at the abattoir. He
tucks the first sheet, on which has been inexpertly sketched
a farmer shovelling eight enormous turnips with a black
spade, under the second, with its floribunda of mop–headed
house plants nodding vacuously in a sinuous vase. The air
tastes thick enough to chew, even with two violent air–con
jets aggressing his neck. Next, Clarke Quay's fêted Häagen–
Dazs kiosk is deftly denuded of another laminated sheet –
this one's boldly coloured in stripes of green, white and red
– and finally they target Maritime Square Terminal, the
Crown's rear axle corkscrewing like billy–o to the smell of
balding Michelins. That's the last of his homemade posters
salvaged. He shuffles forward in his seat, juggling the stiff
stack into some kind of order, while a flurry of Monopoly

money spills impishly onto the teal phony–leather seat.
Harassed now, he stuffs the cash into the cheerless
oriental's face and sashays up the aluminium gangway onto
deck four aft, greeted by a glowering boarding–pass
operative named Hero.

He loses no time in plying himself with a double–
shot latte from Tiffany's Café on deck seven and shambles
his way out onto the sundeck, blinking in the new light, the
slow shift of his shoulders suggesting incipient unease. His
favourite chair beckons the last afternoon rays from
between two bulbous lifeboats, which sway almost
imperceptibly overhead in the non–existent breeze,
underscored every eight seconds by a flaccid mezzo–forte
screech from the straining hinges. Four long, parallel strings
of sallow light stretch from nowhere onto the newly
pampered wooden deck. A slender strip of shadow slowly
cuts across them as if bowed by a faltering violinist intent
on mutilating the serenity.

He sips, puffs and reflects. Only just made it. But it
takes imagination to be late; punctuality is a sign of
inadequacy, probably hereditary and definitely incurable.
The coffee is quickly quaffed and he's on the move again.
First, down to his cabin on deck four to don his glad–rags;
next, through the chicaning crew quarters – anything to
avoid wearisome punters bearing down on him with
anecdotes about Houdini. He narrowly avoids collision with
four giggling Indians pushing a trolley laden with choux
pastry and grapes, and finally climbs the corkscrewing
stairwell leading to Stage Right.

LIFE ON MARS? A CATINEL'S CHANCE

The door's locked. Bastards. Why can't those airheads ever remember to leave it open? It's not as if there's anything to pinch, not unless you've a proclivity for wigs or pink feather pompoms. But thirty seconds later he's inside, scouring the stage floor to confirm the placement of four short strips of blue sticky tape that discreetly punctuate an area between Stage Right and Centre Stage. He glances up at the light burning down at him from the gantry and squints, pretending not to notice the artless Jahangir mincing his way down the purple carpeted steps towards him, sipping from a trough of Pepsi he's been carrying around for the past four hours. 'Oh, it's you, Gid', the man whinnies, as if anyone else aboard Ocean City Three could jimmy open the stage door with such alacrity, or would waste valuable grazing–time bothering. 'And who else?' he mutters, barely disguising his disdain while readjusting his cummerbund under the spotlight. He begins strutting about the stage, sphinx–like yet disquietingly despotic in manner. 'Usual routine tonight, is it, sir?' Jahangir fawns, falling into the rôle of Stage Manager now that he's interpreted the slow–burning agitation pumping out from the star act's sweat–pearled brow. 'And what *else*?' comes the barbed response – the simpering sycophant will need tweezers to locate both of his teeth at this rate; he sniffs haughtily and continues with renewed purpose, 'eight of spades, Italian flag...chrysanthemum'. 'Italian, eh?...makes a change from *German*, sir...been busy with the laminating–machine, have we?' dares Jahangir, unadvisedly. 'Don't pull my chain Mustafa, I'm not in the mood'.

PROLOGUE

With a bucket–full of crystal balls Gideon Pee couldn't predict the number of belly–buttons on a barracuda. A tossed coin would be as likely to land on its edge as on the side he'd forecast, and yet the act he was about to perform to a packed ship's theatre, one hundred miles north of the equator on a muggy evening in January, would portend to a great deal more. He glances at his watch. It's time for the predatory Kylie to check the microphone's working back–stage, a task she embroiders for several minutes, each second providing an opportunity to trespass on his personal space with any part of her anatomy that's readily to hand. Checking her lipstick for any hairline fractures that have appeared in the last thirty seconds she click–clacks her way onto the stage and pumps off her usual perfunctory preamble, upwardly inflecting every other syllable so as to render the Medium's entrance colder than yesterday's carrots. But the crowd's half–soaked; they'd applaud a flushing toilet in their condition.

He stands before them now, stern, unsmiling, a powerful presentiment enshrouding the entire space. 'Tell me', he begins, as if seriously anticipating a response, 'has anyone here got a penchant for piffle...or an eye for minutiae?' One of the three people in the house who's lucid enough to guess what minutiae might mean raises his arm, then quickly shrinks back, dipping his head in shame. But the damage is done. Before he knows it, the unwitting volunteer's on stage, seriously under–dressed and defiantly clutching his plastic pint of ship's shandy. 'Doubtless you'll have seen the sights today, sir' he continues, with something close to a smile settling upon his upper lip, '...you look like

5

the *discerning* culture–vulture type, if you don't mind me saying so?' Clearly the man hasn't contemplated the day's lager–laced exploits in so elevated a light, but nods anyway, if only for the benefit of his fatuous wife, Fatima, herself partial to a glass or two of culture.

With the lights unsubtly subdued and grainy spectral music detonating in the background, five monochrome minutes tick by. The audience is numb with alcohol and indifference. On each of the three jumbo–sized sealed envelopes that have been mounted to a silver board since before the curtains parted has been scrawled a large question mark. In order to accomplish his predictions Gideon Pee needs just three corresponding words from the bashful halfwit, but it's like drawing blood from an anaemic whitebait. Success will solely depend on whether his involuntary volunteer, Ferdie, availed himself of the free shuttle–bus tour of the city that day, and hence visited the downtown hotspots at which everyone had been obliged to alight, which included a majestic colonial hotel and an American ice–cream parlour famed for its dulce de leche flavour. But Ferdie possesses the brainpower of an oxygen–starved ferret, and dredging up the eight of spades from his subconscious memory is proving to be something of a challenge. And the trouble with 'chrysanthemum' is that it has a 'y' where Ferdie least expects one, a stumbling–block that's rather sapping the colour from Pee's floral prediction; he kicks himself – he should have saved his four–syllable variant for the more intellectual Cunard crowd next week. As for the colours of the Italian flag, Ferdie's continental knowledge seems to be suffering from continental drift.

PROLOGUE

The audience has coped without food for nearly half an hour now, and the restlessness is becoming unbearable. Finally, three paltry predictions are ministerially prised from their envelopes and revealed to the audience, each one packing about as much punch as his witless helper's conspicuously obtruding lilac boxer shorts. At last, Ferdie is permitted to return to the sanctity of anonymity, and Pee to his.

◉

The shrunken, drunken Medium consoles himself with a fourth copious G&T, a shadow–laden deck seven once again offering him protection from a passing glance; it's turned blustery now, as they sail vigorously into the South China sea, waves lining up to die thirty metres below him. Traces of foundation powder mingle with the sweat from his nose to form tuppenny–sized orange blots on his freshly pressed chinos. Leaning absentmindedly against a newly varnished railing he nurtures a cigarette in his cupped palm and sends the smoke on a frenzied northerly path, watching it liquefy into a cherry pink horizon. He exhales noisily and flicks away the butt, another feeble capsule of self–respect symbolically jettisoned to the sea forever. Two old ladies limp past him now, heads dipped into the mounting turbulence. They don't notice him loosen his tie or turn his head so as not to be recognised.

LIFE ON MARS? A CATINEL'S CHANCE

'Well, I didn't think he was *that* bad, Jan...better than that god–awful singer with the stoop and the lisp.'

'According to Waynetta, our *terribly* sweet little wine waitress, dear, he predicts the same things in *every* show.'

'Mm...it'll be something to do with the power of *suggestion*, Phyllis. Piece of cake really...although, I must admit, *I* was going to say dahlia, too.'

Draping his black sequinned jacket over one shoulder, he ambles off in the opposite direction, inhales violently and bellows into the night 'chrysanthemum!...*chrys–an–the–mum!*' But the two blue–rinses don't hear him.

For a fleeting moment Gideon Pee sees himself as he really is: a legend in his own lunchtime, a laggard in everyone else's.

1

Death and the Midden

...England, late February...

'I've eaten this pizza before, I reckon' Sam reflected.

'It certainly *looks* like you've eaten it before' slobbered Den, his jaws grating coleslaw like an arthritic llama's.

'Did you know that the water in London's been drunk seven times?' quizzed Sam, five minutes later.

'Mm', nodded Den, studying his glass of cloudy lukewarm liquid, 'I dare say the water *here* has been passed by the Management.'

The two men ploughed methodically through their Meatfeast thin–based pizzas, religiously short–circuiting the crusty rim until all that remained on each plate was a ragged pastry halo. The somewhat strained conversation between them had come full circle too, triggered by their voluptuous waitress, Kim, whose jet–black torpedo nipples offered themselves up like spicy beef morsels from above her contrivedly ill–fitting brassiere.

'Extra topping, Den?' proposed Sam, affecting a grin cheesier than a Quattro Formaggio, while rapidly lining up a succession of equally cheesy puns on the tenuous theme of gristly things you can put in your mouth.

Chesterfield's crooked spire bathed self–importantly in its carroty up–lighting like an accidentally dropped monster ice–cream cone.

'Blimey, Kim's beacons are just as impressive as *that*' drooled Den salaciously, gesturing towards the window, dribbling anchovy oil onto his kipper tie.

'Aye, a jumbo topping on our very own Leaning Tower of...Pizza.'

It was a wonder either man could even contemplate eating, let alone joking about it. Their wonky table was cluttered with unwieldy laminated concertinas; Michael Winner would undoubtedly not approve. Each of the three subtly different menus purported to assist the esurient customer by grouping together components drawn from the others. An index, glossary and cross–reference chart would be needed to coordinate effectively the mouth–watering dishes depicted, not that they matched in artistry, volume or freshness the array of barely consumable consumables spilling onto the lurid plastic table cloth.

An equally vivid image rested against the sticky

accoutrements caddy. It was a close–up photograph of a naked human cadaver, although with half closed eyes the scarred and charred effigy better resembled a voodoo doll. Its mouth and eyes were so widely opened that it appeared to be still in the process of experiencing extreme shock, or perhaps of escaping from something even more horrific than itself. But its skin was so severely ravaged that there could be little doubt it was deader than a griddled dodo. Uneven tufts of tarred hair remained randomly dotted about the body, leaving it as alluring as a warthog suffering from alopecia. Curiously, each limb was arranged deliberately, or so it seemed, to leave the impression of a man who had died while running for his life.

'Lightning?' proposed Den thoughtfully, as he picked up the picture to permit a closer evaluation, while discarding his equally unwholesome pizza to an adjacent table. Sam's eyebrows rose in order to convey a five percent acknowledgement of the idea.

'Seriously, I've heard of people getting fried to death by lightning, and I read about a woman who lost all her hair and fingernails, too. This guy's clothes have been completely burnt away from him, poor sod.'

'Well, most of them' corrected Sam, pointing to the remains of a sock.

'Yeah, so what's this Gentleman Jim type doing so far away from his club, sir?' asked the junior officer, now that the conversation had drifted into the realm of work. He hadn't really expected a straight answer.

'The bowler hat's bloody confusing, isn't it?' scowled Sam. If the chap *had* been struck by lightning it

11

surely would have been the first thing to melt.'

'Ah, but that's not necessarily true sir', responded Den, 'you see, it's all about the *angle* of the strike.'

'The angle?'

'Yeah...have you ever wondered why your nose gets more sunburned than your cheeks?...after all, it's only an inch closer to the sun, isn't it!'

'Well, yeah, but the bone...'

'You see', persisted Den, 'that's why the old saying "lightning never strikes twice" is so bizarrely true. Because, in theory at any rate, land masses, convection patterns, prevailing winds and so on would suggest quite common reoccurrences of lightning strikes, if not precisely down to the nearest inch, of course.'

'Oh, well anyway, it would only have to strike him *once*, for heaven sake' grumbled Sam, sensing an encroaching lecture on meteorology based on Den's patchy recollection of a Discovery Channel programme. But in the absence of an alternative theory he may as well show willing.

'Okay, let's ride with this for a minute then. Have we actually had any lightning in the last couple of days...or rather, have *they*, in the Peaks?'

'I'll check it out sir.'

'I wouldn't be surprised, it was blowing a hooly at my place on Wednesday.'

Detective Inspector Sam Toogood had put up with his colleague's interminable pseudo–encyclopaedic expostulations for the past three days, during the series of seminars they'd attended in Chesterfield, some twenty miles north of their stamping ground in Ripley. Evidently, while

DEATH AND THE MIDDEN

Den Chanter's aspirations were pyramid shaped, his knowledge base was a mile wide and an inch deep. But Sam's dutiful DS did have his uses. One particular facet was his hardwired determination to unearth the tiniest details, even if he invariably struggled to see the wood for the trees and was quite capable of stumbling around in the wrong forest. The partnership had hitherto been quite successful in solving local homicides, with four cases in the past eighteen months drawing them into areas of investigative theory neither of them had tackled before. In each case the motive had been pretty unambiguous and the murder paraphernalia had not eluded them for long. Witnesses had been forthcoming and the trials had flowed through the courts like oil. Hence the two policemen, each in their early forties, partly justified their reputation for diligence. But neither one of them had experienced anything as potentially absorbing as this riddle, not that they read it that way, yet. In fact, they'd not actually seen the site in question for themselves, having only received the batch of somewhat indigestible photographs by email attachment an hour earlier. The rudderless squad back home had nevertheless speedily reached an initial prognosis: suicide or accidental death. DI Toogood had seen the sense in ordering a press embargo, just to head off the inevitable barrage of phone calls from tree–hugging crop–circle weirdoes and supernatural freaks claiming the body had been returned by its pointy–eared kidnappers from Saturn.

The following morning Toogood and Chanter headed straight for the scene, bolting bacon–butties as they bunged their bags into the boot. But the hurriedly scrambled investigation team back in Ripley would have to twiddle with their truncheons until later that morning to receive their belated opening brief. Chanter had charged up his digital camera in readiness for a personal survey of the scene, while his weak–kneed theories hobbled happily along the line of lightning bolts and associated phenomena. Toogood, by contrast, chose a contemplative expression during the picturesque drive to Hollinsclough, barely registering Chanter's self–referential hypotheses. By the time they'd reached the scene at mid morning it was raining in sheets. The approach was eased by the on–board GPS, which enabled them to sidestep the roadblocks positioned to deflect nosey locals.

Relieved to have finally arrived, Toogood accepted the cover of an umbrella and squelched his way along the grass verge that had become cluttered with service vehicles of all types. The largest of these held captive a bunch of recalcitrant squaddies who passed the time listening to a furtively relayed football commentary. A small awning had been erected over the entrance to the field, and a substantial marquee sheltered the body. The familiar stripy tape cordoned off the entire vicinity, lending it the appearance of a low–key garden fête. But there would be no Victoria sponge to mop up the tannin–free tea, and Chanter's adolescent scowl aptly summed up the prevailing mood. The two men entered the tent amidst a restrained kerfuffle of grudgingly employed gendarmerie and squeezed their way past three fragile looking tables laden with dog–eared papers. SOCO had yet to complete their initial sweep of the area immediately surrounding the body, and Pathology were keen to move the corpse to a less compromising environment. From somewhere in the swamp a tenor voice sang out to where the two men now stood, loosening their dripping coats.

'Morning, Sam.'

Toogood turned to greet the crouching pint–sized man busily tucking his trouser bottoms into his wellies.

'Cliff, old horse', sniffed Toogood demurely, 'I'd say it's good to see you, but for the fact that you mix with such *dead smelly* people.'

Toogood lowered his comparatively lean physique to take a closer look at the contorted corpse, pinching his nose as he tweaked the corner of the dainty white plastic sheet.

'Abra–*cadaver*–a…as if by magic eh, Cliff?'

'At least I've got an excuse to be knee high in shit, what's yours?' responded Clifford Morrison, Crown Pathologist, forcing down his last mouthful of polystyrene–infused tea. Before he could think of a suitably irreverent repost, Chanter's ridiculous ring tone stuttered loudly from his jacket pocket. The officer turned away, concealing an embarrassed smile and shuffled off amid muffled giggles. Toogood smiled condescendingly.

'Den's four year–old keeps on fiddling with his mobile, and the daft beggar doesn't know how to change it back again!'

No sooner had he finished scoffing, Toogood's own phone began to ring, or rather, bark, to the sound of Ollie, his octogenarian Labrador. The giggling immediately crescendoed to a full–bodied climax of guffaws as the gaggle of shivering foot soldiers thawed in a welcome moment of levity. Toogood and Chanter scuttled towards the exit of the tent, jabbering loudly into their phones, each man with an index finger buried in his redundant ear. The jocular mood accelerated further in their wake.

'Look, Holmes!' mimicked one, pointing an impromptu magnifying glass at a mess of overlapping footprints, 'an impression of a foot!'

'No time for impressions now, Watson' responded another, in his best Basil Rathbone tone.

The two more senior detectives reconvened outside two minutes later, their ears still ringing from an unavoidable dose of domestic trivia.

'I'll be amazed if any decent forensic exists on this minging mess of a man, Chanter' sighed Toogood at last, lighting a cigarette to help obliterate the pungent pong. 'It's caked in all the crap in creation.'

'I've got a few plods checking the possible entry points into the field, sir' chimed Chanter, attempting a note of optimism. 'But, likewise, I'm doubtful we'll have preserved much, even though we're all wearing these poncy shower hats on our feet.'

'The farmyard perfume's a bit ripe out here, isn't it?' Toogood whinged, struggling to reignite his damp cigarette with soggy matches.

'Apparently, it's an ancient shit–heap, sir.'

'A what?'

'Technically, a dung–ditch, pooh–pit or crap–creek, sir.'

'I thought you'd be on hand with your turd–a–

16

saurus, Chanter. I think you'll find the correct term is a *midden* actually.'

'Have you ever pondered on our preoccupation with matters faecal, sir? Shit smells less offensive when you call it defecation, excretion, manure...'

'Your polyphagous appetite for such matters mildly distresses me, Chanter. You're not related to Marcel Duchamp, by any chance? He got bogged down in lavatorial pursuits, too, as I recall.'

Chanter persisted imperviously. 'Apparently, there are several of these mouldy mounds in the adjoining fields, some more exposed than others.'

'Trust us to be wallowing in this muck. Why couldn't the bugger cop it somewhere a bit more hospitable, preferably near to a service station, or a pub' shuddered Toogood, who was beginning to have premonitions of a fortnight dodging downpours and denuding doo–doo from his boots.

Ollie's feeble bark triggered another perfunctory conversation for Toogood, whose ambivalence was rapidly hardening into profound boredom.

'What?...Yes, we'll take a peek then...where are you now?...Okay, see if you can pinch a brolly would you, for it pisseth down here.'

Chanter's puppy–dog eagerness prised a curt response from his boss.

'Canoes and chip papers...now what, for goodness sake!'

They slopped their way through the awful sludge to the landmark described, an exceptionally proud tree, which

17

stood as if with its arms folded among a thicket of scruffier specimens and random bushes. Two beaming constables greeted them, for whom the discovery of the items in question clearly marked a turning point in their investigative careers, or so they hoped.

'What's all this fuss about a couple of canoes then?' Toogood demanded, not faintly interested in the response.

'There's five actually, sir...they've been shoved into the bushes so no one can see them.'

'Mm, I think you're probably confusing me with someone who gives a shit. They'll have been here for several millennia, won't they? What makes you think they're connected to this tawdry business?'

'Ah, we think you might find this *rather* interesting sir...it's a sea–scout's record of achievement...a lad named Thomas McGuire it seems...the booklet lists *every* task he fulfilled, and...'

Toogood interrupted, shaking his extended phalange like a catatonic headmaster.

'Have you honestly dragged us back out into the rain to discuss the dib–dib–dibs of some leprechaun sea–scout, whose tent probably sank three years ago?'

'Um, well, it *is* potentially a lead, sir' protested the less diffident of the two minions, sensing his fast–track promotion disappearing upstream.

'Yeah', parried Chanter intrepidly, '*any* name at this stage gives us a starting point...even if it does turn out to be some lumbering misfit with the brain of an African antelope.'

'That'll be a gnu, Chanter, not a *canoe*' mumbled

Toogood, struggling with his wilting Marlboro.

They turned and moved back slothfully towards the tent, leaving the two demoralised constables to guard their ridiculed specimens.

'Let's just get the low–down from that pillock Morrison and escape from this wretched mud bath, Chanter' muttered Toogood despairingly.

Following a few non–committal exchanges with the fubsy Welshman, they made a dash for Chanter's car and began threading a passage through the mayhem of vehicles that had queued up behind them. Suddenly a man ran headlong into the side of the car and slumped down to the sodden ground, whimpering like a puppy with toothache.

'What the buggery!' began Chanter, but in an instant Toogood was onto his man, whose clothing was now so muddied he didn't immediately resemble a policeman at all. It was PC Dring, the slightly more promising of the two minions who'd unilaterally assumed the rôle of canoe protector.

'Dring', Toogood snarled, 'just what kind of a dog's dinner are you?'

'Not a *dog's* dinner sir' the poor man struggled to explain, 'a fish and chip dinner.'

'Oh yes' frowned Toogood acidly, 'we'd overlooked that crucial bit of evidence, hadn't we – I expect it'll be the dead man's last supper. My guess is he didn't like vinegar but had a weakness for salt. What do you reckon, Chanter?'

Dring sidestepped the barbed sarcasm, blurting earnestly that actually there had been the vaguest whiff of vinegar, but that the rain had spoiled the evidence, ever so slightly.

'If you've ruined what turns out to have been valuable evidence, Dring, you'll have had your chips!' blasted Toogood, snatching the ball of congealed papier-mâché that might once have contained harvestable DNA. He tossed it casually into the quagmire and skidded off, clipping the heels of two constables propping up a Black Morahia, cheerfully picking over the ramifications of the latest Spurs transfer.

'Now now, sir' giggled Chanter, 'loitering with intent is one matter, *littering* within tent's another.'

'Shut it, you batter brain' sighed Toogood, distancing himself from the chaotic scene not a moment too soon.

They drove guardedly, finding themselves swallowed up by a sudden tempest.

'I dare say you've captured in microscopic detail the full tumult of the ridiculous scene, Chanter' huffed Toogood acerbically, quietly hoping his precocious partner had snapped a few useful pictures to augment the largely useless bundle they'd received the previous evening.

'Well, I did manage some sir, but the light was crap and I'm still getting used to this camera' Chanter responded. 'It's got more buttons than a Trident missile' he continued, assiduously browsing the thumbnails on his viewfinder.

'When we get back to the Nick, we'll keep totally open minded...okay? Let the guys come forward with any off–the–wall ideas they feel like dreaming up' said Toogood, confirming his colleague's suspicion that he was completely clueless. 'But, for goodness sake, spare us your heuristic–

algorithmic crap, and lay off that bloody lightning nonsense too, unless you've got something other than last night's Panorama to back it up.'

'We've got the bowler hat, haven't we sir?' Chanter enquired, suddenly inclined to withhold the latest instalment of his much–maligned theory.

'Not bloody likely, Morrison's taken it for swabs...it's probably our only hope of a hatching a *real* clue this side of Easter.'

'Just how long could the body have been there, sir? Did Morrison have any idea?'

'You've gotta be kidding...there's not a whiff of white smoke from him yet, I'm afraid. You know what he's like, he's spent a lifetime sitting on the fence – it's a wonder it hasn't disappeared up his prosaic posterior. I did drag out of him that our man definitely died "at least two days ago" though, and anything up to a week. He'd detected traces of kerosene too, or some such accelerant, which accounts for that awful stink.'

'Mm' nodded Chanter, indicating this meant something to him. 'Do you remember that geezer who set himself ablaze in Trafalgar Square, some years back, sir? The things some folk will do to get on the box, eh' he continued, shaking his head as if his foundationless contempt amounted to something historically pertinent.

'Well, I've got to admit, suicide is definitely the most likely outcome of this case, although, why would somebody go to the trouble of cremating himself in the middle of a remote field, where no one can even see it happen?'

'He'd have to be a member of some obscure sect, or

else a nutter hearing voices in his head. The long fingers of Opus Dei leaving their prints, perhaps, sir?' proposed the junior officer, wide–eyed.

'Steady, Chanter' sighed Toogood, softening a gargoyle expression, 'my catholic taste doesn't stretch quite that far. No, the burning issue here, if you'll pardon the pun, is the inconsistency of it all; the man's ostentatious suicide – or execution – and the ignominy of his discovery. It just doesn't add up.'

Chanter churned over Toogood's words for a moment, leaning forward in the passenger seat while combing his lank hair, unwittingly flicking globules of greasy water in his driver's face.

'Mm' he replied at last, 'to stage this jumbled scene you'd need one crazy, mixed up mind...it's a bit like finding a box of live crickets in an Eskimo's handbag.'

'If I may say so, that's the most random, cock–eyed simile you've come out with so far; congratulations Chanter. Just keep the lid on your bloody crickets 'til you get back to your igloo.'

'Still, sir, looking on the bright side, we've got lots of evidence, even if none of it's connected yet. It's all grist to the mill.'

'I think you'll find my mill has been more than adequately gristed for one day...furthermore, if that prat Dring reckons there's a gramme of significance to those canoes, then I sure as hell don't. I'd sooner settle for your bloody Eskimo's handbag, crickets 'n all.'

On arrival it took some time for Chanter to pull together the motley coterie, whose collective instinct for camouflage had scattered them into far–flung corners of the Station. Eventually the men, a ragbag dozen, distributed themselves chaotically around the briefing room, a cramped, cheerless place that mirrored the uniform expression on their faces. Pinned unevenly to the wall behind him were amateurish blow–ups of images cobbled together from various sources; sadly, Chanter's paltry contributions were not at all out of place. The facts, such as they were, were alarmingly thin on the ground, a point that made itself transparent upon Toogood's briefest of briefs, which, in blatant contempt of four ostentatiously sited smoking ban notices, he issued using just three modest sized lungfuls of smoke–laced air. A dismal silence followed, broken only by a burp and fart issued ambidextrously by a young PC drifting aimlessly past the open door. Even this timely moment of whimsy was not sufficient to raise a smile from the dozy dozen, whose eyes seemed to sag on cue, this being a practiced tactic to avoid being inadvertently commandeered for on–the–scene duties.

'Don't worry' consoled Toogood, immediately sensing the ruse as one who had himself sat in many such meetings, 'none of you will be needed up there, not just yet anyway. We'll take questions now, but to be honest, I'd prefer sensible suggestions.'

A tentative arm or two rose to half–mast, self–preservation impulses not entirely assuaged.

Detective Constable Danny Blunt, 'Razor' to his colleagues, was the first to cut the apathetic silence.

'This case seems too wacko to be a one–off, sir...what's the database flagged up so far?'

LIFE ON MARS? A CATINEL'S CHANCE

Toogood smiled crookedly, a symbol to the troops that Razor had just nicked his own throat.

'You'll be sure to let us know, with knobs on, Razor...at the next meet, please. Bell me straight away if anything juicy comes to light though.'

Another hiatus hung in the air, mingling with the stale fart that had wandered in from the corridor. Finally, in the wake of the ensuing vacuum, Toogood stole himself to permit Chanter an opportunity to strike with his farcical lightning theory. More baffling than the three–minute oration itself was the unquestioning manner with which the team devoured it; half–witted they might be, but they were shrewd enough to spot a cosy place to hide in the bosom of Chanter's spurious 'lead'. Volunteers scrambled to attach themselves to every strained strand of his theory – anything to evade the threat of accountability. 'Bruiser' Brian, so nicknamed following a recent incident with a paintball that had homed in on his penis with atomic precision, signed himself up to the crucial task of discovering the voltage needed to deep–fry a human being. Not wishing to be requisitioned elsewhere, his sidekick, Kevin, developed a sudden interest in statistics, enquiring as to the probability of encountering such an apocryphal apocalypse in the Derbyshire countryside. 'Crimewatch' Chris, fresh from a non–speaking appearance on the said programme, quickly hooked up with 'Green' Graham, whose new fuel–guzzling wagon took up half of the car park. Their testing task was to uncover any publicised feuds between farmers in the vicinity occurring within the past five years.

By the time Toogood had come to his senses, half

of his team had spirited themselves away quicker than new hubcaps on an old BMW. Feeling like a schoolboy footballer forced to captain a team comprised of three girl prefects and a bespectacled viola player, Toogood sighed noisily and swiftly assigned four semi–sensible rôles. 'Tonsils' Tom, whose adenoids had a habit of rattling like a chain–smoking iguana, copped the on–sight duty that Toogood had denied would be needed. 'Maigrait' Meurig, whose best collar to date was a pickpocket who got off on a technicality, would share the honours. They were to collate any forensic and bagged–up items from the scene. 'Pontius' Pete, who reckoned he was a qualified tiger–moth pilot, would work alongside Dave 'Progesterex' Proctor (whose quest for a new girlfriend had reportedly reached fever–pitch) organising interviews with witnesses, assuming they could drum some up. Meanwhile, Chanter and Toogood sloped off to a meeting called by the Chief Superintendent, fully prepared for a grilling the like of which should only be inflicted on a very dead, naked man, preferably in a far off field.

Half an hour later the two detectives were staring vacantly at a computer screen in Toogood's office. Cold, disenchanted, motionless. Following two minutes silence the screen–saver kicked in; a cartoon character of a policeman danced about the screen, doffing its helmet at regular intervals to reveal an oversized testicle grafted to its forehead. A full minute later Chanter posed the obvious question, more out of courtesy than curiosity. Toogood yawned, rubbed his eyes and interrogated his crotch manfully.

LIFE ON MARS? A CATINEL'S CHANCE

'A secret policeman's ball, naturally', he sniffed, leaning back in his swivel chair and yawning extravagantly.

In pokey rooms dotted about the building, inactivity among Toogood's truculent troop proceeded with dynamic zeal. It was a good job that the Station had recently installed the speediest broadband available to the civilised world, as the wires were soon crammed with a zigabyte of spam pertaining to sacrificial Aztec temples and para–maniac ritualists based in Mississippi. The wanton distraction did bear a little fruit, albeit maggot–ridden. Tonsils and Maigrait had unmasked a Mexican beauty–therapist who'd lost her cherry in the middle of a forest fire in Idaho, while Green and Crimewatch had unearthed a death–metal band from the Banana Republic who'd accidentally set their venue alight while performing their fans' favourite number, 'Voodoo Baby, Take Care 'a My Flamin' Coconuts'.

Progress on the witness front was limited to a half–hearted perusal of the electoral register by Progesterex and a discussion between Pontius and a mate from the Force up in Huddersfield about known 'crazy crims'. Any optimism Toogood was allowing himself was about as rational as candyfloss in a dentist's waiting room. For just two serious avenues of investigation were being pursued: Chanter was triple–checking access points to the field, while Razor quickly found himself knee–deep in computer profiles of parish criminals who'd indulged a similar M.O. But within two days the team was in free–fall, chasing up leads mostly flagged up by 'Yahoo', 'Ask Jeeves' and Progesterex's new girlfriend from the dog–sniffer division, Trudy.

2

The Remains of the Day

somewhere deep in the steely heart of Sheffield, but in a place totally bereft of human spirit, a cornucopia of corpses had been regimentally filed inside grey metal cabinets. An archaic charnel house, holding all the aesthetic charm of Guantanamo Bay, stood in grounds reminiscent of a gothic restoration comedy. Sufficient Unipart body bits were present to put together two rugby teams of Frankenstein monsters, and as many arbitrary arteries oozed their puss–like coagulants into cochineal–tainted plastic bags in readiness for a thorough fossicking. Enough toe and fingernails lingered to fashion a healthy crop of artichoke heads, and hair samples had been classified according to their precise tint of auburn, silver, dappled, stippled or piebald. Eyeballs rolled about drunkenly like sets of pocket billiards in thin glass boxes that could equally well have housed petrified butterflies, and teeth – rated, rooted and routed – chattered together in the inhospitable climate of a dedicated fridge, marked "Incisors With Occlusal Matches Only". Ironically, many of the freshly packaged cadavers were about to undergo a more thorough examination than they had ever been subjected to as living organisms.

Among the pitiful specimens of humanity queuing for the scalpel, hacksaw and forceps lay one Spencer James Day. His name had yet to be ascertained however and so, for the time being, he would be referred to by the label stapled to his left foot: Case 491. Spencer Day's father had never known him, and his mother sure as hell wouldn't know him now, for the task of dismembering the extremities for the post–mortem had already been set in motion – a litany of unspeakably merciless events were etched upon the pathetic soul's remains. Dr Cliff Morrison stood silently, rubber gloves taut like miniature condoms over his podgy fingers, psychologically and emotionally primed to probe areas of Day's anatomy even his nanny would have thought twice about. All in the name of science.

Detective Inspector Toogood listened to the ensuing Coroner's Office Report over the phone with considerably less appetite than Morrison had rallied in compiling it. He might have found a better moment to embark upon his Ginsters pork pie than the one Morrison chose to catalogue the physical trauma inflicted upon the upper torso. In total, a cocktail of four inflammable agents had been scraped and sucked from the body, among them a common domestic fire accelerant and more copious traces of two–star petrol mixed with engine oil. Despite appearances, burning had been quite superficial, the body coming into contact with barely sufficient heat to sauté an adolescent sardine. For anyone capable of garnering more than two grey cells the object of focus ought to have been the deliberate obscuration of the body's identity, not the pernicious infliction of pain upon the man while he was still alive. And yet such a conclusion would drive a coach and horses through DS Chanter's admirably improbable theory of chance lightning strikes, and make less sense still of Bruiser's and Kevin's latest impassioned hypothesis, which consisted of a suicide bequest to the pagan god, Bradthackerray.

'Murder most foul…you should smell it' gloated Morrison, palpably drooling onto his mouthpiece; his own powers of nasal detection had become inured to an acme of clinical dependability, enabling the dispatch of his own lunch, an elegant charcuterie, with comparative relish.

'Take your pick from three possible M.O.s, in my opinion, the most probable being asphyxiation and subsequent heart failure. 491 was healthy enough, until that is, someone strangled him and tried to set him alight, making a bigger balls of it than Akela at the scout barby. Aged in his late thirties or forty, I'd say, an evenly toned eleven stones in weight, five foot ten. Tattoos aplenty – I'm having them flensed and enlarged for you from patches of undamaged epidermis. You'll like them – mostly lurid snakeheads and big–titted mermaids, by the look of it. Hair, well, not much intact except on his love–machine, which itself is only *partly* intact.'

29

'Really?' butted in Toogood, jubilant at the prospect of some perverse sexual axis on which to get the case turning.

'No no, nothing of that sort, more a case of compacted undercarriage, so to speak. The body's been knocked about something chronic, not to mention cauterisation of the left index finger. It's as though the dead guy's been mauled into a hundred yoga positions on a pin board doused in ignited fuel. And then dropped.'

'*Dropped?*'

'Dropped. The absence of muscular swelling, phlebitis, hypostasis, bruising and so forth confirms all this organised anarchy took place *post mortem*.' Morrison stifled a chuckle. 'I reckon he was catapulted from one of those medieval what–do–you–call–its...a *trebuchet*...like a human fireball...He certainly landed squarely on his back, and rolled for sufficient distance to leave body secretions of all types over quite a large area of turf.'

'Are you being serious, Cliff?' asked Toogood, whose aorta had begun shuddering at the very thought of Chanter's lightning theory back on the blackboard.

'No, not really, you silly arse. I'll let you manufacture your own ridiculous scenarios. And I'm sure Chanter will rise to the challenge with his customary sophistication.'

THE REMAINS OF THE DAY

Early that evening Chanter shared a cramped bath with his wife, Tammy. The hot tap dribbled boiling water at a rate that was just tolerable for his left buttock; as usual, he'd copped the dreaded tap end. He stared at the ceiling, which periodically launched tiny condensed water droplets at the same spot on his forehead, an oddly soothing form of torture. Gently gyrating the water with one hand, he occasionally reached out with the other in order to swipe at an overweight kamikaze fly that seemed to be enjoying the tussle in the steam cloud. At the third attempt to bring it to its knees he broke the twenty–minute silence.

'Ponder this, Tam. A man fuelled by a single square of chocolate can walk more than a mile uphill with a heavy backpack. Quite impressive. But a fly...a *fly* can circumnavigate its way around a bathroom at four kilometres per hour, which roughly equates to flying two hundred and eighty times its length in an hour – and all on a molecule of cat shit it ingested yesterday while in search of something more substantial, like a poorly disposed of nappy.'

'You're rambling again, Den' responded Tammy, wearing no expression as she stared at the same bit of ceiling, completely immune to her husband's distressing outpourings.

'How's your deep–fried alien coming on then...did the case conference raise anything interesting?'

Chanter recounted the events of two days earlier, in which Toogood had reluctantly allowed him the floor – though time enough to convince the troops that his lightning theory *did* have legs.

'The pathologist's done his stuff, at last. Apparently, according to Sam, he mentioned the possibility of a freak fireball...which, of course, is merely a gnat's foreskin away from my *own* theory. You wait, I'll show Toogood who's got the bright ideas around here.'

'I'm sure you will, love' Tammy responded with a plaintive sigh, quietly confident he wouldn't.

'The boys are coming up trumps with leads now, too. Some are a bit off the wall, if you ask me, but Green and Progesterex seem to have the right idea.'

Chanter stood at the sink, wiping the mirror and pushing gel into his full complement of hair.

'I just can't help wondering why no one in Derbyshire's reported a missing person that fits our man's description – he must be *someone's* husband, brother or son?'

'And the poor bastard presumably had a name?' mumbled Tammy, suddenly engulfed in a savannah of steam.

'Well, bastards don't *have* a name, do they?'

A loaded sponge duly exploded on the back of his head, by way of reprimand for the glib comment. The pink pair dripped their way inelegantly into the bedroom, and Tammy switched on the light using an elbow. In due course the fly bumbled its way in, now strategically equipped for round two, and settled itself just out of arm's reach. A further twenty minutes limped by without comment, as Tammy irretrievably trashed her sudoku puzzle and Chanter threw missiles of increasing aggression at the belligerent insect.

'What's the average lifespan of a fly, anyway?'

queried Tammy.

     'Around fourteen days, I think.'
     'Commonly known as a fortnight then, Den.'
     'Yes, but the fly doesn't *know* that, does it?'
     'Why is it significant whether the *fly* knows it?'
     'So it knows when to *die*, stupid!'

     A little later that same evening a phone call from an ebullient Crimewatch disrupted Toogood's third futile attempt at an early night, brought on by a lingering lergie. He wasn't best pleased.

     'Sir, a trace of white smoke, at last…we have a name for our victim, or at least, for someone very closely related to him.'

     'Stop talking in riddles, man. Do you have *any* idea what time it is, by the way!...Have we a name, or not?'

     'Um, it's eight twenty–five, sir. Well, you see, the DNA profile of our man, which Morrison centrifuged twice, just to be sure, matches not one, but *two* individuals on the database's mug shot gallery.'

     'Oh, which will kill me first, I wonder' Toogood spluttered, 'the suspense, or this Swine bloody Flu?'

     'The thing is, we can't be absolutely certain which of the two possibilities to chase up, sir: a Charles David Pincombe, aged forty–nine, living in Scarborough, whose qualifications are ABH, GBH; and a Spencer James Day, aged forty–one, from Derby – robbery, fencing stolen goods, threatening behaviour and three counts of GBH worthy of honours status. Both men are handy with shooters and have holidayed more than once at Pentonville.

'Impossible. Morrison's a tit–head. DNA isn't a bloody shoe size that fits a dozen desirous Cinderellas, it's *unique*, that's the whole ruddy point of it.'

'Actually, the two men are brothers, but one changed his surname by deed poll when he moved to Scarborough. Probably wanted to make a fresh start.'

'Now he tells me! So, which one's Morrison's slag on the slab? Only one of them can have gone AWOL, surely?'

'Um, well, funnily enough, they've *both* disappeared, sir.'

'God help me, Crimewatch, perhaps his old man's missing, while we're about it, and maybe there's a hoard of criminally active nephews we could track down, too?'

'The other thing sir, is that Morrison's got shots of the tattoos on their way to us for tomorrow – and, yes sir, I did check the database: both men have a *similar* crop. He's swabbed the bowler hat too, but to use his words sir, "it's just a crock of crap".'

'You can tell the man's educated, can't you?'

'He's sending you a fax about the juicier stuff…wouldn't tell me what it was.'

THE REMAINS OF THE DAY

The second case conference, which took place the following morning, had possibly even less substance to it than the first. It took as its starting point the frustrating new 'juicy' pathology produced by Dr Morrison.

'When is a Day *not* a Day?' Toogood began melodramatically, brandishing a stilton sandwich as if about to propose an alternative method of measuring time, using the degradation of milk as a unit.

'When it's a *night*, sir?' came the inevitable response.

'When it's a *Pincombe*, Bruiser. We wanted a name; well, now we've got *two*. Problem is, Charles Pincombe and Spencer Day are, or have been, literally brothers in arms. They're both missing, not that either had been reported as such, and both are about as popular as perforated piles on a jockey's rectum. Being brothers, their DNA is, of course, virtually identical, so we've no choice but to look into each man's recent history with equal fervour.'

Chanter picked up the reins.

'We're re–assigning you all, as from today; two groups, one for each of our suspected, er, victims. Well, *one* of them is dead, anyway; the other's possibly in danger of ending up the same way.'

Toogood resumed.

'So, we'll be hearing no more off–piste knobishness about thunderbolts, pagan sacrifices or heavy–metal rock groups from Idaho, thank you, Green. The time's come for you all to acquaint yourselves with the tricky concept of joined–up thinking.'

Ostentatious sniggering and paper crumpling confirmed the quality of the research managed thus far by Tonsils and Razor.

'You've got all the details we know for certain in your folders, but I'll draw your attention to two particular pieces of forensic that ought to shape our next move. The first is the victim's left eye, which, apart from its pronounced astigmatism, experienced an odd occurrence around the time of death. The autopsy uncovered a jumping parasitic bug, called a Siphonaptera, that seems to have buried its way under the eyelid at a time soon after our man's death; it was still alive, drawing sustenance from ocular residue. Maggots didn't get a look in. The odd thing is, this tiny flat creature isn't normally a dweller in the area in which the body was discovered – it tends to prefer furred or feathered creatures. Any port in a storm, eh? The point is, the body *may* have been shifted from the site of the killing. The second detail concerns a missing finger – it appears someone's been doling out the pilliwinks on our victim – it had been ripped clean off; however, Pathology took scrapings from his fingernails and interdigital flesh. Inconveniently, and probably deliberately, fingerprint analysis itself will be virtually impossible, given the surface burns our man sustained.'

For a solitary, sobering moment, an expression of interest passed across the faces of the dissolute bunch.

'So, the scrapings, sir?' prompted Green.

'Yes, aside from the seven shades of shite living

under them, were some minute particles of dead skin, resembling dandruff.'

'Well, we knew he was pretty flaky, didn't we sir?' quipped Kevin, unwisely.

'Kevin, your first job will be to chase up Morrison for the DNA on the dead skin, to see if he's matched it to someone other than the victim himself yet', said Chanter, in a tone akin to a French teacher dispensing lines to a mulish schoolboy. 'We'll soon see whether he picks his nose or his arse for a pastime.'

'The most likely killer of a hard–nosed criminal, is another criminal whose hard nose has been put out of joint' Toogood went on. 'The fact that the disappearance of the brothers wasn't reported to us is hardly surprising, whatever the underlying reasons.'

'And so we're working on the basis of a reprisal killing, or killings' competed Chanter. 'Each of these men has more enemies than friends, fewer justifications for living than dying. We want all the background we can drag up folks, so show some front, but watch your backs when dealing with the pond life you'll be dredging up.'

'Yes, *thank you*, Chanter' sighed Toogood, unwilling to endorse his colleague's latest pack of hybrid metaphors. 'Let's make this a no–stop cliché shop, shall we? Get cracking fellas. The Chief Super's silver wedding's next Friday. Let's make his *Day*.'

3

Flights of Fancy

◎

...Seven months earlier...

The only item Felix Abercrombie inherited from his gnarled old grandfather was his gnarled old pipe. He'd grown up around its antique woody aroma, its irresistible contours, even its taste – 'go on then, just one puff, lad'. Although he simply had to have it he wasn't really sure what he should do with it. At first it reposed in an ashtray stuffed with blue–tack, joss sticks protruding like oversized woodlice antennae. But then, one night, Felix's self–induced state of nirvana became shattered when he realised he had made a terrible miscalculation. No tobacco. Panic–stricken he ferreted around, investigating all murky crevices, managing eventually to assemble barely sufficient shag for a fag. But repeated attempts to roll the disembowelled butts into a discernible shape proved unfruitful. It then occurred to him that he could smoke the pathetic heap in granddad's pipe, just the once, for old time's sake. He was amazed at how readily the yellow–pitted mouthpiece fitted his own maloccluded dentition. A genetic throwback, almost certainly. It ignited volcanically but soon calmed to permit a strangely comforting, acrid tasting smoke. The room was instantaneously enshrouded in a blue opaque cloud, which, hanging like a century–old cobweb, seemed to form a vaporous impression of his curmudgeonly granddad – 'aye, just one puff lad' whispered the torpid apparition. Felix indulged himself with a supercilious grin and replied good–humouredly 'good on ya, granddad.' From then on the decrepit puffer featured ever more frequently, not just in times of dire need for weed. His comforting phantasm rematerialized each time he smoked, and sporadic flirtations with mildly illicit herbal substances seemed even more conducive to bouts of hallucinogenic reverie.

It was in such a trance–like state that he'd begun to experience surreal floating sensations, transported on random journeys to places he incompletely recognised, as if watching a homemade aerial video from behind frosted glass. The colours were vivid enough though, the luscious topography resembling the garish Battenberg bedspread his mithering mother had foisted on him. Even these momentary sojourns were a welcome distraction from his unremitting mental pandemonium. One grey afternoon, stressing over some valueless spreadsheet at the office, he allowed himself a brief excursion to his fantasyland, at once gliding timelessly under his own steam. How emancipating it would be, he mused, hand on pipe, to ride real clouds, to sense the crisp air gouge into his smoggy lungs and cleanse his jaundiced eyes. There must be more to life than this self–perpetuating cycle of daily tension and nocturnal release – why not make the dream real? He would have to look into this, right away. Tapping the word 'flying' into the Google search engine triggered an embarrassment of riches, some 7,756 possibilities, in fact. At random he clicked on half a dozen and printed them off for thorough scrutiny later, perhaps over a smoke. A wave of optimism rippled over him. Flying might not be just a pipedream after all.

Now ensconced in his oblong home, a less than sturdy iron–hulled, wood–clad narrow boat called Wagtail, with his perforated socks steaming reassuringly on the warming stove, he carved himself a munificent slab of chocolate cake, shook some egg–flip in the direction of a mug and procured a tiny tinfoil–wrapped capsule from his trouser pocket. At first, the computer–generated blurb seemed rather unpromising: small businesses trying to sell expensive flying suits, bargain–bucket flights to Ibiza and diaries of base–jumping freaks – there was even a queue for the first hypothetical passenger trip to the moon. But then an entry under www.ParaglidingUKderbyshire.com caught his eye. It read: 'If you enrol on a course with us, your childhood dreams of walking on thin air and soaring like a bald eagle are set to become a reality'. An image of a man dangling flaccidly from an enormous banana–shaped parachute wing, wearing what appeared to be an extraterrestrial crash helmet and clumpy ski boots, was certainly eye–catching. Especially so, given that the pilot of this unlikely craft had allowed himself to drift in the general direction of the open sea, with serrated cliff tops grimacing menacingly like condemned teeth behind him. He read on: 'Following the upsurge in foot–launched flying activities post 1980, the spectacular mode of getting airborne known as paragliding has mushroomed, harnessing just the sun and wind to enable pilots flights of several hundred kilometres'.

Felix honoured his promise to himself. Booked into a B&B for a week near to the Paragliding School at Eyam, his spirit was in the clouds already. 'Just bring sturdy ankle boots and gloves, a pair of old jeans, a bottle of water and money for the pub lunches' said the instructor, in a comfortingly practiced way. He could manage that. Amazon nonchalantly furnished him with a copy of 'Flirting with Cloudbase', a sort of paraglider's Hagiographa, bursting at the seams with dos 'n don'ts, sketches of paraphernalia, takeoff and landing techniques, air law, meteorology, navigation etc. He was astonished at how byzantine it all seemed: ominous looking written exams and log books to be completed, detailed descriptions of how to prepare pilot and wing for flight, even cross–country manoeuvres. How can it be, he pondered quixotically, that Man needs so much assistance to accomplish what a butterfly fresh from its chrysalis can master in seconds?

Felix got down to the task with the naïve enthusiasm of a teenager with a willy–shaped kite. Perhaps he could steal a march on all the other pretenders at the first group lesson? What he needed was a wing of his own, just to be getting on with, so he could practise in private, somewhere nearby. Back surfing the Internet he soon found a likely contender that suited his pocket on eBay. It was quickly a done deal, with only a couple of days to wait before winning the bid, a snip at £400. Within a week he was the somewhat befuddled owner of what appeared to be a hiker's rucksack containing a compacted king–sized duvet, bound up with a giant bobbin of twine. He daren't open it indoors in case it erupted like roes from a rotting codfish. Perhaps his first jaunt should be somewhere flat and isolated, he conceded, convinced he was sufficiently appraised with the introductory chapter outlining the black art of 'ground–handling'. He now felt ready to demonstrate to all neophyte butterflies how it should be done.

Already sweating liberally, he emerged from Wagtail on a settled Saturday afternoon carrying his pregnantly bulbous backpack, donning tight–fitting denims, scruffy training shoes and his tweed cap. Bent over double with pipe jutting out and walking with an exaggerated gate, he looked like a cross between Max Wall, Max Headroom and Max Boyce. For half an hour he lacerated himself on barbed–wire fences, negotiated streams and placated randy bulls. All in the name of ground–handling – a compulsory yet baffling pre–flight tussle with the equipment, he'd deduced. At last he felt he'd found just the spot. A gentle breeze cooled the beads of perspiration and here the cowpats, darting dragonflies and gorse bushes were marginally less distracting. Time for a short puff, he proposed, just to line the lungs and sharpen the intellect for the coming drama. His book took three pages to describe the correct procedure for unpacking the wing and checking it over. This he had resolved to carry out faithfully, but he rapidly lost interest in peering inside every wing cell and chasing each corded riser from harness to canopy. Splayed open on the potholed, faeces–infested patch of goat–nibbled scrubland the naked contraption resembled a dissected pterodactyl with its entrails unceremoniously bared. 'How the hell does *this* become *that*?' he puzzled, eyes flitting incredulously between the illustration and his defiled specimen. Not one of the colour–coded risers was completely free of entanglement from its neighbours. And the gentle breeze was still mischievous enough to frustrate his attempts to construct an evenly inflated wing on the ground in front of him, what the book optimistically called a 'wall'. The bloody thing had a mind of its own, and at each attempt to hoist it up there barely seemed time to reach out and adjust any escaping risers. And there was still the daunting business of the harness to contend with.

The multi–strapped, saddle–like contrivance resembled a gargantuan chastity belt. The illustration was quite clearly cockeyed Felix determined after ten minutes of wrestling with it; Houdini couldn't get this sorted – even if he *could* dislocate his genitalia at the drop of a hat. Resting for a while, with sweat gushing freely from his brow to the pipe he was attempting to light, he plunked himself down by a crop of rabbit droppings and extruded a little 'extra' something into the pipe, for good measure. It wasn't actually clear which of the harness orifices were for legs, and which were for arms – either way it was damned tight and about as comfortable as Emory cloth underpants. The

44

smell from the smouldering tobacco was atrocious, and for the first time Felix began to sense his aspirations to fly slip molecularly away from him. He winced at a few gobbets of blood forming at his fingertips, the result of gripping the risers too tightly as they jerked and snatched violently from him in the fitful breeze. If only the scheming thing was a little smaller and more manageable. At the second attempt progress was marginally better, and he'd begun to detect a pattern to the harness design. It still wasn't quite right, he knew that, but at least the risers were free and the wind was now blowing directly over his shoulder, as the manual had directed.

The next stage was to get the whole shooting match flying overhead like a kite, using the so–called 'brakes' in each hand to make fine adjustments to the inflation of the wing. Keeping control of it all was how he imagined a dwarf might feel, taking a Great Dane for a walk in a cyclone. Unfortunately, Felix's second wind didn't prepare him for a sudden gust from behind. In a nanosecond he was flying headlong, arse over elbow, wrapping the spaghetti–like mass around his entire body with death–defying athleticism that Nijinsky couldn't have choreographed. In the panic his pipe, clamped between his jaws, shot free of him, and as he followed its path a loathsome megalith met his forehead square on. Unconscious, there he lay for several minutes, trussed up in his straightjacket like some jinxed bondage fetishist.

Felix came to, greeted by the noxious halitosis of a dozen dishevelled, excrement–encrusted sheep. One of them had taken a fancy to his cap; all supplementary sources of roughage were a welcome variation on the monotonous grass theme, even if the wine coloured plaid stitch–work seemed to have a hypnotic effect on the pitiable beast. In trying to shake off some loose beading that was proving too tough to grind down, it inadvertently found itself modelling the ridiculous thing. Ironically, the ruminant's innate dress sense seemed rather more compelling than Felix's, and yet the cap's nauseating bouquet of sweat and cannabis was evidently more than the disgruntled beast could cope with, however profound the fashion statement. Off it scampered in a state of incalculable embarrassment, emitting staccato squeals as if suffering from some weird strain of Tourette's syndrome and trampling sure–footedly on Felix's testicles in its desire to be distanced from the nightmarish scene. Suffering acutely from the trauma of his bestial encounter and an unnerving formication of the face, Felix was equally keen to escape. He managed to drag himself to his feet, still bound up in his colourful tourniquet of cords, and caught sight of his parachute's shadow, now billowing above him with all the enthusiasm of a drained scrotum. An apt epithet for the whole saga, he sighed to himself, searching earnestly among the clusters of gorse bushes and turds for his precious pipe. At last he traced it, still lit, to a heaving pile of cow shit, the tumbling embers causing minuscule bubbles of sickening gas to form a rising yellow haze. Needing immediate relief from his graceless gymnastics, he wiped off the moistest excreta and drew on his pipe exaggeratedly. After two lung–rattling puffs he felt an uncontrollable mass of vomit surge from his gut, the vestiges of decaying defecation challenging even his iron stomach.

Felix's homeward trek would prove a painfully protracted episode. Manhandling his impromptu aviation equipment through rugged pastures was, he now realised, possibly the nearest he'd ever come to a cross–country flight. His flock of shambolic sheep had warmed to his fusty aroma and no longer questioned the fleshy viscera of fabric flapping anarchically behind him as he lurched along behind them. Having reclaimed his tattered cap from its unwitting bearer he started to retrace his steps home, which turned out to be a good deal harder than finding the site had been in the first place. But his docile companions appeared to know where they were going and Felix accepted the mimesis of sheep and shepherd without question. Even the herd of desultory cows that had seemed so rapt by his presence earlier had lost interest. His shredded jeans and grandiflora of bruises were to be uncomfortable souvenirs of his debacle for days after, and even Icarus would have questioned another attempt at flying with his dismal looking wing. Packing it away was effected with customary ineptitude, the harness now revealing more bald patches than one of his periodic attempts at growing a beard.

Spurred on by groundless pride and criminally deficient judgment, Felix successfully rationalised his abomination of an inaugural flight. Whereas any normal being would have done some post–catastrophe soul–searching, Felix filliped his insecurities by blaming his shoddy equipment for letting him down and the inquisitive sheep for distracting him at the crucial moment. His bird–like mother, a seasoned expert at ameliorating her son's fragile ego, ventured clipped words of support as he regaled his lamentable tale. She'd been drafted in to perform emergency surgery on the gaping wounds in his flying machine, making enterprising use of his primary school brown corduroy trousers and a chiffon scarf she'd brought home from a recent rampage through Sri Lanka with her moribund companion, Pat.

A few days later, while hurtling through Coventry city centre in routine pursuit of a recalcitrant teenager gone AWOL, it occurred to Felix he should have another go with his chequered flying–machine. The short period of enforced calm had healed over his memory of Saturday's travesty, if not the scabs building on his knees and elbows. Where alarm bells might have clanged in any sensible head, in Felix's a romantic film score accompanied images of an epic flight, soaring wing to wing with ospreys, their feet tickled by imperturbable clouds hewn from cotton wool.

Driving randomly around country lanes close to where Wagtail was moored he noted the position of a likely nursery slope and a rather more severe lime rock ridge adjacent to it, a velvety verdigris valley chiselled in between. Curiously, rather more space in his book had been given over to the mind–draining business of ground–handling than to the pithy stuff of takeoff and landing. But he didn't investigate too thoroughly, just in case he discovered a more detailed exposition. He paraphrased the page in his notes: one, commit yourself on takeoff; two, takeoff and landing must be into wind; three, allow plenty of overshoot for landing, free of obstacles, roads and overhead hazards.

Later that night, more than a little pummelled by cheap Chardonnay, he internally rehearsed his sweep across the valley, finessing his way over the curvaceous virescent tapestry smiling beneath him. He waved suavely at the sheep as they admired his butterfly–like descent, his feet barely dusting off the grassy dew. In his mind he performed the entire manoeuvre obsessively, each time building in some expressive nuance, some subtle stylistic variant.

Felix could hardly contain himself that afternoon at Hope House, the inaptly named HQ where he barely functioned as Assistant Coordinator of the Youth Service. But, at last, there he was, poised and erect overlooking his valley, vertiginous and amazed at how accurate his dream–like surveillance of the place had been. He seemed to know every scrub of grass, recognise each panicle of buttercups intimately, and could read the lie of the land as keenly as Tiger Woods on the eighteenth green at Glenneagles.

It was a deliciously temperate July evening, and the fragrant land offered itself up to him submissively. Even the fog of dissolute midges thickening by his nose seemed a charming reminder of omnipotent nature. An extra long draw on his pipe, primed with black Lebanese resin, was just the aperitif his inspiration craved. He recalled the manual's effusive description of the 'magic air' that sits over a hill early on a summer's evening, once all thermal activity has desisted. A breeze, barely a kitten's–breath, trickled up the valley in an attempt to soften his austere demeanour, his eyes closed in affectation of the virtuoso performance he was about to give. Patiently he waited for the optimum moment, a speckled cirrocumulus ambling above, noting the developing cycle of hesitant gusts – long, long, short, long, very long. At the start of the next cycle his lungs began to fill, oxygenating the few receptive cells of his drugged brain: short, long, very long...and in an act of supreme poetic narcosis he was volant, his dismal future delegated to little more than a silk handkerchief.

Felix's eyes didn't open straight away, he simply wanted to savour the feeling of euphoric release a moment longer. When at last he did open them, his dream of flying was realised in a single orgasmic blast. A deferential applause rippled from the balletic butterflies sharing his airspace, and only now did he allow himself to evacuate his aching lungs. But they were just as quickly replete, his freshly accessed adrenaline jolting him back to reality. 'Maintain height and course' a voice of calm cautioned from somewhere; he felt a welcome resistance at his fingertips as the brakes responded to his call to attention. He was climbing now, the massively arching shadow below him pulling back and thinning in the dusky breeze. He gradually extended his left leg and crossed it over his right, shifting his weight seamlessly to initiate the gentlest of turns, the new air whistling a hauntingly mellifluous melody across his frail flying machine. He glanced behind him just in time to watch his Landrover disappear from view.

Mild confusion drifted into Felix's consciousness. He should have been following a straightforward top–to–bottom trajectory, a total flying distance of perhaps three hundred meters. But he'd evidently left behind the valley's soft underbelly and was gliding lugubriously east. He was significantly higher than his launch pad now, and a petulant breeze was starting to tease the left tip of his wing in a most peculiar fashion. His shadow had broadened distortedly, like an unruly cat plucked backwards by a giant hand. The vaguest memory of a paragraph in his book headed 'Going over the Back' formed, and from it pounded an ugly ostinato: 'let it never, *never* happen'. He'd overshot the lee of the valley and only partly understood his peril. Before he could act he suddenly found a new reason to be fearful – for the exposed ridge he had dismissed as too adventurous the previous day was now directly beside and below him, just a couple of hundred feet away. To make matters worse, the semi–collapsed wing had assumed an erratic flight path of its own choosing. He seemed to be descending into a vortex now, a sharper wind stabbing at his half closed eyes and screaming an altogether more sinister strain. He wanted it all to end, but at the same time couldn't bring himself to imagine how it might. He plummeted toward the broadening brocade at an exponential rate, and as his fissiparous survival instincts jostled for position he found himself becoming sucked violently into the clutches of a conspicuously opulent oak tree.

51

LIFE ON MARS? A CATINEL'S CHANCE

Felix's near textbook entry left him dazed, scarred skinless and scared shitless, but alive, and more alert than he'd been at takeoff. His wing had mummified him prior to the crash and had absorbed a fair amount of the impact. Here he laid, prostrate, legs akimbo and more bruised than a barrel full of ripe pears, trying to muster the breath to scream obscenities. Two hours passed and he was now beginning to appreciate the true immanence of his camouflaged tree house. Light was fading fast and the wing in which he was wrapped was beginning to stink of the urine that had been semi–catheterised from him on impact. He spotted the tiny sliver of corduroy that had been fastidiously infibulated into the cloth by his mother, instantly recalling the occasions he'd peed himself as a nervous child at school, wearing the very same shorts. His life had taken him full circle, he philosophised, before sliding into a welcome oblivion.

What broke his coma must have sounded to him like an approaching fire engine. He stared all around him, desperate now for relief from his leafy incarceration. But there was no one to be seen, just a retinue of faintly familiar illuminated sheep, conducting their tireless and silent vigil directly under his sequestered tree. Then he twigged – it was his mobile phone, singing its plaintive melody directly into his tinnitused ear. Fumbling with his one free hand, he prodded the green button, immediately recognising his brother's lairy voice.

'Hi Clay', he moaned, shocked at how strangulated his own voice now sounded.

'Where the hell are you, you half–witted twat?' Clay bawled. 'Let me guess, you're going to say that you've been abducted by fleecy white aliens in deepest Tanzania, and then fell up a tree face–first when trying to escape?'

'Um, sort of' Felix croaked.

'Charming…we're supposed to be going for a curry tonight, remember?'

'Oh yeah.'

'So, you'll be expecting to be cut free from your cocoon, I presume?'

'Um, yeah, please' Felix began to giggle, slightly high still from the Lebanese resin and his narrow escape from the aliens. The last seconds of life had ebbed away from his phone battery during their one–sided, rather inconsequential discussion. There he waited, ensnared in a god–forsaken tree, soaked in his own piss. An eternity had passed before Felix, slowly drifting from numb slumber into abject pain, thought he heard a car screeching around on the gravely area high above the sharp scree slope. Yes, it was Clay, he recognised the blaring Adiemus CD and the dull swipe of the door shutting.

But Felix's enfeebled voice could not carry the distance, his despair heightened at the thought of delaying an imminent rescue. He panicked. 'A smoke signal!…that'll do it.' Managing to retrieve his lighter from his jacket pocket, he set about torching anything that would catch. It worked. But in the minute that it took Clay to realise what was occurring, Felix's purgatory was rapidly becoming his flaming hell.

'What the blazes...' cried Clay, at last appearing at the scene of the alien abduction. From twenty feet above, Felix squirmed in his glowing hammock. Clay, in his desultory bid to reach him, dislodged a few skeletal branches, causing Felix's sudden and spontaneous cascade.

'Shitzenhausen!' cried Clay, beholding the smouldering wreckage of a man at his feet, 'thank buggery I found you in time!'

'Thank buggery for that bloody sheep, more like' Felix croaked, rolling sideways to permit the escape of a sad–faced ewe.

4

Rigger Mortis

@

I t was a heavy, sticky–underpants day in Felix's office, situated two floors above Burger King, were the stereophonic odours of cooked and garbaged food entered by yawning windows, to the front and rear. The usual suspects limped in and out, grunting grudgingly at each other and contributing to the stench of spent breath. A few pallid, balding and brightly T–shirted youth workers prepared wordy documents they'd no intention of implementing, while a group of callow teenagers, reposing after a hard morning of queuing at the 'other' office, prepared to jettison any paperwork that might get thrust upon them. It never occurred to Felix that the wastepaper basket in the cordoned–off waiting area was the most assiduously visited filing cabinet in the office. Here, the art of box–tickery, the curse of our politically correct, patently corrupt age, was manifest. Corrupt in the sense that no one in the entire building, not even the good burghers of Burger King, meant ten percent of what they communicated to each other. 'Have a good day' they would all chant, code for 'get as far away from me as you can, you smelly bastard' and 'for god sake, wash your hair', not that the 'youf' of today would know a 'youfemism' if they tripped over one.

A disturbance from outside, a fracas between two Italian sounding vagrants and a lollipop lady, generated a flurry of enthusiasm in the office. Felix, staring vacuously through his ineffectual fan towards the ensuing mêlée, was reminded of the opening scene in Hitchcock's 'The Rear Window'. Come to think of it, he even looked like Jimmy Stewart, with his leg in plaster, propped up on an empty case of Seven Up. Felix sighed, ineffably ravaged by the shenanigans of the previous week. His every thought seemed in some way connected with the tragic event; even the Thai takeaway opposite was called 'The Happy Valley', its owner, the appropriately named Wing Gong Wong. It was no good, he must distract himself from this self–pity. But he couldn't ignore the gravity of his predicament, even if he ever chose to buck *Einstein's* laws of gravity again. He'd inadvertently become the owner of an excessively expensive duvet; for that was all the shredded wing was good for now. But at least the harness had come in handy as a deck hammock, while the leg was recovering.

Back home on Wagtail, Felix comforted himself with a loaded pipe and a chunk of stale cake, pondering on his joyless flying career to date, his multi–autographed plaster cast diverting the few remaining rays of sun.

Overhead, the faintest buzzing sound became audible, although it had to compete with some stomach–cramping drivel on Classic FM. In desperation he searched out his 'Tranquillity' CD, an hour long sequence of foreplaying finches, canoodling chinchillas, frolicking frogs, potent peacocks and intimate insects, all recorded in their natural habitat by a pretentious botanist by the name of Pierre Eigeldinger, whose PhD, the insert revealed, had investigated the mating habits of leaches. He had to concede he'd achieved a degree of solace in Dr Eigeldinger's researches, while soaking up the vista of his own mini–menagerie, for once content and sober concurrently.

The hum from above was persistent enough to disturb his semi–somnolent condition. What the hell was it, anyway? Peering up through the torn tissue of clouds to the limpid sky beyond, he glimpsed a static looking delta shaped craft, a sort of Batmobile with motorbike attached. He rather liked the look of that, whatever it was. For several minutes he watched, intrigued by its ponderous path – even the chaotic clouds around it seemed to be moving more purposefully. He could barely make out its controller, presumably human, but definitely not the caped hero. The thing took a good five minutes to meander its way, grinding like a lawnmower and engirdling just as inelegantly. He'd read about so–called paramoters – paragliders with ginormous fans strapped to their backs to keep them buoyant in the absence of thermal lift. But the UFO he was following was much more robust, almost an aeroplane. He felt a sense of reinvigoration as he sieved through the list of

4,236 items he'd quickly Googled, discovering almost immediately that he was witnessing the unwieldy yet dignified flight of a flexi–winged microlight.

A close–up picture confirmed that his fanciful notions of lawnmowers, bats and motorbikes were not so far off beat. But this was a serious bit of kit, no duvets, body braces or knotted–up dental floss here. That reminded him – he'd not yet cancelled his paragliding course, due to start the following day in the plague–dodging town of Eyam. He'd reconciled himself to a boozy week with Clay by way of consolation for missing the course. But perhaps he could trade the paragliding classes for one on microlighting? He came upon 'Mervyn's Matlock Microlights' at the third mouse–click. One feverish phone call later Felix had fixed himself up with an innovative method of haemorrhaging both his cash and body fluids. Reclining once again in his al fresco leathery pouch he tweaked up the volume control on the CD, which, appropriately, had arrived at a charismatic track entitled 'Teasing Tsetse Tango'. The remainder of the evening was spent cremating sausages on the barbeque mounted on Wagtail's slender roof, from where periodic attempts to urinate into an old cider flagon proved marginally less hazardous. His injured leg was as erect as a giraffe's neck after nibbling from the apocryphal Viagra tree, and it crossed his slowing mind that he might have mentioned that to his new microlight instructor.

The drive up to Derbyshire was exhilarating and heart–arresting in equal measure. Forced to adopt a side–saddle posture in order to accommodate the preposterous erection, he'd devised a way of operating the clutch with a modified walking stick. Gear changes were expedited gingerly, since the stick had a habit of slipping off the depressed pedal and slamming into his testicles – more a matter of crutch control than clutch control. On arriving at Eyam he had time to kill before hobbling to his room in the pub, so opted for a spot of people–watching in the local Starbucks. He didn't have to wait long for a woman with elephantiasis and varicose veins as protuberant as a brass–rubbing to lollop in, presumably to claim her usual trough of coffee and tray of blueberry muffins. Her unlikely sidekick, a wispy–voiced gentleman with no neck, countable hairs and fewer teeth, acknowledged her hyena–like emissions with a nodding donkey gesture, evidently perfected during many years of failing to squeeze a word in sideways. Although she had presumably perused the menu scores of times she still needed the Starbucks nomenclature to be interpreted by a softly spoken Filipino waiter called Castello, probably an honours graduate in nuclear physics, but confident of earning more here than back home in a laboratory. In the end she just wanted 'a milky coffee, luvvy' evidently unable to contemplate the conjugations for error in a doppio, cappuccino or mocha. Every sentence she uttered was suffixed by an incongruous cackle, her feckless companion doing his best to gauge when the next outburst was coming so that he could coincide his highly expressive mono–movement. Watching her cope with the macaroon was strangely absorbing; more brittle than fossilised antelope crap when dry, soggier than a twice–digested Farley's Rusk when dunked. The remaining tables had been leased long–term to web–browsing nerds and orange–paper–twitching business types, none taking the slightest bit of notice of a piped arrangement of Vivaldi's Four Seasons, pulverised by a band of ill–tuned ocarinas. Felix couldn't help noticing that the first eight lines of the tabloid thrust in his nose by a faceless noisy breather nearly formed an acrostic of the word 'clitoris', but his barely restrained chuckles were taken by his neighbour to be a stifled fart. It had the desired effect anyhow, the Magritte–like acephalous man beating a hasty retreat into the ladies loo. Having endured the merciful culmination of Domingo's excruciating rendition of 'My Way', and glugged his way through two shaving–foam topped goblets, Felix exited.

Opposite the coffee shop, attracting a certain amount of attention, was a puppeteer, vicariously dancing a frenzied fandango through his Punch and Judy characters. But far more captivating for the crowd was the simply brilliant accordion accompanist, whose mercurial virtuosity and glycerine coordination had earned him more in ten minutes than Starbucks had taken during the same period. Impressed sufficiently to hobble across the road, Felix noticed the crowd dispersing, the accordionist taking a well–earned break to count the takings and cool his smoking fingers. But as Felix approached the accordion player, now calming himself with a cigarette, the squatting puppeteer accidentally restarted a cassette machine, hidden from view below. The pseudo accordionist, noting the derision flowing across Felix's face, shrugged his shoulders and pointedly took a sip from his Starbucks mochachino, winking at his sidekick. The instrument tumbled apologetically to the floor while the cassette rollicked on like Charles Aznavure on speed.

'All that glistaz is not *goow–old*' pontificated Felix, in an accent best dismissed as Geordie tinged with Ethiopian.

'Aye, a bit like your fake Durham accent, *mee–ate*' retorted the man, wiping away his creamy moustache and pointing proudly to his Newcastle United shirt.

'Cruel, but fair' Felix shrugged.

At 'The Two Tomtits' Mrs. Kettlety was on hand with terrible tea and tarnished tablecloths, her tacky tapestries adorning every available chipping of peach maquillaged wallpaper. Felix indulged the first half of her treatise on correct showering protocol, then escaped to his room for forty winks, detecting the threat of more insipid earl grey. Mounting the stairs, he encountered an obese cockroach, whose tenancy at the pub clearly predated Mrs K's; it survived repeated attempts to impale it with his walking stick. At the thirty–eighth wink a rude din from below signalled the onslaught of the sixties karaoke evening. Ernie, the bar manager (Mrs. K's son, a forty year–old skinhead with 'mum' touchingly tattooed on his neck) proved indispensable in galvanising the early culprits. Felix sauntered in, clutching a large brandy and nursing his thigh ostentatiously. First to strut their stuff was a succession of Elvis impersonators, few capable of distinguishing 'Jailhouse Rock' from Brighton rock, despite flirting with a whole bunch of keys. The tattoo on the opposite side of

Ernie's neck read 'Jean'. Felix pondered the fate of Jean, presumably a childhood sweetheart whom Ernie wouldn't now recognise; either way, he doubted her continued interest in Ernie's indelible endorsement. Later, Felix struck up a harmless if incomprehensible discussion with Ivan, evidently one of a large Dutch coach party that had unexpectedly poured over the purple–carpeted lounge. The large man's matching sunburn certainly reflected the warmth of his generosity, sustaining the incommutable conveyor belt of lagers and brandy chasers until well past closing time, never allowing a second's fresh air between enthusiastic ejaculations for Felix to de–scramble the boozy babble. An old lady, caked in oxblood lipstick, who'd enjoyed the long and inscrutable exchange from six feet away, whispered confidentially in Felix's ear 'the definition of a bore is someone who talks incessantly about himself, depriving you of the chance to do the same'. She was right, although his companion might just have been translating 'Charlie and the Chocolate Factory' into Madagascarian, for all he knew.

The next morning at breakfast Felix did his best to dent Mrs. K's carnivorous creation, Terry Wogan's interminable postulations doing little to stimulate salivation. Grateful for an excuse to drown out the thumping headache, he enquired affectionately after his Dutch drinking partner, the affable Ivan.

'Oh' said Ernie, fixing a Heinz label onto a well worn bottle of blood red sauce, 'you mean *Ivor* – he's our tame Glaswegian lorry driver. Nice guy, comes here all the time.'

Ernie clutched a wadge of fat books under his artistically evocative arm, and Felix concluded that his host was assembling harebrained questions for that evening's pub quiz.

'Actually, I'm just completing my Masters in Philosophy, Felix' Ernie said in a matter of fact way. Felix pressed him further, somewhat stunned.

'I decided to specialise in Aristotelian logic' he continued, 'you know, the theory that everything exists to have a purpose, ultimately predestined by God Himself.'

'Blimey' stumbled Felix, bemused.

'Even my pet cockroach fulfils an important function in the scheme of things, you see' he went on, glancing devotedly towards the rickety old staircase.

'I suppose a sixties music buff is entitled to indulge his Beatle–mania' quipped Felix, pushing the suddenly less than esculent black pudding to the side of his tray–sized plate.

'But the love of my life would have to be Sartre, Jean–Paul Sartre, who emphasised the will of the individual to determine his own path.'

Ernie pointed reverently at his tattoo. 'The cognoscenti knew him as Jean, of course.'

'Of course' responded Felix.

The short drive to the aerodrome would have taken less time had Felix not paused to drool over every low–flying bee–like craft, summoned home to its hive. The hangar was chock–a–block with planes of every description, fixed and flexi–winged microlights, cesenas, tiger moths, even a stunt pilot's biplane hand–painted in black. Felix marvelled at the way they were parked up in such a close–knit herringbone configuration. The stench of spent oil and developing symphony of engines certainly conveyed an electrifying atmosphere. He noted the predominance of middle–aged men lavishing tenderness on their machines, as if working their way through an aviator's karma–sutra, while their wives deadheaded roses, no doubt. A plethora of Harley–Davidsons, Porsches and other testosterone–fuelled penis–extensions confirmed he had entered the kingdom of the forty year–old teenager.

Felix turned to acknowledge the arrival of a less than magnificent man in his flying machine, the eponymous Mervyn himself, he deduced. The formalities in Mervyn's office brought home to Felix how obsessive his perplexing new passion had become. The walls were dense with diagrams, OS maps and exceedingly complex definitions of obscure aviation terms, what his old Classics teacher would have delighted in dismissing as *ignotum per ignotius*. The conspicuous leg injury didn't unduly concern Mervyn, who'd experienced the complete gamut of oddballs in his time, most notably a poet in search of inspiration, an octogenarian in search of romance and a manic–depressive in search of the after–life.

A glistening, lipstick–red monocoque vessel smiled

back at Felix as he accelerated toward it excitedly, suddenly unencumbered by his plaster cast. The superfluous left trouser leg of his borrowed suit drooped at half–mast, fanning the oily haze that rose from the cooking tarmac. Ushered into the forward seat by his grim–faced instructor – 'Unnervin' Mervyn', as he came to be known – Felix's imagination began to dance. The discotheque of lights and diamante of gizmos shone nearly as brightly as his eyes. Strapped and sardined into the fibreglass shell, his snatched breaths sounded amplified through his headset, interrupted periodically by rapid–fired, ear–splitting radio bulletins. With the benefit of dual controls it would ostensibly be easier to monitor Felix's protruding appendage from behind. More importantly for Felix, it allowed him to assume the persona of Tom Cruise, relishing an opportunity to sport his new reflective sunglasses. Once Mervyn had assumed pillion position and stirred the engine, he began to effuse a long and indifferent spiel, presumably for Felix's benefit. But if Mervyn's true intention had been to erode Felix's flimsy self–confidence, it worked. For before him, both literally and paradoxically, was Felix as a grown man and small boy – the adult, transfixed and intimidated, the child, impatient to raid the sweetshop. Felix nodded energetically, as if following the finer points of his instructor's preliminaries. But his attention had become diverted by a succession of 'touch 'n goes', the essential circuit training of elementary pilots briefly connecting wheels with runway before ascending to rejoin the roundabout five hundred feet above. It seemed to take an age to position the overwrought craft in readiness for takeoff. The two men fried in their chicken foil, waiting for a suitable window.

'So, you're a veteran paraglider, you tell me' initiated Mervyn, apparently alluding to the gammy leg.

'Well, I've had a couple of reasonable flights' responded Felix, unable to contemplate the unpalatable truth.

'Good, you'll know all about the theory of flight, airspeed, groundspeed and stallspeed then.'

'I'm a *bit* rusty actually' said Felix, for once touching base with a part–truth.

'It'll all fall into place – it makes a change to have someone au fait onboard.'

When at last an affirmative monotone mumble was received from ground control, the rotund mosquito rubbed its eyes and prepared for the off. Pre–flight checks were cursorily dispensed with, much to Felix's relief, and seconds later the machine screamed away at full throttle to reach a flying speed of sixty mph. Microlight take–offs had seemed laughably lethargic from the sanctity of his Landrover, but in the hot–seat Felix felt as though he was breaking through Mach II in a steroid–injected wheelchair. The stationary headwind, barely sufficient to stimulate the windsock from its brewer's droop position, had become face–alteringly aggressive. The fully exerted machine became buffeted about like a bingo–caller's ping–pong ball, each of Mervyn's minute inputs massively magnified. Fragments of radio–babble continued to rape Felix's ears and hamper Mervyn's repeated attempts to win his pupil's concentration. The whining engine behind them eventually powered down to a modest Mach I, at last free from the deafening aerial merry–go–round. Consumed still by shock, Felix was incapable of looking down at his right foot, or up at his left, fixating instead on the dizzy dials straight ahead. It was impossible to anticipate the next deluge from a leaking cloud, and yet Mervyn seemed unphased, shielded by Felix's petrified frame. His rôle, more accurately perhaps flying *de*–structor than instructor, involved demonstrating extremes of height gain and loss, unaware of his student's recently acquired expertise in the field. Felix could hear words, but not respond to them, his knuckles glowing white even through his leather gloves. The twenty miles covered in the hour felt more like two hundred, and Felix was as relieved as Mervyn to thread back into the slowly gyrating flock of oddly sized aviates. Touchdown seemed as precise an art as taking a sea urchin for a walk on a piece of elastic; but miraculously, despite wild zigzags five seconds before impact, Mervyn curtailed the mutual misery with an ace landing.

If Felix had possessed a quarter of the knowledge he'd claimed over the phone, another ten lessons would have taken him to the first significant landmark: going solo. As it was, Mervyn's frustration deepened as Felix's frail fortitude dribbled away. He'd pre–booked two lessons per day, an intensive week's tuition, but by day three Mervyn had lost patience, increasingly certain that his student would never fly a microlight as long as he had a hole up his ass. 'Clear the runway, here comes Jake the Peg' would chorus from the makeshift coffee bar, a palpable groan drowning out the engine noise outside. The regulars would delight in watching Felix spend half an hour dislodging the School's student machine, unaccountably always wedged at the back of the hangar whenever his time for a lesson loomed. Five craft needed shifting to create sufficient space to wriggle one free; chess had never been Felix's forte. By day five he had made minimal progress, and still couldn't be trusted to fly a complete circuit without threatening the annihilation of local wildlife. Indeed, Felix's presence in the sky was as welcome as inveterate flatulence in a sauna.

But a spot of good fortune came his way when, on day six, Mervyn didn't show up, leaving his assistant, Larry, to bear the brunt alone. Determined to redeem himself, Felix pulled out all the stops, a few of them right ones, his midnight studies propping up the bar with Ernie at 'The Two Tomtits' at last beginning to pay off. Ernie turned out to be a nascent aviator, as well as maieutic existentialist, hence Felix achieved more with his new instructor, Larry 'The Lamb', in a day, than he had with Mervyn in five. Progress might have been measured in inches, rather than miles, but at least he'd finally moved out of reverse gear. An incentive for Larry came on discovering Felix's intention to acquire a flying machine of his own. Larry's was up for sale; despite not being in the full flush of youth the gold painted plane looked trim and muscular, with all its paperwork up to date, its slender fuselage shining like a newly minted bullet from under a tub of polish. The deal was sealed. And so was his fate.

One month passed, and Felix, finally released from his vexatious plaster cast, had made frequent trips to Matlock. His overindulgence of 'Wagtail II' had become as nauseating as any microlight–widower's, and his faded–dinghy–green Landrover courted the nubile Porsches with all the swagger of a bikinied Lamborghini. Although the summer evenings were withdrawing, and Felix was beginning to think he'd be shackled to the aerodrome forever, his day of glory suddenly arrived. After a few touch 'n goes, with Larry sat soundlessly behind, he was at last granted his début solo flight – nothing too strenuous, just one complete circuit. According to custom, all air traffic was radioed down to watch, and Felix steeled himself to repay Larry's trust: five compressed minutes of fame, but the biggest ego trip of his life nonetheless. Felix took his applause with uncustomary good grace, simultaneously rubbing a dozen noses in the sweaty tarmac. His self–esteem skipped gaily from cloud nine to cloud fourteen in a single move. Even the motley Matlock crew grudgingly acknowledged his accomplishment, though they persisted with the Jake the Peg gag. 'Never mind' his mum consoled him, 'the ruder they are, the more they *like* you, Felix. You know', she continued, 'just remember, your dad was known as a complete *wanker* during his National Service'.

His solo hours were clocking up nicely now, with just five more to log, and his new target became to fly the nest. Larry tentatively suggested a short sortie, perhaps over to Eyam and back. 'But don't push it mate' he warned, 'or the lamb will turn into a wolf'. 'Roger, I mean yeah, Larry' nodded Felix, already mulling over a display of freestyle aerobatics.

'The Dambusters March' soundtrack pounded quadraphonically in Felix's imagination as he sashayed like Julian Clary up to the hangar the following sunny weekend. The Tom Cruise shades only partly concealed his lopsided brow, convinced the success of the next 'mission' lay in his hands alone. It did, of course, for once clear of his aerial micro–community there would be no voice of restraint, no radio communication and no paternal wing to protect him from himself. Felix made a banquet of the pre–flight inspection, his show of fastidiousness attracting a dig from 'Baldy', the silver–locked hippy biplane fanatic.

'You'll wear out that wing, looking at it so hard.'

'Can't be too careful' declaimed Felix, rubbing his old war wound tellingly. With his mental checklist completed and fuel level noted, he was ready to spread his wings. But not before a final consolidatory circuit with Larry. Substitute ballast, in the form of a metal petrol can filled with cement, was then bungeed tightly into the rear seat. Two solo circuits – then once more into the breach.

It felt like zero hour, a vindication of his preposterous impulse to fly, and truly a moment to splice into his mental scrapbook. The final touch 'n go was perfection manifest, and so he fired his golden bullet heroically towards its target, a few degrees west of the corpulent sun. Felix's heart fibrillated as ferociously as a terrier killing a rat, as if in sympathy with his diminutive two–stroke engine. A snatched peak over his shoulder confirmed that his body and soul were free at last and, for the tiniest of moments, Wagtail II was the brightest star in the firmament.

But, having cleared the runway by perhaps four hundred feet, a cacophonous silence suddenly bellowed at him. It was as if someone had inadvertently unplugged his heart from a wall socket, leaving him suspended in time and space. The eternity of his nothingness, which in reality lasted for just a second, was sufficient to turn his short–lived space odyssey into a horrifying earthward plunge. Instantaneously Felix's training kicked in; he wrenched the control bar into his rib cage, somehow managing to confound gravity and point the machine back toward earth. As if given a dose of smelling salts the wing spontaneously began to fly again, this time under its own steam, but at a disconcertingly acute angle. Slowly he released the bar, flattening out the nosedive to something approaching horizontal. At this perilous altitude, effectively now a freight–carrying hang–glider, he knew he would meet his fate within a matter of seconds; his next actions would determine whether he landed like a sprightly field mouse or a geriatric rhinoceros. He'd already chosen his landing field, thankfully still facing into wind, although the disquieting escarpment ahead might yet prove difficult to negotiate. Before he could mobilise his senses, there he was, mowing through the most hirsute field he could have chosen, grinding to an elegant, noiseless halt ten yards in front of a peripheral hedge.

Motionless, he sat there, counting his digits, his limbs and his lucky stars. Gaping with disbelief at his crestfallen machine, he gently rocked it from side to side, his ear pressed close to the tank. It was dryer than a witch's tit. Slowly he pieced together the events that had led to this, his second scurrilous brush with mortality in under three months. 'Holy crackamoli!' he exclaimed, observing the airlock in the carburettor down–pipe. The bloody thing must have been nearly empty before he'd set out, the primitive fuel gauge giving a false reading.

Without a radio to summon assistance Felix had no choice but to trundle back to the aerodrome with his tail and his shrivelled pride dangling between his legs. First he'd need to mark his spot, simple enough with the shaggy hedge running the full length of the expansive field. He turned east to face the aerodrome, expecting to see something at least vaguely familiar – orbiting planes perhaps, or the runway perimeter. Instead, he beheld a panorama of rugged vegetation, glacier–hewn valleys and fields of nodding sunflowers, but not the faintest whiff of humanity in the frowsty air. He may as well have been traipsing the Masai Mara – for it was as if he had been transported from outer space by aliens with a penchant for the bucolic; a tidal wave of déjà vu struck him, if anything, more crushing than the current calamity itself. At least, he consoled himself, massaging his weary leg, history had not *entirely* repeated itself. He resolved to crack on, as disorientated as an aroma–therapist at a wife–swapping party.

The day was one of perhaps five genuinely sweltering days to flatter Derbyshire that August. While most people were de–greasing barbeques in readiness for their annual skirmish with salmonella, or discarding last year's epidermis in favour of this year's colours, Felix stumbled around vacantly, his flying suit awash like a deep–

sea diver's skin–deep urinal. With his top half peeled down to his waist he resembled a Chernobyl victim, random flesh–like ganglions of padded cloth snagging every tooth of barbed wire he encountered. Reminiscences of his ground–handling fiasco were ever present as he hiked slothfully back to the aerodrome – and back to Larry, whose threat to reincarnate himself as a wolf rendered him even more sheepish.

By the time he rematerialised an hour later Felix's cocky swagger had become a feeble stagger, although the reception committee was markedly more appreciative than it had been a month earlier. In contrast, Larry was worryingly taciturn as the two plane–less pilots set off to retrace Felix's incoherent route, Felix not brave enough to expostulate on the self–evident saga. Laden with brimming fuel cans the journey was doubly arduous, and now the first signs of dusk threatened. At last Felix's boyish glee precipitated as they tripped over his carelessly thrown paper dart; Wagtail II's wings trembled fitfully in the casual zephyr, like a newly born chick quietly relieved to be reunited with its parents.

Having fuelled up, Larry set about ploughing a runway, the field appearing rather smaller in the failing light. He careered up and down like a stuttering lawnmower, the long grass matting tightly around the plane's tiny wheels. There'd be no room for Felix, the cramped takeoff area requiring a skilful and assertive solo exit. Out came the ballast, slung into the hedgerow, and off went a buoyant Wagtail II, minus its glum–faced owner. Felix allowed himself a brief moment's respite, companionless, desolate and disconsolate once again. He'd have to make the journey on foot for a third time, now encumbered by the superfluous cans and crash helmet. His leg was protesting vehemently too, and the lunar surface that the aliens had picked out for his second dicey landing was becoming progressively insurmountable.

Upon his return Felix daren't tempt fate by checking in at the dimly illuminated office, too weak to fend off the inevitable ribaldry. But the next morning he plucked up the courage to phone Mervyn, just to warn him he was still alive. The response was predictably curt.

'Where's my bleedin' ballast then, Jake?'

'Ah, well it's still in the field, Merv.'

'I'm gonna need it back...vital bit of kit, that.'

Although it would be less hassle to conjure up a new can, Mervyn had clearly developed an emotional attachment to his old one. There would be little point in arguing.

Back at Matlock, Felix decided to simplify matters, requisitioning an archaic wheelbarrow from the hangar. Negotiating fences might be a struggle, but he felt sure it would lighten the load on the return leg, not to mention his *own* twinging leg. The route didn't seem to get any easier, or familiar. But a few telltale clues, threads from his flying suit and the odd scrap of flesh, added a groundhog–day nuance to his ironic game of paper chase. Finally, after much rooting about to the amusement of meddlesome cattle, he filled his blasted ballast barrow. The noncompliant thing cavorted mischievously over the craggy surface, clearly more adept at the outsized egg–and–spoon race than its operator. His whole body convulsed spastically, his throbbing appendage shooting out at ridiculous angles as he danced the petrol–can–cancan to his ever–perplexed audience of incontinent cattle. Finally, having flown half a mile and walked five, his weekend of misery was mercifully terminated.

'Did you have a good day, dear?' chirruped his mum down the phone later that evening.

'Oh, top flight' Felix replied magniloquently. 'Narrowly escaped getting raped by some silly cow, administered Imodium to an aged bull with a collapsed colon and snagged my tool on an electric fence in the process. But hey, eventually got my leg over, so no complaints.'

'Oh, well done *you*!' she commended volubly, barely diverting her attention from two vile insects copulating slothfully on her Ryvita.

5

Waiting for Godeaux

It was late December, and the shenanigans of Felix's blighted flying campaign had faded from memory during the intervening months. But a rudely coincidental dearth of battery power, gas and coal supplies imposed an evening of tranquillity on the hapless youth worker. Starved of light, warmth and company, time was placed on pause for a few numb hours. Moored a sizeable drive from the grotty city office from where the urban myth of postmodern socialist intervention was perpetuated on a daily basis, Wagtail was cradled in a redolent blanket of incense fumes. Felix's motionless carcass dripped gawkily around a flimsy raffia sofa, his feet rooted to the surface of the lifeless stove from where he was almost convinced warmth was emanating. His mind meandered along paths he suspected his body might never follow again, first to the peak of his luscious valley, the site of a few poignant out–of–body moments, and then up into the swollen clouds, where the faintest vapour of rain had settled on his face like dew to a rose petal. And yet, these moving images quickly became disfigured with angst, reminiscences of his tree incarceration branded ineradicably on a crop of unsuspecting grey cells.

A flickering torch protruded from his mouth as he dribbled unselfconsciously down his chin. With this meagre source of light he indulged a trespassing wave of nostalgia by thumbing through a recently rediscovered photograph album that lay conveniently within arm's reach. In it, college days featured prominently, although the motley anthology of acquaintances only partly registered after all this time. Fragments of his past and present collided as he gawked unblinkingly at pictures of individuals, some of whom he still occasionally bumped into; most, like himself, were now almost entirely bereft of hair. Curiously, among these random images a small brown envelope had been inserted. It instantly reminded him of one his dentist had handed him, aged nine, to safeguard a molar that had just been carved from his head in the name of clear speech. For some reason he must have felt compelled to hang on to it, not that his tongue had been able to make sense of the extra space, even after the tooth fairy had obliged with its tanner. But this particular envelope was free of bloodstains. Nor did it bulge; it had seemingly nestled in among the other inconsequential artefacts in the album as if it had a perfect right to be there. Felix permitted himself a brief snooze; besides, his lower limbs were already half asleep.

He awoke perhaps an hour later, a lancing pain consuming his entire body. Both legs suffered from cramp and a sack–full of pins and needles weighed upon his arms, which clasped the photo album, still open, now swamped in cool saliva. It took half a minute to stir himself from his state of petrifaction, instructing each limb in turn to come to life as if recovering from a minor stroke. The torch, still resolutely clutched between his aching teeth, evidently had also started giving up the will to perform. Moaning pathetically to himself he rummaged around under the sofa and dragged out the paraglider wing that had recently assumed its home there, still partly packed, but sufficiently voluminous to bring a degree of comfort to his racked body. From it an incipient aroma – infantine urine blended with a more contemporary vintage – intruded upon his nostrils; his old antagonist the corduroy trousers, again.

There'd be little succour tonight. He couldn't even boil a kettle; it was worse than being a student. That reminded him, what the hell was in that old envelope? Retrieving a single firelighter match from the ashtray next to him he lit it, inserted it between his lips and prised the envelope from the sanctity of its album. Carefully he opened it, intrigued as to what he would find inside, still unsure how it had got there. A small sliver of banana–tinted paper slipped out into his hand, folded in half three times.

Waiting for his eyes to adjust to the uneven light he eventually managed to focus on some broken red typed print, which read: 'OrthoWorld...We provide braces for straight teeth and beautiful faces...also crowns, bridges, white fillings and veneers...Sanjeev Kasai BDS...etc.' What the gingivitis was *this* doing in his album? The Yellow Pages advert had been excised with surgical precision, but by whom, and why? Sustaining the focus of the dribble–drenched torch stuck fast in his head, Felix repositioned his torso to allow space for a cushion under his creaking coccyx, burying himself among the assorted cloths and tangled cords that now constituted his beleaguered wing. Once more he flirted with sleep, picking up strands of faintly disturbing dreams and daydreams.

But a more coherent thought had begun to take shape, feeding on the vestiges of vulnerability that had weakened him earlier in his solitude. In this semi–lucid condition he started to fantasise a dramatic piece in which a lone protagonist, secluded and defenceless, becomes aware of the presence of someone outside, skulking around in the murky shadows. The menacing figure, using a spotlight to ease its way, inches ever closer, until just feet away from the victim's door. In the background a solo violin repeats a suitably angular and intangible mantra, its halting dissonance confirming the impending peril. All that the quivering, pathetic soul inside can do is cower under the covers, its pleas unanswered, until death, certain and inexorable, becomes an almost merciful release. Felix shuddered timorously, unaccountably persuaded by his melodramatic construction, then passed once more into a trance, the squeaky–gate music never abating.

It might have been seconds, minutes or even hours later that he became aware of his cloaked surroundings once again. But all was not well – for he was soaked from head to toe, his heart racing uncontrollably and his intermittent consciousness desperately seeking some kind of reprieve. What was that! A distant *crrr–aack* resonated in his head – he replayed it in his mind's ear, twice, just to be sure – yes, it was a *real* noise, from outside. He shot upright, ears tuned in for exactly the right frequency. 'There it is again' he gulped, 'oh my god…pull yourself together, Felix', he calmed himself, revisiting the daft storyline he'd fed himself before crashing out, 'it's just a silly nightmare'. But a feeble smirk was hardly sufficient to convince himself he was safe. Slowly, his heart resumed a discernible rhythm as he calmed himself, his sopping wet collar squelching as it met the saturated cushion. His eyes wandered up to the wood–clad ceiling, adorned with the usual canal boat paraphernalia of ancient lavender and dented tin mugs, as a wedge of orange light sidled in from between the partly closed curtains. 'Beautiful moon' he whispered to himself absentmindedly, turning his head to one side, closing his eyes. But when he reopened them seconds later he spotted the *real* moon – the bottom segment of its crescent shape shone dimly but unmistakably a million miles beyond his kitchenette window – no ordinary evection. Someone was out there all right. 'The doors! Oh my god, the bloody doors!' he exclaimed, suddenly recognising the perverseness of the dream playing itself out for real. He pounced from his sofa and crawled at speed to the back door, taking care to duck beneath the line of the windows. He reached up and tackled the latch, rejoicing inwardly at the satisfying click it made. He slumped at the base of the door, finding his breath and staring up at the ceiling once again to see if the ill–omened light was still hovering. It had gone.

While one part of Felix's mentality derided his ridiculous behaviour, another remained horribly shocked and in need of scaffolding from brain–dampening substances. Still flaccid, with his head leaning against the secured door, he assembled an especially generous tuft of cannabis and crammed it into his pipe, taking a few moments' distraction from his distress. The affected smile slowly returned to his face, increasingly confident that his initial thesis had been correct; yes, he had hallucinated the whole damned thing. From his position at the bow of the boat he could just make out part of the window adjacent to the stern door, some distance away. His night–vision was now as sharply focused as his hearing, and he fixated on the window for perhaps a minute. Glancing down at his hand, he realised he was clutching something rather tightly – a small slip of paper. He slowly opened up the crumpled advert, resuming the challenge to link Dr Kasai's orthodontic practice with his unremarkable student snapshots. Evidently, the advert had been mistakenly placed in his album, probably years ago. He turned it over.

On the back, in handwriting as spidery as his centenarian grandmother's, were the words 'I intend to descend near the end, dear friend…4C191208'.

'This gets odder by the moment' mumbled Felix, scanning the cryptic message over and over again, to no avail. Jaded, his eyes drifted back to their initial point of focus: the window. As they did so, to his horror, a shadow poured over the floor like a punctured barrel of black treacle, the curtain only partly filtering the moonlight so that it silhouetted the shape of a head, motionless, facing directly at him. But just as quickly the apparition melted from view like a blowtorched snowman, and Felix heard a soft rustle as an object was slipped under the door. Unable to draw breath he remained slumped, his pipe still glowing unperturbed. Was he still dreaming, or was this the result of his overenthusiastic smoke? Either way, he now realised, the stern door was not locked – he'd been so pleased with himself at reaching the bow door in time that he'd completely overlooked it.

Fretting silently in his tomb–shaped torture chamber Felix considered his diminishing options. He could confront his intruder with a bold act of aggression, though boldness was not featuring keenly now, or he could sit it out – for all his attacker knew, he wasn't even at home; after all, there was none of the customary radio natter and not a single light was on. He could ring the police, yes, that should be done in any case. He moved noiselessly, eventually tracking down his mobile phone. 'Bollocks!' he screamed, internally, failing to achieve a backlight. Of all the times to run out of power. But, hang on, what had happened to his surreptitious caller? Not a gnat's fart had broken the painful stillness for several minutes. Perhaps he should escape? But he couldn't be sure where to exit from, let alone what he'd do once freed. No, the best plan is to play the waiting game, let his assailant make the next move.

Locked in a time capsule, truly a captive in his own home, Felix was all too aware of who was hunter and who was hunted. Nothing had stirred outside and he was forced to sit there, shivering, confused and restless. Should he feel relieved at the prolonged silence or yet more fearful of the pain that might eventually be visited upon him? Either way, control was not his. Over the next twenty minutes or so, uneven patches of sleep seemed to dilute the likelihood of death a little, and it was only the most distant humming sound that jolted him back to the shocking present. What was it? It continued in long, tuneless drones, penetratingly deep and lasting ten seconds each, separated by gaps of equal duration. Felix slid silently up to his knees, level with the window, from where his eyes could sweep wide without even moving his head. But there was nothing to be seen, just the amber light of the half moon waltzing its way across the silvery meadow that partly protected Wagtail from prying eyes. Stealthily he crawled to the stern and surveyed from there. Still nothing. His fear was becoming tinged with frustration.

There had to be some connection between the far off hum and the uninvited caller, for he was so far out in the sticks that two strange happenings in one evening seemed too farfetched. Comforted by this frail conclusion he resolved to investigate. He'd not skulk out like a scorned cat, but march upright and demand to know what his intruder was playing at. The only self–defence tool to hand was his torch, which in any case would be needed to affect his valiant getaway. As a last act of self–distraction Felix donned his balaclava – he could look almost formidable in that. He stood for a second with the door ajar at his fingertips, consuming long breaths and shaking his limbs slightly, like a gymnast preparing to mount the parallel bars. At his feet, among a fluttering pile of receipts and random debris, he caught sight of a blue glossy card with his signature on it: his Court Pass – he'd been looking for that. He slipped it into his back pocket, and as he stormed out of the boat he found himself whistling – something Elgarian – he couldn't think why. After his tenth stride along the path he realised he didn't know in which direction he was headed. But now he was committed. His exuberance ebbed away as he drifted from the path into a neighbouring glade, soot–black and oppressive with round–shouldered, Tolkeinesque trees. He paused for a second, unable to sustain his feigned belligerence, and waited, once more a frightened little boy hiding in a man's body. At least onboard Wagtail there had been a negligee of protection from his intruder. Here, he was truly without the most transparent of defences. He could be exterminated and ditched into the disease–ridden canal in a moment's outrageous madness, or worse still, left to sip sewage amidst a tangled mass of unmentionably squalid objects.

The humming sound, a menacing susurration, had become even more intermittent and infrasonic, and a perfume vivid with saffron and galangal now hung in the atmosphere, lending it the puzzling allure of a Turkish brothel. Before he could make out what it was his ears were filled with a new and incongruous sound, a clanking, intoxicating caterwauling. A voice, startlingly close and confident, suddenly expunged a discursive jumble of incomprehensible notes and words, accompanied by trenchant rhythmical chords from a weird stringed instrument that had a mistily familiar timbre. Eyes staring wider than an insomniac marsupial's, Felix listened in the dark, mesmerised. The invocation meandered its directionless terrain for some time. Then it stopped, as abruptly as it had started. A single cough–like abrasion, a striking match perhaps, followed by a lethargic intake of breath, caused Felix's head to turn anxiously. And there, less than four feet away, crouching on the ground, was his intruder.

The mumbo–jumboing man had casually smoked nearly his entire cigarette before Felix's diminished powers of recognition began to kick in. Before him in the eerie torch light, cloaked in sequined purple and orange fabric like an Amazonian silkworm, was the unmistakable figure of Saleem–Franklin Zaki Qureshi. Eddies of jasmine–tinged smoke formed a thick halo resembling a gently quivering turban about the expressionless man's head. Felix did not know how to react. He just stood there, shaking his head from side to side in a state of nervous befuddlement. Eventually he managed a hoarse whisper.

'Frankie Zaki...you great long streak of porcupine piss!' he stammered, shaking in the biting breeze. 'What the hell are *you* doing here? You scared the living crap out of me!'

'Look, are you going to help me eat this Chicken Mekhani, *or what*?' responded the cross–legged man, eyes to the ground as if nothing out of the ordinary had occurred. Without awaiting a response the elegant figure rose like a snake charmed from its basket and produced a thin white plastic bag dripping with rectangular tin containers. He proceeded purposefully towards the canal path; Felix followed silently, five paces behind. The conversationless march to the boat proved incontestably that Saleem–

Franklin – Frankie for short, being of Indian and American extraction – had been the instigator of this absurdly pointless siege. For he knew the return route more sure–footedly than Felix did, even in the insipid torchlight.

Frankie cut an impressive figure at six foot one, yet his attire was that of a man unsuccessfully suppressing a profound identity–crisis. An intensely embroidered apricot silk kurta flowed gracefully to his bare calves and stopped short of vulgar lime–green training shoes. Struggling valiantly to make itself heard from underneath his loose–fitting upper garment was a dashiki audaciously fashioned out of silver and gold kincob. A bright yellow baseball cap topped off the vivid ensemble. His hair was worn in dumpy dreadlocks that emerged like unruly pinecones from under his cap as he affected a dance–like strut, virtually springing along the canal path. Over his bladed shoulder, brandishing its dozen finger–slicing strings, was his slender necked, ornately decorated instrument: a sitar. Just as Felix was about to demand an explanation for the second time, the wailing resumed at high volume – a plangent plainchant, fractious and raucous. The music, not unlike its perpetrator, straddled a perplexing palette of styles from the East and West – indipop, bangra and bluegrass – a kind of Frankie goes to Bollywood – truly an unnerving and incomprehensible cacophony, gritty and demonic, and his venomous lyrics spat forth like rusty razorblades. With untuned sitar accompaniment it had sounded even more weirdly eclectic – Emenem meets Ravi Shankar perhaps, with a twist of Shaggy and a dash of Sid Vicious thrown in for good measure.

'People used to call me the Rapper—raga—rasta—masta' growled Frankie, interrupting himself mid expulsion. But Felix's silence indicated his continued preference for porcupine piss. Soon the two men were sat together aboard Wagtail in complete darkness. Felix fidgeted impatiently, bemused, waiting for the man to speak so that he could pretend to want to speak first. For something was up, and Frankie's takeaway dinner was obviously just a shallow ruse to curry favour.

In the sickly yellow moonlit living room squatted two men who'd known each other for years but patently didn't know each other at all, and whose camaraderie had at one time seemed fated yet now seemed unconscionable. Each had their reason for skulking behind innuendo, and as a miserly candle dribbled what light it could sustain onto the glistening pile of decimated popadums, fewer grains of truth than grains of rice were brought to the table. Each man pushed tepid chicken into his mouth in preference to tackling the inevitable topic. As if suddenly reminded, Frankie spoke calmly.

'I've just done cold turkey, actually.'

'Really?' blurted Felix, scatter—bombing pilaf rice across the floor. 'I wondered why you smell like the bottom of a birdcage.'

Ignoring the nervous repartee, Frankie suddenly seemed to crave sympathy, speaking with an accent that defied easy categorisation. The man had evidently absorbed a few shavings of dialect from every place he'd lived during the past fifteen years, and his vocabulary too vacillated moment by moment between 'lazy—but—educated' and 'street'. It took the duration of two cigarettes to cover the first few jobs and towns he'd worked in.

'Blimey, your CV must read like a gazetteer, Frankie' stammered Felix obsequiously, grateful for the temporary shelter of an inconsequential topic. Little of his career amounted to much though, Felix found himself thinking, recalling the brazen ambition of his felicitous college buddy. The pair soon dispatched the food, some of it finding their mouths, but as Felix settled into a more comfortable chair his body language communicated a rather different sentiment.

Frankie continued to skirt the issue, embroidering details of an unfruitful job he'd once had satsuma–picking in Spain; apparently, when that had gone pear–shaped, a spell packing chicken breasts had gone tits–up, too.

'Of course, despite my two–two in Geology, I've only ever been *really* good at one thing' said Frankie in a moment of uncompelling sincerity. Felix's static expression was clearly not the response anticipated, but was probably preferable to the ill–judged quip about tutus poised on his tongue.

'Kids', said Frankie.

'Oh…of course' replied Felix, trying to appear intrigued. 'How many have you got then?'

'None, you oaf, I couldn't eat a *whole* one' Frankie snorted. 'But I first realised I could make children's eyes light up when I did a summer season at Butlins.'

'What were you, a Redcoat?' Felix smirked, glancing pointedly at Frankie's costume, his powers of diplomacy waning conspicuously.

'No, collecting deckchair tickets actually.'

'Come again?'

Frankie sighed noisily, partly to register his frustration, but also to evacuate a troublesome cardamom pod from the back of his throat.

'Anyone can make *adults* laugh – you just tell schoolboy jokes and insert the word 'fuck' in judicious places.'

'Fucking right' nodded Felix, glancing with justifiable satisfaction at his recently purchased edition of 'Profanisaurus'.

'But *children's* humour has to be much more robust, much better *thought through.*'

'Fucking right, again' approved Felix, cramming an elusive triangle of Keema Nan into his mouth.

'I polished up a little act of my own, and got my big chance one night when Chortling Charlie cried off with food poisoning' he went on, watching Felix devour the oddly tinted fragment. He sniffed and ejected a bay leaf.

'Charlie always thought he'd get to Broadway on the back of his comedy–conjuring act.'

'So, where is he now?' asked Felix, not remotely interested.

'In Broadmoor, on the back of his criminal act' Frankie sighed peremptorily.

'He used to pickpocket his punters as a 'legit' part of the act, but wasn't always forthcoming when it came to returning a bulging wallet. 'Funky Frankie' wouldn't have been my choice of stage name, but the kids really dug it, and I even trousered some of Charlie's tricks.'

'Bloody hell Frankie, you always were interested in magic, weren't you? I remember now, that phase you went through at college, boring us shitless with silly coin tricks and stuff.'

'Yeah' Frankie replied slowly, reliving an episode in a Bangladeshi corner shop involving a drilled–out fifty pence piece elasticated to his inner sleeve. Felix shuddered too, recalling the silver sword that had appeared from under the counter – in the event, an altogether more impressive piece of conjuring. For a moment then he'd recaptured the old Frankie, or rather, the young Frankie, with whom he'd spent three years pretending to grow up. Yes, there was nearly half as much of the enchanting as of the disreputable about the man.

'Anyway, I made quite a bit of progress in that direction' Frankie continued, eager to develop the topic further. 'For the last five years I've been working the tables at private functions.'

'Beats lap–dancing, I dare say', reflected Felix, not entirely sure what working the tables actually meant, let alone what lap–dancing might involve.

'I attend business do's and stuff, doing slight–of–hand with, well, anything that comes to hand.'

Felix looked almost impressed. 'I hope you dropped the Funky Frankie persona, mate?'

'Damned right. My Equity Card registers me as Jean–Jacques Godeaux, after the famous 1920's Belgian stage illusionist. I'd always worshipped Godeaux, even as a kid.'

'Don't you think your stage name is trying just a *little*

bit too hard, mate?' shrieked Felix, reminded of his old friend's weakness for theatricality. 'It's so frigging long it needs a commercial break in the middle!'

Frankie just smiled in quiet acknowledgement, rocked on the back legs of his spindly chair, and yawned a good deal more melodiously than he'd shown himself capable of singing.

'I'll sing you a song I wrote, in a minute' he threatened.

Felix looked apprehensively towards the jewel–laden sitar, a thing of exquisite beauty, but capable of a life–shortening din when strummed like George Formby's ukulele.

'But first, I should finish what I started' he said, evidently now ready to dust off the topic he'd been keeping at arm's length for more than an hour. Felix faked a yawn. A few more seconds passed as Frankie deftly constructed an alarmingly long joint and proceeded to torch it with a flame tall enough to singe a penguin's pituitary.

'The four of clubs, by the way' he mumbled nonchalantly, reaching ominously for his slender instrument, a billowing reefer dangling perilously from his collapsed lips.

'Your back pocket – *the four of clubs*' he repeated, choosing a slightly more clipped articulation and tentatively plucking out the introduction to his new 'song'. It sounded suspiciously similar to 'Stairway to Heaven', tinged with sequences blatantly lifted from 'Camberwick Green'. Felix submitted to Frankie's eyebrow gestures and delved into his rear pocket. He placed its contents on the indecisively

92

illuminated table, then rolled back in his chair in falsely subdued prolepsis. Frankie stopped plucking suddenly and leaned forward, penetrating the objects with his eyes. With one finger he carefully slid away a single item.

'What of it?' Felix sniffed, hardly registering what he knew to be his dreary C.Y.S. Court Pass.

'Turn it over, Felix' Frankie whispered melodramatically, leaning back.

Felix obliged. It was a miniature playing card: the four of clubs.

'I'm sure I should be amazed Frankie, but somehow, well, I'm not.'

'Ah, that'll be because you never were any good at *dates*' responded Frankie, as though this amounted to some kind of clarification.

'It might also have something to do with being colour blind' simpered Felix pathetically.

'Pah! Colour blind, my candy arse…you always did hide behind that, as if it gives you *carte blanche*.'

'Au contraire, carte *bleu*, avec les trucs *noir*, je crois' corrected Felix in an accent closer to Liverpudlian than French.

'At least you've learned to count, I see…not still playing the dyslex–thick card then?'

'Never mind what frigging cards I might be playing, play yours!' He sent the four of clubs skidding across the table. 'And if you don't come clean soon, I'll push that sitar so far down your epiglottis you'll need a foot long toothbrush to…'

'Okay, okay' calmed Frankie, 'stay in the zone, I'll

explain.'

'Cast your shrink–wrapped brain back to the events of early July 1993' he began, as if dusting off the epilogue to an Agatha Christie whodunit. 'It's a humid evening, graduation day looms, and there are eight of us sat in what passed for a garden in Claude Road.'

Felix allowed himself to relax, now recognising that this whole scenario might be crazy but was probably not life threatening, after all. Frankie continued, ambidextrously constructing a second spliff for his companion with one hand and fiddling with the tuning of his giraffe–necked instrument with the other.

'Each of us had matched our blood level with beer and had puffed enough grass to keep Richard Branson afloat for a fortnight.'

'Just get on with it, mate' Felix groaned, 'some of us have *real* jobs to be up for, remember?'

'As you will doubtless recall, I had been practising my famed magic act all afternoon, knowing how much you all looked forward to it – I knew that, because you always said the opposite.'

Felix's eyebrows rose. He'd heard a similar casuistry before, somewhere.

'My piece of resistance came following a series of, admittedly, less than consummate coin manipulations, during which you'd all shown me as much interest as you would a leftover Christmas sprout; I had all to play for.'

Feeble, beer–clouded images congregated in Felix's mind.

'So, I hit you with my best *ever* illusion, a card trick

94

to crown all card tricks' Frankie sparked enthusiastically. 'Each of you chose a card and put your signature on the back. You replaced them in the pack and I proceeded to burn the full sodding monty in front of your very eyes. But, resisting the impulse to affect a cheesy discovery of the restored cards from cracks in the patio, I handed to each of you a prediction. I then made the solemnest of promises that I would come back and finish the trick, big style, on or near the fiftieth anniversary of Godeaux's tragic death, December 19th, to be precise.'

Felix hooted manically.

'You mean to say we're *all* going to get a visit from mad Frankie Zaki…Jean–Jacques what's–his–face, or whatever the hell you decide to call yourself next? *And* that you expected us to have marked in our diaries a date you gave us fifteen years ago at an al fresco piss–up in Cardiff! I nearly forgot my *own* birthday recently, and I've had thirty–odd chances to get that stuck in my nut!'

A thin veneer of frost seemed to settle on the two characters then, just as the ice had shown signs of thawing, too. The evening had started on a bad note and had slowly acquired greater dissonance; Frankie's unremitting racket resumed its penitent tones with added ardour, as if to underscore the pathos. But a question of some pertinence was beginning to pose itself in Felix's chewed–up mind. It had little to do with *why* Frankie had gone to such perplexing lengths to pull off his magnum opus, for he remembered the zeal with which the guy could approach such things, and more to do with *how*. He began to piece together the evening's events in the order they'd occurred.

First, the disturbance outside that had triggered his panic attack, the shocking silhouette at the window and the furtive rustle under the door. Then the onset of the distant hum that had turned out to be Frankie's doleful intonation, the outrageous singing that followed, and finally the appearance of his fashion–challenged, multiple–named college pal, presumably facing East amidst a heady kedgeree of curry and cannabis.

Frankie suddenly burst the swelling pause, exhaling stilted whiffs of opaque smoke like a speech–impeded dragon.

'Actually Felix, you've missed out several quite significant parts. I knew you would.'

'What?' replied Felix incredulously, not entirely registering that Frankie had read his mind.

'I *knew* you'd skip past the bit about putting the playing card in your pocket, and I *knew* you wouldn't ask yourself how my prediction *is* a prediction unless you've been holding it all this time.'

'Well, I was coming to that' Felix responded unconvincingly, in a daze.

'You see, mental magic is not about misdirection, nor is it to do with left–brain, right–brain eye movement. It comes down to just one, simple thing…*research.*'

Felix inhaled on the reefer he'd just been passed and billowed a rather less imposing dragon cloud.

'Look', Frankie continued, 'a barrister only asks a question of his defendant when he's sure he knows the answer, right? You should know that, with the court hours you've clocked up.'

'Yes, of course…but how did you know I…'

'And so it's a simple matter of planting seeds, nurturing fledgling shoots, and….well, harvesting' said Frankie smugly, the horticultural analogy thoroughly exhausted. Felix's mind turned turgidly from behind a kaleidoscope of part–formed thoughts. He decided to stay schtum; let Frankie have his moment.

'These days, I take my trade *very* seriously' Frankie continued, clearing a little of the accumulating haze. 'I practise it every chance I get, forever refining and perfecting it. There's cash in it, too – the whole E.S.P racket is a license to print the stuff; it's older than prostitution and a good deal sexier. My drug problem woke me up, Felix. It's the best thing that ever happened to me.'

Ironically, Felix's mind had begun swimming faster than Duncan Goodhew on methadone.

'Sure, I can tell' he responded, his old lisp making an unguarded reappearance. 'So, what we're smoking here is standard behind the bike–shed stuff, is it?'

Patently, the weed had a bigger kick to it than a pissed–off donkey.

Felix's leg brushed something jagged as he repositioned his body on the tiny sofa. It was his photo album, strangely damp to the touch. Frankie reached a frenzied instrumental cadenza but watched with one eye as his companion absent–mindedly leafed through it, as if impelled by some external force. He *was* being directed of course, and Frankie waited to see how long it would take Felix to register the photo of the seven college chums who'd partied so hard on that long forgotten night of

97

debauchery in 1993.

Felix got there, eventually, just as Frankie's latest unprepared modulation was about to leave him floundering in the theoretically untenable key of F double–sharp minor. The first clue to strike home was the empty brown envelope, ripped open and now lying crumpled along the spine of the album. Then the photo adjacent to it – he'd missed the significance of it the first time around, but now each of the seven carousing individuals it captured took on fresh meaning. Perhaps he'd have taken more notice of it if Frankie – the eighth member – had been in shot, too? The high–grade spliff had narrowed his vision, but the photograph regressed him back to Cardiff in a single blink, as if hypnotised...

...Frankie's magical soirée was in full swing, although his miserable card tricks were leaving his audience colder than an air–conditioned cinema. Captive they might be, but captivated, no...

...Felix's lightheaded state gently transported his body up to the rafters. From here he monitored the sartorially satirical sitarist's giddying harmonic undulations and could at last take in the full measure of the nonsensical evening. But Frankie was in no mood to allow Felix breathing space, even from the sanctity of the ceiling.

'How on earth *could* I be in the photo, since I *took* it!' sighed Frankie presciently, simultaneously navigating treacherous chromatic terrain with his demonic instrument. From on high Felix grunted a reflex acknowledgement, again underrating Frankie's apparent feat of mind reading.

'You know, Wagner took twenty years to polish up

his Ring. Now that's what I call patience.'

'*God, oh...*please tell me you're not drawing a parallel between Wagner and '*God–eaux*' moaned Felix, never too enfeebled to flag down a passing pun.

'Okay, if it is *that* trivial, how come you fell for every dumb detail I rigged up for you?' responded Frankie sharply. 'Listen, and I'll explain' he said in his most maddening Jackanory tone, preparing to spout a monologue he'd inwardly rehearsed a hundred times.

'Don't you think I'm as aware as you that *no* card trick is worth waiting fifteen years for? Perhaps I had a more subtle point to make? Perhaps I needed to show you all that I was capable of seeing something through, something that none of you would have given me credit for back then? When I performed that card prediction to you all, to tell you the truth, I never really thought I'd follow it up. But I found myself copying across the dates from diary to diary, year after year, and even though I knew you'd all forget about it, I decided I'd see it through to the bitter end. If I've proved nothing to you, I *have* proved something to myself. Of all of you, Felix, you've been the hardest to track down. I found out where you were working easily enough, but I had my work cut out following you back here to case the joint, undetected in the dark, last night. I realised how simple it would be to break in today though, while you were at work, and set things up. You might try locking your door occasionally – you never know what vermin will crawl in.'

Felix's lower mandible crashed like a tray of Martini glasses.

'I didn't break your two portholes, by the way' he

added, pointing to two taped up orifices Felix had long neglected to fix, '*another* of your skeletons must have come out of its closet and beaten me to it.'

Frankie picked up the torch and began flicking the switch.

'I planned every last detail using the props I found hanging around – from placing the photo album under the sofa, to putting a new battery into your torch...to turning off your appliances. I even knocked up a replica of your prediction envelope, assuming you'd have shifted it from the album years ago. I needn't have bothered; it was there all right, exactly where I'd seen you put it a week after the party. I felt a bit mean tossing your last few lumps of coal into the canal, but I had to get you completely freaked out. I was bloody pleased with my plan; everything went like clockwork. Your phone dying like that was a stroke of luck though – you might have raised help – I watched you lose your rag big time then! With nothing better to do with yourself, you'd be certain to chill out in here and browse your crappy old album. I was sure you'd suss me. I'd been trudging around outside like a friggin' antelope for ages before you became suspicious.'

'*Chill out!* You're damn right...you utter bastard' spat Felix, rummaging around for the gas stopcock. 'And you even disconnected the ignition so I couldn't start the bloody engine!'

'No harm done mate, it was only for an hour or so – I got colder than *you* hanging around by those bleedin' trees with nothing but a bag of balti to toast my rocks on!' chuckled Frankie, plucking an errant sprig of parsley from between his front teeth. 'I've not laughed as much since last Diwali, when a cosmically proportioned bluebottle dive–bombed my aunt Sangeeta's sari. Boy, that was one hell of a smash 'n grab.'

Within minutes Frankie had helped Felix to restore power. The pair sat squinting in the new light, Felix unsure whether he'd punch Frankie or hug him. He flattened out the creases in the little envelope, peaked inside it and then remembered the screwed up advert in his pocket.

'Explain this horse shite, mate' said Felix, noticing first the red handwritten scrawl. 'More of your smoke and mirrors piffle, no doubt?' He read it out loud, achieving a suitably supercilious air: 'I intend to descend near the end, dear friend…4C191208…No, don't tell me, some wacko variation on the Fibonacci sequence?'

'December 19th 2008: four of clubs, *of course*!' blurted Frankie, startled by Felix's sluggish pace.

Felix smiled, not at himself but for his obsessive, insecure friend; a prediction fulfilled, a bond restored.

'Why write your prediction on a dentist's ad, anyway?' he asked, still dawdling his way through the fifteen year–old conundrum.

'My old fella's partnership, you wazzock – don't you remember him fixing that temporary cap for you, the year before? Look, it's a doddle. Yellow Pages sent Mr. Kasai, his senior partner, a dozen copies by mistake, so I cut his ad out seven times; a copy for each of you – a *clue*, perhaps?'

Felix nodded, a smile widening to reveal the aforementioned temporary cap, still clinging to life, now yellower than a chihuahua's eyeballs.

'I hereby wipe your karma scoreboard clean and leave you in peace, Felix' Frankie smiled, climbing his way into the sitar's shoulder strap. 'I've two more manic missions still to complete, you know.'

'I predict they'll go swimmingly, Frankie' Felix smiled, generously. 'Say hi to the guys for me.'

He didn't mean it, but Frankie already knew that.

The two friends shook hands. No false promises of reunions were exchanged, no glib prophecies for the future. Little more was said as the jovial jongleur slipped away into the blackness, his spangled instrument nodding happily in anticipation of more nocturnal visits in the hands of its madcap virtuoso.

'Can you actually *play* that bloody thing?' Felix sniped, from the safety of his longboat.

Frankie turned and shouted as he evaporated into the moonlight. 'Only well enough to make you weep, mate.'

Felix tumbled into a bittersweet silence, relieved to be alone but saddened at losing what he now realised had once been his best friend, for the second time. As he tugged back his duvet he discovered two small presents – a lump of coal and a small brown envelope. On its reverse, hurriedly scribbled in one of Felix's glitter–pens, were nine maudlin words framed within the outline of a Christmas tree: 'I intend to be your friend, to the end'.

'Soppy Indian sod' muttered Felix, wrestling with a strong–willed joss stick and turning out the light.

6

Atrax Robustus

It was some time later that Felix would have cause to reconsider the security of his boat. For much of Wagtail's time was spent languishing sedately among itinerant wildlife and brushy fauna, perhaps twelve miles away from where its owner acted out his fraught daily business. An impressive food chain organised itself under the slender boat's water line, and only an occasional cursory lick of paint would undermine the miniature beasts' conspiracy to stake permanent squatting rights. Troops of militarily marshalled birds spent their waking hours patrolling Wagtail's small territory of canal, which happened to lie on a due west–east line. Like Felix, they seemed to draw comfort from the inevitability of awakening to the caramel sun, however short–lived it proved to be. Unlike Felix, usually departing for work at dawn's crack, they could occasionally enjoy Wagtail's sundial effect as a fattening shadow cast itself across the spindly line of water. This particular patch of canal had been his home for several weeks, Felix keeping a vigil for the ever–present threat of mooring fees. He liked it here. It was about a quarter of a mile from the nearest point of vehicular entry, but the daily trudge across the candy smelling fields would top up his flagging sugar levels and enliven his dulled senses; a welcome chance to reconnect with his disconnected world.

Christmas had passed without undue strain on his bank balance or sensibilities. A mercifully brief family visit to the boat had incurred only marginal breakage and distress to the neighbouring eco–structure. New Year's resolutions were showing early cracks and Felix's perspective of life was gradually easing back to a state of healthy cynicism. The climate was one of cold, unchallenging and unchanging predictability. He sat alone, quite contentedly, listening to his new Herbie Hancock CD, the one inoffensive Christmas offering from his brother, Clayton. Its 72.5 minutes duration had been subtly calibrated to accommodate a typical couch–potato's caffeine and carbohydrate requirement, which presumably accounted for its enduring popularity in his spiritual home, Starbucks. He'd been appreciating the music's cyclical charm for several hours as he went about his pointless pottering.

A loud thump on the roof was barely sufficient to turn his head towards the front door, which swung open abruptly to confirm the arrival of his brother. Clay's new T–shirt, clashing splendidly over his sweatshirt, was marginally less uncouth than earlier vintages; Felix had chosen it well.

It read: 'I am a bomb technician – if you see me running, try to keep up'. Clay's arrival confirmed the time had come to share an annual burden that, for each of them, was moderated slightly by contrasting ulterior motives: a New Year's visit to their uncle Albert. For Felix, it was a chance to check out the seventy year–old's impressive record collection, which embraced everything from twee 1920's musicals to that inevitably transient jazz genre known as 'modern' – the collection halted abruptly here, in the 1960's, as if nothing of consequence had emerged subsequently. For Albert this was indeed the case. He'd suffered a partly debilitating stroke aged thirty–six, and so the dutiful visits offered Felix, for one paltry hour each January, a glimpse of his own fragile mortality. For Clay however, the trip presented an opportunity to monitor his uncle's ongoing financial position, ever optimistic that a lucrative health insurance payout all those years ago had been invested wisely. Clay's approach had evolved over the years from feigning impecuniousness to more brazen requests for handouts. Neither tactic had yet borne fruit, but Clay's tenacity had ample ambit.

The truth was that Albert's flat had few luxuries aside from a home–assembled valve amplifier and a pair of Wharfedale speakers that had been warm to the touch for four decades. Albert shared Felix's craving for solitude, but also his paradoxical need for companionship. He welcomed them, as he always did, with a half smile, a lingering palsy that immediately reminded both nephews of the premature damage he had sustained. This visit would last just twenty minutes as Albert was already gearing himself up for an afternoon's indoor bowls. While Clay carefully surveyed the flat for contemporary clues to his inheritance prospects, Felix hovered in the kitchen chatting to Albert, waiting for the kettle to condescend to boil. The man swiftly assembled two small belated Christmas presents. His visceral understanding of the mismatched brothers manifested as a 78 acrylic of Gershwin's 'Rhapsody in Blue' for Felix and a puny cheque for Clay. Neither gift hit its mark, and soon the peremptory yawns and the donning of Albert's white cap punctuated the passing of another year, another box ticked.

As Clay availed himself of Albert's makeshift toilet Felix spotted a little brown medicine bottle on the kitchen table. He picked it up and read its faded prescription out loud.

'Sennacod: to be taken twice daily. Use before April 1999...I didn't know you had problems in *that* direction' Felix winced, not wishing to appear unduly anal about it.

'Oh, I haven't, Felix' came the reply, as quick as a flash.

'So, why have you got these, then?'

'Well, I discovered them in my cabinet and noticed the use–by date had passed a decade ago. Anyway, I thought I'd give them a go, just to see if they're still okay. I've taken one a day for the past week, and I've suffered no side–effects *at all!*' he exclaimed, palpably chuffed at this revelation.

'But surely, Unc' restrained Felix, 'you shouldn't be *taking* them at all, if you aren't actually constipated?'

'But that's just it, I'm *still not* constipated, Felix' he

smiled.

'Come on bro, for sanity's sake' muttered Clay under his breath, standing by the open door, sneering at the derisory figure etched on his cheque. The three shook hands and Albert slipped off to the sanctity of his bowls match. Felix had found a moment to discreetly replace the old 78 back onto its shelf in readiness for its presentation next January, while Clay had gleaned a few figures to check in his copy of the FT, which he should hardly have needed to confirm the pitiful position of Albert's 500 BT shares.

Half an hour later, Clay's BMW returned Felix to his mobile country residence. The car's sleek physique glided suavely up the stony lane, arriving at the point where only the keenest pedestrians would be likely to continue their peregrinations. 'Cheers mate' said Felix, enjoying one last sumptuous swish of the door. Clay nodded distractedly and dissolved like a Tardis, leaving Felix to whistle his way along the route he knew so well, a narrow and meandering path arched by high–reaching pine trees. Semi-darkness had arrived unnervingly early; it was just 6:30, and Felix began mulling over the options for his evening repast. As he mooched along the ever–thinning path he glanced to his right and admired Wagtail, leaning majestically against her mooring, dark and impressive in the half distance. He approached without haste, fishing for his keys as he herringboned up the gangplank. Then he stopped, just two feet from the door, arm outstretched. Something was not right.

Where there had once been a neat little brass lock there was now a hole in the wood and a pronounced indentation in the frame next to it; the door was ajar by a few degrees. In twelve years of living alone he had never experienced anything of this sort, just the inevitable marauding group of drunken yobos larking about on a Saturday night. He crept off the boat to see what else he might adduce. But on peeking through the windows he found nothing except what appeared to be minimal evidence of furniture movement. He didn't know whether to feel outraged or plain scared. He certainly felt violated, and went back onboard as soon as he was positive he was alone, anxious to rid his boat of its residual ambience. What was he to do, ring the police? They'd take till next Thursday to find the boat, let alone do anything about it.

Strangely, upon closer examination, nothing much had disappeared anyway, just a few quid he'd piled up on the kitchenette table while performing the annual tidying blitz. One or two drawers were open around the place, but Felix knew that didn't necessarily mean anyone had been nosing, since canal boats have a habit of rocking as other vessels pass. Slowly he calmed himself, realising that his laptop, briefcase and work papers were safely where he'd left them, strewn about the bedroom floor in accordance with his somewhat idiosyncratic filing system. But then it dawned on him that he may have only just avoided a confrontation, for if the intruders had seen him leave, they'd quite probably have spotted him return. After all, he and Clay had been gone an hour and a half at most.

A few hours of recovery time pierced the pall of the invasion a little, and Felix soon found himself whistling inanely while concocting something that resembled a stir—fry but smelt more like an escaping camembert. Radio Four had drawn him into a captivating argument about incarcerated pandas, a subject not especially close to his heart, yet one he felt qualified to contribute to at high volume. The deglutition of his meal was speedily affected, subliminally troubled by the outstanding issue of security. His brother offered little support – 'get yourself a dog...or a hyena' he screeched nesciently down the phone. But Felix had an allergy to any pet that ate, slept or fornicated more than he did. The remaining possibilities amounted to a toucan trained to chant 'bugger off or I'll bite your balls', a snake with constricting tendencies, or an agoraphobic bat.

Or...a spider. Now this option might not occur to many recently burgled canal dwellers, since spiders don't bark, attack to order, or have any primordial sense of defending its owner's premises. 'Ah', thought Felix out loud, 'but who else would think all of that through on a dark, cold evening in the middle of nowhere?' He permitted himself a little indulgence of fantasy, picturing a ferocious spider trained to crawl up suspicious looking trouser legs with a view to demobilising any objects of a pendulous disposition. 'No, this is the wrong tack' he mumbled, shaking his head in the shivering light of three gold—painted Christmas candles. Surely the answer lay in the idea of what *might* be lying in wait for an intruder, rather than what he could construct as a plausible fake. Following this path a little further raised the possibility of a spider silhouetted against night–lights, projected perhaps from behind an obliquely illuminated draught curtain. Yes, this was a more lucrative approach. Felix loved a project that depended upon multiple levels of ingenuity rather than a single level of practicability. He busied himself for the remainder of the evening with a gamut of Heath Robinsonian possibilities involving revolving projector screens and cardboard cut–outs shaped like bird–eating monsters. He slept on it, or rather, he slept on a broken tennis racket that might yet have to serve as a weapon of self–defence.

Felix awoke with dented confidence. How could he power his contraption in the event of a catastrophic drop in battery power? Another unannounced visit from Frankie would scupper him, too. As he watched the silvery meniscus of his stewed coffee fold into the cup, he hit on it; the perfect subterfuge. The plan had its roots in that timeless masterpiece, the 'beware of the dog' sign, a strategy commonly attributed to farcically small dwellings, where there can self–evidently be nothing more potent than an intellectually gifted dachshund in residence. Out here however, Felix felt confident he could get away with something quite daring. He formulated the remaining details while absorbing caffeine faster than a bath load of sun–dried tarantulas. He would grease his rusty Blue Peter skills later, at the office.

ATRAX ROBUSTUS

By that evening Felix's sign was complete. It looked almost authoritative in its laminated sleeve, typed in large font and Blu–Tacked conspicuously to the window of his newly appointed front door. It read:

This is to certify that the owner of 'Wagtail', Felix Abercrombie Esq., licensed under ruling 4667349 by the British Academic Body of Specimen Arachnid Research Developers (BABSARD ©), is permitted to hold 6 specimens of <u>ATRAX ROBUSTUS</u>. This shall be exclusively for the purpose of obtaining measurements associated with the A.R.'s extensive jaw extension capacities in pursuing its natural food source, the Southern Chilean mongoose.

NB: This particular species of tropical spider has unique attributes, principally its daily habit of eating twice its own body weight at a single sitting. <u>On no account</u> should persons unauthorised, or not wearing British Standard Teflon arachnid protection gloves (see appendix 3a) handle these creatures. Respiratory equipment is advisable.

VERY DANGEROUS. KEEP OFF THESE PREMISES!

Felix was so chuffed at having cocked a snoop at perspective burglars, he almost wished one would turn up. Despite its astonishingly obvious hoax factor, he seemed to sleep easier at night. He felt reassured, able to leave the boat at any time of the day or evening, convinced that his tactic was close to perfect, conceptually. Gilding the lily slightly, he'd attached a plausibly large plastic spider to the draught curtain, so that a wandering torchlight might pick it up. Wagtail had never felt so secure, and she too languished more easily in her beauty spot. A month on, the sign had become so familiar he scarcely took notice of it anymore. Clay's predictable derision of it merely fuelled Felix's conviction: Wagtail was truly impenetrable.

Until, that is, he was proved wrong. For like all flawless plans, it'll never go wrong, until it *does*. Felix arrived home one bitterly cold evening, dragging a sack of coal along the uneven path, humping the damned thing with ever–smaller gaps between breathers. Panting the icy air like an asthmatic Labrador, he relived the horror of a month earlier. For the door was ajar. The lock didn't appear to be jimmied – had he merely forgotten to lock up properly that morning? It wasn't until he'd installed himself indoors that he became sure this was a break–in, although the evidence was a little more compelling on this occasion. Not that the items taken were any more significant – it was just that a few rather odd objects had been pointlessly disturbed. Two of his dainty porthole curtains now dangled from a single point on their rails, and the objects that would normally be parked just inside the door – an umbrella stand and a hen–shaped magazine rack – had been displaced randomly. Felix was dismayed, as much by the patent failure of his bespoke sign as by the fact that he'd been ransacked a second time. He slammed the door violently behind him and retired to bed, not even bothering to tackle the freezing stove.

ATRAX ROBUSTUS

Another bitter morning struck with alarming alacrity, a predictably spiteful initiation to the day. Getting out of bed proved to be rather less enticing than climbing into it had been. Pissing in the sink while attempting to shave, he sighed like an old horse and assessed the need for a shower by sniffing an armpit. Needing immediate consolation he chewed over the prospect of a massive breakfast adjacent to a raging stove. By eight o clock the fry–up was progressing well, but the stoke–up was proving more problematic – somehow, in the ensuing chaos of the previous evening his elegant hand–painted coalscuttle had become misplaced. He searched for it in vain. He'd indulged its mischievous game of hide 'n seek several times recently, usually discovering the pesky thing skulking by the rubbish bag, camouflaged in ash. He did the job by hand, cursing even more lividly, then sat down to a plate of bendy toast, runny eggs and hard bacon. A smouldering cigarette leaned precariously against the filthy plate he was eating from, while his blackened hands dispersed charcoal traces around his harassed face. He coughed and spluttered like a pensioned–off coal miner, scattering ashes over his punctured eggs and dropping clotted ketchup onto his sleeve.

The case of the missing coalscuttle returned to him intermittently that day. It should hardly have merited such consideration in the normal course of events, yet somehow he felt its discovery might bind together other fragmentary clues to the latest invasion. Upon his return that night Wagtail welcomed him more warmly than she had the previous evening, the enthusiastic stove at last permeating the less hospitable corners of the boat. Felix took to his bed exceptionally early, indulging in a spot of light reading but quickly succumbing to sleep under the half–hearted radiance of a 40W bulb.

He awoke to the prospect of a bubbling new lead, triggered by Ruth Rendell, no doubt. Why he'd even contemplated the book was the biggest mystery; his own tawdry existence surely generated sufficient turmoil and anguish. Curiously, it seems other people's petty predicaments are generally more alluring and worthy than one's own. Nevertheless, the first thirty pages had fulfilled their principal obligation – the story had proved to be an even better cure for insomnia than Geoff Boycott's autobiography, with which Felix seemed to remember reaching page thirty–one before passing it on to his granddad, who reportedly soldiered on to page forty–six. (Mrs. Boycott probably ventured as far as page forty–seven before donating it to Age Concern). And yet the mystery had succeeded in de–icing an area of his loofah–like brain that could occasionally dabble in logic. Troubled by his unresolved predicament he embarked on a pompous oration, out loud, his Bagpuss hot water bottle feigning a measure of attentiveness.

'If everything we do or say trips inevitably from something that's happened already', he mused, 'we ought to be able to reverse–engineer every inconsequential comment, every throwaway line to find its derivation, probably in itself equally trite and capable of being retraced.'

As he pondered on the ramifications of his strangled philosophy his mother phoned, a purveyor of random thought, if ever there was one.

'I need a holiday, Felix' she chirruped with her staccato tongue.

'Ah…it's been raining then' replied Felix without an instant's delay.

'That's right dear', she sang, no hint of astonishment colouring her tone. 'Clay's taking me and Pat off to Majorca to see Bessie for a couple of days – just thought I'd let you know dear. Bye, dear…'

As Felix fashioned something faintly resembling scrambled eggs, accompanied by a penetrating radio discussion of water–hog hibernation tactics, his brain realigned itself with his earlier line of thought. Yes, his theory of cause and effect amounted to playing chess in reverse. He now realised his mother's phone call was a perfect illustration of this substantial insight, for she'd taken his response to her holiday news as a casual reference to bad weather lowering her spirits.

'But actually', he proclaimed, Bagpuss still not inclined to play devil's advocate, 'I went back *four* logical steps in a single fluent move! One: if mum's wanting a holiday, it's because she's been chatting to her gossipy neighbour, Maggie, who she's in continual competition with – Maggie's probably just got back from the Valley of the Kings, or somewhere exotic. Now, Mum avoids Maggie as much as possible, so there had to be a specific reason for their conversation. Two: there would be one of only two possible reasons for knocking on Maggie's door – to pinch some sugar, or to borrow her stepladder.' (Since he remembered his mother had given up sugar the year before, it must be the ladder). 'Three: she'd need the ladder for one of the two DIY jobs she'd conceive of doing herself: painting the fascia above the kitchen, or fixing the drainpipe above the front door, which was in the habit of unhinging itself. Four: since it's not the weather for painting, it had to be the drainpipe, which generally gives up under the strain of rainwater. Ipso bleedin' facto...*rain* equals *holiday.*'

Felix smiled conceitedly, folded his arms and tested the waterlogged eggs, which might have benefited from a bit of reverse engineering, too.

Reassured by his burgeoning powers of reasoning, he began to tackle an issue still awaiting satisfactory resolution.

'What if', he proposed to himself, issuing a thunderous egg–flavoured belch, pipe glowing in hand, 'we assume that *two* bungling burglars had been at the centre of this intrigue, not one?'

This he felt was a reasonable assumption, given that a lookout would be desirable in the event of his unexpected return.

'Having already crashed the premises a month earlier, they've established what's worth returning to steal, as well as a reasonable feel for the layout. They're confident of my late return as it's the middle of the week, and they've been observing my movements.'

Naturally, he assumed, the burglars had been attracted to the boat on the first occasion because of the Landrover's presence – for only a boat keeper would park so far out from town. He pictured two men clad in dark costume, driving slowly up to the parking area and alighting their vehicle adjacent to where his own would normally reside. He took a generous draw on the pipe and continued.

'This time they're better equipped – a torch...and bags for the booty. They pause for several minutes within eyeshot of the darkened boat to confirm it's not occupied, then move swiftly but silently onboard. While each man appears under control, one of them is distinctly less self–assured. He covers this up by adopting an overly cavalier, jocular front. They've brought the crowbar again, anticipating a break–in, but are amazed to discover it's not needed, for the idiotic owner hasn't locked his door!'

A shiver travelled down his spine and halted just short of his clenched buttocks.

'While the confident one illuminates the door handle with his torch, the insecure one reaches tentatively forward to open it. As he does this, his eye catches something neither of them had spotted at their first visit to the boat: a white sheet of paper, fixed to the window. The confident one urges his cohort forward, but the insecure one is immediately suspicious. Directing the light at the sign, he reads it out loud, emphasising the underlined words with a growing sense of foreboding. "Spiders, nonsense!" cries the confident one, "it's just a ruse". "Yeah, of *course* it is" titters the other, barely able to contain himself. "Spiders, huh, he's 'avin' a laugh!" The two men move forward, the confident one noticing the spider crouching on the curtain but keeping silent, aware that his companion needs no further provocation at this pivotal moment. As they advance to the point at which the living area meets the kitchenette the insecure one, inching tentatively forward, brushes his brow on a sprig of dried lavender that hangs from the ceiling above the stove. His impulse to scream is suddenly beyond his control – his bottled up nerves find immediate release. "Shit, it's…it's a spider!" he cries, leaping back and colliding with his friend. At this point the confident one experiences a sudden catastrophic lapse in composure, too. His gut reaction is to avail himself of the nearest flat object he can lay his hands on – a coalscuttle, which happens to be lying within easy reach on top of the stove – and sets about swatting violently around him. Losing his balance momentarily, he reaches out for something to steady himself, but finding only a flimsy curtain, this immediately gives way at one end of the rail. The two men continue their frantic flailing around in the dark for several seconds, a second curtain copping the full impact of the coalscuttle as the spider reappears menacingly in the darting torch light…In desperation they bolt for the door, knocking to the ground the umbrella stand and magazine rack they'd so carefully steered clear of on entering the boat. Empty handed they slip away faster than a flushed Vindaloo, both men frantically inspecting themselves for creepy crawlies at the slightest tickle.'

Felix nodded to himself contentedly, re–igniting his pipe for the fourth time since breakfast. He felt more at ease now. In his mind he'd regained a measure of control and rationalised the employment of his spider paraphernalia – he couldn't wait to rub his brother's nose in it, not that Clay's nose ever showed an inclination to be rubbed in anything but his bank manager's backside – 'Felix, you don't know shit from Christmas cake, mate. The number of people on this planet who'd be taken in by that daft notice could be counted on the fingers of one...*finger*!'

Nevertheless, Wagtail continued to be protected by free–roaming Atrax Robustuses, and once again a level of normality resumed onboard.

It wasn't until he came to replenish the stove the following evening that Felix's thoughts strayed to the one missing piece of the jigsaw – his coalscuttle. Again he scoured the boat, re–enacting the scenario in his mind as he did so. A thought began to occur to him as he sat calmly amidst a dense haze of pipe smoke. Rehearsing his hypothesis out loud somehow accorded it greater gravitas, and Bagpuss seemed in no mind to argue.

'Well, if I'm right about the order of events', he began, struggling to keep the thing alight, 'the coalscuttle would still be here somewhere...or, would it?' He picked up the tail end of the scenario again.

'The two men, led by the nervous one naturally, pelt at breakneck speed from the boat; the braver one is still clutching the scuttle as he scampers to dry land. Within a few minutes they reach their vehicle. They breathe a colossal sigh of relief as they pull away from the parking area, but as the car is reversing, the confident one, probably the driver, realises he is still gripping the scuttle. He winds down the window and...assuming he's right–handed...shuttles the scuttle far into the darkness. Finally, the two men flee from the scene.'

Despite its many–pronged presumptions, Felix's theory had an underlying simplicity to it; he just had to check it out. Trotting along the path leading to where his

LIFE ON MARS? A CATINEL'S CHANCE

Landrover dosed in the twilight, his breath slowed as he assumed the position of a stationary vehicle, using the Landrover's rotund shadow as a datum. Felix stepped slowly backwards, as if reversing out. With a look of wild intent spread across his face he pictured the man winding down the window and hurling the scuttle as hard as he could towards the coppice of tall trees marking the entrance to the path. He plotted the trajectory from the imaginary car window and, deploying a stone of approximately the same weight as the scuttle, estimated the distance travelled. His stone carried smoothly, immediately disappearing from view. Marching up to the most thickset tree along the flight path he stopped at its base. Sifting through the mulch of soggy pinecones and kicking away the composted leaves that softened the surrounding ground unearthed nothing. But as his gaze returned to head height his eyes leapt to the ends of their springs – for there, hovering in a branch at an angle of forty–five degrees to the tree trunk, wearing what might best be described as a deadpan expression, was a coalscuttle, glossed in black, an intricately painted azalea dancing along its handle. Felix skipped a tarantella back to Wagtail. As he neared the boat he realised something had been teasing with his wrist. Glancing down he caught sight of a svelte spider abseiling happily from its hurriedly constructed web at the entrance to the coalscuttle's hollow handle. He stopped for a moment, smiled and watched the gangly thing hurry away to safety in the shimmering grass. 'An Attractive–but–not–so–Robust–Robustus, if I'm not mistaken' he smiled, whimsically flicking off an archaic dog turd from the scuttle and resuming the battle with his pipe.

120

7

Small Medium at Large

◎

Felix had every right to assume he'd seen the back of Frankie Godeaux for at least another fifteen years. And so a second appearance from the faddish fool within a few weeks was going to prove challenging. It was early spring, the time of year Felix revelled most in his solitude but, ironically, suffered the most from it. He'd planned to move further down the canal towards Leamington, following the second break–in, but never quite got around to it. He'd warded off some half–hearted hostility from a mooring owner and resolved to hold his favoured spot until the summer. Wagtail looked a picture – quite literally – a local postcard publisher had taken a fancy to her idyllic situation and Felix had accepted a few dozen copies by way of royalty payoff. These he'd scattered like seeds to anyone who faintly knew him by way of recompense for a decade of overlooked birthdays and

Christmases. Wild snowdrops and hellebores dripped extravagantly from the fields around him, and clusters of dwarf daffodils were showing early precocity too, the most confident specimens flattering a patch right alongside Wagtail. While his roof floribunda bulged with potential, a recent bout of depression receded in equal measure. A week's holiday leave brought with it the exigent prospect of repainting the boat. Wagtail's skin had reached retirement age, her premature decline in part due to her owner's slapdash effort two years previously. Work anxieties had not subsided, and yet his resolve to stare them in the face seemed in resonance with the nubile life sprouting all around him. Lambing season was around the corner, and it was hard to sustain a stony demeanour embraced by so sanguine a scene.

The weather was hardly shirtsleeves, and yet Felix's jubilance kept his blood rotating as he hung precariously from the roof rail in order to reach the off–side of the boat with his lissom priming brush. The sanding down stage had progressed well and he was confident of completing the job within the time he had left. He'd temporarily traded Radio 4 and his motley collection of classical CDs for an album of Beach Boys favourites, which perhaps explained his irrational indulgence in sunglasses. The better weather also brought with it renewed interest in Wagtail II; she'd hibernated through the winter in the darkest recesses of Mervyn's hangar, up in Matlock. He planned to bring her down in time for the summer and, with this in mind, had begun customising an old towing platform he'd picked up cheap at a car boot sale.

Compared with the high jinx of December, Frankie's return would seem decidedly tame. He arrived unannounced one afternoon as Felix was approaching completion of the nearside of his boat. Felix was stunned more by Frankie's radically new appearance than by his *re–appearance* – the dreadlocks had virtually vanished leaving behind an amorphous mop, the Indian robes had evolved into a denim jacket and his Hushpuppies seemed remarkably demure compared with the puce trainers he'd last sported. The old friend's histrionics had softened too, indeed his whole persona seemed to have metamorphosed into something altogether more mellow.

'What's up then, mate?' Felix asked, as the two slurped their second mug of strong tea, perched on the roof among a plethora of assorted paint pots and stencils.

'Well, the thing is, I need your help, Felix' began Frankie, adopting a seriousness of tone Felix couldn't quite tune in to.

'You see, I teamed up with an old friend, Giuseppe, recently. He's been in the business…oh, for *ever*.'

Half a packet of Gingersnaps triggered little further enlightenment.

'It's one thing to be a nutcracker, and another to be a *successful* nutcracker' Frankie clarified, most unclearly. Felix's inflated shrug confirmed Frankie's successful

123

obfuscation.

'Nutcracker as in Tchaikovsky, or as in Brazil?' Felix probed mischievously.

'As in mind reader, you wazzock' sighed Frankie, 'or should I say, *assistant* mind reader?'

'There's a pretty high bollocks factor in all that, isn't there?' provoked Felix, pursuing a Hobnob with shiny green fingers.

'Yes, mind reading, as I seem to recall explaining to you before', continued Frankie, 'is made up of more bollocks than your average faggot. But it is nevertheless highly skilled bollocks. When you observe an illusionist at work, you imagine you're watching him perform a trick – but you're *actually* being treated to a whole succession of smaller illusions that fold back on each other so seamlessly you're convinced of what is not possible. Anyway, the real skill of the nutcracker is practiced days or even weeks before a show. In prestigious gigs it can involve a tight–knit group of researchers, all weevilling away from their particular angle, uncovering details that between them amount to something tangible.'

Felix's body language revealed a glimmer of interest. 'A sort of Nutcracker *Suite*', he quipped. Frankie continued, undaunted.

'Let's take a hypothetical situation' he said, flinging poisonous fumes from his flaring nostrils. 'A hit–list of punters who've purchased tickets for a show is compiled, as usual.'

Felix's frown prompted further detail.

'Look, the easiest person to convert to Christianity

124

is the one you've persuaded to attend the local church "just to *see*", right?' proposed Frankie. 'So, anyone attending a 'mentalism' event has straight away demonstrated a capacity to be convinced spiritual communication is possible, however inclined he might be to assert the opposite.'

Frankie lined his cavernous lungs with cannabis, pointedly not checking Felix's face for acknowledgement. 'It's just entertainment, after all – mentalists use the same booking agents as clowns like Chortling Charlie, for heaven sake. Anyway, stage two is where the real work begins. Electoral registers, phone books and the internet corroborate that Bloggs the ticket holder really *is* Bloggs, and basic background information about him is assembled. The team are looking for characters with a faintly interesting past, people who've been recently bereaved or dangerously ill perhaps...folk who've been featured in the local rag for saving a shiatsu from a three inch puddle, or whatever. Then, finally, they want that "golden nugget" element, some off–the–wall detail that seems at once irrelevant and yet brilliantly insightful. They'll prise out two, maybe three such individuals from a shortlist, just in case of non–attendance on the night, all of whom live far enough apart to be confident they don't know each other. It's easy for the mentalist to wallow in persiflage when he knows already whose nut's been cracked.'

'Ah, but what happens if someone they *didn't* research responds to the call from the "other side"?' enquired Felix, his curiosity lifting fractionally in response to further biscuit stimuli.

'Simple, you pitch a curveball – "Oh...I'm losing

my connection with your husband Mrs. Cartright...but your favourite colour *is* lilac, isn't it?' Frankie affected. 'You only need to have fully honed up one, maybe two punters from the audience to round off a big event. The rest of the show is bluff 'n bluster, gypsy stuff really, just a load of crystal balls.'

Frankie paused for a much–needed inhalation before expunging smoke sufficient to cure a bathtub of haddock.

'You see, if every card in your pack is the nine of hearts, prediction becomes a bit easier, doesn't it? There you go – an example. My overblown trick in Cardiff came down to a switch of packs after the initial shuffle, not a *prediction* at all.'

Felix smiled, unable to resist a momentary interlude from Frankie's diatribe. His own recent small–scale act of diversion, which had preyed on arachnophobic burglars, tapped resources Frankie would undoubtedly appreciate.

'Clearly, I've been proffering shit to a dung beetle' grinned Frankie, scanning Felix's laminated sign; strangely, the man's approval amounted to something meaningful. 'We've not grown so far apart after all, I see!' he shrugged. His next breath would be sufficient to set an alpine horn in motion.

'Now, Giuseppe is the son of a private investigator, Salvatore. That's how he learned his trade, ferreting through dustbins, rifling through people's tawdry little lives in search of incriminating material – in fact, the perfect background for working the mentalism circuit. He began nutcracking for a few quite prominent mentalists – he even got a bit of TV stuff lately – you know, that Russian faker who's making his comeback now that his cash has unaccountably drained away and he's run out of wonky spoons. Paradoxically Giuseppe became well known in the business, and yet of course, completely unheard of outside it. All went well for him until about ten days ago. The gig was a biggy, top of the bill at the Coventry Playhouse – the mentalist in question had begun making quite a splash on cruise ships. Anyway, five days earlier Giuseppe had short–listed several contenders for him, among them a malfeasant civil servant whose estranged brother had been a vicar with a charmingly liberated drink problem, and an ex–con – a poacher–turned–gamekeeper type, now on the lecture circuit at institutions for young offenders.'

Felix's mood changed.

'The nugget appeal with the posh old geezer was his amazing compendium of tattoos, which naturally he'd wanted to keep covered up, but Giuseppe eyeballed them on a spying mission to the local swimming bath. The nugget with the ex–con, a dodgy dude by the name of Spencer Day, was much, much more intriguing though. You see, he was still at it, *thieving*, I mean. Giuseppe followed Day on a second sortie, assuming he was en route to his seedy snooker haunt again, but ended up at a small lockup on the outskirts of the village of Mugginton, ten miles out from Derby. The inside of the lockup looked like the stock room at Harrods – everything from silverware to software, beanbags to bum–bags. It was definitely hooky gear, too; Giuseppe said Day hung around for ages before opening the swing–over door. At first, Giuseppe was stumped.

Should he shop the guy to the police now, or keep him on line 'til after the show, since he was such a juicy catch?'

'But surely' Felix interrupted, shaking his head disdainfully, 'Day would hardly pipe up in public anyway, would he?'

'True', replied Frankie, helping himself to an almond encrusted specimen, 'but that's hardly the point. In the show the mentalist could tiptoe gently around the fact that Day had had a shady past, and dodge the recent stuff. Then, *after* the show, he'd hit the headlines with his celestial powers of ESP – "Day's more recent crimes came to me later, as if in a dream", etc.'

'Huh, if I were this Spencer geezer, I wouldn't be seen dead at the show. So, go on then, what happened?'

'Well, this is where it gets hairier than a barmaid's bum. The day after his Mugginton mission, just a few days before the gig, Giuseppe got the shock of his life…a reciprocal visit, *from Spencer Day!*'

'Bloody hell!' cried Felix, 'but, how did he…'

Frankie interrupted with a silent shrug, 'I just know he was confronted by the bloke at his front door. Day had obviously twigged he'd been followed and turned the tables on Giuseppe.

'Sounds like this chap Day's E.S.P is a tad more reliable than your guy's…what's his name?'

'Gideon Pee. Yeah, I know, sounds like a urine infection, doesn't it? Giuseppe of course swore blind he'd never followed the bloke, and just about managed to get away with a few nudges and a cut lip – scary shit for the little guy though.'

'I hope Giuseppe just cashed in his chips then, and walked away – plumped for the old git with "I love Doris" tattooed on his arse' said Felix.

'I'm afraid not – by now, Giuseppe was like a dog with another dog's turd. So he fed all the information to Pee, missing out the part about having been rumbled, and urged him to go for it, live!'

'What a dozy twat!' echoed Felix, reaching out to grab a lungful of Frankie's smoke in exchange for a crumbling caramel wafer.

'You see, Giuseppe's as much of a mentalist at heart as the *mentalist* is, isn't he – minus the stage presence bit. At any rate, he knows a money spinner when he's onto one.'

'More of a mental *case* than a mentalist too, by the sound of it', posited Felix.

The shared spliff unexpectedly expired. Frankie adroitly set about crafting its replacement.

'Anyway, out of the blue, *I* got a call from Giuseppe. The man was a bag of nerves – it was the night before the gig and he'd successfully sold the ex–con idea to Pee. But now he was having second thoughts. And the tattoo freak had been airlifted to hospital with a strained hernia, so he'd definitely cut himself out of the equation. But the *real* problem was our man, Day. It seems he'd completely sussed the game...perhaps he'd smelt a rat following Giuseppe's spying incident? Anyhow, he'd returned his ticket to the theatre.'

'That was a bit of luck, then' mumbled Felix.

'Well, Giuseppe was a bit stuffed actually, 'cos he'd focused all his attention on Day and "leopard man", and let the other contenders drift out of his sight.'

'But surely, there was no harm done' said Felix, 'I mean, Giuseppe could quickly scrape a few ropey nuggets together...like the colour of Mr Pratley's car, or the name of Mrs Davis's daughter's milkman, or whatever.'

'You're missing the point again, mate', snapped Frankie. 'Giuseppe was frightened Day might come back and nobble him properly this time – let's face it, the guy's got a garage that's bulging like Peter Pan's cod–piece. Giuseppe had let his guard down big time, and a crook with Day's credentials might well turn his hand to things we wouldn't even contemplate.'

Frankie made a scissors gestures to his ear.

'He should have thought of that before, the silly sod.'

'Let me finish', insisted Frankie. 'This is where I come into it. Giuseppe wanted *me* to do some eleventh hour background stuff on the remaining shortlist, while he cowered behind the wardrobe and protected his hairy little arse. I did help him out of course, and I even went to the show myself, just to see how effective my research had been. I was quite pleased actually – I'd discovered a woman, Mrs Brontie, a mother of twins, who'd named the girls Emily and Charlotte, silly cow. Her shitty little two–up–two–down in Dudley was called Heath Cliff and she called her dog Lockwood – can you believe it? Anyway, there I was, having a beer with that cretinous creep Pee after the show, when I spotted a shifty looking geezer hanging around near the green room. I don't know why really, but I just got the wind up a bit and called Giuseppe. Sure enough,

SMALL MEDIUM AT LARGE

my description of him tallied with none other than Spencer bleedin' Day! I'd already squared things with Pee myself, before the gig I mean – Giuseppe hadn't been in a fit state – he couldn't face explaining why our reckless recidivist had voted with his feet. Pee was really pissed off actually – swore he'd never use Giuseppe again. Anyway, I decided to bugger off back to Giuseppe's place pronto, so we could *both* hide behind his bleedin' wardrobe. We stewed away like dumplings all night, chewing the fat about Spencer and wondering what he might do to us if he felt like indulging a spot of DIY surgery.'

Frankie's cross–legged pose brought back recent memories of chilly stakeouts, lukewarm chicken and cold–turkey. He tapped at the roof incessantly with his long fingernails, unleashing a giddy fusion of Indian raga rhythms and pent–up nervous tension. Felix repositioned himself too as he teed up the obvious question.

'Why didn't you just ring the police – look, you'd blown Day out of the show anyway, and Giuseppe was already running scared – he'd nothing to lose, had he?'

'It's obvious you've never been in showbiz, mate. He couldn't blow the gaff on Pee's behind the scenes tactic, could he? Imagine it, Giuseppe, a paid spy working for an up and coming mind reader!...Pee would be as open to abuse as our man with hot stuff in cold storage. No, we had to be a bit subtle about it, so we decided we'd wait for Spencer to show up at the lockup to stash more gear, then wheel in the cops anonymously. He'd be taken care of, Giuseppe would be off the hook and Pee would be out of the soup.'

Felix looked puzzled.

'But you could have been waiting for *ages* to get your chance – for all you knew, he might only visit the lockup once in a month, by which time he could have done a Van Gogh on Giuseppe and a Leon Trotsky on *you*.'

'Well, I never said *I* thought it was a great move – anyway, we decided to sit tight. We knew Spencer would be doubly wary of stalkers, especially since he'd clearly suspected Giuseppe's show was some kind of elaborate setup. We parked up in a white Transit van I'd acquired through one of my less fussy acquaintances and ploughed our way through a bucket of Jaffa Cakes, thirty yards away from the lockup. It felt like a legit under–cover operation – and, in a way, I suppose it was. We'd brought binoculars, and we even had false registration plates, care of Giuseppe's old man.'

Frankie's gleeful gaze switched abruptly to one of consternation. He calmed himself with an oddly misshapen reefer retrieved from an inside pocket designed to hold a pen, and began brandishing it portentously as if about to usher in the trumpet fanfare at the start of Mahler's Fifth.

'We got the shock of our lives when Day finally showed up after two nights keeping watch in the van. I don't know what we thought it would be like. We just froze. Giuseppe whispered incomprehensible bull crap down the phone to the police...as if Day could possibly have heard him! We waited for what seemed like five minutes – it was probably two. Nobody arrived and Giuseppe was already panicking. He decided he'd try to get a photo of Day red–handed using his mobile phone, but that meant getting bloody close to the door, where there was only the tiniest gap left at the top. I told him he was berserk. We'd phoned the police and, for better or worse, it was now down to them to deal with the slippery sod. But things really cocked up when Giuseppe's mobile rang, just as he was taking the photo, standing on tiptoes! Ironically, it turned out to be the police wanting a bit of clarity. I knew Giuseppe had had his chips, so I fired up the engine and pulled up outside the lockup. Things really went the shape of the pear then! Day grabbed hold of Giuseppe and dragged him into the lockup, hands over his mouth. To be honest, I just sat there revving the engine, feeling about as much use as a condom in a convent. There wasn't time to call the police again – I just prayed for them to arrive, tearing my hair out.'

'I wondered what had happened to it' reflected Felix.

Frankie dropped his gaze and stopped his tapping, clearly weakened by his memory of the diabolical debacle. 'I might be a magician, but I'm no sodding wizard. No mojos or potions were going to save Giuseppe now – I just had to wade in, sharpish. As I barged my way into the lockup I found Giuseppe on the ground with his hands in front of his face. Day was attacking him with an umbrella – the poor guy was squealing like a pig in a mincer. There was a struggle, which resulted in all three of us scrabbling around on the ground like pissed–up break–dancers. Somehow Giuseppe got hold of the brolly and was bearing down on Day's neck with it, while I tarted about like a complete jackass. By the time I'd realised it was my job to hold the bloke down, it became obvious the bastard had already stopped moving; froth was dribbling from his disgustingly contorted mouth. He looked grotesque, with his face whiter than George Bush's teeth and his teeth yellowier than Bush's face.

'My god, you mean you'd killed the bastard?'

'Yeah! Well, we *thought* we had.'

He lit the reefer, which immediately returned a little colour to his cheeks.

'We bundled Day up in a sheet he'd been using to cover up some of his gear and shoved him in the van. It was ridiculous, not another human being had passed by for nearly an hour. We could have danced a naked satanic tango around him and no one would have seen a bleedin' thing! A cool place for a lockup, I've got to admit. I was for leaving Spencer to rot where he was, but Giuseppe probably felt more vulnerable since he'd actually done the deed. We drove further and further out into the country with Day lying on the backseat – I put my foot down and just kept it there. It was weird, Felix – before I knew it, I realised I was hammering along in the direction of your boat. Funny really. We stopped just outside the village of Barton in the Beans and caught our breath for ten minutes, shivering with shock.'

'Hang on just a cotton–picking minute, Frankie' Felix intervened, 'I've a horrible feeling I know where this is all heading – you've brought a dead body to me out here, haven't you?…you're gonna piss up my pastoral paradise, you dippy banjo–plucker!'

'Look, this all happened a couple of days ago remember. But, well…yes, Day *is* here…'

134

'You'd better be pulling my chain, mate' pleaded Felix, acquiring a tortured jowl. But there was no sign of a chain, let alone one with bells on it.

'That night, we ditched him in the corner of a field several miles from any decent road, still rolled up in his sheet. We figured the police would tie the murder to some criminal assignation or other.'

'You know, for a bright guy Frankie, you're thicker than a lorry load of colostomy bags.'

'Thanks for that vote of confidence, mate.'

'Heard of DNA profiling? Heard of *pathology*?'

Frankie slumped back, leaning on his hands, his fingers and heels chuntering chaotically on the linoleum roof. He wasn't of a mind to retaliate.

'So we beat it back to Giuseppe's place and carried on doing what we did best, hiding behind wardrobes. We *knew* he was dead of course, but we were still in recoil I suppose. But we couldn't sleep, so at about three in the morning Giuseppe suggested we took a shovel back to where we'd dumped the body and bury the bugger properly…delay his discovery for a bit longer, maybe. And this time we'd get kitted up with gloves and stuff. We even took a sponge and a jerry can of water to scrub him down, just to remove any really obvious clues.'

'At last, an atom of sense.'

'Thing was, Felix, we got there in the pitch black only to find Spencer had vamoosed! I became convinced he'd not died at the lockup at all, and had somehow managed to stagger cross country from where we'd dumped him. Giuseppe insisted he must be dead and that we'd just forgotten where we'd dumped the odious bastard. Anyway, we wandered around with our torches for maybe half an hour, like titties in a trance. We were on the point of giving up actually, when suddenly I spotted him…Day…sat huddled under the sheet, quite visible from the roadside. He was dead all right, stiff as a deep–fried rat, already disfigured and horribly clammy looking. Must have been praying for a passing vehicle, I suppose.'

'So you were right then, he *hadn't* been dead when you taxied him out into the sticks! But I suppose he was so feeble after the suffocation incident that the cold air soon polished him off.'

'Yeah. I'm not sure if I was relieved, or what…anyway, we stuck him back in the van and whizzed off. Burying him out there didn't seem so clever, after all. I realised I was driving like a lunatic, but we'd both lost it, big time.'

A raft of troubling points had tottered to the front of Felix's mind during Frankie's morbid monologue.

'Wait a friggin' moment, Frankie, the police have now got Giuseppe's mobile number, right? So they'll have been onto him the moment he started using it again!'

'Ah, well, luckily it's registered to somebody fictitious, thanks to Giuseppe's old man…in his line of work he's often had to make calls anonymously. And when Giuseppe called the police, thank god he had the wit to give a false name. The voicemail's activated, but not customised, so the police left a fairly non–committal message when they called back.'

'Where the hell *is* this Giuseppe tart, anyhow? Why

isn't he with you – you're really sticking your neck out for that pilchard!'

'Friends are important, Felix – just think what I might be prepared to do for *you* one day…Right, I'm ready for a nosebag. What have you got?'

A prolonged hiatus afforded time for Felix to put together his famed club sandwich ensemble, which combined components as disparate and unsavoury as Frankie's mood swings. The two reconvened on the roof, chomping noisily, while Felix tried to make sense of it all. Frankie picked up the story.

'Giuseppe's lying low, not too far away, but far enough to safeguard the integrity of his nose and ears, the current disposition of which he holds in singular affection.'

'He'd be better off at home wouldn't he? It'll look more suspicious if the cops are able to make some connection, however tenuous' said Felix, anxious to limit the number of high–maintenance mediums he might have to baby–sit.

Having demolished the less volatile components of his assemblage, Felix returned to the favour Frankie had alluded to at the start.

'Go on then, ask', he said with an air of impending doom, squeezing the final corner of his abominable sandwich into his face.

'Well' said Frankie, with a spurious optimism colouring his voice, 'what better place to lose a body…than in a *canal?*'

'You've got to be bloody joking, mate – if you want to use the canal, go ahead, about a hundred miles from here preferably...how about Manchester? I appreciate your glass is always half full, but what with...koala piss?'

'The thing is mate, you're the geezer when it comes to canals. We just need...advice...on where to stick the bastard, preferably so he's not discovered 'til the next ice age.'

'Sure', nodded Felix sarcastically, 'it'll be as simple as that, won't it? Marksmen are probably lined up behind those bleedin' bushes as we speak!'

'Hardly, Felix' Frankie protested, sidestepping Felix's barbed sarcasm, 'I've been so bloody paranoid since Thursday that I'm prepared to bet Giuseppe's *life* on it.'

'Let's take a walk' proposed Felix, leaping manfully to the path in a single manoeuvre. 'I'll offer you one or two reasons why your idea stinks worse than your aftershave.'

The pair walked in the late afternoon air, as cold, crisp and incisive as Felix had suddenly become. He sighed.

'You know, the human brain accounts for under two percent of total body weight, but uses twenty percent of its energy. In the case of *your* brain, I suspect, the equation might be profitably reconsidered in relation to the composition of a sausage: two percent meat, twenty percent breadcrumbs and seventy–eight percent pure, unmitigated bollocks...Listen, unless you're going to get into the grizzly business of decapitation and dismembering, a *whole* corpse is quite likely to reappear at some point. Canals are like living things, mate, as I would have thought you'd know, what with your degree in sandcastle building – or was it Geology? A canal's characteristics chime with the seasons and, in places, it can pretty well dry up if we get a hot summer. Even thick coppers waving dowsing rods will trip over the bastard then. Anyhow, an isolated stretch such as this gets a fair amount of traffic over the course of a year, and you could never guarantee to keep Day's ghastly carcass from breaking its ties.'

Frankie looked a little nonplussed.

'The other thing' he continued, pointing proprietarily at his beloved canal, 'is that there's enough crap in here *already*! It does get dredged – not as regularly as it should, but often enough to screw up your chances of a porridge–free retirement…Anyhow' continued Felix thoughtfully, 'I think you're on the wrong track, mate…I reckon you should be actually aiming to have the body discovered as soon as possible.'

'What?' squealed Frankie, whose watery grave idea had patently failed to take account of canal garbology.

'Because the longer Spencer Day is unaccountably absent, the more vociferous the investigating team will be forced to become. They'll pour over every damned detail, and that's when some bright–spark no–life will emerge with a home video of Laurel and Hardy sat in a van outside some burglar's garage, scoffing Jaffa Cakes!'

'So, what do you propose, Sherlock?'

'I'll run this idea up the flagpole and see who salutes

139

it' pontificated Felix, unashamedly revelling in the fact that someone had finally taken note of his appreciable strategic resources.

The walking pace quickened as they approached a more open section of the canal, where 'B' roads and walkways unfettered the view to the broadening hills either side. Felix resumed his iteration following a minute's cogitation, lungs primed with fresh smoke.

'Okay, mate. Here's the deal. In two days time an ex–criminal, who mysteriously disappeared from his home some days before, is found dead. *Not* in a canal, not wrapped in a sheet, but in the middle of a field, somewhere completely off the beaten track. The body is strangely charred...and naked. There are broken bones, bruises and lacerations. A few objects are discovered close to the scene that appear, on the face of it, very specific and yet, at the same time, are tantalisingly abstruse. At first the corpse cannot be identified, but fairly quickly the investigating team acquire the necessary pathology and our man is given a name.'

Felix glanced at Frankie for his input.

'Day', he muttered sheepishly, as if giving evidence in court, 'Spencer Day.'

Felix released a mushroom cloud, a reliable barometer of his renewed mental buoyancy.

'Now, Spencer Day is by all accounts not a likeable man. Indeed, some think he bears an uncanny resemblance to the recently obsoleted American President, and his duplicity at having turned over a new leaf has damaged some newly established reputations on the Labour government's criminal rehabilitation programme. But, despite all this, Spencer Day's killer needs to be found, especially under such peculiar circumstances.'

They walked on, feeling the first of a little rain that dribbled from between a phalanx of buttressed clouds.

'Pieces of the jigsaw begin to come together, although these tend to flag up completely superfluous leads – the team become distracted in anticipation of closing a whole filing cabinet of unsolved crimes in one fell swoop. They assume the bizarre circumstances in which Day was discovered have some significance, some meaningful explanation that is bound to make itself clear eventually. Giuseppe's incoherent phone conversation to the police will be put down to some fellow criminal's petty vindictive behaviour – nothing to do with Day's death at all – they don't fully understand it, but in any case can't follow it up.'

Felix's smugness radiated fluorescently – his improbable yet remotely plausible plan had taken shape frighteningly easily. Frankie took a moment to absorb the full weight of the emerging hypothesis, stealing the pipe briefly in the hope it might mobilise his grey cells, too.

'It's pretty fiendish, perverse and impossibly Machiavellian…I like it' Frankie nodded. 'But if I might just tackle you on one or two details' he continued, ejecting the second–hand spittle from the pipe onto the grass, 'why a burnt, naked body?'

'Simple', replied Felix, keen to pile it on, 'it's a no–brainer, mate. It'll have the hallmark of an obsessive, twisted killer who enjoys taunting the police with his eccentric predilections. If we were to just dump the body without

141

ceremony on the roadside near his home, the killing would look more impulsive, more random, which of course, it was.'

'But in a field?'

'This part's more strategic' said Felix haughtily, 'and possibly a tad more abstract. Imagine that the field represents, symbiotically as it were, a blank canvas for the body – a frame around which the killer's destructive and yet *creative* act reflects his nascent inner turmoil, a turmoil that...'

'All right, all right, I've got the drift' relented Frankie, unable to countenance further godwottery. 'What are these objects left at the scene then?'

'Mm, I'm not fully decided on that detail yet...but I would think a bowler hat and a pair of plastic handcuffs, wouldn't you?'

'What! Which tree are you barking up now, for Pete's sake?'

'Again, it's a necessary bit of machinery in the subterfuge' Felix responded, mercilessly rubbing Frankie's nose in his steaming pile of sophistry. 'It will be self–evident to any criminal psychologist that these items are *meaningful*. They're not intended to be read as enigmatic clues to the murder motive per se, but as indicators of the killer's unhinged mind.'

'You're frightening me now, Felix – I'll never get on the wrong side of *you*!'

'The bowler hat is, frankly Frankie, pure Vaudeville...that's the point. But remember that our criminal psychologist won't rest until he's attached some metaphysical definition, some *purpose* to it – the man who mistook his *life* for a hat, perhaps? Likewise, the plastic handcuffs could be read as an oblique reference to the man's distant past....or even his more recent past, of course. Even if they suspect it's all a ridiculous distraction, they'll have to account for these details *somehow*. And time spent chasing up false leads is time *not* spent looking for Laurel and bleedin' Hardy. Savvy?'

'Okay, so precisely where should we dump the body?' asked Frankie, unaccountably converted to the cogency of Felix's scenario.

'Ah, this is my masterstroke, mate' radiated Felix, a newfound speciousness invading his tone. 'We'll study some OS maps of the Peak District, paying particular attention to the area around Hollinsclough, just south of Buxton, I reckon. We'll home in on a crop of fields that are barely approachable, either on foot or by conventional road traffic – in other words, one that implies an off–road or farm vehicle of some description.'

'I presume you're trying to implicate a herd of dairy cows now' sighed Frankie.

'Persiflage dear boy, persiflage. Naturally, the nearest inhabitants will cop the first wave of enquiry – and our seemingly explicit placement of the body will narrow down the field of suspects...or, should that be, narrow the suspects down to a field?'

'Okay smart–ass, I've thought of a problem. If our dumping ground is that bloody difficult to access, how will *we* manage it? We don't want Farmer Giles poking his nose in just as we're humping Day across his precious cornfield!'

Felix had been looking forward to this moment, but

being a veteran procrastinator he'd stretch Frankie's patience just a shade further.

'Well, I suppose we'd need some kind of mountain bike, or trike' he mused, affecting his most earnest tone. With a well–stocked pipe in his cupped hand he was already allowing his imagination to drift upwards towards the sky, the clouds, the birds...

'I suggest you camp down with me 'til this is cooked, proposed Felix. 'We may need to act swiftly.'

'Sweet', acknowledged Frankie, promptly crashing his size tens on Felix's flimsy table. The pair spent the early evening wrestling with oversized maps. When at last Frankie thought he'd found a likely site to dump the body he pointed avidly at an area vaguely northwest of Coventry, about a mile into open country.

'No no', dismissed Felix, casting just half an eye, 'too much traffic.'

'Traffic, here?' exclaimed Frankie, 'there isn't even a decent road!'

'No, traffic as in *air* traffic, mate.' Frankie looked deliciously perplexed. The time had come for Felix to reveal his trump card; his ballistic bailiwick.

'While you've been uncharitably plucking rabbits from hats they've no business sleeping in, I've been flying on my magic carpet, mate. I'll be introducing you to

Wagtail's flightier half–sister tomorrow. She lives up in Derbyshire at the moment – I bought her from a mate of mine up there, my instructor, actually.'

If Larry the Lamb only knew what dastardly plan was being hatched he'd probably have taken up maypole dancing and denied ever even sitting in a microlight with Felix, let alone selling him one. And yet Felix's selective memory permitted a remarkably anodyne version of his flying career to trip from his lips, one that judiciously bypassed embarrassing details of fuel starvation and squatting in blazing bushes soaked in his own piss. Instead, he unreeled tales of bonding with birds at great altitudes and spiritually 'finding himself' in secret pockets of the countryside. Frankie was incredulous to limits Felix couldn't have hoped for, and the remainder of the evening was spent lavishing ever more implausible details. Amidst the heady haze one sensible conclusion was reached, however: there would be insufficient time to bring Wagtail II down to the Midlands – they must aim to get the job done within twenty–four hours and would need to travel up to Matlock at first light. Spencer Day's body would be discovered in Derbyshire after all.

Aeronautical maps of the area immediately surrounding the aerodrome flagged up a few prospective sites for the drop, but Felix was anxious to distance the discovery of the body from the aerodrome a little. He eventually plumped for a cluster of sprawling fields, with what appeared to be a few ancient monuments or Saxon burial grounds dotted about. Broad overshoot areas would further decrease the potential for disaster. But a significant problem was going to be rendezvousing with Frankie within a short flying distance of the drop zone. For an intense period of perhaps five minutes there would be three people onboard – for Day would have to be strapped in on top of Frankie in the pillion seat. The approach and climb out would be cruelly taxing with such an abnormally heavy load; an extra generous take–off area would be needed – not an easy manoeuvre even for a competent pilot, let alone Felix, with just the one brilliantly bungled sortie on his CV.

The next morning Felix and Frankie assembled what they thought they'd be needing for their intrepid act of large–scale misdirection: Felix's hotchpotch flying kit, warm clothes and hats, walking boots, maps, a dozen orange traffic cones pinched from a service station, a double blanket and three heavy fuel cans. They chose Felix's Landrover, not wishing to draw undue attention to themselves by appearing at Mervyn's flying school in an unfamiliar vehicle. But first, they must extract Spencer Day's unyielding corpse from Frankie's purloined Transit van. It wasn't going to come easily. An act of caesarean would be required, and the paint–spattered tarpaulin they'd taken from the lockup would prove indispensable. But the tarp's odour–retaining capacity was hopelessly inadequate. Felix nearly parted company with his breakfast while shifting the body. And yet, in fulfilment of his plan, they must now strip the body and set it alight – a task that would take some time, for the bugger just wouldn't ignite, even with repeated dousings. In the end they resorted to wrapping the naked corpse in the fuel–soaked tarp before setting it ablaze, finally administering an outer sheet once the flames had subsided.

The napalmed body, laid bare on the grass beside Wagtail, induced a scene of sickening macabre, human skin excoriated and spitting like cheap pancetta. Compressing Day's festering edifice into the back of the vehicle would prove to be an equally revolting process – the pong of his partial cremation remained unspeakably pungent. Despite the cold weather they drove up to Matlock with all windows open, never quite managing to ignore the hideous ambience.

'You know, Spencer is more dangerous to us dead than he ever was alive' reflected Frankie, teeth chattering away in the icy breeze and fingers clicking on the dashboard like a hysterical Geiger counter. 'Remember how they caught Peter Sutcliffe – a random vehicle spot check, and not so far from here either!'

'Bugger!' yelled Felix, as they neared Stoke–on–Trent, 'we've forgotten something crucial – the props to drop with the body!'

They slipped off the M6 and spent an hour searching out novelty shops that might sell handcuffs and a charity outlet that could rustle up a bowler hat. At last they were back on course for Matlock, and it wasn't long before the familiar buzz of microlights and cesenas began to trickle in through the gaping windows. The wind speed was low to moderate, as indicated by the gently nodding windsocks, although its effect was as jagged as ice beneath the glassy, cerulean sky – ideal flying conditions for the season.

'The first time I came here I had a stiff leg to contend with' joked Felix as they neared the aerodrome entrance. 'Now I've a stiff *lag*.'

His emotional state darted violently between exuberance and reticence – not unlike his first visit, in fact. The Landrover eased contentedly into its slot in the lunar surfaced car park and Felix soon clocked a few of his tenuous acquaintances engaging in various stages of flight foreplay.

'Right, Frankie, this is how we'll play it' scowled Felix, winding up the windows and pinching his nose as the old odour instantly invaded their nostrils. 'First off, we'll get her out and dust her down. I'll have to give her a thorough check over and fuel her up. Then I'll log in at the office and minimise the small talk. I'll knock off a couple of circuits and fly northwest in the direction of Longnor and Hollinsclough. You drive up to checkpoint one and prepare to signal me by the entrance to the fields – remember it's the B5053 midway between the A515 and the A53, just this side of a little bridge crossing the River Dove. It shouldn't take you more than half an hour, so you'll be in situ before I've even left. Send me a text when you're nearly there. Come to think of it, text me a second time once you've done a recky to tell me whether it's on or off – we won't be able to hear each other on the mobiles. We need to be sure we've got a good venue for this bit of theatre. You'll see me circling overhead and then I'll land as close as I can to you. Wave something bright and voluminous in the air, like your Y–fronts, to help show the wind direction; there shouldn't be too many pylons or telegraph poles in that wilderness, fingers crossed. But if you spot any hazards, mark them with the cones, there's a good chap.'

They'd spent the latter part of the previous evening

refining the procedure for offloading the body – military efficiency would be paramount, and the fewer the clues to a hellish drop from the heavens, the more baffling Day's reappearance would be. Now it was for real. A valedictory handshake between wartime bombing aces and the pair parted company, a moment's unguarded apprehension telling on their faces.

'Right then, are you hot to trot? I'll see you later, mate' said Felix.

'Not if I see you first...*mate*' mumbled Frankie, the gallows humour failing to crack his friend's frowning phizog.

Wagtail II was every bit as worthy of postcard immortalisation as Wagtail I had shown herself to be. The sun ricocheted off the hangar's southern face and rubbed its corrugated rays gently over the tiny machine, which cooed excitedly at the prospect of an outing. Larry had maintained her well, and she needed little encouragement to cough away the dust from her little lungs. Fuel levels were healthy and the controls were all registering normally. Frankie had departed in the Landrover as planned, leaving Felix to brush off one or two discourteous mutterings from mirror–polishing old–timers escaping decorating their spare rooms. For once, Felix was relieved at the little interest shown in his presence. Neither Mervyn nor Larry was visible during the twenty minutes it took him to get organised, so he didn't even have to log in. A busy morning for lessons, it seemed, and accordingly the hangar was free of its customary congestion. Felix pressed on with the preliminaries and was soon back in the swing of things. He felt comfortable in his new machine – it had a sturdy, lived–in quality that immediately lifted his mood. A little of Larry's patience might have rubbed off too, for he took pains to check every wrinkle in the wing and every rivet in the bodywork. He waited calmly for Frankie's text as he laid up in a small queue of flying machines on the approach to runway 180. When the text arrived it was succinct: 'sweet'.

Two touch 'n goes in his bionic bee were reeled off with consummate ease and within ten minutes of strapping himself in he'd left the circuit and was heading south–east, 120°, at an altitude of fifteen hundred feet, sixty–five mph into a ten mph headwind. He monitored the dials closely, injecting tiny doses of input by foot and by hand. This was almost fun, except that he'd overlooked the need for ballast, so Wagtail II became progressively buffeted about as she tracked her way along an extended line of trees. If only he'd been as assiduous earlier in his flying career, he reflected; yes, all was progressing according to plan. He should try to enjoy this exercise, a *real* mission that would depend entirely on his pilot skill and judgment.

Having left the crowded aerodrome behind him Felix surveyed the immediate airspace and was relieved to see no other traffic. He quickly passed the first two landmarks – a defunct tin mine and an outward–bound centre – and estimated his arrival at the third, a small reservoir, to be about ten minutes off. The temperature was a few degrees cooler at this altitude and the wind–chill factor soon fixed a purposeful grin on his face, his sunglasses hardly deflecting the thinnest patches of sporadic vapour.

SMALL MEDIUM AT LARGE

As Felix seesawed towards what his map showed him to be the landing zone his mood swung like a pendulum between courage and cowardice. He quickly shed significant altitude, falling to around seven hundred feet in order to get a better view of the frieze–like terrain below the splintered clouds, encountering a stomach–churning bout of turbulence as he flattened out, wing tips slicing along the horizon. Ahead of him on his new bearing of 190° was a squally patch of rain, so gingerly he nudged the nose round to 300° and sank further to five hundred feet, initiating a large arc around the quilted arena below him. He was now looking out for his Landrover, which would appear as little more than a dustgreen postage stamp. He'd hoped Frankie might have used some initiative and placed the traffic cones conspicuously along a possible landing path, but as yet nothing was visible.

The giddying corkscrew magnified the geomorphology below him, and eventually he spotted the vehicle, tucked in close to a high hedge that encompassed a succession of flat un–cropped fields – an ideal cluster of landing sites. Felix had been uncommonly conscientious in his observations, interpreting the subtle clues on the landscape that betray the prevailing wind direction. A farmer burning rubbish in the distance, the swaying of the treetops and the rippling shades of the grass shifting like schools of whitebait assisted rapid assimilation: a light southwesterly. He could see Frankie now, moving around the vehicle and gesticulating crazily, a tic–tac that didn't seem to serve any discernible purpose. At this crucial stage in the flight Felix was preparing himself to execute a

151

manoeuvre that would be doubly hazardous once the plane was fully loaded up. The optimum dumping ground for the body would need to be ten or twenty fields away from wherever he now landed. In his mind's eye he'd chalked a large rectangular circuit around the adjoining fields, with 'finals' leading down to a smooth, featureless sheet of green baize, just a few hundred yards from where Frankie now stood, manically shaking a sheet.

As he dropped to around three hundred feet Felix could make out the position of the cones – but instead of suggesting a landing route Frankie had configured them to spell an even more clipped message than in his text: 'NO'. Felix was baffled. 'What does he mean, *no*?...I can't stop now!' he shrieked. A rapid judgment was needed – what would *Larry* do? 'Sod it, I'm landing here, and that's that!' he shouted to himself, drowned out by the whining engine. The ten–foot high hedges at his ankles resembled bonsai trees from this altitude, but Felix allowed himself plenty of leeway. He was descending rapidly now, his makeshift landing strip rushing ever closer into focus. This was as easy as landing at Wimbledon – what was Frankie talking about?

Within seconds his demented machine was committed, its wheels scoring into the reassuringly yielding turf, ahead of him an endless carpet of immaculate emerald. Felix immediately turned 360° and chugged back in the direction of the hedged border from where Frankie could be seen running at full pelt towards him.

'Am I pleased to see you!' he bellowed breathlessly, not waiting for Felix to turn off the ignition and dismount.

'Likewise, mate' responded Felix, equally winded,

reaching out to grip the hand of his partner in crime. Felix alighted and they speedily tugged the microlight back to the hedge where a gap between two sizeable trees afforded a convenient hidey–hole. Without further comment they dragged Frankie's large sheet over her and dipped the delta shaped wing down into the breeze that sauntered half–heartedly across the meadow. Felix removed his helmet and let out a belated whoop of exhilaration. He'd made it! The pair reclined on the moist sward, congratulating themselves on a perfect stage–one execution.

But five minutes later Felix revisited his outrage at Frankie's inscrutable cone–code.

'Hey, why did you try to warn me off then, you numbskull nutcracker?'

'What are you on about?' grunted Frankie, stabbing at his hair with stiffened fingers.

'You spelt 'NO' with the cones...and nearly made me crash into the frigging hedge!'

'I know you're dyslexic Felix, but you did ask me to confirm it was a goer...'

A faint bleeping sound interrupted him. Felix glanced down at the mobile phone dangling from his neck, which declared itself in possession of a new text message, an unequivocal two–letter palindrome: 'ON'.

LIFE ON MARS? A CATINEL'S CHANCE

The weather had become moodier. A fractionally more resilient breeze elbowed in, accompanied by increasingly confident attempts at rain. A doom–laden cloud positioned itself resolutely overhead and the two men began to shuffle restlessly under Wagtail II; she too sought a little shelter from the trees. The time was two o' clock and, until now at least, the worsening prospects for flight seemed to have worked in their favour, for there had been no inquisitive eyes to fluster them.

'We should crack on with this' mumbled Frankie, nervously.

'Yeah, this is the dodgy bit...I can't keep you under my wing forever, you know!' sniggered Felix unconvincingly, flicking a tiny puddle of water that had collected in the stretched cloth above his head.

'It's time for you to work your magic' pronounced Felix, rubbing his friend's shoulders in a slightly disjointed display of camaraderie. Spencer Day was quickly released from his makeshift hearse. A disgusting brown cassareep had seeped through to the outer sheet, sweating a sticky, shiny film along the thin plastic seat. The head looked as if it had been reclaimed from a prehistoric Norwegian peat bog, its skewed jaw assuming menacing Mick Jagger tendencies. The maggot–ridden corpse was consigned to the damp grass for a moment while Felix and Frankie animatedly discussed the detail of the second, far more hazardous leg of the campaign. Frankie would have to time the drop precisely to coincide with the moment of lowest altitude; contact must not be made with the grass, or they'd give their game away. One chance only – make or break.

With a bit of luck, no air traffic would pass over the field once they'd completed the drop – but even if it did, at normal altitude it was unlikely a randomly placed body would attract attention.

'Just one thing, Felix' gibbered Frankie, wiping a bulbous bead of sweat from his oddly quivering nose, 'I'm *slightly* afraid of heights...'

'Tough...get over it, mate' sang Felix curtly.

Fortunately, Day was not an exceptionally large man, yet the three of them together would place unprecedented strain on the poor bird. Felix checked his map cursorily, praying he'd pinpointed the drop zone accurately. He pondered the flight plan for a minute, a disconcerting rictus trespassing onto his face as he dared to imagine what the pair would soon endure.

'The thing is mate, this is going to be bloody tricky' he stumbled anxiously. 'You see, the lower you fly, and the heavier the load, the faster you've got to go to stay stable...and the faster you fly, the harder it is to hit your target.'

'Mm, with you so far....' responded Frankie.

'And the harder it is to hit your target once...the harder it is to hit it twice.'

'Twice? Why do we want to hit it *twice*?'

'To lob the hat and handcuffs, of course' said Felix, as if this were self–evident. 'We're wanting to give the impression that a deranged twat has targeted a specific field for Day's reincarnation in order to fulfil some bizarre fantasy.'

'I reckon we'll have achieved that then!' burst

Frankie, a good octave higher than normal.

'Once the bugger's been dropped, the plane will get suddenly lighter, see, which means it'll get suddenly faster – it'll bounce around at a dangerously low altitude, like Zebedi on HRT.'

'Oh, let's just stick the hat on the sad bastard's head and stuff the handcuffs inside the sheet' sighed Frankie.

'Sweet...I mean, good thinking, Frankie' smiled Felix, 'that'll be close enough grouping.'

'Hey, I've just thought', continued Frankie cautiously, 'what's our exit strategy after the drop?'

'I was coming to that' responded Felix, who'd completely overlooked the need to plot his bearings for the return leg. He hurriedly scribbled some figures on his map.

'Simple, just reverse the process. We dump Day, fly straight back here, land, you drive up to Matlock, I fly back, park the old lady in the garage – and Rashid's your uncle.'

'It's Mahmood, actually' muttered Frankie.

A deafening sound–loop of Indian rap music suddenly pounded from somewhere close by. This time it was Frankie's mobile.

'Watcha, mate!' shouted Frankie, swivelling on his heels to improve the reception.

'Yes, it's as good as cooked – your old man would be proud!' he continued, grinning like a Cheshire twat. 'I'm with my old mate Felix in Derbyshire...we've stripped and cremated the body and now we're gonna fly over some random field and dump it...oh yeah, with an old hat and some fake handcuffs...then we'll fly back and celebrate with egg–flip on a canal boat near Coventry, and...'

156

He'd been headed off by a somewhat flabbergasted Giuseppe, who'd imagined that by now Frankie would have carried out their mundanely sensible plan to submerge the body in an overlooked section of canal.

'No, no don't come down here, for heaven sake' protested Frankie, 'just keep fiddling with your Nintendo for a few more days, then start scouring the tabloids for humour–free headlines about dead strip–artistes.'

But Giuseppe's two–minute tirade clearly hit the spot.

'Ah, I suppose that does change things a bit…but make bloody sure you're not followed…we're in heavy enough shit as it is, and life's about to get a bloody sight harder.'

Doling out directions to Hollinsclough became progressively hindered by the damp maps that fluttered like monster moths around the draughty Landrover. Frankie loosened his collar and frowned like a trapped trout.

'Last night Giuseppe paid a solo visit to Day's lockup. I guess he just wanted to check whether the cops had got round to following up the information from Day's "anonymous" grass. He sat in the car for half an hour, then sneaked up to the lockup and peeked in – he found nothing – just a crappy old cabinet with a few dodgy trinkets on it. Either the local scallies had been in there or else Day's ghost had shifted the gear somewhere safer.'

'Or the cops have acted as they'd be bound to and impounded the lot as hot property' stabbed Felix.

'Well, this is the odd bit' continued Frankie. 'If they *had*, they left the garage unlocked – the police wouldn't raid a place and then leave it unsecured like that, surely?'

'What's the big deal, Frankie? The stuff's gone, yeah?...Day's gone and pretty soon *we'll* be gone, too...or, at least, that's what we'd planned. I'm getting the willies – why did you have to let Giuseppe come out here? I don't need another mindless mind–reader cramping my style.'

'Yeah, well, he's on his way, so get over it. He's utterly convinced Day's got a side–kick whose covered over his tracks.'

Felix looked dazed.

'If Day had a mate who's acted so promptly, he must know that his friend's dead...and if that's true, he could well know *who* killed him...'

'Exactement, mon ami, zoze leetle grrey cells are steel fonctioneeng aftair all!' mocked Frankie, sounding more like a drunken Welsh bricklayer than a prissy Belgian sleuth.

Frankie quickly brought Felix up to speed. Giuseppe had outstayed his welcome at his friend's gaff and had left an hour ago driving his dad's old Volvo estate, still hooked up to its nest of knackered sea–scout canoes. He'd arrive within the hour.

'God help us' moaned Felix, wearily. 'If this field gets any more populated we'll have to apply for gypsies camping rights.'

More alarming than the rain, which had become quite insistent, was the piercing wind. Flying under these conditions would be unthinkable. Moreover, the wet grass would not stand up to being treated as a launch pad now, let alone a landing strip. A rethink of strategy was needed, especially in light of Giuseppe's imminent arrival. But after another hour alternating between ducking under the trees and mopping up condensation in the Landrover, Giuseppe's appearance seemed less likely after all. Little light ventured out from the mass of bruised clouds that had stacked up above them; it felt more like ten o' clock than four. At around five Giuseppe appeared at last, stressed, irascible and paranoid. An interminable ping–pong of texts and mobile discussions severed at vital moments had led him a not so merry dance around the knotted 'B' roads of the Peak District National Park. Coaxing a smile from him would prove as likely as contracting diphtheria from a punctured waterbed. He produced a stack of beef burgers and a grease–swamped bag of fish and chips that had been congealing like a nest of slugs on the passenger seat for over two hours.

The three men sat morosely in the Landrover, picking at their lacklustre meal, windows open again in a hopeless attempt to exorcise Day's ghostly aura. The stench of anaemic beef, wilted haddock and frazzled human flesh blended to produce a ghoulish variant on surf 'n turf, while the ghoul itself continued to exude a nicotine–like substance onto the sodden grass just a few yards away. The Volvo, squatting next to them on the boggy grass, might have been the more obvious vehicle in which to sit, but the risk of

159

chip fat contamination to his father's tan upholstery was more than Giuseppe was prepared to countenance, cadaver or no cadaver. Its windows were festooned with multi–coloured flags and stickers, which proudly asserted his allegiance to the scout troop he'd led for decades.

Each of the doleful accomplices was thinking a similar thought as he pushed chip slugs around on his lap, but Felix was the first to articulate it.

'So, what the buggery are we gonna do now then?'

'I've got an idea' said Frankie, several minutes later, screwing his half full chip wrapping into a ball and tossing it through the window. 'We can't fly now, right?'

'Right', they chorused.

'We can't stay here, right?'

'Right.'

'We can't leave Day here, right?'

'Right.'

'So, how about this…we sit the bugger in the back of the bionic bird, which we trade with the canoes from Giuseppe's dad's trailer, drive both cars and the winged wonder back to the boat and return early tomorrow, praying for a drier spell overnight.'

Felix shrugged his shoulders and communicated a doubtful grimace to Giuseppe.

Frankie continued. 'If we're unlucky with the weather, at least we can lie low 'til it picks up – it's gotta be better than sorting chips from maggots here all night, and I'm sick of the sight of Johnny Rotten over there.'

'We'll never get Wagtail II onto the trailer, surely?' Felix frowned…we'd need to fully de–rig her.'

160

'No sweat, the wing can come apart, can't it?' asked Frankie.

'Yeah', sighed Felix, recalling the trouble he'd had packing away his comparatively simple paraglider wing.

'We'd better get on with it then' Frankie commanded, 'get your tool out, Giuseppe.'

They started up both vehicles and pointed their lights at Wagtail II, suddenly oblivious to the risk of attracting attention. With the right tools, practical skills, experience and patience the job could take twenty–five minutes. But it would take them nearly two hours to remove the wing, strap it to the roof rack and bungee the cockpit onto the trailer. By this point, even Day looked dead bored, sat in the back seat of the microlight with a strangely twitching black bag placed over his head.

The drive home was perilous, precarious and ponderous. The wind nagged at the poorly secured wing while the cockpit wobbled sporadically – thankfully, Day proved to be a docile pillion, although the stench of putrefaction remained more powerful than anything the wind could temper. By the time they'd returned it was nearly time to be thinking of setting off again. But a few hours rest had begun to cleanse their minds of the spectre so that the trip back to Fenny Drayton was relatively unhindered by erroneous turns. The three glum–faced men sat motionless in the Volvo listening to a succession of banal commercials and trailers for programmes they'd no intention of hearing on Classic FM's breakfast show. Frankie's prayers for a change in the weather seemed to have been answered, a crystalline sky signalling an improvement to their fortunes.

A road block five miles out from the first rendezvous point provoked a few nervous twitches however, and reminded Felix that they'd forgotten to dispose of Frankie's topsy–turvy traffic cone message. They arrived early enough to be confident of an expeditious corpse drop, with as yet no air traffic to hinder progress. Wagtail II's re–assembly consumed only an hour, and soon Felix was ready once again to prick the skies. Giuseppe, yawning incessantly, helped to maul Day into position and the engine was tickled into life. Felix speedily reacquainted himself with the intended drop zone on his map and aligned the machine ready for take–off into hardly any headwind.

Frankie tapped Felix on the shoulder and shouted above the noisy engine. 'Bondage kit?'

'Not *now*, darling' he replied, but quickly came to his senses.

'Oh shit' he cussed, gesturing to Giuseppe to bring over the handcuffs and hat. Day's overnight deterioration was horrendous, the ill–fitting hat screwed onto his malleable head and the black bin–bag now removed in preparation for what was to be the man's mysterious reappearance. Frankie had acquired a blanket to protect him from the worst of the putrid discharge that had begun to slide like molten toffee down the sides of the cockpit. But the growing heat from the engine heightened the dripping odour of death and further accelerated the rate of decay; maggots popped up visibly like boils on a punk rocker's arse. And so it was with a sense of relief tinged with apprehension that Wagtail II began her inelegant pass along the iridescent grass.

Frankie braced himself for the most impolite of initiations into the world of aviation as the distraught machine struggled to achieve flying speed. Then, in a moment of unbridled heroicism Felix hoisted back the bar and persuaded the wheels to part company with civilization. Immediately the plane veered violently to one side, momentarily clipping a wing tip on the ground. It took all of Felix's will and strength to remain committed, his foot anchored steadfastly to the tiny throttle. The sound of the engine and Frankie screaming in unison was nearly enough to wake the dead, although ironically Day's presence thereafter seemed to have a moderately stabilising effect. Despite Felix's valiant protestations the wilful machine held its unilaterally adopted trajectory and the sudden appearance of a wild hedge looming on their immediate flight path was more than Frankie could bear. Day had begun to escape from his wedged position, which further exaggerated the roll and yaw of the plane. Wagtail II stoically nosed herself upwards until eventually the ground shrank to form the impression of a circuit board at their feet. Felix glanced back at Frankie, intending to give a somewhat pre–emptory thumbs–up, but found Day's maggot–nibbled backside dancing cheek to cheek with Frankie's ashen face – he was staring into the bowels of grim death itself and bellowed at Felix 'I can't hold on much longer, just get us down, for pity's sake!'

Felix had no idea where they were, nor did he care. He was just glad to be still alive, despite the grim odour of death wafting forward. A minute later he estimated they'd travelled far enough from the vehicle to target a revised drop site. He'd levelled off at eight hundred feet in order to scan for a suitable spot and pointed down to a group of fields showing potential. Takeoff and landing areas seemed gloriously abundant and there wasn't a hint of a farm. But a second glimpse of Frankie's transfixed vomit–smeared face, now firmly wedged between Day's quivering buttocks, confirmed his accomplice's current ambivalence in matters of geography. They descended slowly, tracing a progressive arc. Felix felt in control until about one hundred feet from the field, which was when he remembered his own cautionary lecture on low altitude flying. He simply couldn't go faster without climbing, or slower without dropping too rapidly. The ground–rush effect was nose–grindingly authentic, yet he pushed on, resisting the plane's impulse to lift, and when they'd levelled at thirty feet he shouted 'let him go! *Let the bugger go!*'

The hat tumbled first, enthusiastically pursued by Day's speckled corpse, now free of its festering cocoon of sheets, which lingered, billowing dangerously close to the screaming propeller. Spencer Day looked almost graceful for the second or two it took him to plummet to the grass, landing noiselessly on his back and rolling briefly before coming to rest in a swastika position. Fortuitously, the handcuffs had slipped from Frankie's grasp too, although the sheet and blanket had quickly become knotted around his upper body. 'Don't let that frigging sheet touch the prop!' hollered Felix as they began climbing at what now seemed jet speed. The immediate problem was how to find their way back to Giuseppe, who'd been anticipating a minor explosion ever since the tumultuous takeoff six minutes earlier.

A flight without bearings is likely to get a person exponentially more lost than over the same period in a road vehicle, especially when that person can barely remember his takeoff position in relation to the sun. Felix had spotted one or two other microlights bobbing on the pink horizon and was eager to get down out of view. At last Frankie came good, nodding excitedly and pointing towards some fields with familiar looking trees and hedges around their periphery. They were lucky, the breeze had remained light and ran along the most extended of the fields in which Giuseppe could now be seen, scampering haphazardly like a nitro–glycerined ant on a billiard table. Felix approached what would have to serve as a runway and affected his re–entry with uncustomary coolness, now a hundred and fifty kilos the lighter.

The de–brief would have to wait; Felix wanted to tie up the loose ends quickly, before they were spotted by a growing crop of pilots circling in the mid distance.

'You know', he began, catching his breath, 'I think we should de–rig her and get her home now – I was going to bring her down anyway, and I'm worried who I'll bump into back at Mervyn's, 'cos it's turning into such a perfect flying day.'

The others grudgingly agreed, despite the fact that it would mean re–engaging combat with the errant wing. The thing consumed the Volvo's roof, accentuating the slightest soupçon of a crosswind and rendering the vehicle as manoeuvrable as a beehive on a Vespa. By 9:45 the triumphant trio were ambling back in the direction of

Felix's boat. Compared with the melancholic journey a few hours previously the mood had become rhapsodic. Even Day's odour had finally begun to subside. They avoided the roadblock they'd encountered before, near Leicester, choosing a more circuitous route that took in the immeasurable aesthetic magnetism of Ashby–de–la–Zouch. Apart from a minor tussle with a window cleaner's ladder and a trifling skirmish with a viaduct, the homeward journey seemed simplicity itself.

'Holy bilge–water!' Giuseppe shrieked, keen to drink up the minutiae of life onboard Wagtail. 'On Planet Longboat they'd call this longboat *Sir*!'

Frankie had heard it all before, in cumbersome detail, two days earlier. Likewise, the bond between the two Wagtails, introduced to each other at last, was quickly as strong as that between the three hot–headed hotspurs. Egg and bacon sandwiches quickly fortified their frames, while hyperbolic reminiscences gradually reconstituted their egos.

'We should burn all of our clothes and hose down the plane', insisted Giuseppe, with yoke spilling from his lip, 'we could so easily end up with egg on our faces you know.'

'My fashion sense isn't *that* bad, is it?' smiled Felix.

'Frankly, yes, although avoiding a life–sentence is marginally more to the point. And we should sort out self–corroborating alibis, too' embellished Frankie, the least likely contender for the position of team leader.

There was a stink of smouldering pastrami. Felix appeared, bearing torched chitterlings.

'Right landlubbers...who's for sausages?'

8

Captain Pirelli's Mangled Inn

At 11:28 on Monday evening the last sinews of smoke snaked away from the bar area of the Constipated Cobra public house and curled sleepily around its sticky brown rafters. Viewed from an angle of forty–five degrees the ceiling had become stained in six subtle, yet clearly discernible shades, which resembled a kind of colour–chart; Farrow and Ball might be tempted to call it '*Marron Rustique*: evocative French hues'. Clive sat alone, his gaze glued to the most oily brown variant, and exhaled the kind of sigh that signifies a long evening's labour drawn to a welcome close. The eighteen year–old erstwhile fitness fanatic was a non–smoking, twenty–a–day passive–smoker prone to bouts of non–passive drinking. Snorting from somewhere far back in his sinuses he shuddered at the thought of the Creosote–like mucous his lungs would discharge, sliced up on a morticians slab like a medium–rare haggis. This numbing wave of delirium had swelled during an hour–long ear–bashing from a voluble anti–smoking Scottish acupuncturist whose tongue was sharper than any pin in her cushion; but she'd been preaching to the converted. Clive ushered away the memory of the evening, tugging himself upright and straining to access an itch that had been bothering him since administering last orders. It was his job to lock up, yet again, since the owner had gone on leave for a week and didn't trust either of the other hired hands, Trish and Brice, who'd slipped away the moment the coasters were cleared. All three had recently arrived from Pretoria, ostensibly to fulfil vicarious cultural ambitions held by their patently uncultured parents, but inevitably the gap–year had relaxed into more of a slack–year. Clive glanced up at the cuckoo clock as it sprang to life fleetingly, and performed his daily time–zone arithmetic. Being the last one to leave the pub did have a couple of perks – a few gratis jars of Stella Artois and a freebie phone conversation with his girlfriend, Stephanie, who should by now be tumbling out of bed, back home. He'd risk calling her a little earlier than usual, having succeeded in emptying the bar with unaccustomed alacrity. But, as he reached for the cordless handset, it rang and gave him quite a shock. He answered it curtly, "Cobra", making it sound more like a question than a greeting. The caller seemed equally surprised his call had been answered and did not speak for a few seconds. Prompted by a second, even more clipped "Cobra!" a guarded voice responded.

'Um, can I speak to Toni please?'

'Na, sorry mate, he's on holiday...can I help?'

Another pause tested Clive's patience.

'Well, maybe. So, are you managing the pub this week then?'

'Sort of...unofficially, anyway.'

'Right...do you happen to know if Tom is still working there? I'm, er, a friend of his.'

'Couldn't say mate – he's certainly not been here for the past, what, four weeks...oh, is he the thin, lanky guy in the photos behind the bar?'

'Um, yeah, almost certainly.'

'Right, well he's off sailing I reckon...Northway... Norfway?'

'Norfolk?'

'*Norfawk*, that's the one. I reckon he'll be back fairly soon, maybe a week, 'cos none of us gappies are hangin' around here much longer than that, if we can help it. We've got some serious partying to do down in London with the Durban crew. I'd offer to take a message, but I doubt he'd find it – the paperwork's reached Table Mountain proportions here.'

'Oh, don't worry, I'll call back in a day or two and speak to Toni; he'll probably be more up to speed.'

Relieved to have dispatched the anonymous caller, Clive positioned himself prostrate along the pool table and gossiped avidly to Stephanie while absent–mindedly performing short–circuits of the corner pocket with the cue ball. Within a minute he'd forgotten the disjointed conversation that had just taken place. But the caller had not.

LIFE ON MARS? A CATINEL'S CHANCE

Two days later in the Constipated Cobra, at the occasion of a particularly fractious ladies darts match, a young man sat alone, wedged between an expressionless one–legged vicar and an ostentatious one–armed bandit. The commotion was quickly becoming unbearable, with cries of 'come on darlin', let's see your double top' emitting from an adjacent table, followed by guttural male 'phwoas'. The young man fixed his gaze for some five minutes, but in the opposite direction to everybody else, towards the bar, where Clive was busy impressing a woman called Mavis from the visitors' team with lewd allusions to his scoring potency. The object of distraction for the man, although barely visible to him, was a photograph featuring a ginger–haired surfer leaning casually against his giant board, which protruded phallically from the sand by its tail end. Occasionally the man's eyes would lower to his hand, which clutched another photograph. In it a young motorcyclist straddled his Japanese power–house, arms folded nonchalantly, helmet suspended precariously on the mirror.

Toni, a fifty–something year–old olive–skinned man, almost suave despite his horse teeth and cauliflower ears, ambled into the bar from the kitchen nibbling what looked like a cross between a chorizo sausage and a banana fritter. He took a slurp from a coffee cup next to the till, lifted the hinged bar top and sidled up to the vicar, who'd seized an unexpected opportunity to shuffle himself forwards to the bar, thus achieving marginal relief from the projectile pandemonium. He too seemed preoccupied by a photograph and hardly acknowledged Toni's affable slap on the shoulder.

'What have you got there, Sinjohn?' asked Toni, a tone of curiosity barely prevailing over his pearly, Italian sounding accent. 'I see you've found a slightly safer position, away from the Sick Parrot chicks.'

'Well, you know how it is Toni, you spend your teens chasing girls and your sixties escaping from old ladies, or in my case, hopping.'

'Even one foot can make a difference, eh!' laughed Toni, glancing pointedly to the vicar's absent pin.

'Getting my leg over this stool is about as exciting as it gets for me these days, but no matter Toni, you see, you develop more cerebral passions as you get older, such as patronising godless infidels in public houses. The church teaches you that life's not just about *sex*.'

The animated conversation behind them desisted momentarily, triggered by the word 'sex', as if it somehow amounted to more, falling from the lips of a man of the cloth, for whom sex would presumably constitute a tandem knee–trembler on a pogo stick. The vicar flattened out a wadge of papers clasped together by a bulldog clip, and pointed reverently to a picture.

'My god, what's that bastard?' frowned Toni incredulously.

'That, my good friend, is a Poison Dart Frog, from the family Dendrobatidae.' He began reading aloud from his handwritten notes, evidently quoting from an embryonic sermon based on the diversity of life. 'Sometimes referred to simply as "Dart Frogs", these are indubitably among the most fine looking of all the South American Rainforest specimens. They range in length from just over three centimetres, as with the Raspberry Poison Dart Frog (Dendrobates pumilio), to the more voluminous four–inch Dyeing Poison Frog (Dendrobates tinctorius). South American Tribesmen employed these secretions to fashion lethal poison darts.'

The vicar became distracted and broke off suddenly, glancing in astonishment at a chronically obese, daringly decorated women bearing down upon the ocky with such force her dart would surely have slain a mature albatross. He shook his head scornfully.

'You know, I can't help observing that her backside presents an unfair test of the strength of modern textiles.'

'Mutton dressed as lamb, Sinjohn?' whispered Toni, aware of the woman's compatriot whose buttocks straddled two stools, just a few feet away.

'Mutton dressed as *spam*, more like', fired the vicar, not remotely muted by Toni's nervous eye signal. 'Observe the girth of those *legs* – God's teeth!...they're like tree trunks! A case of acute VPL, I fear.'

'VPL?'

'Visible panty–line...or in her case, ingrained.'

'Otherwise known as Podgkinson's Disease...and just look at that jewellery, she must have got it from a *bling* 'n buy sale' giggled Toni uneasily, sensing her head turning slowly towards them.

'Mm, I expect you can tell her age by counting the

172

number of rings, you know' nodded the vicar facetiously.

Having demonstrated his aptitude for erudite and benevolent social commentary, the unholy vicar returned to the substance of his text, coughing showily by way of overture.

'The Native Indians favoured the appositely named "Goldenbolz Poison Dart Frog", Phyllobollakas terribilis. It is said that there is sufficient venom or "Batrachotoxins" in the secretions to slay perhaps 17,000 rodents or a dozen men.'

He took a gulp from his ginger beer and sloshed it vigorously around his mouth, as if rinsing after a dental scrape.

Toni looked puzzled, but said nothing.

The vicar moved without further encouragement to the central, somewhat inevitable, pillar of his sermon.

'They're all God's creatures, Toni, and they've only evolved in this way because they need to withstand attack from beasts even more formidable than themselves.'

Toni sniffed distractedly. 'I had a gerbil once. It got stuck in a toilet roll and died with its head sticking out of one end and its feet from the other. It lived a week.'

It was the vicar's turn to look bemused.

'Another ginger beer, when you're ready, Toni.'

Meanwhile, having become subliminally distracted by the vicar's wilfully arcane homily, the solitary young man resumed his study of the two photographs. Before long he turned to the vicar with whom, despite the lack of eye contact, he felt he was sufficiently acquainted to ask 'excuse me sir, but do you happen to know the name of the chap in that photograph?' He gestured towards the wall.

'Surely – it's young Tommy, a nice lad, but' (unaccountably lowering his voice, as vicars are in all probability trained to do) 'not quite "all there", if you catch my meaning.'

'Right', responded the man, drawing the vicar's attention to the picture he held in his hand. 'So, this would be him, too?' he enquired tentatively.

'It would indeed...so what's the fellow done, he's not been poaching again, has he?'

'Poaching, sir?'

'Oh, nothing too serious, from what I can recall, just a bit of petty pilfering he and his older brother got up to at one time. Tommy's straight enough now, I hear, but his brother Luke's another story. He got himself arrested for handling stolen vehicles about a year ago, and then was had up for the arson of a chip shop. Never did find out what happened to him for that. Terrible how a young life can turn Picasso.'

The young man nodded, as if mentally filing away some significance that he wasn't going to share.

'Where's this Tommy character now then...off sailing instead of tying up his A level projects, I'll guess.'

'Probably, you know what they're like', pontificated the vicar, 'surf 'til the day before the deadline, then download someone else's essay from Wikipedia. Mind you, I can talk, I've just researched next Sunday's sermon using the Net...it's taking as its starting point the much misunderstood Dendrobates tinctorius...'

'Do you happen to know his surname – Tommy's, I

mean?' interrupted the man, unable to endure further pronouncement about South American frog secretions.

'Mm, not certain...McGrath, perhaps?'

The young man smiled laconically, nodded his head and thanked the vapid vicar, muttering something incomprehensible about Celtic misfits as he put on his coat, and disappeared.

When an accidental fire caught deep in the bowels of the Constipated Cobra just three days later, causing near death to a family in the neighbouring property, Toni Pirelli's pub was put out of commission for a full fortnight. Parochial investigations proceeded along two entirely profitless tracks with unflagging determination. The most tenuous of these was connected to an incident eighteen months earlier, which involved a relative of Toni who'd become entangled in some peculiar impersonation scandal. The other centred on a mysterious figure whom, on at least two separate occasions during the past week, had taken an uncommon interest in the alleged criminal activities of an eighteen year–old part–time barman, whose name was also familiar to the police: Tommy McGuire. The inquirer, whose identity was not known, had been direct and specific in his solicitation; he'd left without engaging in chitchat or hinting at his purpose. The principal source of these details was the Rev. Sinjohn Forsythe whom, in his sixty–one years ministering had single–handedly christened, conjoined and cremated fifty–three percent of the population of Penistone.

Unbeknown to each other, two overwrought but intellectually underweight Derbyshire investigation teams were concurrently penetrating their focus–less inquiries with all the incisiveness of a pond–soaked tennis ball. While one sought clues to the misadventure of a seared corpse, the other tracked a manifestly unsuspicious inferno caused by the spontaneous combustion of a systematically neglected Baxi boiler. Meanwhile, working methodically, independently and covertly, one man was pursuing a line of enquiry that just might lead somewhere important. The young mercenary, PC Perry Dring, was of course himself the subject of one of these dysfunctional investigations. Had he known this, he would have been quietly self–satisfied; his mother, anxious to see him shinny to glory up the Chief Superintendent's slippery pole at any price, would have been apoplectic with pride. Detective Inspector Toogood had been blind to the value of those canoes, but *he'd* seen them for what they were, time–capsules left high and dry, one almost certainly concealing a unique clue to a wretched man's grisly demise, alone in the wilderness, robbed of every ounce of dignity, not to mention his underpants.

CAPTAIN PIRELLI'S MANGLED INN

Dring sat deep in thought on his single bed in the diminutive, manicured semi that belonged to his sixty year–old mother, while Eastenders boiled up its latest implausible stew of tragic happenstance on the wide–screen plasma TV downstairs. An impoverished investigation folder lying open on his bedside table contained the two potentially illuminating pieces of evidence his random investigations had so far unearthed. The first item, a barely readable sea–scout's record book, had of course already flagged up Thomas McGuire's boyhood canoeing prowess, although the few remaining details left him precious little still to follow up. From his assiduous internet enquiries two days earlier Dring had discovered that one of the canoe awards stamped on the record book, the British Canoe Union's Two Star Award, had been rendered obsolete two and a half years earlier; by a combination of logic and guesswork he'd concluded that the book could be no older than seven years, and probably not more recent than two or three. At any rate, such competence was unlikely to have been achieved by a scout under the age of sixteen. No one could be sure how long the canoes had rested in their final position, and no one but himself seemed faintly interested – but even if Toogood's disparagement had been near the mark, Dring would be looking for a young man now in his late teens, perhaps nudging twenty. He'd quickly short–listed seven Thomas, Tom or Tommy McGuires currently domiciled in England that fitted the age bracket. Since only one of these contenders was a native of Derbyshire, his route to the ginger–topped surf–bum barman at the Constipated Cobra had been relatively plain sailing.

LIFE ON MARS? A CATINEL'S CHANCE

Dring's second piece of evidence was a transcript he'd made of his conversation with Father Sinjohn at the Cobra during which an outline of McGuire's early criminal history had come to light, although this amounted to little more than petty arson and theft. So, Dring asked himself, buffing up his glasses with a companionless sock, what had he gleaned from his initial enquiries? He could think better in bullet–points, and reached for his notebook. One: Tommy McGuire had disappeared leaving only scanty details of his sailing holiday, and at a crucial moment in the official investigation, too (two asterisks). Two: motive; now that was going to be the tricky part – somehow, he'd need to establish a connection between McGuire and the dumped corpse (two question marks). Three: had either of the McGuires *ever* been near the scene of the body's discovery? Four: might either one of them have ties with extremist groups, right–wing factions of Greenpeace or CND, perhaps? Dring briefly snoozed at point number six, where he'd intended to write: check out Toni Pirelli. At his reconnaissance trip to the pub he'd noticed a framed photograph hanging in the Gents' lav, taken perhaps a few years earlier. It featured Pirelli, stood to attention and dressed in some inscrutable mode of sailor's uniform, while another man, who might have been his brother, had contrived to appear as shabby as possible, perched on the bonnet of an old banger.

It had been a long day for PC Dring, running errands for two officers, one deluged by humdrum traffic directives, the other making headway of a comparably pedestrian pace in the murder case. Although he'd tried to enlist the assistance of his chinless mate, PC William Young, better known as 'Old Bill', in his undercover operation, the response had been predictably tepid; compared to Dring, Bill had fewer aspirations than a fairground goldfish. No matter, this way the glory would be all his.

On returning to the Constipated Cobra two days later, confident of procuring the Pirelli photo for further analysis, Dring was perplexed to find a sign pinned to the door, which was resolutely bolted. It read: 'Due to extensive fire damage last Thursday evening, the Management regrets to report the temporary closure of the Constipated Cobra. If anyone has any knowledge of the events leading to this deliberate act of sabotage, please inform the police using the number given below.'

Dring stopped in his tracks but made a mental note of the officer assigned to the incident, Detective Inspector Frank Paradis. He'd also hoped to drag a bit more detail from Sinjohn Forsythe, the malevolent monopod minister, who clearly spent much of his time rehearsing flimsy vocalizations on anyone imprudent enough to sit within earshot. But, in a way, he'd learned more from discovering the pub incinerated. The next day Dring did a spot of unofficial sleuthing, assisted by a couple of the more amenable members of the 'official' murder squad, Bruiser and Progesterex, whose canteen gossip had revealed the investigating team's groundless suspicion of a firebomb attack, evidently ignoring the distinctly more plausible hypothesis that a dickey boiler had triggered the blaze. Dring also learned that a young man closely matching his own description had been poking his nose into McGuire's private affairs and had appeared particularly interested in the teenager's criminal credentials. DI Paradis, with feet of clay and a demeanour to match, headed up a team of considerable ineptness. No tie–up between the Cobra incident and the murder investigation looked in prospect, leaving Dring's irrepressible imagination to run as wild as a pessary on a radiator.

9

Mourning 'til Night

A t 11:00 AM on Saturday Wagtail shook contentedly to the refrain of three snoring men. This was partly a symptom of some late night poker playing, in which Felix had relinquished ownership of his boat on at least six occasions in a desperate bid to succeed at double or quits. But it also signified a certain level of restored equanimity onboard that had been rudely shattered by the activities of Felix's oldest pal, the immodestly clad Frankie, and his newest acquaintance, the modestly proportioned Giuseppe. Soon the rumble of pedestrian–paced traffic on the canal, guided absent–mindedly by coffee–swilling middle–aged men wearing FCUK sweatshirts, nudged them gently above the first plateau of consciousness. Giuseppe's vociferous bowel movements had to share cabin space with Felix, whose showering prospects had become dampened by

Frankie's heavy cake of matted hair, which had clogged up the drain hole as effectively as a pummelled porcupine. Just a few paces away, Frankie was now busy preparing variations on a theme of cremated pig, simultaneously deploying the whistling kettle as a hair dryer to preen his recently trimmed dreadlocks. A good–humoured hubbub prevailed through to brunch on the roof, where evidence of the previous night's debauchery was very much in evidence.

The topic of conversation that had been all pervading just days earlier had lapsed into a temporary state of exhaustion. Yet it was never too far away from their minds; it hovered about them menacingly, not unlike Giuseppe's latest poisonous flatulent emission, a problem that had its suspected roots in an exceptionally angry looking tub of hummus festering in Felix's lukewarm fridge. Close by, twinkling in the uncertain sunlight of that March morning, the three vehicles had been scoured virtually to the level of their undercoats, and every grain of gravel and grit had been prised from the tyres. The windows had been chamoised shinier than a freshly shaved armpit, the carpets toothcombed down to the rubber, the ashtrays rigorously ear–budded and every moulded crease in the synthetic trims ironed smooth. Every nook and cranny was spick and span. Wagtail II had been exfoliated to within an inch of her life too, vintage dead flies individually flicked off and every nuance of human matter lifted away. New footwear seemed to symbolise a precipitate sense of optimism.

From the roof grill, gristly sausages, crispy eggs and rind–laden bacon tasted almost acceptable that morning, the warmer weather inducing an orgy of colours all around them. Sat together, cross–legged on the thin strip of roof, they drank in their blissful surroundings and bathed in their blissful ignorance, Grieg's Peer Gynt Suite thumping out irrelevantly from underneath them.

The news blackout regarding the peculiar discovery of a naked, flash–fried man deep in the Derbyshire countryside had inevitably been only partly effective, but it had penetrated as far as Felix's lush green haven. Giuseppe's daily Internet survey provided scanty and conflicting information that didn't even make clear whether the body was male or female, let alone how or when it might have materialised, as if from nowhere. Radio Four's news bulletins continued to be reassuringly anodyne and noncommittal; the doggerel had become so predictable that the three would sing along to it in perfect unison, as if rehearsing a patter–song from the Mikado.

'Tell me', said Giuseppe unexpectedly, in a moment chosen to coincide with loading his fork with medium–rare black sausage, 'did you ever take a dump, and feel like you'd slept for a week?'

'You *just did*' came the unison response – '*both.*'

Paying no heed to Giuseppe's random observation, Felix returned their attention to more salient matters.

'They'll track down Day's identity sooner or later, you know' he muttered, between mouthfuls of fatty scraps. 'Then they'll figure out he was as bent as a nine–bob note.'

Frankie quickly tuned into the negative vibe, groaning as his bacon bap wept ketchup onto his trouser leg.

'His lockup will be discovered, eventually, and

183

they'll show a toothpick to every inch of it, looking for evidence.'

'What could they find, anyway?' asked Giuseppe in a half nonchalant, half earnest tone.

'Exactly, Giuseppe', frowned Felix, 'and anyway, Frankie said you'd sniffed out the lockup directly after the Day debacle, and that it had been completely empty!'

'There again, it's possible someone other than the police was responsible for that…They could find plenty, actually; those buggers are so clued up these days – they'll be bottling *air* for DNA before we know it.'

'So, do you reckon we should get up there and hose it down?' asked Frankie, his left eyebrow twitching as if being controlled from above by a system of pulleys and levers.

'I suppose we could' conceded Giuseppe grudgingly, 'the News would have mentioned the lockup by now if the police had got that far in the investigation, surely?'

'Of course not!' erupted Felix, determined to avoid contact with the scene if he could possibly help it. 'Look, the News bods will have been fed nothing but the barest of bones. For all *they* know, the police are close to closing the case. You two go if you must, I'll stay here and…rearrange my etchings or something. My neck's already fully stretched, thank you very much.'

MOURNING 'TIL NIGHT

It was probably the need to be doing *something*, however pointless or risky, that in the end motivated them to drive the fifty miles to Mugginton late that same evening. Felix was onboard too, dragooned into the comparatively sheltered rôle of lookout. They'd brought with them a bucket, two firm–bristled scrubbing brushes, a litre of Domestos and a hefty torch. By the time they'd arrived the weather had turned petulant, wind and rain whipping up apace. They parked some distance away, further than Frankie had lingered on that first occasion, but near enough to be within eyeshot. Defended ineffectively by wind–contorted umbrellas and clutching their improvised cleaning kit, the two shifty looking men marched with a speed that was inversely proportional to the prevailing level of confidence. Acting on the questionable assumption that the lockup would still be accessible to them, they progressed to the cluster of 1980s red–brick buildings with compounding consternation, heads dipped into the lashing rain.

As they approached, an automatic light briefly tripped into life near to Day's lockup. It startled them momentarily, but soon timed itself out and did not impede them again. By the time Giuseppe's night–eyes had returned, his fingers were at the door handle. Sure enough, it did not resist, and within seconds of receiving the go ahead, courtesy of Felix's torch signal, the pair were inside with the door tugged shut tight behind them.

From Felix's vantage point in the Landrover, what happened next probably seemed more baffling than concerning. According to the plan they'd concocted en route, Frankie and Giuseppe would operate solely by

185

torchlight. They would be in and out within two minutes, three at the outside, barely long enough to remove the more obvious forensic traces of their involvement in Day's accidental demise. But after what Felix estimated had been five minutes of complete stillness he felt compelled to venture from his comfort zone. He moved uneasily, with no particular haste, and cowered outside the closed aluminium door from under which, by now, he might have expected a trickle or two of frothy cleaning fluid to have mingled with the rain bouncing at his feet. No human sound was audible to him, just the symphonic percussion of rain upon corrugated iron that rushed madly across his plastic cap and down to the nape of his neck, and not a tendril of light crept out from around the door seams. Felix waited for a further minute, his hand moving periodically towards and away from the handle, unable to galvanise the courage to open it.

When he finally did, it was as though he'd stumbled upon a surrealist's construal of the 'Lion, the Witch and the Wardrobe'. His quivering torch first picked out a large Formica cabinet stuffed solid with oddities – silverware, trinkets, jewellery boxes and the like. A life–sized lion, stuffed and growling, mounted upon a marble plinth, glowered at him with mad intent in its eyes. Its teeth had become yellowed and chipped with age, but there could be no doubting their former efficiency. Giuseppe hadn't mentioned anything about a lion; probably just as well. His torchlight then washed over the oil–stained concrete floor and across to the other side of the lockup, one centimetre at a time.

There was a spicy stench of disinfectant about the place, and the brushes they'd brought along were there, resting next to a nest of metallic painted racing cycles, but there was still no sign of his crazy crew; Frankie and Giuseppe had vanished into a cubic area no larger than Wagtail. Felix moved forward cautiously, unsure of whether to announce his presence with a projected whisper. He stumbled over stack upon stack of random objects that clearly ought to have been lining other people's living rooms, until he finally reached the back wall of the lockup. Here, two striking pictures of Lord and Lady Byron, incongruously framed in baroque gold, looking especially farcical mounted directly onto the naked breezeblocks, peered down at him registering their distinct disapproval. Glancing over to his right Felix noticed a faint puddle of light a little distance away. He walked slowly towards it, expecting at any moment to be consumed by some awful duende from the fuliginous darkness. Here he would finally discover his two compatriots: upright, silent, transfixed.

Frankie and Giuseppe hadn't noticed Felix's tentative approach. It could hardly have mattered less; for within a second of confronting the hellish vision sat there, stiff as a caber, Felix was motionless and breathless, too.

'Deja bleedin' vous, mate' whispered Frankie.

'I've heard you say that before, somewhere' muttered Giuseppe.

'Who in the name of Kris Kristopherson, *is that*? Felix at last managed to squawk under his breath.

'If we hadn't already torched the bastard, I'd *swear* it was Day', exclaimed Giuseppe.

187

There was indeed an uncanny likeness between Spencer Day and the pallid man, bound and gagged, strapped into a bishop's seat, fingers clamped around the armrests as if to alleviate the stress of unanaesthetised dental surgery. His unflinching gaze returned Felix's torchlight as intensely as the lion's had, although no sane taxidermist could wantonly recreate such a gruesome spectacle. They watched on, as though there might be something further to gain from doing so, as a single line of black blood tracked lugubriously from under the dead man's chin; it collected into a globule the size of a ten–penny piece and fell to the ground with a sickening splat. Having sustained an absurd minute's silence, the three men spoke at once. Although the words were unintelligible, the consensus was clear.

'Let's get the buggery away from here!' gestured Giuseppe, tripping over a large garden ornamental figurine as he led the way out of the adjacent lockup via the small gap in the wall that had not at first been evident. Felix found the presence of mind to grab the buckets, which sloshed their sharp smelling cleaning fluid over Frankie's trousers as they retreated gracelessly, only half succeeding in closing the door behind him. They ran the fifty yards back to the Landrover looking like drug–crazed window cleaners, persecuted relentlessly by blades of horizontal rain. Its sidelights glowed timidly, and fortunately the doors were unlocked. As they screeched off, Felix at the wheel with a bucket inadvisably clenched between his knees, they narrowly avoided clipping the side of a silver VW. It had appeared from nowhere and had been the first sign of life to pass by during the threesome's brief sortie to the lockup.

'The new model's got brakes, indicators and everything!' snarled Frankie, pointedly mopping his trousers.

Felix was in no mood to deflect Frankie's derision. He continued to move at such speed the entire vehicle was soon contaminated by the foul foaming fluid, which attacked their skin with the ferocity of boiling petrol. The roads seemed much busier than before, or perhaps the three men were more conscious of eyes turning towards them at traffic lights and assiduous rear mirror analysis by the car in front.

'I *warned* you this was a cretinous move, you pair of wrinkle–rectum baboons!' shouted Felix, windows open, as they shifted south along the A52 at a spine–compressing seventy–five mph. Progress had self evidently not been made: one of their freshly spruced vehicles had been irredeemably soiled, they'd implicated themselves with a second death scene that was even more gothic than the first and, perhaps worst of all, their getaway may have been witnessed. An escalating torrent of mutual abuse corresponded with the chaos unfolding outside – at full velocity the windscreen wipers were about as effective as a chamois leather on the Chrysler Building.

LIFE ON MARS? A CATINEL'S CHANCE

Midnight supper on Wagtail bore more than a passing resemblance to breakfast. Amorphous semi–solids awaited rejuvenation under a thick film of brown–flecked sausage fat; under moderate heat they slid away from the egg scrapings with little persuasion and rolled easily into butter–stacked wedges of bread. The food was for comfort, not for nutrition or gastronomic stimulation. Frankie stared at his mobile phone as he chomped noisily, holding it at varying distances from his face and turning it ninety degrees, before inviting the others to share the surprisingly crisp image of corpse number two that he'd managed to capture ahead of Felix's pusillanimous arrival. He quickly revealed the image to the others, zooming in and out to the accompaniment of sighs, groans and sharp intakes of breath. They were mid way through their dessert of chocolate marshmallow biscuits before Felix noticed something odd in one of his own pictures – not the grotesque, blooded visage itself, but a small, curiously conspicuous object wedged in among a small clutter of stolen items. The shot had captured an open–shelved cabinet angled obliquely to the side wall, positioned at the other end of the lockup from where the body had been seated.

'If that's not a camcorder, then my name is Magnus Magnusson' he said, affecting a commanding tone.

'What if it is, Magnus?' responded Frankie, busily prising out grit from his front teeth.

'I've started, so I'll finish' he continued, sustaining a barely excusable Scottish accent, let alone an Icelandic one. 'Look!...I'll zoom in...a couple of millimetres above that bust of Beethoven.'

The slightly pixilated image indeed revealed a camcorder perched on a tiny tripod, angled optimally to film the seated corpse – and positioned directly in line with the point they'd stood to gawp at it.

'And the bleedin' green light's on, look!' cried Giuseppe.

They stared at each other, stood up sharply as if the headmaster had just walked in on an illegal smoking session, and hurried from the boat with panic and HP sauce painted all over their faces.

Theories varying from the faintly conceivable to the downright absurd abounded on the return journey to the lockup, but at least the three were agreed on their purpose: that camera *had* to be retrieved. The wind and rain violated the open windows but only partly dissipated the residual whiff of Domestos.

'It's gotta be a setup, Felix' yelled Frankie, combating the noise from outside by tapping a frenzied rhythm on the headrest in front of him.

'Just leave off the bongos, for god's sake, you're sending me into a nervous fever.'

'Someone's exterminated the bloke as he sat strapped in that chair...and filmed himself in the act!'

'Or else, left the camera hooked up to some kind of surveillance device to nab any nosey bastards coming in after him' lamented Felix.

'Yeah, like us, you mean' moaned Giuseppe. We've just *got* to get it before any other bugger claps eyes on it.'

'Anyway, who is this guy, why has he been topped

off...and why *there*, of all places, too?' demanded Felix, clipping a pavement while expediting a bold turn.

'Whoever's done this must know about us, mustn't he?' blurted Giuseppe.

'Why?' hollered Frankie.

'Because it's a cloaked message to us...don't you get it, you mad rapper?' bellowed Felix over his shoulder. 'We're meant to learn our own fate from this. *We* killed Day, now someone else has been slain in the adjacent lockup. Someone's assumed *he* was Day's killer. But when they discover he wasn't, *we'll* be sliced up bitches 'n all!'

'This is baloney, you mean a cocked–up reprisal murder?' yelled Giuseppe.

'Yep, and we're really in the crapper now; if that camcorder's got us on tape, its owner will be on to us like mosquitoes on a weeping cold sore.'

They were becoming all too familiar with the route up to Day's lockup. Not that the lockup ever seemed to *be* locked up; it was a wonder no one had pilfered the remaining tat, considering the persistent intrusions of the past week. The rain had weakened somewhat, mercifully; the air was dank and smelt sour, with just the gentlest murmur of wind to contend with as an ominous stillness cloaked the scene. According to Felix's Landrover clock the time was 2:33 AM as they alighted close by and meandered up to the lockup door. On clicked the security light for its customary two seconds as Giuseppe's hand reached for the door handle and turned it unquestioningly. It didn't budge. A second attempt by Felix also yielded nothing. Only then did Frankie notice they'd been standing at the wrong door.

192

'Wait a minute', whispered Felix as they ambled the few paces to the adjacent lockup, 'why would Day have two linked lockups but fill only one of them with hot gear? The one with the body is virtually empty, apart from that cabinet.'

'And in any case, in daylight the gap in the wall at the back wouldn't be exactly hard to spot, would it? But I suppose if I wanted to execute someone like that I'd chose the lockup with elbow room, too' rationalised Giuseppe, realising his solo mission earlier in the week had landed him at the virtually empty adjoining lockup by mistake.

'Let's just grab the camera and get away from here...only one of us needs to go in...Giuseppe, you're the cause of all this mayhem, in you go' ordered Felix.

Giuseppe meekly complied and crept in with just a micro–torch for illumination. The handle was reassuringly free of its catch, suggesting that no one had been there since their visit a few hours earlier. Within thirty seconds Giuseppe was back, looking petrified but pleased with himself, clutching his trophy, a small silver Sony camcorder, still connected to its six–inch tripod but no longer in possession of its green light. They were gone in the time it took to pull the door to and wipe around the handle.

The return drive was accomplished in a comparatively subdued atmosphere, despite Frankie's tiresome puzzlement over the lack of videotape in the camera and Felix's uncommonly reticent mood; he drove carefully, even slowly, as if to make amends for the Domestos fiasco, the aftermath of which was still in evidence every time one of them picked his nose.

193

The first thing Giuseppe did upon their return was to cram each of their mobile phone adapters into the camcorder's charging socket in the hope of coaxing it to life, for the battery was flatter than a stingray's jowls.

'I don't know why you're fretting anyway, mate' snapped Frankie, once it had become clear success was not in prospect. 'There was no mains lead attached to the thing, let alone a tape inside it, so I guess my hunch about the surveillance must have been wrong after all.'

'Pass it here' said Felix softly, snapping his fingers, his first words since leaving the lockup. He scrutinised the camera for some time, pawing at it, peering inside it, shaking it, as if expecting to entice a microscopic Japanese genie from one of its hidden ports.

'3 inch display...12 megapixels...10 x digital zoom...USB connection...200 Gigabyte hard–drive data storage' he read from its collage of multi–coloured stickers. 'This machine records to disc, as well as to tape. If we can charge her up there's still a chance there's something of interest on the drive, even though I don't see it being *us*.'

They scouted about for sacrificial AA batteries to feed it, raiding two clocks and a virgin milk–frother before persuading the machine to stutter and blink encouragingly. Eventually a church organ, grinding like a stressed bulldozer through its internal speakers, indicated they'd stumbled over the machine's on–board memory.

The display had kicked into life mid way through a crematorium service, over which the camerawoman wailed so incessantly that the chaplain's simpering monotone oration was virtually incomprehensible, let alone what might have been her sister's attempt at a running commentary. Only when the same woman, still breathless and overwrought, was called upon to blub her way through a particularly abstruse Jeremiah reading did the film become fractionally more coherent. The coverage then shifted abruptly to the wake, an unnervingly irreverent occasion with more clinking of champagne glasses than you'd expect at a wedding and fewer tears than you'd see at a christening. A heart–shaped wreath with the word 'Dad' fussily pinned to its centre in pink carnations, balanced unbecomingly on a crate of Budweiser bottles, lent little poignancy to the show of paternal affection.

'Stop!' cried Frankie suddenly, 'stop it right there!'

Felix scrambled for the pause button, which freeze–framed at a curious point in the proceedings. Two men, whom they were certainly not expecting they'd recognise, were in the middle of an animated contretemps, and perhaps on the cusp of something more vociferous. One held a half raised finger to the other, whose response seemed to be one of contempt, arms folded, head tilted to one side.

'Spencer....*sodding*...Day!' spluttered Frankie hoarsely, his slender fingers flying about uncontrollably.

'And could that be...Day's *sodding*...brother?' stammered Giuseppe.

Felix nodded knowingly, '...AKA corpse number two', and released the pause button, whereupon a cortège in varying stages of dishevelment and inebriation paraded before the camera, feigning kisses and exchanging phone numbers in what could just as easily have been the closing stages to an office party.

Felix pressed 'stop', noting the prematurely dwindling batteries, and looked up at Giuseppe, whose cavernous eyes had become every bit as expressive as Frankie's progressively distracting upper body spasms. Giuseppe began cracking open a cooker igniter for additional batteries to placate the hungry machine, while Felix calmly switched it off, placed it to one side of his mug of diet Coke and silently exhaled a cloud of pipe smoke, filling the space between himself and his numb–tongued friends. But before he was permitted a chance to expunge his hypothesis, Giuseppe had replenished the camcorder and re–pressed 'play'.

The coverage shifted violently, once again, to depict an altogether more intriguing scene. The space was dark and austere, with no furniture, carpet or curtains to soften its edges, and no background sound audible except the occasional echoing footsteps of the videographer. Evidently the camera had been set to record and then placed randomly on its side directly on the concrete, presumably awaiting a more suitable position. Lighting seemed excessively frugal, in fact there was just the meagrest copper glow to suggest that this might be a dungeon, attic or cellar. The three men stared at the little screen with some frustration, and Giuseppe was about to hit the 'fast forward' button when yet another unannounced change of scene occurred. The camera was on the move now, and a few seconds later someone was attempting to fix it into a small space on a shelf. The coverage jolted sharply to a shocking and immediately compelling subject, and a voice simultaneously cut dead the previous two–minute's stasis; it was cold, controlled, and incandescent. The volume level wavered wildly at first, then settled to permit broken comprehension. But before the tidal wave of reaction could consume them, Giuseppe's mobile rang. It was his father, whose clipped delivery attacked the earpiece like a peashooter.

'Okay, Pop...not sure, does it matter?...Well, I'm pretty busy on a job with Frankie...*what*? Oh, um, well I can explain all that...we could do with your help actually...look, can I call you back in a bit?'

The tidal wave crashed with the power of an airdropped sperm whale. It was obvious in a millisecond what was unfolding in the amateurishly taken footage, and why the feng–shui of the surroundings had seemed so macabre. But, ironically, the image of a man gripped so tightly by his chair that his jugular wobbled palpably, appeared magnified through the camera display the size of a lemon puff. The gag used to cover the man's mouth, which had struck Frankie and Giuseppe so forcibly on their face–to–face encounter two hours earlier, had not yet been applied; in any case, the man seemed incapable of speech. A woman of masculine dominance, with big, uncontrolled hair and a mouth to match, bustled noisily in and out of shot. Dressed in waterproofs and galoshes, she was unquestionably built for the kill. Between bouts of near hyperventilation she unfurled a barbed tirade, patently for her own satisfaction as much as for her captive or the camera trained upon him. Although only one in five of her sentences was intelligible the man's eyelids, constantly surveying his immediate space, assisted comprehension by juddering in response to words of especial significance. One such moment occurred when his assailant uttered the word 'crossbow'; another was triggered by the word 'nipples'. Felix's antenna seemed marginally better tuned in to her manly tessitura than the others, so he paraphrased every few seconds.

'...You pile of steaming horse crap...you always hated Spence...brighter than you...better looking, too. Spence loved you...and you *humiliated* him...*burned* him...*murdered* him...Why? *Why*?'

Presumably it was the prospect of receiving a left nipple massage from a loaded crossbow directed at him that prevented the man from formulating a considered response. But in any case, the audible trickle of urine puddling at his conjoined feet expressed his sentiments more than adequately.

'I can mourn for Spence, and for poor old Dad...but who'll mourn for *you*, you callous, jealous bastard?'

Felix continued, his impersonation quite commendable.

A single word spilled from the man's quivering lips, '...Paula...'

'Don't *Paula* me, you pathetic prick, or I'll *poleaxe* your *prostate* for you!'

The man complied; he would never speak another word, confirmation indeed that his prostate didn't require poleaxing. A fiendish misandry resonated in the dominatrix's voice as she aimed the crossbow at the man's groin. 'Tell me why I shouldn't do it...tell me why you deserve *any* mercy?'

The arrow, once freed, was swift, artful and incisive; it caught the executer as much by surprise as the executed. In fact it wasn't immediately obvious through the camera's display whether the arrow had penetrated, missed or even been discharged from its carriage. After five seconds the woman, evidently herself unsure of what had just happened, moved languorously up to her paralysed victim and stood there, shaking and whimpering quietly, like a small child that had just discovered its mauled hamster.

The first indicator of the woman's escalating panic was her decision to unshackle the man's hands and feet, as if this might in some way lessen the perceived vindictiveness of the crime she'd inadvertently committed. She changed her mind half way though and hurriedly retied her knots, bleating like a whipped donkey and crying 'no! no! not like this, not like *this*!' A second indicator was her decision to fashion a gag from a stray cloth, even though protruding from his pursed lips was what appeared to be the butt end of a green feather; the shot had impaled him to the wall as deftly as a meat hook through a brace of pheasants.

Paula had gone nuclear. So turbulent was the woman's state of mind that she scurried about, fitting and yelping like a cat force–fed a jalapeno. Her one lucid move was to decant the camcorder of its cassette, never to appreciate its superfluous state. Her twitching face, drained of any femininity it might once have been capable of, rained droplets of perspiration directly onto the lens as the camcorder continued to record the pitiable scene. She

199

fumbled randomly, eventually triggered the eject button and thus brought to a close a tragic video diary she would never bring herself to watch.

The plain absence of shock, or even of curiosity on Felix's face, only served to antagonise the others; their own incredulity prompted as many reviews of the final manic sequence as the camcorder's batteries could allow.

'Well, why are you looking so bleedin' smug?' interrogated Giuseppe, finally permitting the machine a moment's respite. 'I suppose *you'd* guessed all this?'

'No' responded Felix unflappably, 'I'd suspected a man actually, possibly exhibiting a female capacity for bearing a grudge and a childlike obsession for melodrama. Instead, we have a woman possessing all the charm of an inflamed urinary tract, the sexual allure of a Hobbit and as much raging testosterone as your average Etonian wrestler. It's better this way round though...let's thank god she's an emotional wreck, an oversized half–wit, who's probably more scared of herself now than *we* need to be.'

'I take it she's the blubbing bird at her old man's funeral' said Frankie coldly. 'Her plastic shell–suit didn't do much for her figure, did it?'

'This apparel, notwithstanding the rain earlier on, is indubitably indicative of a most twisted and complex personality' continued Felix, striking a familiar air of condescension. 'Nobody wears galoshes unless they're fishing, bating, emptying a cesspit or revenging their husband's killer with a crossbow. And yet, given her emotional volte–face in the video, I'm pretty confident she'd not planned to do more than scare her brother–in–law into an admission of guilt.'

'How did she...Paula, I mean...manage to lure him to the lockup do you suppose?' enquired Frankie.

'Who knows' shrugged Felix, 'but the whole family presumably knew of its location – and he'd hardly have suspected reprisal for a murder he hadn't committed.'

'Holy shitburger in a box, chaps, where does this leave us?' stumbled Giuseppe exasperatedly.

'In the shitburger, along with the chips and the manky lettuce' responded Frankie.

'It leaves us in a perfect position to drag ourselves out of the swamp *we* are in, actually' corrected Felix. 'Look, the daft rubber–ridden wench thinks she's in possession of the only incriminating documentation that'll ever exist. She's unlikely to check out the tape – would you? That buys us a little time.'

'Time...to do what, exactly?' pursued Frankie, still infuriated by Felix's impossible composure.

'The time to stitch her up like a kipper, for the *first* accidental killing, that is – *ours.*'

'Yin–yang, I suppose mate? Something positive in opposition to something negative?' conjectured Giuseppe, unsure he'd caught the drift.

'In one. Well, in two, actually – two stages, I mean' teased Felix.

Felix lit his pipe and passed it among his stunned companions.

'You're developing an *eye* for this, Felix', conceded Frankie, blinking exaggeratedly.

'He *knows* that, the cocky bastard' chuckled

Giuseppe, firing smoke from a single nostril.

'Go on then, we're all *ears*' they chortled in unison, flicking each other's lobes in a long overdue moment of regression.

10

Malice, a Four Thought

Giuseppe's Pop, Salvatore, a rotund, unassuming man of sixty–six, turned out to have an impressive lexicon of complexes and yet a naively simple take on life. He hit it off with Felix in an instant. For a seasoned private investigator his sleuthing powers were not immediately manifest but perhaps, as Felix reflected, a PI would need to give off an impression of harmlessness to remain effective. The Sicilian was blessed with a vocabulary that was striking in its delightful non–appearance of sophistication, intensified by an accent as broad as if he'd lived a quarter of the time in England. He'd taken an inordinate time to make his way to the boat, despite innumerable phone directions, but, just as his son had done, he'd appeared bearing a bounty of goodies, driving a beat– up yet pristine old Volvo that was the spit of its twin, the rather less mollycoddled model entrusted to Giuseppe. It was just as well he hadn't seemed to notice the conspicuous disappearance of his beloved canoes. Parked next to Felix's antiquated Landrover and Frankie's Mk 1 Transit, they might have been hosting a vintage automobile rally.

'Blimey, Salvatore', cackled Frankie mischievously, casting an eye over the peculiar vehicle, 'I must have gone five years without spotting a single Volvo Estate 740 GL on the road, and here, in the most secluded corner of the country I've ever found myself in, I bump into a man who's proud to own *two*. You're not... Swedish, I take it?'

'Ah ha, two reasons for thees' Salvatore explained earnestly, *'wan*: I've halways gotta spares; and *tu*: heet makes geraita cover.'

'Cover?'

'Yesa! People canna never be sure heef I'm abouta, or notta – I canna be hinna two places hata the sama tima, or somewhere *hentirely* different; like the Scarlet Peempernella, yesa?...They seeka heema heera, they seeka heema thera, they seeka heema *facking everywhera*, eh?'

Salvatore even giggled with a Sicilian twang. He clapped his hands and rubbed them together as if crushing the life from a disoriented daddy–longlegs, stood up and declared 'now, I have some gooda news and... some *notta* so gooda newsa. But firsta, I fixa the pasta, boys, eh?'

The cuisine made economical use of fresh ingredients but was extravagant in respect of dried pasta shells and nondescript cheese, with which Felix was awash. The atmosphere was reassuringly insouciant; it was hard to see how Salvatore's bad news could amount to much. After all, he'd only just arrived, only just made the acquaintance of Felix and Frankie, and they'd purposely kept the details of the two Day demises sketchy over the phone. So, when at last he'd cast off the portion of caponata that had clung to his chin since his first mouthful, belched manfully and returned to the subject, the reaction among the others fell somewhere between bewilderment and amusement.

'Now, boys, today I hava to take a slasha, onna the motorwayee, see, and a leetle, *leetle* thought crossed my minda.'

'Whata?' probed Frankie naughtily.

Felix thumped him and smiled at Salvatore, whose skin was clearly thicker than any moustachioed walrus's.

'Seerious boys, *seerious*' smiled Salvatore, 'heen my job I follow many peoples, *many* peoples, and I know h— when I ham being followed, you understanda?'

'But who'd be interested in following you, here, I mean?' quibbled Felix reasonably.

Salvatore shrugged his shoulders and sparked a Capstan full–strength cigarette. His first tiny inhalation resulted in an astonishingly elongated flood of blue smoke that lasted through to the conclusion of his next three inscrutable sentences.

'Yesterday, I went to hasda for the heggs and hole– le–meal' he continued.

'Wait, wait...*whaf*?' demanded Frankie, smothering hysterics.

Giuseppe helped him out, sighing, 'he went to Asda to buy eggs and wholemeal bread.'

'Thees I already say, no?' protested Salvatore.

They all nodded.

'Behind the freezy place for the leetle feeshes, I see a mana. He look at me funnya, but I don'ta laugha, *ha ha!* No, I heegnore heem completely – well, I *pretend* to heegnore heem. Really, I keepa the tabs onna heem and take the photographa with my phona from behinda the Rica Chrispies!'

He proudly revealed a somewhat outmoded mobile phone, the weight of a brick and with the functionality of same.

'Thees came in h–handy today. Any–h–way boysa, you maka me forgeta my slasha, at the motorwayee thervethes...I wait a longa tima, a longa *longa* time for a slasha 'cos every mana in the thervethes needs a slasha too, see, and I am worried I ama lata to see my favourite stupid boy, Giuseppe.'

Salvatore began laughing uncontrollably as he kissed Giuseppe's head showily. They braced themselves.

'The mana next to me, he wait a longa tima too...he say to me, "I coulda wash my hands *first*, I suppose, to sava tima!" *Ha ha ha!* He *very* funny mana.'

Frankie and Felix laughed compassionately; Giuseppe smiled the smile of a son who'd long forgotten how to feel embarrassed about his father, and could access a mode of calm resignation at the flick of a switch.

'...So, I hava my slasha, then I sit in my cara to eat my chocky muffin...anda I see *heem*, the hasda mana!'

'Mm, so, let me get this straight' said Felix, shaking his head and struggling with his pipe. 'You're saying that the man you thought was ogling oddly at you in the store yesterday is the same man you spotted in the motorway services today. Is that right?'

Salvatore paused and sucked in smoke sufficient to fuel his next disjointed iteration.

'Thees I notta justa say, boys?'

They nodded.

'Coincidence' dismissed Frankie sneeringly, 'or else, you've got the faces muddled.'

'Maybe' said Felix, looking to Giuseppe for further clarification.

'Look, Dad's not the best at remembering names, and he's worse still at pronouncing them. But he's as sharp as a microwaved piccolo when it comes to recalling faces. He's unbelievable; you can believe him...*believe me.*'

'But, as I said, who'd have *reason* to follow you?'

'Have you been rogering the Asda manager's missus, mate?' snorted Frankie, snapping his knuckles vaguely in time with his rhythmic nasal emissions. 'You wanna watch out, mate – she's probably twice your size from gorging her husband's pilfered broken biscuits!'

'Ah...brok–ed–ie biscuits, why you saya thees?' exhaled Salvatore into Frankie's face, 'I *only* eata the Bourbona or Garibaldi.'

The annular topic of supermarkets, strange men lurking in public toilets and economy biscuits had orbited for as long as could be sanely permitted. The conversation moved to the comparably painful business of appraising Salvatore with the details surrounding their mutual predicament. A pause to recuperate became imperative, during which tobacco displaying a variety of aromatic properties was pooled, blended and ignited.

Eventually the sluggish Sicilian was brought up to date, reaching a top speed commensurate with his pair of twenty–five year–old Volvos.

'Ay, ay, ay boys. You are uppa the shitters'a creeka, witha no bog paper anda no paddle…yes, truly.'

They nodded and began scrutinising the patchy pictorial evidence they'd captured on their mobiles. Salvatore's contribution consisted of an image so burnt out and poorly focused that his mystery follower might equally well have been Cindy Lauper's mum or Lord Lucan's dad. Felix's choice of moment to launch his plan of action was poorly taken also, for it coincided with Salvatore's unanticipated claim to authority. He clapped his hands to steal their attention.

'Okaya boys. Thees is whata we musta do. We *cannota* piss abouta with thees anoraka lady. She is mada, mada, *mada*.' He leaned forward and muttered confidentially '…and I tell you thees…I woulda rather maka the love to a calzone pepperoni, yesa?'

'Steady, Salvatore! Gird those Latin loins, or we'll have to cool you down with a ladle of gazpacho' joked Felix, still hoping to distract his new rival from an ominously sensible sounding strategy. But the Sicilian was not to be upstaged.

'We musta go to the police, tomorrow.'

'What!' barked Frankie with unexpected asperity, 'I think you must be an olive short of a pasta pesto, mate. Your favourite stupid son is guilty of *homicide*, not library book larceny! And even though I can confirm he's got all the killer instinct of an unscrupulous budgerigar, the fact is we're all submerged in your shitters' creek...and I ain't planning to spend the rest of my life running errands for a butch queen in Broadmoor.'

Salvatore nodded as if in agreement.

'I understanda thees, my frienda. I hata the butcha Queena, too – all thata "mamma–mia, mamma–mia, won't–you–do–the–fan–dan–go"' he yodelled in resonance with the song's incontestable metaphysical connotations.

Frankie couldn't resist joining in with the Mercurial racket, stretching the moment's light relief to just under a minute and a half, but faltering at the third poignant verse, where the song's improbable hero delivers a typically hollow promise to visit his mum "sometime tomorrow".

Salvatore persisted. 'If you admit heem boys, you weel hava the shorter sentence, see? I don'ta wanta to visit my stupida boy in the clinka – *it was han haccidenta*, wasn't eeta? Righta, then you musta give it upa now, while you cana still maka the bargain of the *pleee*, yes?'

'Look, Salvatore' said Felix, clearly on the cusp of an act of defenestration, 'I rather think you're having your torta and eating it...I'm afraid *you* are tied up with this every bit as much as Giuseppe. The body's been in *your* car remember, and now you reckon *you've* been followed en route to us! The Carabinieri wouldn't like that, you know.'

Giuseppe shrugged his shoulders by way of grudging acknowledgement.

'Sadly my frienda, you mighta be righta' he stammered, imposing another kiss on his son. For once, Giuseppe's reciprocation was sincere.

LIFE ON MARS? A CATINEL'S CHANCE

'It looks like we'll be doing the fandango together, mate' consoled Frankie, but lapsing inevitably, 'it's turning into the Italian Job this, isn't it?'

The others looked at him with pity in their eyes as Salvatore slipped off to engage in chemical warfare with the chemical toilet, singing mournfully "Hi–ham–justa–the–poor–boy, froma–the–poor–famil–eee".

Upon his return, having pre–emptively ridded himself of his *pasta con fromaggia nebulina*, the shrunken Sicilian took his turn at the pipe of humility and assumed his docile new rôle. Felix's ascension to top dog was correspondingly swift; his scatty scheme could wait no longer.

'I think we're agreed that we *do* need to tackle Paula, the plastic–packed bunny–boiler from hell. She's our ticket out of here, for definite, and the fact that she's blatantly bonkers is surely to our advantage. Look, imagine you're the investigating officers in this weird case. First, you discover a frazzled, bollock–naked body that's a tad hard to identify – and even harder to make sense of – smack in the middle of some random field. Next, a week or so later, you discover that the victim's brother's been bumped off too, even more bizarrely...he's been garrotted by an arrow in the lockup adjacent to the one long–leased by his brother. The presence of a second victim at the hands of a sadistic killer –– now apparently harbouring Robin Hood delusions – proves that the first death wasn't the result of an accident, which, just conceivably, it might have been. So, it comes down to a double–murder, committed by the same frenzied freak. And remember, there's no evidence to suggest *Spencer* died at the lockup…or at least, we hope.'

Felix sniffed his palm, grimacing at the faintly detectable trace of Domestos, and paused to steal an interim draw on the sizeable spliff glowing like a poker between Frankie's convulsing fingers.

'Anyway, just as you're growing in despair at the supreme weirdness of it all, you receive hard evidence from an anonymous source, *eh hem*, that links the first victim's death to his psycho of a wife whom, it's safe to suggest, isn't exactly a candidate for the Mother Theresa Peace Prize. You follow it up and, just as things are beginning to fall sweetly into your lap, the double whammy arrives – video evidence of the *second* murder…Now, you ask yourself, how many crazed, vindictive bastards can there be queuing up to kill these brothers? Accordingly, the perfidious Paula cops the two murder charges and we slip quietly away to resume our sad but hitherto inoffensive little lives, with just the faintest whiff of diesel and detergent as a memento of the whole tawdry business.'

Salvatore might just as well have heard Hank Marvin reel off a Shakespeare sonnet in Urdu, for all the sense Felix's commentary had made to him.

'Right, so what's the deal here?' snapped Frankie, progressing from mouth–percussion to table–tapping, a measure of his qualified conversion. 'And anyway, what's this 'first' bit of information we leak to the police?'

'Well, we'll have to plant something from Day's lockup at Paula's, I guess' he responded carelessly, 'something hooky, naturally.'

'Felix, have you been popping those psychedelic

211

Smarties again? Paula was Spencer Day's *wife*, remember! Of course there'd be stuff from his lockup at the house – it was probably all fenced from home in the first place!' slammed Frankie, chuffed to have sifted the first flaw from Felix's plan.

Salvatore's head dipped as the reality of the situation at last filtered through to him. In his most sotto voce tone, not really intended for the others to hear, he mumbled 'so, whata we needa, is the veedeo of the firsta murder, yesa?'

'Well! What bleedin' *veedeo* would that be, mate?' demanded Frankie caustically.

A depressing hiatus ensued, broken abruptly by Giuseppe, who clapped his hands and simultaneously leapt to his feet.

'Pop!' he cried, kissing his father's head for the second time in a decade, 'you've bloody well got it…a video of *Spencer* Day's murder! Felix is right…look, we simply fake it, using Paula's own camcorder, and courier the cassette to the cop–shop, pronto.'

'Woosh!' shouted Felix, his plan safely back on course after a brief wobble.

'This is perfect, boys' screeched Giuseppe like a castigated castrato. 'Since the *second* tape is completely genuine, the *first* – which we keep really slim on details – will pass muster easily, savvy?'

From the plume of euphoria that quickly swallowed them up Frankie enquired 'so, what's the *gooda newsa* then, Salvatore? No no, let me guess…the Pope's reversed his vasectomy and had a lovechild with Madonna, called *Clitoreesa.*'

'You bladdy fool, Frankie' hooted the Latin laggard uncontrollably, 'the Popa, he can *never* finda Madonna's cleetorisa...she is a *mana*, too, no? Ha ha ha!'

The others nodded.

'Hactually, my friendsa, we gonna hava the *beeg* party, witha mucha booze and many lovely ladies, mm, yesa.'

'Hang on Pop, we're not out of the woods yet, you know...we've only just found the frigging path!'

'Ah, screwa your wooden path, boy. Your uncle Antonio, hees beega seextieth birthday ees two daysa tima. We all gonna go, yes? Hees notta lika me...no no, hees a *very* nica man. He speaka the perfecta *Eengleesha*, too.'

Giuseppe assisted.

'Uncle Toni's got a pub, up in Penistone, near Barnsley...he gets lots of boaty types there, even though it's got to be a good fifty miles from the east coast...it's quite a cool place actually; I used to hang out there when I was a kid. Pop did a lot of his sailing around Hull at one time, eh Pop?'

'Hull! Hardly the Straits of Messina, is it?' Felix sniffed.

'Well, at least they got around to building their bleedin' bridge' defended Giuseppe feebly.

'Sweet' nodded Frankie, boogieing in his seat. 'First we frame Cruella de Ville...then take a free chill–pill and pig–swill.'

'Well, something like that' muttered Felix, struggling to keep a lid on Frankie's alter ego.

'Where are we going to do this bit of dodgy filming

213

then, chaps? asked Giuseppe. 'It needs to be somewhere dark, gloomy and featureless.'

'How about your place then?' sniggered Frankie.

'With just a chair or two in view' continued Giuseppe, undeterred.

'And a rope' added Felix.

'A rope?'

'Day One was throttled to death, right?...Oh, and we'll place a Geri can just in view too, just to tie in with the frying of the body – we've got to link our videotape to the M.O. the police know was used with Day Two.'

Frankie nodded, picking his nose with an elegant pirouette of his little finger.

'Wicked.'

However simple the task of searching out a derelict out–building might have seemed to them, rooting about in the sticks, their endeavours came to naught. In the end, it came down to following Salvatore's first sensible suggestion so far: to use his brother's place, arriving a day early for the party. The journey to Penistone would be made in one of Salvatore's antique Volvos, since this would not attract interrogation from anyone witnessing their arrival at the party. The film props were assembled and two new videotapes purchased for the camcorder, one of which soon contained a complete, unedited version of Paula's Packamac

Massacre. The blank one awaited commission at Toni's place.

'Right! Film crew, let's get rolling!' commanded Felix.

'Have you found your bloody torch yet, Giuseppe?' demanded Frankie, 'we'll be needing it.'

'Yeah, I looked bleedin' *everywhere* for that sodding thing' Giuseppe responded dejectedly. 'And do you know what…it was in the very *last* place I looked!'

'It would be, you dozy picaroon' burbled Felix, 'you'd hardly carry on looking for it *after* you'd found the stupid thing, would you?'

They chose a scenic route up to Penistone, a trip made more tedious by Salvatore's funereal pace behind the wheel of his indestructible hearse, which he insisted was the best model Volvo had ever produced owing to its 'hextra smoothy hengine.' Its tan leatherette seats had certainly aged better than its owner's complexion, but the prehistoric sound system was probably due for a new rose–thorn stylus. It didn't much matter, for Frankie's personal stereo was about as personal as Deaf Leopard's PA system. They decided to stop off for a bite to eat. Salvatore pulled over at a crumby little Italian joint called 'Stefano's Grill', painted predominantly in green with plastic flags and lurid synthetic ivy dancing along the front window, behind which not a soul could be seen eating. Fixed to the window was a sign which read "Bring your own wine: corking charge levied". Giuseppe struggled to open the front door, eventually noticing that a tiny, handwritten 'closed' sign was dangling above his head.

215

'Closed! Great...nice choice Salvatore' hissed Frankie, 'I suppose we have to bring our own *food*, too – with a *cooking* charge levied?'

They were about to slope off in disgust when an eager tap from inside the glazed door raised hopes of life but dampened Frankie's chances of a cheeseburger from the neighbouring McDonald's.

'I hopen, I hopen!' came a pearly voice, resonating at once with Salvatore, who responded cheerfully 'hokay, hokay, we waita!'

A little olive oil wouldn't have gone amiss on the door hinge, which screeched three notes in ascending pitch. Frankie picked up the cue, his wolf–whistle version of 'Edelweiss' and offbeat reggae grunts sapping the melody of its latent Swiss charm. The sense of welcome was excessively abstemious, and the only moving object in sight, aside from the stout Stefano himself, was an excessively rotund woman, hunched maladroitly on a bar stool, a thick black loose–knitted shawl draped over her shoulders. The newspaper she was reading mopped up whatever light dribbled from the crookedly mounted fake–candle–with–shade arrangement, a travesty of interior design perpetrated elsewhere in the small room creating the atmosphere of a medieval chancel. The woman turned her head for long enough to grunt two syllables that sounded like 'up yours' but apparently meant 'good evening', since Salvatore responded with disproportionate effusiveness. The four were heartily ushered over to a large central table with bread sticks attempting to jump out of a ludicrously petite jug; from whatever angle one viewed it, an unmistakable 'V' sign toned in well with the general ambience. The menus were presented with an immodest grin, and the foursome's attention was drawn to the 'special' of the day – a loose leaf of photocopied paper upon which was scribbled the words 'Steak Mignon with choice of sauces: pepper, cheese or red wine; served with jacket potato or deep fried potato wedges; salad garnish or vegetables.' Frankie lost no time ordering the special, which arrived almost before the others had finished registering their orders for variations on a tagliatelle theme. Without a second's hesitation he plucked two slices of thin bread from the basket, placed the decidedly mignon steak in between, collected up the feeble salad and shoved it below the meat, above the bottom slice of bread. As a final concession to stylishness he peeled away the cheese sauce that had prematurely adhered itself to the rim of his oblong plate and curled it like a rat's intestine upon the steak, now housed firmly in its bread casing. He plumped up the pile of potato wedges, drenched them in balsamic vinegar and clumps of sea salt.

'There you are, chaps, cheese burger and chips. Just what I wanted.'

'H–wanker' sniffed Salvatore, nibbling noisily at a poppy seed studded bread roll that bore more than a passing resemblance to his chin.

'McDonald's would charge one ninety–nine for this' moaned Frankie, whose meaty mess had suddenly undergone a fascinating chemical reaction with the garnish to produce a thin, greasy residue that made its way speedily along his naked elbow and onto Felix's plate.

Stefano sidled up to them, glanced over his shoulder

at the woman now moving slothfully towards the ladies loo, and whispered 'my wifa, she have a *bada* tima...hera poppa has died...drowned in hees sweeming poola in Napoli. She maka the notice in the Engleesh newsa paper...the obritra, obitrari...'

Giuseppe's practiced ear for linguistic impediments facilitated rapid assistance.

'I think you mean ob–it–u–a–ry, sir.'

'Ah, yesa, that eesa thees. Look, she writa thees.'

He handed them a page from the previous day's Times and pointed to a circled entry, which read: 'Franceschini, Angelo, 76; tragic accidental death; leaves two grieving daughters; Fiat for sale.'

'I suppose this makes a change from pasty and chips, mate?' said Giuseppe, lassoing his tagliatelle with the skill of a Texan rancher and gesturing towards Felix's heaving pile of angel–hair.

'Oh, I love Italian food actually, although I'm not...anti–*pasty* either, you understand.'

Salvatore laughed so ecstatically at Felix's crap quip that he fired a semi–masticated meatball onto the centre of Giuseppe's disobedient lariat of spaghetti. The unwitting recipient, suddenly absorbed by a Canaletto print above his head that had faded to three shades of blue, mistook the meatball for an olive and appropriated it without comment.

The clipped patois pinging between Stefano and Salvatore was notable for its multiple possibilities of meaning. The words emerged as a hybrid of Southern Italian and Northern English, short packets of sounds rather than intelligible sentences, like chiffchaffs politely awaiting their turn to sound off across a suburban garden. As they prepared to leave, Stefano gaped pointedly through the Venetian blind that had been fluttering like a Lambretta in the dreadful draught, and engaged his new friend with English small talk.

'Eesn't it weendy?'

'No...it'sa *thersdaya*' replied Salvatore in his plumiest tone.

'So am I...we musta have the drinka some soma tima, yesa?'

They nodded in full comprehension.

11

With Nail and Eye

◉

As PC Dring drove to work, in plenty of time for the start of his late morning shift, he decided to make a detour to the Constipated Cobra. Although the pub would not reopen for another couple of weeks it contained one small piece of evidence that might nudge his independent investigation onto the next plane: a photograph. He'd been struggling to recall the detail of the image on the WC door, but could only vaguely reconstruct the two figures it featured; there had been a faint but discernible family resemblance. One of the men was undoubtedly the establishment's owner, Toni Pirelli, whom Dring assumed from his attire had at one time been a middle–ranking seaman, while the other's gratuitous scruffiness had made an equally striking impression. One aspect of the photograph had lingered but not fully registered; it had something to do with Tommy McGuire, the conveniently absent teenage barman with boyish canoeing aspirations. It had been McGuire who'd led him to the Cobra, of course, although at that stage he'd no reason to be interested in the lad's employer, let alone the man's dishevelled brother. However, Dring had since ascertained via Green and Razor that Salvatore Pirelli concealed a skeleton; he'd been inconclusively investigated by the West Ridings Squad some eighteen months earlier for his part in a peculiar case of assuming identity. The identity in question belonged to an oversexed central heating engineer named Gary Parker. Parker had been chivalrously stoking the fires of numerous shivering damsels, so it transpired. Pirelli's penetration, on Parker's wife's behalf, was rumbled by one of the engineer's golfing buddies – he'd been rooting about for phone numbers in Parker's changing room locker. Although Pirelli wasn't a registered Private Investigator, he could show he'd acted as an agent, and since Parker's wife had provided the locker key, Pirelli was off the hook.

While Dring remained mildly intrigued by Pirelli's subversive behaviour a more concrete thought was forming – might McGuire be connected with the Pirelli brothers even more tangibly than he'd first thought? The Cobra's resident busybody Vicar had indicated that the McGuire family concealed inbred arsonist tendencies, although he'd not had a chance to uncover more detail on that. Nevertheless, a suspected pyromaniac working in a recently torched pub run by a nautically minded Sicilian whose brother was slipperier than a jellied anguilliforme, must surely add up to something more solid than his initial tenuous lead from the ditched canoes? Dring felt confident he'd time to assemble a convincing case; there seemed no immediate danger of Toogood and Chanter poaching his lead, for the pair had become hopelessly distracted by the team's unwholesome Internet fixation.

Indeed, thus far, Toogood's moronic minions had assembled only a few paltry scraps of kosher evidence: the body dumped in the field belonged to Spencer Day, an enterprising ex–con whose brother had at one time also been a professional burglar. The brother, Neil, who'd conspicuously changed his surname to Pincombe on moving to Scarborough, had gone AWOL too, even more conspicuously, shortly after the death of his brother; he was now assumed to be in danger. Day's death had been by asphyxiation, subsequently masked by surface burning inflicted to deprive the investigation of reliable fingerprints. DNA possibly belonging to the killer was limited to random skin swabs extracted from under the fingernails, but frustratingly these didn't match up with any on file; peculiarly, too, one of the man's fingers had become severed during his protracted trauma; it had not subsequently turned up at the scene. Tattoos covering the body were not in themselves informative, beyond highlighting the man's juvenile fascination for feminine mythological characters and phallic weaponry. There was, however the distinct possibility that the dead man's body had been subjected to a fall prior to its chance discovery by a local farmer, Les Hepleston. Moreover, an insect not normally resident in the discovery zone had been found dozing under the man's eyelid, its presence indicative of a moving of the body post–mortem. Other items discovered at the scene – a bowler hat bearing a PDSA label and some novelty–shop handcuffs – were dismissed as curious but inconsequential.

Meanwhile, Detective Inspector Paradis, heading up the pub arson investigation, had been contentedly hashing things up, too. He'd been unable to establish whether the fire in the basement had been triggered by an unstable boiler or unstable personality; either way, the premises had been inopportunely unmanned at the time. And he'd failed to follow up what ought to have seemed two compelling clues: one of the current bar staff, Thomas McGuire, had previously been implicated in arson; and the landlord's brother, Salvatore Pirelli, had recently had a brief skirmish with the police.

Unsurprisingly therefore, the connection between the two ongoing cases, albeit tenuous, had so far eluded both Toogood and Paradis. Ironically, it had been PC Dring's remarkable incapacity for cynical thought, his willingness to take mundane matters at face value, that had permitted his comparatively good progress from canoe to cobra, and so from vituperative vicar to fusty photo. A copy of that photo would give him something more substantial to chew on though; his case file was still alarmingly slender.

As he drew nearer to the pub car park, with the humble–bumble of his inherited Honda tiring to a dawdling drone, he couldn't fail to observe evidence of the repair work so far carried out. Strewn about everywhere were tarred kitchen units and rolls of melted carpets, crates of shattered bottles and other publican paraphernalia in various stages of disintegration.

Dring looked plausible in his civvies and had considered his strategy carefully. Naturally, he wouldn't declare his status as a policeman; this called for a far more nuanced approach. As he ambled up to the partly cordoned–off area leading to the side entrance he quickly confirmed the lack of police presence. A solid, swarthy individual loped in and out, gainfully employed as far as a passing glance could detect, but pausing frequently outside to quaff the relatively unsullied air. Dring, now on foot and removing his helmet, shifted up a gear and strode confidently up to the man, adopting a practiced, strained expression.

'Hi mate, look, I couldn't just use the bog, could I? I know the pub's closed, but...'

'Do what you bleedin' like...just bleedin' 'urry up about it. I'm stoppin' for me bleedin' lunch in a minute. There's only one door open...on yer left, and watch yer bleedin' step, mate.'

'Gottcha, you're a star...been busting to let one out for ages.'

'Siphon the bleedin' python at the Constipated Cobra, eh!' came the unexpectedly perspicacious response.

Dring took advantage of the precious moment he'd been granted to avail himself of the charred facilities, and simultaneously scoured the walls for the photograph. Alas, his luck seemed to have dribbled down the urinal, along

225

with the Ribena he'd been struggling to keep at bay for the past half an hour. All that remained was an old poster, positioned above the sink, which read: 'Now wash your hands – violators will be shot, survivors will be shot again'. Having relieved himself he was about to leave empty handed, when he noticed a fractured frame protruding from a split bin–bag by the WC exit; he knew what it was straight away. Damage to the photograph's lower region was more severe than elsewhere, which was fortunate given the positioning of the two salient characters. He slipped the photo into his bag, denuded of its frame, portions of sooty glass still clinging purposelessly to it.

Meanwhile, outside, the liberal labourer sat chomping his conservative lunch. He'd finally submitted to the allure of the car park's walled perimeter and was already three bites into his wilted sandwich, judiciously augmented with a bottle of stout pilfered from a discarded crate. This, along with two exhumed packets of pork–scratchings, must have tasted acceptable, as he'd lost no time in sifting for other consumables. Dring, suddenly conscious of the need to be on his way, mumbled unimpassioned gratitude and disappeared, forcing on his orange–peaked skidlid and fastening his fly. As he buzzed away from the car park, simultaneously buckling his bonnet and reacquainting his backside with its plastic seat, a dark Shogun finessed its way in; it contained two people, one of whom was undoubtedly the pub's manager, Toni Pirelli. Dring exited unnoticed and immediately parked his bike on the adjacent road in the first available slot. He jogged back to the car park and found a small hole in the hedge to peer through from the pavement.

Pirelli had alighted and was busy removing a sizeable stash of wine and beer from the boot. Another man, much younger, wiry and good looking, assisted him; he was singing loudly and badly enough to stir the lounging labourer into action as he emerged tugging at a pack of dry–roasted peanuts. Dring studied the two men closely; suddenly his powers of detection came alive in an unfettered surge of brilliance. For the second man was almost certainly Thomas McGuire, canoeing prodigy, surf–bum, semi–qualified arsonist and ginger–bonced barman.

Dring was euphoric – this was *real* detecting. The two men talked animatedly over the car stereo, which was blaring out an inexcusably awful version of Bizet's 'The Pearl Fishers', sung by a chorus of shrill choirboys accompanied by what sounded like an inebriated reggae band. McGuire spoke, mustering a full, cavernous timbre that would be less incongruous in a man twice his mass, adjusting his baseball cap with one hand and levering out a litre of Crème de Menthe with the other.

'Blimey, Toni, I hope my sixtieth bash is 'alf as good as yours is gonna be! You realise I'm missing the *footy* for this, don't you!'

Toni smiled complacently, said nothing and continued pulling bottles from behind the seats. It seemed a little odd to Dring that the manager of a pub should need to purchase alcohol from Threshers, but there again, he'd just suffered a major setback and wouldn't be accepting deliveries for some time yet. Holding his position behind the bush, Dring felt rather perplexed and thwarted. Not only had McGuire reappeared from his holiday, calm as you

227

like, evidently oblivious to the possibility of being blamed for torching his boss's pub, but Pirelli plainly had no qualms about engaging his assistance – actions hardly consistent with a disgruntled employee or peeved employer. But, looking on the bright side, Dring had learned of Pirelli's imminent celebration at which it would be reasonable to assume close friends and relations would be present, including perhaps his elusive brother, Salvatore. Besides, just because Pirelli displayed no overt suspicions didn't automatically mean McGuire was off the hook. Dring shuffled off back to his bike, keen to begin study of the photograph slowly desiccating in his bag.

◎

Having scanned it onto his laptop back at the Station, Dring magnified every pixel for clues. Clues to what, he still wasn't sure – anything that would unify the fragmented scenario that presented itself to him. The bedraggled second man, whom Dring was increasingly confident must be Pirelli's brother, Salvatore, was seated coolly with one buttock on the bumper of a car. The registration plate was just about readable under extreme magnification, but he couldn't be sure whether the X was a Y, or the J a T; in fact, the conjugations were too numerous to take him further forward. He'd enlist his mate Brian tomorrow, an ace at crosswords and an incurable

'Countdown' fanatic. But first he'd probe a little deeper into an issue that had been troubling him from the very beginning: the abandoned canoes. He'd been so keen to chase up McGuire on discovering the sea–scout record book that he'd neglected to establish how long the canoes had actually been at the scene.

A phone call to DC Spink at the Crime Scene Investigation Store was alarming and intriguing in equal measure.

'Canoes...what bloody *canoes*?' came the response from the officer whose bovine indifference confirmed the absence of anything as penile in profile quiescent upon his overburdened shelves. Dring, stunned wordless, realised that Toogood's appalling oversight played straight into his hands; he recoiled sharply and affected a misunderstanding, which Spink was only too willing to accept. Dring replaced the receiver slowly and casually surveyed the inhabitants of his open–plan office to confirm a prevailing level of semi–consciousness; he whistled a long, drooping note that petered out as the door opened.

A man entered holding a multi–coloured stack of papers; he caught Dring's eye and moved toward him with a disquieting sense of purpose.

'Dring, who are you on with this avvy?' enquired the officer, sweating under the weight.

'Um, I'm down to go with...Sergeant...Sm...'

'Good, well, this can take priority. It's the petition for the proposed zebra–crossing at Culver Hampton. They need adding up and compressing into a meaningful document lasting no more than one side of A4. There are a few objections to account for, too. By start of play tomorrow, please…I've got four more zebras and a pelican knocking on my door, so think yourself lucky. Knock off early and finish it at home, if you want.'

Within four minutes, Dring had guesstimated the number of petitions in his pile and compressed his findings in a meaningless document lasting a little over one paragraph. He was out of the office and astride the hind of his aged Honda C70 before you could shake a stick at a moulting Abyssinian tomcat.

As he screamed his way along the A6 west towards Buxton, Dring cobbled together a plan. He'd need to be back from inspecting the canoes in time to inventory the arrival of guests at Pirelli's shindig, an awkward journey that would feel more like four hundred miles that the forty according to his map. The football match alluded to by McGuire could only be the Argentina v Germany game, which he'd learned would be covered that same evening on Satellite TV. As he shambled his way with a few essentials stuffed into his velcroed pockets, fearless in the face of uncharitable elements, Dring had much to occupy his mind. He pondered the speed at which grass can grow, considered the impact of insect manifestation, puzzled at the likely disintegration rate of a laminated record book and troubled himself over the outlandishly inapt orientation of canoes in a far–flung meadow. For somewhere here, in the solutions to these seemingly piffling mysteries, must lay the information he sought, the thread to connect his random clues and the key to a brighter future.

The journey was in itself a major test of

resourcefulness and tenacity. At least he'd managed to nobble a decent OS map of the site. Dring could obey maps unfalteringly – and in the time it would take him to scour the sprawling, featureless terrain for the blessed canoes, he could probably have drawn one himself. On arrival at the scene he'd been amazed that police activity had fizzled to zero. Nothing but a series of recovering mud patches indicating recent heavy foot traffic remained – not even a sign stating something like 'Incident at Hollinsclough, please contact...'. It was as though nothing out of the ordinary had occurred here in this craggy, deceitful landscape. Still, for Dring, being a foot soldier had had its advantages on that first night. Unlike the big cheeses, who'd been pampered with umbrellas while pretending to take control of the case, Dring had stood for hours in the rain with his sourpuss colleague, Old Bill; together they'd ventured well beyond the periphery of the marquee, performing essential ground work such as replenishing coffee urns and guarding canoes – not that Toogood would recognise a decent clue if it crawled out of his porridge.

Were it not for a stray polystyrene cup, buffeted gently against the foot of an exceptionally patulous tree near a small clearing, Dring would probably not have rediscovered the canoes at all. But here he was, helmet in hand, once again sharing the drenched thicket with five fibreglass vessels resembling inflated kazoos. He got down to his task immediately; no time to waste. First, he measured the area of the grass covered by the canoes and wrote it down. Then he assessed the average height of the grass butting up to them, and over them, and under them, and in them, and wrote that down. Next, he scooped insects, grass and rabbit dung from under the bottommost canoe into a transparent bag. Finally he tipped each vessel on its end and shook it violently, just in case anything emerged, which he duly bagged up. As an afterthought, he placed a hulking limb of a tree on the grass – at some point his dim–witted colleagues would need a marker. 'A special *branch* for *Special* Branch' he mumbled as he mounted his stoical steed, and sped off to gatecrash Pirelli's party.

Dring paid no further heed to the weather, which did its best to persuade him from the road into the ditch as he approached the A628 from Glossop. He was too engrossed in his clandestine campaign, which had progressed from whim to hardening reality in a few days. As he drove, neck braced and eyes stabbed by the serrated rain, his gut feeling strengthened – the canoes could only have been there a relatively short time. Surely, the vegetation would have virtually consumed them in a matter of months, even at this time of year? Laden with bagged–up fescue and fauna, Dring aimed his Honda resolutely into the savage rain and scuttled southwards, quickly inured to the nefarious wind. Two hours later, in a dreamlike stupor, looking as though he'd ridden to Greenland and back, he arrived at the Constipated Cobra, the driest watering hole in town, with more booze in the car park than in the bar and the crispest crisps Smith's had ever countenanced.

He needn't have hurried, for the Cobra's car park was entirely bereft of vehicles. Even Toni Pirelli's four–by–four had vanished. Dring sat cross–legged on his not so mean machine, valiantly restraining his desire to water his horse in the bush he'd peered through earlier. He felt dejected and saddle–sore after his marathon circuit, but at least the wind and rain had finally waned, too. The Honda's engine was so hot it fizzed, setting off a stench like boiled turnips. After ten minutes he'd spent all his patience and crept around the side of the pub in search of a possible piss–port.

As he stood there in a cloud of rising salty steam, a deafening ballyhoo from above suddenly startled him; his left trouser leg copped the worst of the fallout, but thankfully his horse had nearly finished watering. He stood there, leaning back his head in an attempt to see what had caused such a clamour. Then, glancing at his watch as he mopped his trousers with a handkerchief, he realised. The football match must have ended – those partying plonkers must have been watching it after all! He ambled around the corner and discovered an overspill car park on the entrance to which one of Pirelli's minions had posted a notice in blue marker pen that had haemorrhaged all over itself in the rain: 'Please use this car park – other one's buggered'. Dring sighed at himself in exasperation but was relieved to see Pirelli's Shogun nestled in among a dozen other vehicles.

The party itself was clearly taking place upstairs in Pirelli's private quarters due to the carnage in the public bar area, and this, Dring decided, was to his advantage. The football match, now concluded, had temporarily upstaged the host's sixtieth birthday celebration, just as it would have done to five hundred similar celebrations up and down the country that evening. But by now they'd be back on the booze, for sure. Under cover of a tall, unglazed wall his

233

covert operations in the car park would not be overlooked, so he hurriedly jotted down the registration plates for inclusion in his reassuringly distending case file. As he squatted on a stumpy wall, enjoying a brief moment's respite, Dring's eyes drifted dozily across the row of cars and his mind returned to the photograph he'd procured from the pub loo, with its tatty vehicle and partly obscured registration plate. He looked down at his notebook on which he'd listed the permutations and was surprisingly quickly able to find a potential match.

The car in question positively shimmered in the rain – every one of its thousand pits and craters glowed haughtily; it was certainly the shiniest wreck of a Volvo he'd ever clapped eyes on. But it was the car's absurdly decorated windscreen that confirmed to him he was looking at the right vehicle – flags of Lanzarote and Bognor Regis, badges and logos of all shapes denoting the owner's staunch commitment to the sea–scout movement. Funnily enough, although he'd subliminally registered the overly endowed windscreen when the photo was in situ, he'd become somewhat absorbed with discovering the vehicle's registration that morning. A quick phone call to the control desk was in order.

Doris, or 'Mum' as she'd affectionately become known to any plod under the age of thirty–five, obliged, and within thirty seconds Dring had extracted from her the details he needed: the vehicle was owned by a Salvatore Marco Pirelli, aged sixty–six; he'd been in possession of the vehicle for nine of its twenty–five years. Dring was about to ring off when Mum exercised her familiar matriarchal caution – 'do you want details of other vehicles owned by Mr. Pirelli, Perry?' Dring grunted in the affirmative and duly noted the specification of a remarkably similar Volvo to the one he'd just been hearing about; same model, same year, different colour.

'Cooking on gas!' Dring grinned to himself, peeping through each of the Volvo's windows for anything else that might remotely constitute a clue. Resting on the back seat was a short length of rope and a bulbous torch among a hoard of other unremarkable items spilling out of two rucksacks, while on the overcrowded dashboard was a stack of CDs covering a somewhat narrow artistic gamut: Gnarls Barkley, The Pussycat Dolls and Snoop Dog. In any case, the vehicle barely had wheels, let alone a CD player. A sudden downpour curtailed Dring's bemusement at what looked more like characters from a children's TV show than chart–topping musicians. He took refuge under a piece of ill–fitting plastic guttering ten yards away that channelled water past his ear to a clogged–up grill at his feet. As he hopped to one side of it he became aware of a presence nearby. A man was emerging, whistling hesitantly and unmusically, as if only partly convinced by his display of contentedness. Curiously, the man, holding his easygoing pace, appeared blissfully unaware of the deleterious effect the downpour was having on his beige corduroy jacket.

Dring watched, computed, but scored nothing. The man arrived at the car that had been parked adjacent to the shabby–chic Volvo, a spanking new silver Saab, and sat nonchalantly on its bonnet facing the opposite direction to where Dring looked on. He took out his mobile phone and dialled a number, still oblivious to the torrent of rain thrashing on the metal roofs around him. He was obliged to shout.

'Clay?..Hey!...What's the crack, buddy?'

The response comfortably filled a minute.

'What can you tell me about lighting for a small space?'

The response comfortably filled three minutes.

'No, not feng sodding *shui*, dummy, lighting for *filming.*'

The man deflected what was evidently another shot fired from the hip.

'We've *tried* the cellar light, it hums too loudly...We've *tried* a torchlight, it's far too dim...We've *tried* candles, but they make it look like a Mandarin wedding...'

The conversation cut off prematurely, which in any case had evidently been spiralling into an unprofitable void. The man, in his late thirties, was bordering on bald and definitely overweight. On turning around it became apparent he was wearing clothes deserving of prosecution by the contemporary fashion police, for beneath the leather–patched elbows of his jacket were trousers made from a statically charged fabric formerly known as Crimpolene (eventually to become superseded by Lycra) which, aside from posing a latent electrical hazard, has the characteristic of shining like a plastic shoe after three washes. The man swore to himself in a well bred, subdued tone, slipped the phone back into his pocket and ambled back in the direction of the door from which he'd appeared, resuming the asinine whistling and continuing to ignore the deluge. Half way back he changed his mind, swung around on his heels and walked back towards the car, retrieving a key from his pocket. Dring quickly pulled himself into the guttering. But as he approached the Saab the man turned instead towards the Volvo. He unlocked the driver's door without pausing.

Dring's blood–sugar level had by now plummeted to the level of a rice biscuit, but he snapped alert as the man proceeded to open the rear door while kneeling on the front seat in order to access a particularly bulky article. He took a little time to push the thing under his jacket and walked blithely back into the pub, neglecting to lock the car door. Dring waited a moment, then nipped back to the Volvo to see what had been removed. But the driving rain hampered visibility and as he wasn't yet brave enough to open the door he retreated to his position beneath the dislocated gutter to await a more opportune moment. As he leaned against the wall, deafened by the cascade of water bouncing up from the tarmac, something standing up on the Volvo's dappled dashboard caught his eye – a red booklet with some kind of braiding around it. Dring couldn't resist. Twenty seconds later he'd snatched the thing and stuffed it into his pocket. He lost no time in putting his helmet on and scurried back to the bike, ignition key at the ready.

LIFE ON MARS? A CATINEL'S CHANCE

The day had been an unprecedented success for upwardly mobile PC Dring. He'd gained possession of a key photograph, retrieved salient material for dating the appearance of the canoes at the site of the body's discovery, and, care of Mum, identified both of Salvatore Pirelli's vehicles as well as the man's home address and a potentially significant item from his car. Not bad for a low–grade copper with two GCSEs and a four–length breaststroke certificate to rub together. As he revved up his bike, which was still smarting from its turbulent trip, Dring puzzled over the identity of the man he'd watched gaining access to the Volvo; it definitely hadn't been Salvatore, not unless he'd shaved his head, had a nose job and done teacher training since the photo had been taken. Besides, this guy was at least twenty years too young and about as Sicilian as Bertie Wooster.

Dring suddenly craved the soothing properties of alcohol and decided to remunerate himself for his five hours astride the Honda with a short visit to the Constipated Cobra's nearest rival free house, the Fuzzy Duck, at Piddlewash St Maud's. As he pulled up to the car park, the rain now virtually abated, a surprising number of furtive mobile phone conversations were taking place outside, indicating the ongoing status of the weekly quiz night. His case notes needed consolidating and he now had an intriguing red booklet to peruse. In his haste to get away from the Volvo he hadn't noticed that the thing was actually a mini photograph album. Flicking through it would require a commendable feat of multi–tasking involving beer, a Café Creme cigarillo and two packets of Twiglets.

WITH NAIL AND EYE

The untitled album turned out to be even less inspiring than his excessively flat pint of Courage Best; the gist of it, not unlike the beer, was water – cups, trophies and rosettes – a prosaic series of indulgent memorabilia dating from as far back as Noah's granddad's first trip on a peddalo at Paignton. White–water rafts piloted by imprudent pensioners and muscle–bulging power–freaks falling out of catamarans were interspersed with gentler folk operating more traditional craft including dinghies, canoes and windsurfers. Human beings were relevant only in relation to the vessels they attempted to manoeuvre. An exception to this was a clutch of exceedingly dull team photos near the back pages that featured Salvatore in the rôle of leader/organiser; the progression from dodgy moustaches to dodgier goatees and sideburns, complemented by a preposterous palette of spectacles, provided adequate clues to the shifting timescale.

In one of the rogues' galleries a figure squatting at the front, showing off a silver salvo, caught Dring's eye. The boy's grin revealed more teeth than a double–dentated logging saw and his flourishing shock of ginger hair could have kept an alpaca comfortable through an extended Peruvian winter. Dring compared the image side by side with the one he'd taken with him to the Cobra on his first reconnaissance mission; this he'd managed to procure from McGuire's old school with unnerving ease. The match was beyond doubt. All the other water babies, aged about nine, were girls, except one rather older lad with striking brown eyes, a side–parting and teeth like chimney stacks, sat next to Salvatore. Dring removed the photo and was about to enter it into his case file when he noticed some faint pencil writing on the rear. Clearly the names of the canoeists had been added some considerable time after the picture had been taken, and by someone not wholly familiar with the team members, since several question marks had been inserted. But, in the line–up Dring was pleased to find confirmation of a T. McGuire, a G. Pirelli and, sat next to him, an S. Pirelli.

Having laden the ashtray with knotted crisp packets, Dring looked at the time and tried to gauge the progress back at Pirelli's party. It would be good to round off his day with a little more detail on Salvatore's companion, the absentminded fashion victim who'd chosen the privacy of a rain–soaked car park to discuss the dreary business of photography lighting. It was just after nine, but to Dring it felt like midnight. He closed his eyes and gave in to his need for a short doze, Neil Diamond scratching along inconsolably in the background.

Felix awoke much earlier than the others the morning after Toni Pirelli's party. The whiff of charcoaled carpets and windows scorched to matchwood below them was intolerable. Ironically, a fresh injection of cigarette fumes into Pirelli's private apartment the previous evening had partly distracted the twenty or so guests from the pervading pong. The party had concluded with a series of embarrassing alcohol induced episodes and several speeches that had disappeared up their own backsides, not that anyone noticed. Salvatore's ten–minute emotional outpouring had collapsed into a tearful rendition of 'Hee ain'ta h–heavee, hee my *brather*', accompanied in an adjacent key by Frankie on a guitar with three strings. By 3:00 AM sleep had been not so much desirable as irresistible. Giuseppe was sharing quarters with his father upstairs in an attic conversion barely large enough to house a snake's wisdom teeth, while Felix and Frankie found themselves crammed into a box room that would have been double the size were it not for Toni's collection of gaudy silk scarves. For most of the comatose guests sprinkled randomly on the landing and stairs, sleep was experienced as if in a slowly revolving kaleidoscope. But by 7:30 Felix had emerged from the haze, still as pissed as a polecat, but conscious enough to be worrying about details; details of the video yet to be rigged, details regarding its safe deportment to the police, and details of the ways they might all suffer in the event of Paula Day's maniacal intervention, armed with a refreshed crossbow.

Such details had gate–crashed Frankie's dream, too; his trembling eyelids indicated that he was being chased along a warren of nightmarish proportions, the sweat from his quivering forehead bringing a patina to his lanky locks. Felix closed his eyes and struggled in vain to plunge himself in a bubble of nothingness. For he knew that, while asleep, options remain open – from the moment you've arisen, they begin to diminish, and nonsensical fears of masculine women bearing down on you with medieval weaponry become shockingly rational possibilities. But Felix couldn't hold off his need to urinate any longer and headed tentatively along the corridor in his frangipani boxer shorts, passing a bewildering pile of appurtenances that would soon be called upon to return the flame–licked chamber downstairs into a convivial public bar. Once dressed, and evidently still alone in his dawning state of sobriety, he decided to slip away from the pub for an hour or so, taking advantage of Salvatore's Volvo to which, oddly enough, he still seemed to have the key.

Ten minutes later, having parked the lumbering wagon across two spaces, Felix strolled away from a Lidl car park, transparently giving the ticket machine a wide berth. The car park was ostensibly being policed by an iPoded seventeen year–old whose concept of individuality extended as far as wearing his yellow store tie at quarter mast, allowing his studded dog collar a chance to assert itself from around his scrawny neck. Felix strolled around the corner and followed his nose into the former coalmining town of Barnsley, a place he'd never imagined he'd visit unless handcuffed and gagged. Even at this unearthly hour, a time Felix would normally prefer to designate as night, McDonald's was doing roaring trade with its McHashbrowns and McScrambled eggs. There was a reassuring weekend ambivalence about the town itself; few people moved with any desperate impulsion towards work. Felix considered his options for an inaugural caffeine injection, which at first glance consisted of a Costa Coffee bucket or an inviscid Marks & Spencer thimble.

WITH NAIL AND EYE

As he wandered about, strangely wooed by the undistinguished grey 1930s buildings breaching the heavy black skyline, Felix caught a brief glimpse of a middle–aged man wearing a blue artist style smock and knee length patch–pocket trousers. The man, a round–shouldered, slightly down at heel figure, had passed him by before he knew it. Coincidentally, he saw the man again, just a couple of minutes later, as he searched hopelessly for the Costa Coffee shop that had unaccountably vanished. On this occasion the man had cranked up his pace considerably and adopted a more brooding expression, but was gone again in an instant. Felix wondered what the odd looking bloke was so troubled by, moping aimlessly around the unpretentious little town, for the intensity of his distraction had itself become quite distracting. When Felix, now bound resignedly for M&S, encountered the same lost soul for a third time ten minutes later, he was moving earnestly past the glazed entrance to John Lewis. The man looked even more absorbed now, diligently poking his nose with one hand and rearranging his manhood with the other. Only then did Felix realise that, on reflection, he knew the man quite well. It was himself.

The M&S thimble of Bovril–coloured water wasn't exactly a snip at one pound ninety–five, and Felix's enthusiasm for his saccharine surroundings only lasted as long as it took to expedite three hesitant tongue insertions. He exited by the snail–paced escalator, which simultaneously shuttled up a steady stream of eagle–eyed, silver–haired SAGA–louts, and found his way to a mall, a precursor to the modern American concept, containing no more than a dozen shops. The only store of conceivable interest, wedged between Accessorize and Lush Handmade Cosmetics, was a Fourbuoys Newsagent, run by one lethargic boy and three feisty ladies of a certain age. Felix browsed the impressive chocolate racks for some time before homing in on an Aero bar and a king–sized Yorkie. Only as he was paying for these did his eyes fall to the waist–high pile of newspapers he'd been resting his glasses on. Competing for column space with two unfeasibly endowed mammary–madams from Celebrity Big Brother, one of its headlines read: 'Second murder victim found – police suspect gangland vendetta'. Felix snatched a copy of the News of the World and hastily made his way out of the shop, suddenly conscious of eyes burning into him from all directions. He soon came across a small public park boasting a few lopsided swings and a rather pathetic border sated with impotent pansies and delinquent saxifrage arranged in rank to form three incoherent words: "Pansy i blm". Barnsley in bloom indeed.

Felix read the article with wide eyes and ebony lips. It turned out to be no more plausible than the mammoth mounds spilling over from Big Brother's bouncing babes, and about as informative. In fact, so fanciful was the commentary that, but for the names of the two executed brothers, Felix might have mistaken the story for an entirely different one. No mention was made of any specific 'outside' involvement, in fact, according to the reporter, just two people were currently assisting the police with their enquiries: a close acquaintance of Neil Pincombe (formerly Neil Day) named Jethro Farr, and Spencer Day's "distraught and inconsolable" wife, Paula. Naturally, details of the kind responsible for disrupting Felix's sleep pattern had been kept deliberately scanty, although reference was erroneously made to the attempted cremation of *both* bodies. No mention of a murder weapon was made however, and Felix was relieved to learn that no suspicious vehicles had been reported. Detective Inspector Sam Toogood was in charge of the case. He reported "steady progress indicating the involvement of a network of felons with appropriate motives and familiar criminal histories". Toogood was plainly quoting from official document 42b, paragraph 14, of the P.P.P. (Police Prevarication Procedures), which committed to nothing, promised nothing and revealed less.

Felix swallowed the last square of his Yorkie bar. He felt calmer now that the morning's sugar quota had been restored to a more plausible level and better able to re–engage with unresolved cinematographic difficulties. The nub of the problem, which PC Dring had partly overheard him discussing the previous evening, concerned the business of illuminating Toni Pirelli's cellar. Regrettably, Salvatore had not been able to gain access to his brother's garage because Toni had filled it with salvageable equipment from the bar pending completion of the renovation work. In the fake video the impression needed to be given of a dimly lit lockup, since the police knew the location of the second death and would be encouraged to think the first had been committed along similar lines. Surely this should be a simple matter, or so he'd thought – if you want to convey a lockup, film in a lockup. But mimicking the precise camera orientation Paula had randomly arrived at had so far proved elusive. And the margin between too little light, and too much, seemed infinitesimal with just a torch and a box of candles to work with. The important thing, it seemed to Felix, was that the police are tricked into thinking the conditions for both killings were broadly similar, even if subtler details didn't quite match upon closer inspection. After all, even cold–blooded murderers can be allowed an occasional refinement of procedure.

Felix considered other possibilities of illumination as he trudged along the myriad urine–soaked ginnels and snickets that led from the park back to John Lewis, quietly accepting the presence of the familiar, oddly clad figure who continued to shadow him as keenly as ever. He eventually passed a shop selling garden furniture and the like, and something of interest called out to him from the gravelled area outside. It was a pack of plastic solar lights, knee high, the sort that are either so effective they aggravate the neighbours all night long, or so dim they fail to attract even the most light deprived Lepidoptera. A tenner well spent, Felix smiled to himself, as he strode back to the Lidl car park in time to fend off the diffident teenager with canine aspirations; fortunately, the youth was infinitely more interested in searching for Twisted Sister tracks on his 60 Gb iPod than in brandishing his burgeoning individuality.

The Cobra's cellar was dank, reeking and inhospitable – indeed, an ideal setting for staging a gothic murder scene. The rambling space, which had long been given over to storage, had been cruelly ravaged by the fire, and the walls had become coated in a thick, oily tar that hung in swirling patterns like Artex. Felix had high hopes for his bespoke solar lights. During his absence the others had tried out various camera angles, determined to improve on their aborted efforts of the previous day. They'd laid their hands on an ancient wooden chair that was perfect in every respect except its height. This factor, they judged, was inconsequential. In their bogus video the 'victim' – a rôle conferred to Felix, since his physique most nearly matched Spencer Day's – would be hunched over, hooded and bound; naturally, neither he nor his fellow actors would utter a word in the crescendo to his execution. Furthermore, they rationalised, if they shot the scene replicating the trajectory Paula had used in hers, details such as shelves groaning with stolen trinkets, busted busts of Beethoven etc., would not need to be accounted for.

Felix sat in the cellar cogitating over whether they should fake a commentary of some kind, too; but Paula's tormented voice had an unmistakable timbre – surely they couldn't dupe the police with any skulduggery in that area? Giuseppe sat patiently reviewing the copy they'd made of the death scene Paula had unwittingly committed to the camcorder's hard disc. He fast–forwarded through the first part of the funeral service with the organ whining away in Mickey Mouse mode, then to the unduly celebratory wake, and finally on to the chilling performance itself in the

247

concrete pantheon of death. Felix suddenly became agitated, moved over to the camcorder and hit the pause button.

'Okay, so we can't *fake* her voice...but we could *copy* it from elsewhere on her recording – I'll bet she says something in all innocence that could be understood differently, depending on where we splice it in!'

Salvatore would need several passes at that one.

'Doesn't she say something like "I'll never be able to forget seeing you like this", referring to her dad in his coffin?'

Frankie looked unmoved while Salvatore continued to show no glimmer of comprehension.

'Look, it doesn't need to be anything particularly incriminating, or even relevant, for that matter – it's a deictic – in other words, the context determines the impact, got it? The police will never see the funeral sequence we've copied our extract from, only the slaying. Viewed side by side, our two tapes will be pretty convincing, the more links between them the better. So, all we need to do is borrow *another camcorder*, and use it to play our sound bite from the first tape *while* we're acting out the fake murder on Paula's machine!'

Salvatore, now irredeemably confused, nevertheless agreed to ask his brother if he had a camcorder they might borrow. He returned five minutes later, shaking his head frenziedly.

'Toni, hee nairvous, hee thinka hees brather isa the *pervairta.*'

'The only thing you're perverting is the course of justice. Or at least, I hope that's the case' mumbled Frankie.

'No camcorder, I take it?'

Gadgets were anathema to the Constipated Cobra, a pub forever trapped in a technological abyss, the remains of its mechanical cash registers and bar–billiards table proudly asserting the prevailing level of low–tech sophistication. Toni's personal stereo system consisted of a Boots own–brand cassette machine that Giuseppe had bought him for his fiftieth birthday, an occasion not dissimilar in alcoholic proportions to the previous evening. So, if Felix's dubbing idea were to work, they'd have to revise it a little – first they'd decant the chosen sound extract to a cassette in Toni's machine, then run it simultaneously with the camcorder while recording the murder scene. The resulting loss in sound quality would cover the risk of detection.

Felix's new solar props as yet produced only the weakest orange flicker, although the accumulative effect of six mushroom shaped beacons dotted strategically around the cellar walls conveyed the more promising ambience of a catacomb. The novice film crew eventually fixed on a suitable position to seat the hooded body, and began shooting. The first half dozen attempts became fatally screwed up by extraneous noises–off; the clanking of the upstairs toilet was followed by a sustained assault on Felix's bare calf by a pair of humongous spiders that, having somehow survived the all–consuming flames of the previous week, were not about to succumb to a crap actor's hysterical lashing out. Dubbing in the sound from Toni's tape recorder proved to be a major source of stress too, and only a few words from the salient extract survived the process intact: 'I'll...never...seeing...like...this...'

interspersed with sporadic crackles and spits; the whole thing might just as well have been shot in Joe's Café. And yet Felix's rendition of a broken man about to lose his life at the hand of his pathological wife was memorably moving; in the final take he'd cultivated a most compelling judder of the head and roll of the shoulder as the cloaked figure (Salvatore) emerging from his side drew in the rope that had been loosely placed around his neck.

Amid the fits of nervous laughter that gushed from them upon reviewing the forty seconds worth of successful footage, Felix seemed somewhat pensive.

'What do you suppose Paula's motive would have been, anyway?' tossed off Giuseppe casually, as the four men prepared to depart for home an hour later.

'I mean, we're suggesting she despised her own husband enough to throttle him on camera, right...'

'Shit!' exclaimed Felix, 'you've made me think of something...we'll have to completely scrub the sound from Paula's video when we come to edit it on my laptop, because in it she accuses Neil of killing her husband, and we're about to claim *she* did it!'

'I don'ta hunderstanda thees, boysa' protested Salvatore, struggling to come to terms with the fact that he'd just executed Felix in his brother's burnt out cellar – the rôle of flabby murderess accentuated by padding from four towels – to the accompaniment of intermittent dwarf lights and vindictive monster arachnoids. In truth, Salvatore's inarticulate articulation summed up their collective grasp of the situation.

The two senior Pirellis slapped each other's backs

250

for a good two minutes in the car park, while Felix busied himself with the bags, anxious to shield himself from their ostentatious show of affection. Despite the fact that there were no plans to reunite unless either Toni ever reached his seventieth birthday or one of them died (whichever came first), the sentimentality was crushingly overblown.

'Get a *grip*, Pirelli, I'm...*tyred*' groaned Frankie from the back seat, paradiddling impatiently on the headrest.

'*Tred* carefully mate, we don't want him *skidding* on his *bald* patch' sneered Felix, further cheapening the repartee from the back seat. Giuseppe, who'd promptly taken up his position in the front, wore an unconvincing smile as he too protected himself from behind a half closed window. He'd not had much of a chance to engage with his uncle at this visit, for the man's mental state had vacillated somewhere between half cut and fully hammered from the moment they'd arrived two days ago. In any case, Giuseppe's sailing days had long since melted into the mists of time, dragging with them fuzzy memories of under–age drinking sessions that would inevitably culminate in a Jackson Pollock shocker in the pub loo.

Having successfully escaped Toni's tearful clutches they disappeared cheerfully down the M1, leaving little evidence of their visit aside from a sizeable dent in Toni's beer reservoir and a cassette tape in his tape recorder containing Paula's six misappropriated words. They'd done their best with the fake videotape, and now the focus turned to the timing of its leaking to the police. A simple enough task, it would seem, and yet, for Felix at least, worries remained. The process of acting out the first murder had

251

crystallised his senses somewhat. The central problem was why Paula Day would wish to film herself killing two men, one of them her husband, and then calmly release the videotapes to the police. Bravado is one thing, suicide another. Alternatively, if the intention was to suggest that somebody else shot the two scenes, how could he, the cameraman, have rigged things up without Paula knowing? For she'd hardly have broadcast her intentions to someone bent on shopping her to the police.

'I'm wondering if we need to big things up a bit, boys, in the form of a covering letter for each of the tapes' reflected Felix.

Frankie's head dropped, detecting the onset of some misguided convolution. 'Oh god, spare me a *little* hope...'

'You see, the way the police will figure it, Paula must have had a confidante, someone to whom she divulged her intention to slay both men...but for some reason this person decided to shop her, after all...for there's no other possible explanation for the materialisation of the tapes, is there? Even though *we* know that Paula slaughtered Neil as an erroneous act of reprisal, we want the police to think she bumped off the pair of them for some other twisted reason.'

'Please Felix, not random letters cut from newspapers and glued skew–whiff on Kleenex to read "I'm Jack, I did 'em good 'n propa with me noose and me bow 'n arra"' sighed Giuseppe.

'No mate, for that would be just a *tissue* of lies. I was thinking more along the lines of a subtle, enigmatic one–liner, something like "I was to be next on Paula's list, so I nailed the bitch before she could resist".'

'Felix, you haloumi–headed Herbert, there are times I think you've lived your life from the sanctity of a yogurt commercial' groaned Frankie. 'Don't you think we've got our work cut out already, stitching up Paula? Now you're intent on implicating some other random bastard as well!'

'Obfuscation, dear chap, obfuscation.'

'Huh, *odd–fuckation*, more like' snarled Frankie, slapping his forehead repeatedly with the heel of his wrist.

'Look, the more red herrings the police reel in, the better. Don't you see? This only seems far–fetched to us because, well, because *we* know it's all bollocks.'

'So, who might this shadowy figure, this unduly bollock–endowed red herring, be anyway?' snapped Giuseppe.

Felix shrugged his shoulders in despair.

'Oh, I don't know...her stepbrother? Santa? Who cares? It's just a distraction, mate; look, first Paula shoots the films, for her own satisfaction, and then someone else sends them to the police to satisfy his own screwball agenda – as long as *we're* overlooked, I don't care if *Doris* Day is implicated!'

DI Toogood had indeed overlooked the possibility of the fatuous four. But he wouldn't have wanted the case to become any more complicated than it already had.

253

Despite the mountain of stolen objects recovered from the first lockup incriminating Spencer Day in the rôle of consummate if indiscriminate thief, tangible clues to his and his brother's murder seemed pretty patchy. But Toogood had panned a grain or two of fools' gold along the way, aided by his diligent if wayward compatriot, Chanter. About time too, for he was now in active pursuit of a double murderer – a *real* power player, not some random crackpot pagan ritualist. Any suspicions he'd quietly held that Spencer Day's aloof brother, Neil, was the killer, had been soundly squashed by the rude reappearance of the said brother with a bolt through his brain and the expression of a harpooned tuna fish spread over his face. Both brothers had to have been nobbled by the same madman.

Toogood had been instructed by CS Flemming to isolate the two murders in order to minimise the risk of jumping to unsafe conclusions, but it was hard to see beyond the rather obvious links. Indeed it was thanks to a tangible, indeed concrete link – the passageway between Day's lockups – that Toogood and Chanter had just spent two hours poking about in cardboard boxes packed with Capodimonte swans and teasing out dust encrusted Pewter mugs from overstocked shelves. Admittedly, there was something slightly odd about the fact that the body, resembling a gruesome artefact from Madame Tussaud's, had been executed in the second virtually empty lockup, not the replete one that two teenagers had been tempted to enter en route to bunking off school, although it was fortunate they'd done so. Now that the body had been bagged up and stretchered off to the mortuary all that remained was a large bookcase lining the back wall, containing mostly junk, and the blood–sated wooden chair into which Neil Day had been strapped prior to his sadistic dispatch.

Chanter had installed himself with his customary zeal; he was in his element, measuring every conceivable dimension of the lockup in anticipation of further structural concealments, shining his torch into fissures in the breezeblocks hoping for hair samples and scratching at unsavoury stains that had long since maculated the concrete floor. All of this had, of course, been thoroughly expedited already by the forensic team the moment the body had come to light, but Chanter needed to assuage his passion for detail, find fodder for future fantasy. And one promising discovery had rewarded the officer's fastidious fossicking: a *third* interconnected lockup. A concealed MDF door, which had been camouflaged in a remarkably effective fake breezeblock veneer, was sited approximately one third of the way back from the rear wall of the second lockup, presumably so as not merely to extend a corridor connecting the first two. Paradoxically, if the function of the second lockup had so far eluded them, the discovery of a third – this one almost completely clean – was entirely baffling. But Chanter quite enjoyed being baffled; it provided endless scope for fact–finding missions and preposterous hypotheses with which he might antagonise his boss. As yet, Toogood had been spared Chanter's strained insights, but not for much longer.

'Sir, I've a theory regarding the third lockup' he ventured, struggling to control his thermos flask.

'Yes, I rather suspected you might' responded Toogood, accessing a practiced tone of disinterest.

'I reckon it's a sort of guerrilla distraction strategy. I've read quite a lot about this in respect of the ongoing crisis in Afghanistan.'

'Oh yes' muttered Toogood, maintaining the ambivalent tone.

'Actually, the Russians did something similar when the Nazis wanted to get their mitts on Peter the Great's Marble Room. The theory goes something like this. First you find a really good place to stash your stuff, away from any obvious associations – we'll call that area 'A' – and this is where you deposit most of it. Next, you hide a few significant pieces some distance away, in 'B'; these you are prepared to sacrifice in order to safeguard the greater part, should it become absolutely necessary. Finally, somewhere near to the first two points, 'C', you leave clues pointing to 'B', to suggest that it is here that the remaining objects are to be found.'

'Never mind the Bolsheviks, Chanter, I think *you* are the one who's lost his bleedin' marbles', quipped Toogood. 'And besides, it was amber, not marble.'

'But that's just it sir, the Russians *kept* the thing largely intact, due to the ingenuity of their secretion. The Germans only ever managed to capture a few relatively small sections, too few to be of value to them.'

'What's this, the ABC murders, eh? Trust you to reduce this scenario to an episode of Sesame Street, Chanter.'

The officer looked crestfallen for a full four

seconds, but squared up to his cynical boss. The pair stood at the entrance to the first lockup close to where, unbeknown to them, Spencer Day had met with his unpremeditated death ten days earlier surrounded by his stockpile of paltry pilferings.

'*This*, of course' continued Chanter, recovering his conviction, 'would be area 'B'.'

He strode purposefully to the rear of the lockup and led the way through to the adjacent one, which held little of interest now except the old wooden chair, its ugly history self evident from the body fluids spattered all over it. A freshly made hole directly behind and above the chair, approximately the size of a bullet, had metaphorically placed a full stop at the end of Neil Day's tawdry little life, and the glaucous guacamole pasted all over the stone wall tracked the trajectory of his lower cerebellum.

'Now we're in 'C', sir...and finally, we progress to 'A'.'

They walked through the hidden door leading to the third lockup and stood there in the deathly dampness of their surroundings. Toogood was evidently not impressed.

'Hang on; I thought you said the sacrificial area was called 'B' – so are you implying the 'real' stuff is in *here*?'

Chanter nodded smugly.

'You must have read all this crap in some sheep's entrails...or perhaps it fell out of a fortune cookie? Precisely how does a rickety old chair, in 'C', distract us from 'A', which in any case is *completely bleedin' empty*?'

'Um, well, I'm not sure about that yet, sir...but of course the victim was murdered in that chair, and I'm

257

suggesting its location in 'C' leads us back to where we started, that is, in 'B' sir, not 'A'.'

'You're flying your kite again, Chanter. For god's sake, just keep hold of what we know for certain here – Robin Hood's latest victim – who just happens to be Spencer Day's brother, Neil what's–his–name.'

'Pincombe, sir...actually, I think you're probably confusing the reputedly virtuous and courageous Robin Hood with the vengeful and diabolical Guy of Gisborne, sir. Not that Guy, the melodramatic villain and arch rival, would have misrepresented the motives of his mythical employer – the Sheriff of Nottingham – quite so blatantly as to impale a fellow citizen to a garage wall, rather than simply arrest him, sir.'

Incandescence contorted Toogood's face, persuading Chanter to shift to matters less abstract.

'It's just that, well, we now know that *Spencer* Day rented these premises under his wife's name, and had been using it as a place to store his knocked–off gear for the past fourteen years; we'd been under the incorrect impression he'd gone into retirement. But anyway, first he gets himself killed by some maniac who dumps his body in the wilderness, then his brother, whom we'd suspected from the start might be in danger too, turns up with an arrow through his oesophagus here, in 'C.'

'In *'A'*, Chanter, *listen* to me. The very existence of the third, empty lockup means *it* is 'C.''

'Only if the third lockup turns out to be as empty as you seem to think it is, sir.'

Although Toogood had kept his rag quite well until

258

then, suddenly it shrank to the size of a postage stamp. But that wouldn't dissuade Chanter from pushing the envelope.

'The thing is, sir, why would Spencer go to such lengths to conceal his third lockup unless he had something really significant to hide?'

'What, like an old car battery? 'cos that's all there is in here now...open your ruddy eyes man!'

'Possibly sir, possibly, but the absence of *proof* isn't necessarily the proof of *absence*...I mean, who knows what else he'd kept here before all this murder business kicked off?'

'Listen, I couldn't care less if Myra Hindley once sublet this necropolistic hellhole from Spencer in order to house her bagged–up body bits...Chanter, your third bloody *lockup* only serves to triple your chance of an all–mighty *cock–up*! Face it man, your 'B's' and 'C's are at sixes and sevens.'

Toogood couldn't indulge his partner's harebrained theories a moment longer.

'Make yourself useful and snap some pictures of this farcical scene for the case conference this afternoon; we'll have to wait for *Granny* Day to be topped off – perhaps here, in the third lockup! – before SOCO come up with anything of use. I've already had the Chief Super tugging at my shirttails today. He wants to see some action. And frankly Chanter, so do I!'

Toogood's torpedo was perhaps excusable given the weight of random evidence queuing for his attention, not to mention Chanter's offbeat musings. What he needed now was digestible, unequivocal evidence; his cohort's penchant for eighteenth century mythical figures was about as helpful as a hole in the head. He left Chanter to finish up and made the journey back to the Station, accompanied by officers Green and Bruiser, whose disquieting silence at least afforded him time to assemble a few disjointed thoughts for the case conference.

By the time he'd arrived, Toogood's fatigued mind had percolated through a painfully long list of details relating to his two murder victims. His head felt like a box of bird–droppings; little of the information he'd been wrestling with remained intact for long enough to work it through properly. But one thing seemed clear enough to him. Forensic evidence, aside from anything arising from the latest swabs from Neil Day's body and Chanter's spurious bag of bacteria scratched from the third lockup, still came down to the two areas emerging from Spencer Day's murder: in essence, a nail and an eye. For the number of fingerprints lifted from Neil Day's death chamber amounted to zero, and early indications were that even the gruesome gore sprayed across the back wall was cleaner than Cliff Richard's underpants. Ongoing door–to–door investigations might yet bear fruit, but Toogood had a bad feeling in his water. No one will have noticed a damned thing – if they had, it wouldn't have been left to two fourteen year–olds skiving chemistry to discover the body impaled to the wall that morning. The nail evidence, or rather *nails* evidence, suggested to him two things: the one missing altogether, along with the forefinger itself, seemed indicative of a torture episode prior to death. Clifford Morrison, the singing pathologist, hadn't ruled out that possibility, but since the finger wasn't actually in their possession, this remained an entirely subjective proposition. And the skin under three of the remaining nails on the same hand probably belonged to the murderer since it definitely didn't belong to Spencer himself. But since the harvested DNA wasn't on file, this too could only be added to a list of things they could be sure they *didn't* know. The incongruous beetle hibernating under the dead man's eyelid merely served to confirm that the body hadn't met its fate where it had been discovered, lying starkers in a field. It didn't tell him where to begin searching. It didn't help him to understand how Spencer Day had met his peculiar death, let alone why. And now the man's muscle–headed brother had muscled into the equation too, his demise making every bit as dramatic a statement, if only he knew what it meant.

As he jotted down woolly ideas for the briefing in ten minutes time, Toogood suffered in silence. But his pain was about to become marginally less acute. A phone call roused him; instinctively he knew it would be from Chanter. Reacting quickly, he pretended to be an answer machine, his voice falling somewhere between Sylvester Stallone and Graham Norton: 'You've reached Guy of Gisborne. Unless your name is Maid Marion, fuck off.'

Chanter didn't miss a beat.

'Friar Tuck here, sir. For your delectation, I bring news of cheer and unrivalled happiness.'

'Get on with it then, I'm briefing Little John and the other Merry Men in two minutes.'

'I've been researching our mysterious beetle, sir.'

'Ah yes, the elusive *Beatle*, that'll be...Stu Sutcliffe,

bass player in...let me guess...nineteen....*sixty'* mocked Toogood.

'Or to give its correct name, sir, the Siphonaptera. It resides in four discrete spots in Derbyshire, principally, but in one especially, and that's a patch of land sandwiched between Bakewell and Leek on the southern fringe of the Peaks.'

'So, it likes good, sturdy northern grub then, this bug?'

'Sorry sir?'

'Never mind – how big an area is that, then?' asked Toogood, aiming to sound a smidgen more indulgent.

'Roughly fifteen square miles sir, quite a small area, when you think what it might have been.'

'It *might* have been *one* square mile Chanter, and then you could be standing on the spot where Spencer was killed, instead of brown–nosing me for twenty plods to toothcomb the sodding Serengeti.'

'According to my SatNav, there's only one decent road that passes the spot. I could take a peak on my way back to the factory, if you want me to, sir.'

'Oh, go on then, but don't traipse about randomly like a jackass, knackering up any clues...And don't fall asleep on the job, or a rare breed of lice known as the copper–todger might just nibble your nads off.'

12

Snot Rocket Science

Details of the second murder had been trickling in to PC Dring at an uneven pace. He wasn't sure whether to be elated by it, or deflated at the prospect of coordinated efforts to catch the pitiless killer he felt he was now on to. Dring's mundane daily duties had taken him progressively away from the case that still dominated his every waking thought. But now that he'd revisited the canoes and procured a bag teeming with indigenous insects, excrement and foliage, the time had come to call in a rapid favour from his buddy Rick in the Forensic Science Laboratory. The propinquity with Dr Rick Aldhaus was an odd one; it had formed through their efforts in the squad's biennial pantomime, ostensibly a charity gig, but in reality an excuse to fanny around on stage like a lot of halfwits, wearing brassieres that could comfortably strap a bag of puppies to a lamppost. Rick most certainly wasn't a halfwit however – he'd acquired a decade's experience seconded to the CID while assisting a number of other forces on matters criminal, pathological and microbiological. Following their chance meeting two years earlier, it transpired that the two men had become involved in another voluntary capacity – working for the Samaritans – an occupation as far removed from the peculiar lunacy of amateur dramatics as it is possible to conceive of. The two men coincided periodically when their shifts happened to overlap, their personal aspirations overlapping rather less often, needless to say. And yet, something about having one's head pressed against another man's rear end for ten consecutive evenings every six months, coordinating horse canters and whinnies with a retired policeman operating scooped–out coconut shells off stage, had revealed a different aspect of each man, so to speak.

Acting on Dring's curry bribe, Rick had performed rudimentary tests on the wayward constable's lucky–dip bag; knowing Dring as he did, he'd expressed little concern for why he was being asked to sift through such an odd assortment of detritus, the contents of which ranged from rabbit and goat faeces to weeds and grass of varying lengths and types. But a few items were proving more troublesome to elucidate, presented as they were within the somewhat narrow context of an unlabelled specimen bag.

'One can learn a lot from shit', began Rick in an impassive tone. 'What an animal eats in its habitat, it will shit in its habitat. Where it lays its turds will be pretty close to where it will lay its head, and where it kips and shits is likely to be where it's happiest procreating too. Especially if it keeps a clean toilet. The older and more numerous the examples of life, the better matched to its environment an animal might be said to be.'

'Can we know whether a solid object resting at the point where this lot was collected, let's say, for argument's sake...a canoe...dates from the time the *oldest* specimens do?'

'I'm not entirely sure where you're coming from, Perry. You mean you extracted this motley assembly from inside a canoe?'

'Hypothetically, yes. Well, under it, over it and around it, actually.'

'Since you can't tell me the relative position of each turd and every blade of grass, and bearing in mind I've never even seen your hypothetical canoe, that's a bit like asking me to carbon–date a missing blackboard from the evidence of the chalk thought to have been used to write on it.'

Dring swiftly produced his notes and handed over the measurements he'd taken at the site. Rick smiled as one might at a seven year–old who's just brought a half–eaten mouse into the kitchen.

'I always thought you were a bit 'tweed' on the inside, Perry. I'll say this though. None of the samples is terribly old, and the yellowing grass from under the canoe would appear to have had its growth stifled by the placement thereupon of same, assuming that it would otherwise have reached the height of the other samples taken from the locality.'

Dring allowed himself to look placated, if mildly confused. 'And how long might that be, roughly?'

265

'A month, possibly two or three, depending on whether the farmer ever cuts his grass – it's not got the same growth behaviour pattern as common or garden suburban grass, you see.'

Rick didn't react to the infantile smile that had consumed most of Dring's face, but swung around on his swivel chair to pick up a plastic tray.

'And that just leaves the chocolate, the snail and the lettuce.'

'*What?*' shrieked Dring, striking a soprano's tessitura. 'Sounds more like a trendy wine bar in Notting Hill!'

'There's a tiny amount of Arugula Eruca Sativa, or what we commonly call 'rocket', in amongst this lot. I'd say it was a good deal more contemporary than the other vegetation though. Luckily, the local wildlife disliked its taste as much as the human who'd begun eating it.'

'Ah, now you're talking!' beamed Dring, 'what could...how might...'

'Rocket is a relatively easy plant to grow, of course – it self–seeds at the drop of a hat, if left alone in a sheltered spot. But, no, your sample had too many lingering lypocene and viscoelastic properties on it to permit that, I'm afraid.'

'I expect you'll tell me what those are, just as soon as I threaten to withdraw my promise of a peshwari naan' snarled Dring.

'Tomato ketchup, Perry.'

'And now talk to me about snails and chocolate, before I force feed the bloody bag load down your face.'

'It's very much a case of *snails of the unexpected* – a

Catinel Cuppediae, a fine specimen; congratulations.'

Dring leaned back on his haunches, holding Rick's tray at arm's length.

'I take it you wouldn't normally expect to find such a creature in this neck of the woods?'

'No, the nearest sighting I can recall hearing about came from Braunton Burrows, of all places. But there's no real reason why it couldn't have been living quite beatifically in your patch, I suppose – in the hundreds or even thousands. It has a distant relation, if my taxonomy serves me well, a big bastard that lives somewhere in Africa, I believe. Your fella's sometimes confused with the arenaria variety of catinella, a sand–bowl critter that doesn't get up to much.'

'Mm, okay, now, matters chocolate?'

'Um, well I'll wager it's the scrag–end of a Mars bar; it's rotted down to a blob the size of a goat's stool and its degradation process is quite interesting as regards the formation of a hard sugary coating. The odd thing is, our chum Catinel has taken a morbid liking to it, for some reason I can't fathom. It took quite some time to prise the fellow off; he's left a curious gooey slime all around it. Take a look. And I'd been thinking he was a discerning fellow, too – he didn't go for the rocket or ketchup…My debridement has revealed a residue containing inhomogeneities of a higher viscosity than the Catinel's natural trail–forming mucous – it's a bit like human snot in its consistency actually."

'Sounds like a charming creature, Rick.'

'They'd *eat* them in France – your average Frog

downs a cargo of escargots for his elevenses, you know. In fact, truth is, that's been the cause of much of the overpopulating that's occurred everywhere between here and California in recent years. Presumably the chocolate was offered some protection from the canoe then, Perry?'

'Um, yeah, I suppose so; is it the same vintage as the other stuff?'

Rick shrugged his shoulders, as if to indicate he'd speculated enough to earn his chicken shashlick already.

'I doubt if chocolate degradation studies have been much of a research priority in a world still suffering from AIDS and droughts.'

'Well I don't know Rick, enough money was blasted on refining 'E' numbers for the sodding chocky bars, I dare say.'

'My limited knowledge of cladistics leads me to guess at weeks rather than months; that's all I'd be prepared to say, without putting the thing through some pretty mesmerising chemistry. And I'm no food–techy either, you know.'

'Good enough for me, Rick, old sausage – weeks but *definitely* not years.'

'Now' said Rick arriving at his peroration, 'while we're in the field of confectionary, so to speak, feast your eyes on *this*.'

Another plastic tray emerged, this one containing an even smaller specimen peppered in something hairy.

'Blimey Rick! Your portions are even stingier than that Michelin–starred joint on the Ripley road.'

'But marginally more refined, *peut–être*? We're talking

coconut. At first I thought Waggon Wheel, then eased towards something less malleable – Club? – and ended up with Bounty.'

'Look at those frigging things, Rick!' exclaimed Dring, realising that the alien matter embedded in the horrid thing was made up of crystallised ants.

'Mm, Pachycondyla verenae, I fancy' nodded Rick knowingly, 'your common or garden worker ant. Must have beaten your friend Catinel to it.'

'Took his eye off the ball, eh Rick' Dring frowned in disgust.

'When they get nasty, Queenie doesn't get a look in either – a colony can turn on her if she has the wrong perfume.'

'Blimey' scowled Dring, 'I've heard of Mutiny on the Bounty, but…life on Mars?'

'A Catinel's chance, Perry, a Catinel's chance…'

Not unlike his myopic boss, the moonlighting Dring now found himself juggling an embarrassment of riches. If they'd pooled their resources the two officers might have been able to close the book on both murder cases – and the arson that never was – inside forty–eight hours. But as it was, they'd have to tread their own paths and commit their own tragic acts of incompetence. Nevertheless, Dring's bag of catalogued excreta had propelled him forward with redoubled courage; he hadn't yet paused to consider how he was going to cope with Toogood's inevitable claim to the spoils, assuming he ever did get around to closing the case single–handedly. But at least now he could be confident that the edifices of manmade food – something fried, wrapped in greasy paper and a couple of squandered chocky bars – had been partly consumed while in a position close to, or even inside, one of the canoes. The person responsible for bringing the canoes to the site was almost certainly the perpetrator of Spencer Day's death. And Dring's money remained firmly on McGuire and the Pirellis.

The morning after Toogood's monochrome case conference a small package bulging with potential arrived at the Police Station, delivered by hand from a freelance motorcycle courier. Scrawled along the Jiffy bag itself were three words only: 'Detective Inspector Toogood'. The contents, a single mini videotape intended for use in a digital camcorder, unlabelled, was accompanied by a succinct, cryptic covering note:

Paula Day has the might of a man. Stop her now, while you still can.

SNOT ROCKET SCIENCE

The words had been printed so as to be only just legible across a strip of newspaper excised from a certain News of the World feature, the contents of which were all too familiar to the two impotent policeman. Toogood and Chanter eventually got their apparatus sorted out and subdued the lighting in the small studio dedicated to the scrutiny of inscrutable media–based evidence, the imaginatively named Audio–Visual Aids Studio. Neither officer felt confident enough to prejudge what was about to appear in front of them, but both geared up to claim the benefit of hindsight.

The tape leapt into life without announcement or preamble. The sound quality was atrocious; the scene, a blacked–out room resembling a cave or attic, had more than a little sense of the surreal about it. The footage was grainy and static, yet marred by as much hiss as you'd get from a mangled snake. The lighting was so pared down as to be ascetic, and yet it was clear someone was sat directly in front of the camera, head draped in a dark gown or sack, and hardly moving. Echoes from feet movement elsewhere in the vicinity had the opposite effect to normal, or so it seemed; each sound became progressively amplified and looped back on itself like an experimental piece by Karlheinz Stockhausen.

Sixteen seconds into the footage there came a loud 'clunk', followed immediately by an overwrought woman's voice. It was so badly distorted that she might have been saying anything, although several sharp intakes of breath and continuous pronounced sniffling gave the impression of a tearful, impassioned rendering. Another abrupt 'clunk'

271

followed, whereupon the hitherto motionless figure adopted a bewildering stuttering gesticulation, as though an earthquake was imminent. The figure did not speak throughout, but continued to judder until, from the right of the picture, there appeared another darkened figure, bulky, quivering too and uncertain in its motion towards the seated one.

The intentions of this second, lumbering figure, then became a little clearer. A sideways gesture of its arm exposed a noose that had been waiting to perform its duty around the neck of the seated one, and this was now drawn in, as if in slow motion, by the tall, skinny figure now hovering menacingly in the shadows. In the awkward scene that followed, stifled sounds of strangulation competed with rather more distracting noises–off from elsewhere in the room, each boom reverberating madly to confirm the impression of a cave.

The remaining coverage was almost comedically chaotic. It took another fifteen seconds or so to reach its climax, as the seated figure affected a somewhat deliberate collapse to the ground. The executor then glided out of shot, leaving an empty wooden chair that cast a faint silhouette on the wall behind it. The footage ended as it had started, with a wineglass–shattering screech.

Chanter was the first out of the blocks. He'd managed to restrain himself for more than half a minute.

'We'll need to watch it again, several times, I'm sure' he said finding his most ministerial voice. 'But it does what it says on the can, sir – the film clearly shows Paula Day strangling her husband to death in his own lockup. In fact, if I might be so bold sir, the location of the murder does look more like the *third* lockup than the second, which would seem to bolster my assertion yesterday of *it* being area 'A'.'

'I've got just two words to say to you, Chanter: *Armitage Shanks*.'

Chanter twitched nervously, anticipating a more thorough admonishment for his platitudinous observation.

'For that was, without a doubt, the most unutterably unconvincing *sewage* I've ever been forced to watch. The only scary aspect is the fact that you've been taken in by it…I've encountered more discerning bacteria than you!'

'But sir, of course it *looks* amateurish. I'd be more concerned if it looked pro. You can't rehearse a live *death*…I mean…you can't rehearse a live videotaped *murder*, can you? You can't ask your victim to try a little harder to be convincing while you shoot the scene another dozen times. The murderer is capturing a moment on the fly, a video diary…a snuff movie, if you will.'

'I most certainly do *not* will, Chanter. And why are you assuming she'd want to distil her craziness onto videotape anyway? A diary of that sort is the last thing I'd want to have. Anyway, if we're to believe this laughably asinine note, someone else shot the film in order to make sure she cops it! No, Paula Day never did feature high on my list; she's slipped even lower now. Someone's got it in for her all right; whoever it is, he's a bloody dreadful poet and an even worse cameraman – he ought to be hung, *himself*.'

'Hanged, sir' corrected Chanter. 'The past participle

273

of hang is hanged, in this context.'

'Ah, but what if our hangman is *well hung*, eh, Chanter?' retaliated Toogood, unsure of how to proceed, so going for the base humour option. 'Perhaps he shoots homemade grunt movies, too!'

'Okay, I accept it's unlikely *she* shot the film' conceded Chanter, 'unless she's incredibly unlucky and it straight away slipped into the wrong hands. But surely sir, if we're agreed someone other than Paula filmed this, then he or she is still a real witness to a real murder.'

'A real witness to a *staged* murder, more like. And besides, since we never see her...*its*...face...let alone Spencer's...the tape's about as compelling as pineapple chunks on a pizza.'

Toogood was in no mood to review the tape again; it would come down to Chanter's best efforts, a task he would relish. By the end of the morning he'd produced a transcript detailing all material and immaterial events, occurrences of significant background noise etc. He'd also attempted to unscramble the voice that had blurted out so stridently, precisely eighteen seconds into the film. The best he could come up with was: "Neil...lover...seeing...like this". It didn't make much sense, even if 'lover' were traded for 'brother' or 'seeing' for 'seething'. On the other hand, he speculated, if Paula had been trapped in a love triangle involving Spencer's brother, the missing words might conceivably be slotted in to mean: "Neil (is my) lover; (we couldn't have you) seeing (us) like this".

Chanter whimpered as he surveyed the mind–boggling sequence for the fourteenth time in order to check that his time–line was pinpoint accurate. But he wasn't going to make a crime passionnel fit, however hard he tried. It dawned on him that Toogood did have a point about a frame–up; Paula would surely never have sanctioned a video of herself murdering her husband, only to have is sent to the police a few days later accompanied by an unequivocal squib. Even so, he couldn't really understand his boss's obstinacy over the veracity of the tape itself. Being the wife of a convicted burglar may well have heightened the tension between the charmless couple; in any case, there were no other candidates to pursue. Paula had been interviewed by Toogood directly following the discovery of her husband's body, and although his questioning had been notably half–hearted, coy even, it had flagged up the fact that no one other than she and Neil even knew of the existence of Spencer's lockup, let alone its whereabouts up in Mugginton. Furthermore, Paula's interview with Toogood would have presented the ideal opportunity for her to implicate somebody else – the simple–minded Jethro Farr perhaps? She mightn't have been aware of the videotape's damning footage, but could hardly fail to read the writing on the wall now.

There was a way forward for Chanter, he now recognised. He would need to establish a copper–bottomed match between Paula's voice and the one on the videotape. Then it wouldn't matter what she'd actually said on camera, or even whether *she'd* shot the film – she'd still be bang to rights. But he knew he'd have his work cut out persuading Toogood to support him in rigging up a covert operation, especially since he'd failed to discover anything at the beetle site the previous evening, despite spending two hours ferreting about in the rain with his torch. The more he thought about it, the less fanciful the newspaper headline had been in proposing a gangland vendetta. Long–term friction between the Day brothers might conceivably lie at the heart of the case.

Then he had a brainwave. A tape recording would have been made of Paula's interview with his boss, as a matter of routine police procedure. If he could get his hands on it, it would be a simple enough job to have it investigated by the voice analysis expert and compared alongside the video sequence. He set about it. Toogood could go and boil his head.

Meanwhile, PC Dring's progress boiled down to a wilted lettuce leaf, a snail with an unaccountably sweet tooth and two oddly festering chocolate bars, for these alone placed the canoes at the scene of the crime, or at least in the discovery zone, at the salient time. But the plucky plasm's unsavoury liking for confectionary brought with it one or two imponderables. After all, proof of a recent visit to the site didn't automatically implicate either one of the Pirellis as murderers, and Dring was even further from pinning anything on Tommy McGuire, whose gravest misdemeanour so far had been to leave his sea–scout record book to disintegrate in a canoe. And the gory details of Neil

Day's crossbow execution had scarcely even registered on his obsessed little mind. What he needed was something that would irrefutably link one of his suspects to Spencer Day's macabre reappearance. A motive wouldn't go amiss either. Indeed, he had yet to establish any connection at all between the Days and the Pirellis. And something about Toni Pirelli's unworldliness, his apparent lack of suspicion regarding McGuire's possible rôle as arsonist, inclined him toward Toni's elusive brother, Salvatore. After all, in the rôle of instructor he'd be the most likely owner of the woebegone canoes. If he could somehow cajole Salvatore into admitting to an acquaintance with one of the Days, however fleeting, that would stir things up nicely. A bold gesture would be called for, something quite audacious; after all, he could make contact any time he liked.

  Dring considered his opponent for a while. How might Pee best harness his scanty profile of Salvatore Pirelli? He'd discovered the man's occupation easily enough, but setting up a full–on fishing expedition wouldn't be as simple a matter. He couldn't afford the time to execute a stakeout; Toogood and Chanter would be snapping at his heels at any moment. He could inveigle Salvatore into some neutral place, but then what? He had no bargaining chips, no incentive to offer the small–time PI for incriminating himself, McGuire or anybody else. And if Salvatore really were the murderer he'd be needing a bullet–proof fig–leaf to safeguard his lineage; his ambition didn't extend to getting himself kebabed and paraded naked to satisfy some sadistic predilection. Better not to come face to face with the man. Keep his distance.

Dring's trump card was the canoes. That much was obvious. Putting to one side for a moment the reason for their being dumped at all, why had the killer allowed them to remain in the field *after* the body had been discovered? It didn't make any sense. What's more, Salvatore was intensely proud of his nautical pedigree, the purloined photo album demonstrated that, if nothing else. At least Toogood's disinterest in them was understandable – a golfer would hardly ditch his old clubs in a lake! It was as if Pirelli didn't *know* they were there. But who else would have reason to deposit them to coincide with the arrival of a dead body? Dring needed answers fast; he'd have to wing it. An anonymous letter to Salvatore's home address might tip the balance. It would need to shock the man, provoke him into an act of recklessness. But first he'd need to rattle the cage a little, see if the man had any interesting history.

The police intranet file that Dring sneaked a peak at made interesting reading, not least because he hadn't expected Salvatore would have an entry at all; he kicked himself for not checking it out earlier. A green flashing icon indicated that Pirelli had recently been implicated in an ongoing investigation conducted by the Derbyshire squad, and two more mouse–clicks revealed that this was being coordinated by Detective Inspector Paradis. How odd – Paradis had been heading up the Constipated Cobra arson investigation, and he'd been under the impression it had hit sand. So why on earth could Salvatore still be of interest to Paradis? No further information was accessible on file, so a phone call to the incident room would be his only hope.

'Why do you need to know about Pirelli, Perry?'

278

interrogated DS Hales, for whom the Cobra case already seemed ancient history. 'He's old news, well, not that he was ever really *news* at all.'

'Oh, it's just that I had to deal with one of his brother's employees, a young chap called Tommy...'

'Would that be Thomas McGuire by any chance?' butted in Hales, abrasively.

'...Blimey Serg, how did you know that?' stumbled Dring, mildly destabilised.

'Well, it's just that he called us too, *again*, earlier today, as it happens. Don't take any notice of him, Perry. He shouldn't be hassling you either, I'm sorry you had to fend him off. If he rings you again, tell him to bugger off. He's worrying about nothing.'

Dring was startled but did his best to sound unphased.

'What did he want, then?' he bluffed, affecting a yawn of unconcern. 'Same as he did with me, I assume.'

'Yeah, he wanted to know why we'd been asking after him while he'd been away on his sailing trip. But the thing is, we *hadn't*. We'd clocked him right enough, after the pub got torched, of course, thanks to the local bush telegraph, but all that led to was a pile of piffle about him setting a bunch of caravans alight when he was a nipper. Truth is, we followed it up but Paradis wasn't interested, so we dropped it. Apparently it was his elder brother who'd done the gypsy job anyway, and the kid just went along for the ride; you know what younger brothers are like. And as I recall, the older one's now in the clink for something completely unrelated anyway.'

Dring managed to sound surprised.

'Oh, you mean McGuire thought you wanted him for the *pub* job...but if he was away on holiday he couldn't have done it anyway, could he?'

'Exactly. Just forget about him. He's just a twitchy twat. What's your angle on Pirelli anyway...you got something tasty?'

'Um, no, it's just that the case file shows that the investigation is still open on him, and McGuire happened to mention his name when he was offloading to me...I...I thought I'd better follow it up, you know, just to be efficient, like.'

Hales soughed brashly. 'Look, if you're that interested I'll drop the file off later...just get it back sharpish, 'cos Paradis is a control freak when it comes to stuff like that. Must dash.'

Dring was dumbstruck: two juicy titbits for the price of one. For all his contrived coolness McGuire turned out to be paranoid, and not too astute. Fancy drawing attention to himself like that, he thought, although it was lucky for him that he had.

Later that afternoon a feverishly ebullient PC Dring positioned himself face to face with his cold insensate PC; it flickered into life, the screensaver reluctantly dissolving to leave a winking cursor. The letter he was about to compose would call upon all his powers of inventiveness and manipulation. It would draw him still further from any instinct for self–preservation he may once have had. From the case notes Hales had slipped him he'd read with glee of Pirelli's freakish behaviour in the rôle of private investigator some months previously, and of the man's narrow escape from being lynched for gaining false entry to a golfer's dressing room locker. But Pirelli's subterfuge had been pretty tame, in the scheme of things, and in any case insufficient to warrant further scrutiny, least of all in respect of Paradis's prematurely defunct arson investigation. The story nevertheless lent power to Dring's elbow, a cubital joint that would need beefing up if he ever found himself head to head with the person capable of such animal–like acts as had been inflicted on Spencer Day. His letter would be blunt and yet provocative. And he wouldn't be able to resist a swipe at that young tyke McGuire while he was about it.

> *Salvatore Pirelli,*
>
> *Okay, so you got there first. Congratulations. You saved me a job. I've got hard proof you killed that petty pilfering ponce. And I know you torched the pub with that half–witted paddy paddler you used to splash about with. You'd better have enough cash to pay me off or you'll both pay a steeper price. I want 50k in used tenners or the video goes to Toogood. Bring the money to the field in an unsealed shoebox – you know a place it will stay dry. Do as I say and the tape will be in the same place twenty–four hours later. Friday at 9 pm. Not before. Not after.*

Dring was more than a little dismayed at how much he'd enjoyed constructing the nasty little blackmail note. It was a wildcard, to be sure, but it might succeed in smoking out Pirelli. If he were completely off beam then neither Pirelli nor McGuire would have the vaguest clue what the

281

letter was all about, and they might even contact the police. But if they knew which field to go to, then, de facto, they'd have to know how it implicated them in Spencer Day's death. And if they were guilty, they would undoubtedly have kept abreast with news reports of Detective Inspector Toogood's ineffectual direction. The bit about the videotape was mere window–dressing – but it might just stir up Pirelli enough to come to the party. Pirelli would have two days to react, barely long enough to raise the loot, but easily long enough to raise the alarm – and if he did, so be it.

Dring was calculating on Pirelli making a trip to the canoes on the Thursday evening, a day in advance of his demand; if he were indeed Spencer Day's killer, surely the man would want to comb the canoes for any incriminating clues ahead of the rendezvous? He might even be inclined to rig up a surveillance device, after all, the man was a PI, if not a terribly competent one. Since the field was so remote, accessible by a single road, Pirelli wouldn't be able to bring any heavies along without him immediately becoming aware; he'd select his vantage point with great care, that very evening.

It hadn't occurred to Dring that he'd no plan of action beyond summoning his suspect – what would he actually *do* with Pirelli, or indeed McGuire, assuming either of them showed up? His plan could so easily boomerang, and the last thing he was prepared for was a cardboard box brimming with cash; that would hardly secure his promotion prospects. Indeed, he was only just waking up to the fact that he'd soon need to come clean to Toogood. His covert operation was now irreversibly headed toward a fork in the road: adulation or castration.

@

At 10:00 AM a second parcel arrived by motorcycle courier marked for the attention of Detective Inspector Toogood. As with the first, two days earlier, the covering note was oblique, except that this one had been typed on a small slip of plain white paper, not scribbled across a newspaper article, as before:

I said she'd do it, and now she has. It's on your head, you stupid ass!

The miniature videotape squeezed into the Jiffy bag was a Phillips brand, just as before. It had been wound to the beginning of side A, unlabelled, just as before. Toogood's appetite for further fallacious interference was predictably small. He slung the package onto the table that separated him from Chanter, whose hunger for it was predictably gluttonous. Toogood watched his partner feed the tape into the uppermost machine in a stack of largely superfluous gadgetry and set it in motion.

The film started slightly differently from the first, in that there were at least twenty seconds of digital nothingness, so–called white noise, which only served to heighten the impact of what was to follow. The tape jolted into life sharply. Although there was no ear–splitting noise to aggress them as in the first tape – for there was no sound at all – the image of a human life, fragile and vulnerable, about to be nullified, was immediately compelling. Toogood sat up, unexpectedly captivated by the power of what he was seeing. The setting was dark and cavernous – a hangar perhaps, or dungeon – a veritable chamber of horrors. There were obvious parallels with the first tape in that the doleful figure, dimly lit, had been positioned in precisely the same spot relative to the camera, except that here there could be no doubting the stench of silent misery wafting from the man as he sat slouched, his head dipped in anticipation of something quite terrible. No attempt to obscure the man's identity had been made, no play of ambiguity.

The man was, beyond any doubt, Neil Day. A second figure, a large and imposing creature, dressed from head to toe in plastic galoshes or fishing garb, presided. Its sex was not immediately self–evident since it was endlessly moving in and out of shot. An obvious contrast between the two videotapes was the weight of detail. While both films had been shot from a single static position, somehow this one succeeded in capturing a more absorbing documentary, an altogether more diabolical chronicle. Toogood and Chanter knew the space well, for they'd spent long enough devouring the detail of Spencer Day's second lockup, two days earlier.

Now, from nowhere, a crossbow appeared. Wedged tightly between its gaping jaws, a long, steely arrow delighted in the little artificial light that could find it. Its state of hypertension brought about a similar reaction in Toogood, whose breathing accelerated palpably to spasmodic snatches. Knowing intuitively what was coming next could not adequately prepare him; nor could anything mollify Neil Day, a man whose neck looked set to undergo a DIY tracheotomy.

The only clue to the clinically lethal event itself was a fractional convulsion of the footage, hardly detectable given the distance between the victim and the camera. For Neil Day's head barely moved on impact, such was the efficacy of his impalement. But a clearer signal that something life–altering had just taken place came from the killer. The reaction was one of simple apoplexy. In an instant the crossbow, now spent of its charge, had leapt in stature from instrument of precision to homicidal weapon. In the desperate scene that ensued, the untying and retying of redundant rope from around the impaled man's body was every bit as harrowing to witness as the execution itself had been. For only now, with the benefit of a more steady focus, was it apparent that the killer crouching at Neil Day's feet, panicking over unrelenting knots, was the dead man's sister in law, Paula Day. Ironically, she had in that instant become as much a victim. She stood now, fumbling hopelessly with the machine, desperate to stop it filming, as if by doing so she might conveniently airbrush away the miserable event. Here the scene reached a merciful close; two short minutes of interminable horror.

The viewing at an end, Toogood's face concealed his emotion little better than Paula Day's had. He gawped

285

blankly past his DS, temporarily incapable of finding appropriate words to initiate discussion, let alone to consider the more awkward process of back–pedalling. Finally, aggressing his stubble with both thumbs, he spoke.

'You know, by the time this is all over, we'll be different people, Chanter; too ready to expect the worst in others, less able to keep an open mind.'

Toogood's profundity bypassed Chanter, who'd been using the valuable seconds to prepare a thought–provoking repost.

'Why do people invariably point to their wrist when asking for the time, but never point to their groin when they ask where the bathroom is?'

Toogood looked aghast at the uniqueness of his colleague's banality.

'I mean, you don't need to allude to something if you're going to articulate it anyway, do you?' he continued. '...Let me put it another way, sir. Why would Paula Day go to such lengths to send us video diaries of these slayings – two intensely personal accounts – but only allow us to see the identity of *one* of the victims? She knows that *we* know who each one is, right?'

Toogood exhaled loudly as he wrestled with Chanter's spurious conundrum while continuing to explore his complexion with the nib of a biro.

'I'm increasingly unsure *you* know anything, Chanter, for you've an intellect roughly commensurate with my potting shed. Will you agree with me on one tiny, insignificant, piffling little detail? Neil Day was definitely slaughtered in lockup number two. Or, if I indulge your

286

bizarre nomenclature, *area sodding A!*

'But sir' protested Chanter, 'I never claimed that Neil Day was murdered anywhere other than lockup number two, merely that more lies in store for us in number thr...'

'The reason for the first victim being hooded must be that...that it *wasn't* a victim...or at any rate, it wasn't *our* victim.'

'Eh? You're not suggesting there's a *third* victim sir, one that's out of sequence, and that we're about to receive the *real* Spencer Day videotape next?'

'No. No, I'm not' whispered Toogood exasperatedly, arresting an incipient rage. 'God, this is like trying to get shit from a rocking horse...I'm implying that *nobody* died in the first video. Read the note: "I said she'd do it, etc." A third party is claiming responsibility on Paula's behalf – *she's* not. And the fact that the first 'victim' was hooded when the second wasn't *proves* the first tape wasn't ever intended to be for private consumption! Face it Chanter, Paula Day killed Neil all right, but she didn't kill her husband. And if it weren't for someone else's twisted agenda, I'm positive we wouldn't have been sent the tapes at all.'

Toogood was making frustratingly good sense, it seemed; Chanter might have to diversify.

'It's also interesting, sir, that the sound on the first video is so bloody lousy, whereas on the second, which is so much more visually descriptive, there's no soundtrack at all. Actually sir, I've done a little homework on the first tape, and unfortunately the sound quality is too rough to be

287

analysable. It comes down to subjectivity; we either believe it's her voice, or we don't.' He didn't await a response. 'So, what do we do now then, apart from arrest Paula, obviously?'

'No, *not* obviously. I think we'll just drag our brogues on that one. Our best hope of catching murderer number one is to leave murderer number two to stew for a bit. She's not going anywhere – and I'll wager she doesn't have the vaguest clue we've got her tape.'

Chanter spent that evening watching TV documentaries. His already impressive fund of trivia called for continuous replenishment, his resourcefulness widening with every programme he viewed, whether it be about plate tectonics, parasitic invasion of water buffalo or the construction of Malaysian subway systems. Indeed, he'd just been engrossed by a particularly riveting account of the life of an Antipodean grasshopper; a number of scientific speculations, such as the creature's metabolic temperament and its calorific value when deep–fried in sesame oil, had been woven in, much to Chanter's childlike enthusiasm. Naturally, he would need to rehearse his new data at the earliest opportunity, an inclination his wife had developed a commendable resistance to during the couple's five year marriage.

'Tam, did you know that if you count the number of chirrups a snowy cricket gives in twenty–five seconds, then subtract fourteen, you get the temperature in degrees Centigrade?'

'Of course, Den, I thought *everyone* knew that.'

'And this fluctuates according to a formula that....'

'Goodnight Den, I'm going up now. Don't stay up too late, will you.'

But Chanter's appetite for the kind of intellectual esoterica best consigned to the manufacturers of bargain–basement Christmas crackers, had not yet been fully assuaged. He trawled through the detritus of Reality TV programmes and wasteland of satellite channels, skipping past the forty–eighth re–run of 'The top 100 people to shag before you die' and eventually paused at a programme given over to cold cases – unsolved murders consigned to the backburner that are periodically awoken only to be promptly put back in the refrigerator for another decade. The case in question concerned a body that had hitherto not been satisfactorily identified or classified according to conventional resources of pathology. But a psychic, aptly named Lucrecia, claimed she'd had a vision of a killing that had taken place some eighteen years previously in a multi–storey car park just outside Chepstow. The assailant, a mentally unstable character whose name began with a 'T', or perhaps a 'D', had led an otherwise unremarkable life. Predictably enough, Lucrecia had been able to pass on other vital scraps to the investigation team that subsequently led to the arrest and conviction of Trevor Davis, an outwardly benign middle–aged tax office worker from Bolton.

If there was a redeeming feature to Chanter's obsessiveness, it was that his mindlessness was open–minded and his judgments generally non–judgmental. He could access a rare capacity for tangential thought to match that of any probationer hairstylist, and was equally incapable of dismissing as implausible stories that would reduce most people to a state of helpless hysteria. These qualities had taken time and diligence to distil. He wasn't about to negate them now.

13

The Wrong Day-View for a Rendezvous

Felix flicked open his Filofax and navigated to the current week. In it he'd made three significant entries: Clay's birthday; Landrover MOT; meeting with Clive Bird. This last entry, scheduled at short notice for 8:30 the next morning, was causing him a little angst, for his boss was prone to bouts of sense–of–humour failure when his senior employees absented themselves without notice, as Felix had done for the past full week; he'd failed to respond to a blizzard of voicemails and texts, which will have further ruffled the Bird's feathers. But Felix had his excuses lined up and was prepared to slide shamelessly down the list, one by one, as his boss whittled them away. There's a limit to the number of deaths in the family one can reasonably have though, and Felix had endured more than most; indeed, his allocation of hospitalised grandmothers had already been seriously overstepped.

In one sense the recent goings on had done him good, shaken him up a little; there's nothing like being hunted for murder for putting your tawdry life into better perspective. He'd missed the solitude aboard Wagtail though, as the company of his three compatriots had brought with it a disturbing palette of stress inducers. He'd permitted himself a quiet evening alone. The Pirelli pair had eventually been persuaded to go home and Frankie had pretended to have worthy distractions of his own, up in Sheffield. But the abrupt peace did not sit comfortably with him; he'd forgotten how to luxuriate in it. His granddad's old puffer seemed a promising starting point. He packed it, lit it and was straight away transported to an unfamiliar place, a miscegenation of Coventry and Calcutta perhaps, with blocks of black fog sitting in the air around him like monsoon clouds set to wring themselves dry. If this was sleep, it was exhausting; characters whom he'd never met seemed to know him well enough, and yet his own relatives seemed to question his identity. The mysteriously mundane setting for this out of body experience, his mother's hermetically sealed garage, had acquired a disquieting air. He couldn't figure out why she would be wearing a diving suit as she vacuumed the stone floor, with oven gloves on her feet and a helmet on her head. He knew it was her, because the sopranino singing couldn't be coming from anyone else with a clear conscience. And yet she hardly turned her head to acknowledge his usual greeting; perhaps the din of the

Hoover scraping along the sidewall was impairing her hearing? And why didn't she have the light on in there? She could hardly see which of the old paint pots needed dusting with the pink feathery device clenched under her armpit. Eventually she piped up, the machine still complaining noisily at her feet.

'Put your helmet on, dear...*your helmet!*'

A few more inhalations would carry him still further from corporeality, to a meadow laced with jubilantly green grass and above it terraced grey clouds that carved up the skyline into sharp potato wedges. He strolled, perhaps alone, he couldn't be sure, past towering trees, like spindly old men who had a calmer vision of the world but no one with which to share it. There, among long shadowy streaks he shuddered, wondering why he wanted to drink them up; places best not to dawdle in case you find what you think you're looking for. Now, suddenly, he was above everything, blackened scallops of cloud spitting at him as he dared to scratch at them with his booted feet. And then, just as suddenly, back among the knowing trees, looking for nothing in particular but scrutinised by everybody. The vagueness of everything seemed crystal clear to him, and yet he couldn't be sure of the little he knew. If only it would stop raining he'd be able to worry about the sun melting his wings. At least then he'd have an excuse to crash, better than to drift or be sucked further into someone else's freedom...

The telephone jangling on the toilet cistern did little to jolt Felix back to the questionable sanctity of the real world, a world in which fried dead men fall headlong into open fields, and where Indian conjurers are more interested in planting brown envelopes in photo albums than in sorting out their pathetic little lives. It rang and rang, and yet only a despondent Venus Flytrap appeared to take the slightest bit of notice. Felix's evanescent reverie leapt sporadically from fragment to fragment; and still it rang. An orange ember tumbling to his lap, small enough to be carried by a lusty bee, was actually what roused him, but quickly he realised he'd frustrated an impatient caller's best attempts to rouse him.

Felix eased himself gently into a state of noncommittal lucidity. His head throbbed and his mouth tasted as if some small animal had curled up and died in there. He filled the kettle and listened to it swoop crazily above the uneven flame, negotiating a Jaffa Cake with one hand while scouring the mobile's call history with his other. It informed him he'd missed three calls – all from Giuseppe. Couldn't he be left alone for five minutes? The first had occurred more than two hours earlier, just after the initial wave of cannabis had started to ossify his brain. Reluctantly he pressed 'dial' and was taken by surprise at the speed of the response.

'Shit, Felix...I thought you'd been hijacked by some abominable creature!'

'I was beginning to think the same thing, mate. What do you want, anyway? You can't have been home long' he said, checking his watch needlessly as he poured boiling water into a mug with no handle.

'Are you sat down?'

'It can be arranged.'

'Arrange it then. Now, Felix, what would be the scariest kind of response we could get, now that our videotapes have been sent to the cop shop, I mean?'

'Ooh, I don't know...um, a letter saying "stop pulling my chain, arsehole, I know you guys did it"' he tittered.

There was an extended pause, during which Giuseppe had clearly felt compelled to sit down himself.

'Bugger me...are you sure *you* didn't write it!'

Felix amplified his yawn. 'Huh! Giuseppe, are *you* sure you're not the cheerless bastard that's just been tampering with my dream? You sound very familiar, in a fuzzy kinda way.'

'Stop pissing about, Felix. I'm dead serious. Pop's just been sent a poison pen letter – anonymous and typewritten, postmarked Ripley and dated Tuesday the fourteenth. I'm truly spooked by it, and I reckon Pop would be too, if only he could understand it.'

Giuseppe read it out loud, twice, once for Felix's benefit and once more for his father, whom he'd just joined in the attic, from where the signal promptly collapsed to an intermittent crackle. Felix rubbed his eyes and groaned; he still couldn't be sure he wasn't being pursued by a character from his prematurely curtailed nightmare, and sank into his wicker settee, scalding his hand with un–milked instant coffee. The searing pain and abysmal taste of the curdling sludge shunted him into consciousness. He considered Giuseppe's letter for a moment before speaking.

'It must be the cops, mustn't it?...I mean, who else would be in a position to cobble together these facts, if facts they are, of course?'

'Mm, well, I'm not sure, Felix – I mean, it's more as if our first tape has fallen into the wrong hands, don't you think? Notice no reference is made to the killing of *Neil* Day, nor to the existence of the second video. And yet we couriered it to Toogood *yesterday*, the day Pop's note was posted.'

'No, I still reckon it's a knee–jerk reaction by Toogood, mate' replied Felix, systematically working in errant coffee grains with the arm of his spectacles. 'He mightn't have had a chance to watch the second tape yet, or else the two just overlapped in the internal post; if he had received tape number two he'd have wanted to scoop a double whammy, wouldn't he? Look, let's start from the top shall we? First off, what's all that hoo–ha about a torched pub, and who the hell is the "paddy" your old man is supposed to have "splashed about" with? I didn't know Salvatore was into Irish peat–bog fighting!'

'Can't think who he is. Pop must have dragged a thousand people onto water when he was younger – canoeists, windsurfers...it could be any of them – even me...shit, Felix, I've just realised, the pub's gotta be *Toni's*...the note's referring to the Constipated Cobra!' Giuseppe whinnied. 'Toogood's put two and two together and come up with hedgehog! – for some reason he's connected my uncle's basement fire with Spencer Day's murder!'

'But this is all too fantastic, mate. Look, both of the incidents referred to in the note were *accidents* – at his party, we all heard Toni admit he'd not bothered having that antique boiler serviced for ten years, and that he'd only let the police follow it up in order to substantiate his insurance claim. If the author of the note has the resources to assemble such a giddying compendium of random details, including your Pop's address, how come he doesn't know *that*?'

'We're missing an important bit of detail, too, mate. The author's threatening to send the tape to Toogood, which suggests the cops *don't* have it now.'

'Oh, come off it, it's just Toogood pretending he's somebody else! That way, he gets to keep his distance. I mean, it's technically entrapment, or something decidedly in contravention of PACE, to fire off blackmail notes to suspected criminals, surely?'

'Look, the important thing is to decide what we're gonna do now...or rather, on Friday. I suppose it's obvious which field to go to, but then what do we do?'

'Well, the writer mentioned a place we're supposed to know of, where the cash will keep dry?'

'But what are we gonna do about raising the fifty grand? We can't go empty handed.'

Felix kindled his pipe in the hope of gaining aesthetic relief.

'Well, we're agreed the note's written by Toogood, or one of his sidekicks, yeah? If it is, he won't actually want the money, will he? He's just luring us there, wherever *there* is precisely, so the bastard can nobble us for double murder. Forget the money, mate. I expect we can stretch to a shoebox stuffed with newspaper though.'

'But Felix, surely he doesn't mean there...as in...*there*,

297

where we dropped the body?'

'No...no, he doesn't, Giuseppe – I've got an idea forming. Get your old man out of the garage and into his car – *molto, molto prestissimo!* In fact, take *both* Volvos. I'll meet you on the A53 as soon as I can get there; I've got more to assemble than you two...I'll call you in an hour. Oh, and ring Frankie would you? Get him to meet us there, sharpish.'

'Okay Felix' responded Giuseppe, unaccountably persuaded by Felix's veneer of confidence. 'Oh, by the way, Pop's not in the garage; he's in the attic, looking for his gun.'

The fact was, Dring knew nothing of the two videos that had been couriered to Toogood, nor of the accompanying portentous poetry intended to bolster the case against Paula Day, a woman he'd never even heard of. And he was as unsure of how to proceed as Felix, despite the latter's cavalier sign–off to Giuseppe. But Dring's off the cuff (and entirely spurious) allusion to a videotape in his blackmail note would turn out to be inspired. He now had just forty–eight hours to get his act together and come up with a workable strategy for netting Pirelli at the field. Then he must win over DI Toogood; either that, or he'd lose everything he'd wished for, worked for and sinned for.

Felix was equally aware of the ramifications his team's next move would have. The leadership rôle that the others had been only too happy to confer upon him, in tacit acceptance of their collective ineptitude, bestowed upon him unenviable responsibilities. The pipe of obfuscation thus became the pipe of clarification; here it rested in his cupped hand, a docile, sympathetic servant. As he moved at speed around the boat, collecting together a few essential items, Felix's sharpened senses turned to the detail of Salvatore's cryptic letter. He couldn't help wondering why Salvatore had been Toogood's target – albeit anonymously – rather than Giuseppe, Spencer Day's unwitting killer, or indeed Frankie or himself. Might Salvatore have left careless clues, or else drawn attention to himself by some unguarded Sicilian silliness? Unlikely – for Salvatore hadn't actually been present at the killing, nor for much of its aftermath; he'd joined the party only *after* the action had taken place. And the man's grip on the case was somewhat tenuous anyway; surely he'd been no more dangerous to them than he'd been helpful? He pondered over Salvatore's story of the man whom he'd suspected of stalking him, first at a supermarket and later as he visited a service station toilet. But even if his suspicions were correct, this had occurred *before* he'd become materially involved in the case – in fact, several days in advance of Neil Day's shocking appearance.

LIFE ON MARS? A CATINEL'S CHANCE

As he began loading up his Landrover, a tiny memory capsule dislodged itself from Felix's brain – it snowballed forward, landing abruptly at his tongue to form the words 'buggery! The *canoes*...they've been *there* all the time!' They'd requisitioned the trailer for Wagtail II's homeward run from Hollinsclough, and the act of dragging the canoes into the overgrown foliage abutting the field prior to dumping the body had been so hasty he'd clean forgotten they were there. Surely the police would have removed them for analysis by now? Either way, here must lay the key to Salvatore's detection – a nameplate perhaps, or some other identifying feature. It was a pity Salvatore couldn't recall the mystery Irishman he'd once sailed with though. Still, he now felt certain Toogood had written the letter, a man whom he'd never met, knew virtually nothing about, but was now about to engage with in mortal combat.

Intoxicated by his epiphanic moment Felix smiled quietly to himself and continued packing the vehicle. Another snowball promptly hurtled forward and crashed at his lips. This time he greeted it with somewhat diminished enthusiasm; it stopped him in his tracks.

'Bugger my auntie! The canoes must mark the spot we're meant to deposit the cash...which means they *are* still where we left them...which means the police *didn't* take them...which means...*who the hell else knows about the bloody canoes?*'

The farmer whose land they'd used for aerial fly–tipping Spencer Day's body would hardly have been capable of such dastardly scheming, however pissed off he'd been at having his field carved up by an army of plods–a–plodding.

And the place was hardly on the beaten track for dog walkers or ramblers.

As he paused for breath Felix's eye fell fondly to Wagtail II; her left wing tip rested coyly on the grass to protect her fragile bones from catching a chill. Felix caressed her curvy posterior, buffed up her altimeter and was sure he heard himself mumble 'who's my lovely lady then?'

He knew, in the instant she twitched and cooed with pleasure, that she wanted to play her part in releasing him from his torment. He didn't hesitate in acceding to her request, and set about marrying her to Salvatore's trailer. An hour later, just as he'd finished strapping, bungeeing and manhandling her into position, his phone rang. It was an irate Frankie.

'Okay, so first you snatch away my only chance of a half–decent Tarka Daal all week, and then you keep me waiting by a perishing, godforsaken field that I'd promised myself I'd never clap eyes on again. The Pirelli plonkers are nowhere to be seen either. What's up Felix?...I couldn't get any sense out of Salvatore on the phone earlier. The man's two ciabattas short of a scampagnata basket, if you ask me.'

'All will become clear shortly, my friend. The plonkers should be with you any time soon. Now, while I'm en route you can suss out one or two details for me. I want you to reacquaint me with the local geography and the nature of the terrain, in particular the proximity of the unmarked roads linking the A515 to the A53, coming from all directions, and the height of the adjoining hedgerows nearest to where we made our drop. Time the routes for me would you, point to point?...there's a good rapper.'

Felix had rung off before Frankie's expletives could impact. Quite what he'd do with the statistics Frankie had been commissioned to gather, he wasn't sure, but it was important his quarrelsome quorum sensed his fingers were hovering somewhere near the pulse.

The pulse that had been nagging in Felix's neck left a sickening feeling as he finished shoring up Wagtail I and pulled away hooked up to Wagtail II. His anxieties were well founded. But there was something about a flight in prospect that immediately raised his spirits; he didn't fully understand why he was dragging a microlight up the M6 in the middle of the night when his very liberty was at stake, but he wasn't about to let details ruin the opportunity to get airborne after what had seemed an eternity. Or perhaps he simply craved the consolation of an old ally? But he'd forgotten how difficult it was to drive with a fully rigged delta wing on the roof, tugging an oversized tripod on a trailer built to hold a few fibreglass canoes. He drove solicitously; the last thing he needed was to be nabbed by the police for unlawful aerobatics in a Landrover. He knew the best route now, largely making use of lanes and back roads.

People choose 'B' roads in preference to more direct routes for any number of plausible and less plausible reasons, and carrying a flight–ready microlight on the roof of a Landrover in the thick of night might be considered to be among the more fanciful possibilities. But, as improbable as it may seem, the short stretch of road called the B6105 (but known locally as Panadol Drive as it was such a headache to negotiate, even in broad daylight) some fourteen miles east of Stockport, was concurrently being put to an equally unlikely purpose, a coincidence heightened by what was to become the inexorable fusion of the two parties twenty–four hours later.

The motorcade of grating, lumbering vehicles belonged to the Farkas's, a small family of Rumanians whose business in the country straddled legal boundaries as uncomfortably as the vehicles they used to conveyance the jumbled tools of their trade. Few of these were recognisable from under heavy canvas, stretched beyond its limits in all directions like Cher's lipo–sucked buttocks. But the outline of a cage robust enough to constrain a big cat on heat is as difficult to camouflage as a cheetah's roar is to stifle; even from fifty paces, both clues were unmistakable. The Farkas's had become progressively dispirited, disenfranchised and disaffected, their predicament steadily worsening during the season they'd spent on loan to the Jaberwocky Circus Company, itself a splinter from a rather more illustrious family circus that had for decades lived up to its name, out–Smart–ing its rivals with wilier manoeuvres to counter the inconvenient tide of animal rights activism. For here the trafficking of humans and animals thrives unabated, stage–managed by a handful of portable entertainment outfits, none slipperier than the raft of duplicitous regulatory bodies positioned to sensor such activity. Not that Zoltán, the head of the Farkas family, would have considered himself or his animals victims, or even particularly poorly treated, casualisation no more than an occupational hazard, a pre–eminent feature of his fickle industry. He had learned, like Chimera his usually docile cheetah, to expect food only when it was actually in front of him. His family too had come to terms with a life vacillating between the limelight of the sprawling circus ring and the lime–scale of the tiny bathtub they took everywhere with them. They had settled at their particular spot not for its rustic grandiloquence or proximity to a gastro–pub in neighbouring Glossop, but precisely for its aloofness. However, luck had conspired against them. A farmer's muck–spreading activities in an adjacent field had startled them into quitting the little haven that had been home to them for the past couple of days. They would move southwards, to where Jacob, the eldest son, had at one time sustained a friendship with a fingerless lion tamer nicknamed 'the pianist'.

By the time of Felix's arrival, just after midnight, the small stretch of road off of the B5053 was becoming inordinately cluttered. Frankie's van was parked behind the two Volvos, each with its lights on but emitting no sound. The impulse to be sociable was plainly not as intense as the call for sleep, and Frankie's feet, crossed at the ankles on his steering wheel, summed up his derision. Felix switched off his engine, opened Frankie's passenger door and sat himself down, sweeping to the floor a pile of long spent food debris. While gravity kept his mouth wide open, Frankie's eyes remained steadfastly shut; he made a point of not moving a muscle for thirty seconds, but eventually sniffed, turned his head away from Felix and muttered something incomprehensible. Felix helped himself to a mint humbug and picked up a scrap of paper from the dashboard on which Frankie had scribbled a lot of numbers and letters that conformed to no immediately discernible scheme.

'What's with all the hieroglyphics then, mate?' he snapped, impatiently.

'What you asked for – a bunch of stupid measurements, and much good may they do you, too...the police have probably been fielding calls for the past half an hour from drivers who suspect I'm a blind curb crawler. Fortunately, the only thing on the game round here is ringworm.'

Felix leaned across and flicked the high–beam lever a few times to attract Giuseppe's attention in the nearest of the two Volvos. Here a similar lack of urgency prevailed, but eventually Salvatore sauntered down to them from the Volvo in front of Giuseppe's. His eyes did not meet Felix's, but he calmly took a seat in the back and closed the door quietly, as if conscious of sleeping residents, the closest of which would be a good three miles away in Hollinsclough village. He hadn't seemed to notice that there was half an aeroplane mounted on Felix's roof, and his gaunt gaze was not conducive to small talk. Felix relented first.

'So, Salvatore, you'll have brought the letter with you, yeah?'

'Ah, yesa...the lettera...let me find heem...Here...hee...eesa.'

Salvatore handed over an A5 sheet, folded into quarters, already stained red from the evening meal. Felix read it silently, moving it slowly towards and away from his face as though expecting a three–dimensional image of Hong Kong to appear at some point. Reading the letter for the first time was quite a shock to him; even though he'd been mulling over its contents incessantly for the past few hours, he hadn't expected it to appear quite so clinical on the page. And, not unlike a cryptic crossword, the more he scrutinised it the less clear its meaning became.

'You know guys, I think we learn more from what's *not* included here than what is. I mean, if I were to write such a letter, wishing to instil the fear of god in somebody, I'd be really specific about the details – I'd want the reader to know that *I* know the minutiae of his secrets. I wouldn't ponce about with allusions and barely decipherable references, would you?'

Frankie sighed the sigh of one who had been here before.

'Perhaps he knows Jack Shit...*like us*' he mumbled, still not budging an inch or deigning to open his eyes.

'Yesa, I theenka hee speaka the sheet of the cowa' posited Salvatore thoughtfully, '...I hava *the experienca of thees*, you know?'

Frankie and Felix turned to him in unison.

'Oh, we know all right' mocked Frankie, immediately resuming his pose.

Felix continued.

'It leaves me with the impression he's trying to make a little go a long way. And, assuming my hunch about Toogood is correct, if only he'd waited a further twenty–four hours he'd have had decidedly more to allude to, wouldn't he?'

'Felix, if it was written by the cops, either officially *or* unofficially, wouldn't you expect there to be some kind of police presence here, now?' said Frankie impatiently, '...Don't fret, I'm pretty sure there isn't, 'cos I parked some way off and had a scout around when I got here. The place is deader than a donkey's dildo.'

Two minutes passed while Felix pretended to be absorbing Frankie's inscrutable data, nodding his head periodically to reinforce the impression. Not that Frankie was looking. Salvatore leaned forward meekly, as if about to ask daddy for a sweetie.

'Why ara wee heera?'

There was a pause, during which Felix drew an exaggerated breath in preparation for a long and lengthy expostulation. But, halting himself, he released it in a single gust.

'Sorry?'

'Whata we do, heera?'

'Well, I'd have thought your letter makes it perfectly clear, Salvatore – we're supposed to deposit a box full of cash in one of the canoes, which are here, where we, er, carefully placed them for safe keeping, not far away, in the

307

bushes.'

'I know *thees* – Giuseppe, hee tolda me already...you *forgotted* thema, heera.'

'...So, what's your question?'

'I no aska why ara wee *heera*? I aska, *why* ara wee heera?'

There was a more prolonged hiatus, during which Felix snatched two shallow breaths. Frankie headed him off.

'He's right, you know!...our silly–arsed, silicon– headed Sicilian...*is right.*' Frankie held out his hand for Salvatore to shake it; Salvatore tentatively obliged, bewildered, and accepted his reward of a humbug, while Frankie got into his stride.

'Look, you don't mean to tell me we went to all that trouble to rig up a fake videotape, coughing our guts up in a burnt out cellar crawling with feral furries, *then* delivered the sodding thing to the cop in charge of nailing the culprit...only to *then* risk incarceration getting it back again! We *want* Toogood to have the tape, don't we?'

'Ah, well, we *do*, but surely we also want to know who the hell is on our case here, don't we? Look, whoever it is seems to think we've incriminated ourselves in the tape, or in other words, we achieve the opposite of what we set out to do.'

Frankie fixed a sarcastic snarl.

'Exactly, which means he or she has seen just how farcical our tape really is!' he bellowed.

'But if he or she is so sure the tape is a fake, then, ipso bleedin' facto, they must think they know who really *did* kill Spencer Day!...and if that's *us*, then, as I said, why don't they just sodding well say so, in the letter?'

Having partly wriggled free from the bobbin of bastardised Cartesian logic he'd tied himself up in, Felix slumped in his seat and began flicking the gear stick.

'Okay Bubba' demanded Frankie who'd begun beating out a tiresome compound cross–rhythm on the windscreen, 'but Salvatore's question remains valid – what the buggering bungee–jumpers are we hoping to achieve here?…'cos I reckon we stand to lose more than gain.'

'If this guy's pissing in the wind, let's catch the pillock with his pants down and his tool out of its box' responded Felix pugnaciously.

Despite Felix's eagerness to begin rehearsing their moves for the following evening, the team mutinied and resolved to rest overnight. Little more would be achieved at this late hour; Giuseppe had been comatose since the moment they'd arrived, Salvatore's meagre capacities had ebbed to a dull stupor and Frankie was becoming more diffident by the second. But there would be no sleep for Felix, yet; for the waters of paternal pressure channelled deep into his consciousness. He hadn't noticed that the two biggest clowns in this chaotic circus, Giuseppe and Frankie, had collapsed into their sleepy holes quickest of all. He was too busy visualising, revising, fantasising. But slowly, frenzied thoughts gave way to sleep, gave way to utter stillness.

A brilliant coruscation upstaged his slumber. A lambent moon the size of a wok appeared to teeter precariously on the bonnet of his Landrover; it quickly sautéed the few lacklustre clouds that limped past it, as if with its hands in its pockets. The others hadn't seen it sharpen into focus during the last thirty minutes, but there again, they'd have missed the landing of a strobe–lit space ship, so lost were they in their selfish sleep. Felix shuddered, yawned, rose like a grizzly bear and walked. He needed some air, some distance from the stagnant, petrol– contaminated ambience of his ancient vehicle. Its spontaneous creeks and groans suggested it too was experiencing difficulty resting out there in the oppressive haze. A cursory torch–lit reconnaissance confirmed to him that his choice of site for dumping Spencer Day's body, an episode that had begun to melt into misty memory despite occurring only days previously, had been highly appropriate. For they could scarcely have found a more soulless place, one less mauled by the fingers of humanity. The terrain resisted any impulse to manicure it; its spirit remained cruel and impregnable, shaking off their impudent invasion without turning a hair of its shaggy landscape. He located the canoes quickly enough, still languishing where they'd ditched them, under the thick clump of trees invisible from the roadside. And in the dim light there seemed nothing to indicate they'd been tinkered with.

By 7:00 AM the air traffic was sufficient to prod even the heaviest sleeper into life. It mainly consisted of fixed and flexi–winged microlights making the most of a crisp, icy clear sky, whiter and thinner than was conceivable given the recalcitrant fog of two hours earlier. But he'd become concerned that their four vehicles – his own sheltering beneath Wagtail II's sprawling magnificence – might be spotted and reported back to Mervyn at the aerodrome, which lay just a few miles away to the north. He rapped uncharitably on the windscreens and received a retaliation rude enough to offend the dozen sparrows that had arranged themselves in an improbably neat line along a nearby branch. They must leave, right now; no time to debate the best route. Two minutes later the convoy choked its way from the roadside, which, reassuringly, had brought only one lorry and a motorcycle past them all night. Felix soon pulled over and took his time lodging the Landrover, complete with fully–rigged microlight, in the entrance to a large field; the whole area was overgrown and unlikely to attract unwanted interest. Removing a tarpaulin from the back seat he made a fist of covering up part of the wing, jumped into Giuseppe's car and the convoy continued forward. Despite the vexed chill in the air, long threads of sweat had built on both foreheads, as much a barometer of their perilously low caffeine levels as of any pedestrian instincts for self–preservation. The two greeted each other with a nod but not a sound, and twenty minutes later the outstanding coffee issue finally showed signs of a resolution.

They'd arrived at Stoke–On–Trent just as the place was reluctantly coming to life. The others parked up behind Giuseppe and Felix, obscuring the double yellow lines that ran like a seam, the full length of the road. They alighted, stretching and contorting their aching bodies like monkey trees while emitting strange, strangulated sound effects, imitated commendably by three passing teenagers. The ubiquitous Starbucks, groaning under the weight of hardening cholesterol, beckoned them from across the street, its green and white logo strategically positioned to overwhelm Ann Summers and completely obliterate Timpsons. Felix paused momentarily at the window of the cobblers to adjust the few remaining hairs on his head, just so that he could appear consistent when dallying in front of the cherry–lined lingerie paraded by headless, ambivalent plastic females next door. They sidled into Starbucks and deftly requisitioned the few remaining padded seats, while Giuseppe proceeded to make a hash of ordering. A tall youth, sleeping loudly nearby and patently oblivious of the temperature outside, was wearing yellow shorts and a T–shirt. His head was bent back over his chair at an angle of almost 90° and a motionless strand of saliva dangled from his chin, shining like silver. His T–shirt read: 'This is what cool looks like'. The first consignment of drinks and snacks arrived at their table in due course and were attacked with Neanderthal zeal.

'We're parked illegally, you know' observed Frankie, anticipating something other than the look of indifference that had settled over Felix's face.

'You reckon?' asked Giuseppe, fending off an assault from a strong–willed Frappacino lid.

'Yeah, well, that's what my barista told me' he continued.

'I didn't realise *he* was here' humoured Felix '...murdered anyone lately?'

Salvatore hadn't expected enlightenment, but Felix took pity.

'The waiters here are known as *baristas*...a misnomer to camouflage a general paucity of GCSEs and a disturbingly incipient fetish for rat poison. To his credit, our man did spot a member of the yellow–rimmed Gestapo skulking behind a butcher's van, brandishing his portable cash register.'

Salvatore looked none the wiser for Felix's elucidation.

'Pop nearly needed a barrister recently, didn't you!' teased Giuseppe, denuding his nose of whipped cream. 'A case of, eh hem, mistaken identity shall we say, on one of his last cases, eh Pop?'

Salvatore declined to answer on the grounds he might incriminate himself. But Giuseppe couldn't resist regaling the saga of the louche plumber permanently on heat whose wife had decided against tightening up his stopcock with a torque wrench in favour of employing a PI to dig the dirt.

'Now, about tonight, guys' interjected Felix, steering the conversation towards more pressing matters. 'There's something important we need to agree on. And that's whether the author of the letter is expecting us to show up today, or tomorrow.'

He confiscated Salvatore's crumpled letter and read it out, slowing for emphasis at the last sentences:

…The tape will be in the same place twenty–four hours later. Friday at 9 pm. Not before. Not after.

'My point is, is he saying that Friday's the day for the cash to be delivered, or that Friday's when he'll exchange the 50k for the videotape?'

Frankie looked noncommittal and Salvatore remained nonplussed.

'...I reckon it means Friday for the cash...Saturday for the tape' responded Giuseppe eventually.

'But if it turns out to be *tonight* for the dosh, we'll have missed the chance to nab our man!' insisted Felix, '...let's assume tonight's the night, and if it's not, it can be a dress rehearsal.'

'And just what is there to rehearse anyway, Felix?' sighed Frankie, preparing himself for a plan landing somewhere between ardent naivety and crass lunacy.

'Love Walked In' ambled inoffensively in the background, over which Frankie had begun pounding out an astonishingly incongruous rhythm on four empty cups, perverting the tune irreconcilably for the old couple on the adjacent table.

'Is *any* melody sacred to you, Frankie, or is everything fair game?'

Frankie shrugged his shoulders, executed a demonic 'fill' and promptly brought his impromptu drum kit tumbling onto the laps of his irreverent audience.

'As I was saying' attempted Felix above the trouser–mopping expletives, 'we all need to know our rôles, or this thing will go tits up, a bit like your Cozy Powell impersonation, mate.'

Felix began assembling props from Frankie's carnage and set out his war campaign.

'Now, these two coasters represent the Volvos; I'll position them one hundred yards from the ends of the two piddly access routes to the field south of the river and north of Longnor, which, according to Frankie's detailed calculations ought to be about point six of a mile. Over on the other side, this espresso cup represents Frankie's van. I'll put it...here...for now, but actually it'll be in constant transit, surveying the circuit linking the A53 to the B5053, a journey that, as Frankie knows all too well, should take him around twelve minutes with a heavy foot, or fifteen if he keeps the dial below five thousand revs...Finally, this half eaten muffin can be me...'

'Figures...' mumbled Frankie, 'and where are you going to be, Mr. Muffin–Man, Abergavenny?'

'I wish. No, I'll be sat in Wagtail II on the old south–west apron of the aerodrome – I need a direct flight path to the field...there'll be no time to do any circuiting once you've scrambled me. I'll just have to beat it.'

'And just what the buggery will you be doing up there that's so vitally important?' demanded Frankie, determined to piss on Felix's fireworks.

'Only Felix could contrive an excuse to bring his flying hours up to date while the rest of us dance with death' explained Giuseppe sardonically, as if explanations were necessary following the team's already impressive lexicon of disasters.

'I'll be doing the aerial equivalent of Frankie's job actually, maintaining continuous reconnaissance of the routes that could become congested as you make your exit...and monitoring any on–going police activities. At least there's only one approach road to worry about.'

Felix paused and slid his soapbox into position.

'Let's assume for a moment that the letter *is* the

work of the police. Now, Toogood's men will be expecting Salvatore to turn up alone, or perhaps with a minder or two, but they'll hardly be prepared for our mob–handed assault. We'll smell the bastards coming from miles away.'

'Okay, but what if our man *isn't* a cop, but some opportunist twat hoping to pay off his time–share in the Canaries? We won't find *him* as easy to keep track of, will we?' protested Giuseppe.

Before Felix could retaliate Salvatore had stirred himself, tentatively leaning forward but meeting nobody's eyes.

'And...whata eef our mana, she eesa the *womana*?' he whispered melodramatically.

A pained expression settled on their faces.

'How abouta eefa the lettera eesa from *Paula*?' he persisted, still unable to win a glimmer of comprehension. 'Paula hasa the motiva! She hasa the will of the cunninga, cruela, *bastardetta*...no?'

'How on earth could she have intercepted our videotape?' snapped Felix, restraining the impulse to submerge Salvatore's head in an ice cold Mocha that had just been deposited in the middle of his war campaign by Frankie's new barista buddy, Darol.

'Who's for the intravenous espresso trip–shot?' enquired the Mohicaned thirty year–old, pretending not to be ear–wigging the conversation.

'It's not such a silly point, is it?' defended Giuseppe. 'I mean, we still don't fully understand Paula's reasons for making her video diary, do we?...She could conceivably have struck a deal of some kind with the police...'

316

Felix shook his head disparagingly.

'Nice try, but no cigar. Paula's not our woman...*or* our man.'

He began sucking up the beige bilge with a double–barrelled straw, his eyes darting in pursuit of acknowledgement.

'Now, if a single vehicle, marked or unmarked, moves in our direction, one of us will spot it and we can take appropriate action.'

'Like castration or beheading, you mean?' growled Giuseppe, 'or a petrol bomb?'

'Like forcing him to spill the beans, so we can make sure our next move hits the spot' said Felix.

'Cutting the bastard's tongue out hits the spot for me' ventured Frankie, simultaneously miming his order of a double caramel latte to Darol.

'We'll keep in continuous contact...in fact, we should sort out mobile phone conferencing; that way, we can fine–tune our approach. I think we ought to aim at moving our tanks up to the war zone for twenty–hundred hours...we want to mimic the level of darkness we'll encounter tomorrow, assuming we survive that long.'

A minute's silence was observed to mull over Felix's scary plan. Worryingly, he'd meant every word of it. Finally, Salvatore dared to speak.

'...And...how abouta...*me*?'

'Ah, good point, Salvatore...you're doing the drop, naturally' Felix smiled.

Salvatore seemed to understand that part quite quickly.

'You'll be in position in the hedgerow, as close as you dare to the canoes. With your gun.'

'Hang on a minute, Felix, we never said anything about shooting the bastard!' yelled Giuseppe.

'Don't panic, mate, the gun's for firing off flares...I've brought some with me...I knew they'd come in handy one day – you'd be amazed at some of the epic balls ups people make dealing with canal locks. Assuming I'm right about tonight being a run through, Salvatore will fire off a single flare when he hears me pass overhead for the first time, just in case the signal drops on our phones. This is to indicate all is as it should be; I'll then proceed to my second lap. If, for some unholy reason there are major problems, like we're under siege by the SAS, Salvatore will let off two flares.'

'Yeah, right' scoffed Frankie, '*you* fly off home in time to catch the "I Claudius" re–run, while *we* get pepper–potted by a squad of marksmen amid Salvatore's pathetic firework display. Smart plan!'

'Arguably, guys, *I've* got the riskiest job. Microlights aren't allowed to fly at night, and for very good reason...they don't have lights. Nor do they possess radar or satellite navigation devices to direct them; they fly what's called VFR: visual flight rules. I've got to take off and land in pitch darkness, and fly close enough to see where the hell I am...which is low enough to be popped off by one of your bleedin' marksmen, that's for sure. *You* fly and I'll sit in the van, if you prefer!'

Later that afternoon, as the convoy shambled north in the direction of Buxton, Felix chose his moment to turn to Giuseppe, fixing a somewhat strained expression.

'I didn't want to mention it to the others this morning, but, well, there's something that ought to be said.'

Giuseppe looked suitably dejected.

'It's just that there's the smallest chance we'll get nobbled by the cops tonight, or tomorrow. And if we do, we'll need to be able to demonstrate that we didn't play any part in Neil Day's death, even if we did cack–handedly deep–fry his brother. We should be prepared to hand over everything: Paula's camcorder, her original videotape…oh, and even the cassette we used to fake the sound on our first videotape. Now, the thing is mate, I've looked everywhere for that damned tape…it's, um, disappeared!'

Giuseppe shrugged his shoulders, 'I don't suppose it's still up at the Cobra, sat in uncle Toni's crappy old tape recorder, is it?'

'Suffering succotash…if it is, we need to get it off him in time for tonight's showdown.'

LIFE ON MARS? A CATINEL'S CHANCE

By 7:30 that evening Felix had moved Wagtail II into something like optimum position on the outskirts of the airfield. Frankie had already performed the first patrol lap in his van, and the two Volvos were in position, half a mile apart on the roadside with their sidelights on. Salvatore was pretending to be scouring a map, while a further half a mile away his son distracted himself with two crumpled pages from yesterday's Telegraph. They'd spent the afternoon honing telephonic procedures, each member of the team refining his moves and memorising everyone else's. The cassette tape's location had been quickly confirmed and was on its way down to Giuseppe, care of one of Toni's minions. Everything conceivable had been conceived of, everything discussable discussed, everything frettable over fretted over. Felix's pre–flight checks had been affected with uncustomary diligence and the plane had been fuelled to overspill. He sank into the pod of his machine, allowing his mind to lapse into a near meditative state. He must take his rest now, for he instinctively knew that if disposing of Spencer Day's body had been a struggle, the task in hand would stir up a crucible of hazards.

It had been over a week since his last aeronautical skirmish; his recollection of it was strangely positive, given the subtext – for despite Frankie's uncooperative whinges they'd succeeded in pulling off a trick not to be tackled by the faint–hearted, lily–livered or level–headed. But night flying was an altogether different proposition. At least on this occasion he'd be flying solo, not three–up with a fusty cadaver dribbling treacly mucous down his neck. He pull–chorded the engine, which gleefully struck up its comforting

320

refrain. The controls felt uncommonly alive and responsive and the wing stretched out optimistically overhead, painting its imposing silhouette across the pockmarked tarmac in front of him. The light had already faded to a point where the surrounding fields had become entirely drenched in an oppressive cobalt shadow. Felix searched in vain for a moon as his imagination set in motion the first tentative fragments of his imminent death–defying sortie, Wagner's Flight of the Valkyries further macerating his withering sensibilities. Earlier that afternoon he'd rigged up a cradle for his mobile phone so he could keep an eye on the fluctuating signal strength; he'd be operating at an insanely low altitude – between two and five hundred feet. He dialled up Giuseppe and tuned into the banal chitchat bouncing between the two Pirelli vehicles, a conversation employing a bewildering bastardisation of etymologies comprehended by them alone.

Suddenly Salvatore seemed more alert, cutting curtly into Giuseppe's nervous rambling. He'd spotted something. A large vehicle had been creeping along the road with its lights on full beam, plainly in search of something, or someone, but it wasn't until the thing was upon him that he'd recognise who was driving.

'Aha!' he sparked at last, 'I theenka...eet eesa my olda frienda...yesa...*eet's Tommya*!'

The two men greeted each other as if the reunion followed a lapse of twenty years, not twenty hours. For Salvatore, embracing an old friend to within an inch of his life came as naturally as breathing, and yet his brother's recent party had been somewhat slim on opportunities, his attempts at conversation with Tommy diffused by the prevailing drunken haze. Tommy addressed his old canoe instructor with touching reverence.

'I can't think why you're so desperate to have this tape, Mr. Pirelli...I trust you've not recorded anything saucy with me and Shirley on it!'

Salvatore cackled nervously.

As Felix eavesdropped on the inconsequential twaddle, the clarity of which was severely impaired by the distance they'd been standing from the driver's door, an intangible thought began to solidify. He'd been considering Salvatore's anonymous letter, its peculiar combination of the highly specific and wilfully vague. An idea came upon him in a blaze of unbridled brilliance. He blurted into the mouthpiece, desperate to attract Salvatore's attention.

'Salvatore...*Salvatore*! If you can hear me...Tommy's our man, our Paddy Paddler! Ask him if he's got any Irish rel...'

The signal plummeted, just as an important piece of the jigsaw was about to lock into place. But luckily Giuseppe had speedily pieced together Felix's desiccated brainstorm.

'Pop...*Pop...listen!*' he blurted into the mouthpiece.

But Salvatore's effervescence would thwart his attempts, too. Giuseppe swiftly exited the Volvo and trotted towards his father's car. He arrived a few minutes later, breathless and effusive.

'Tommy! How odd to...to...see you again, so soon...mate.'

'Yeah, likewise. Toni offered me the choice of

scrubbing down the forecourt or doing a mission of mercy for Mr. Pirelli...I hadn't realised *you'd* be here, too. God, Toni's Shogun's got SatNav 'n shit, but it was still a bugger to find you guys out here! Why did we have to meet in such an awful place...it's all a bit cloak and dagger, isn't it?'

'Well...actually' said Giuseppe, still catching his breath, '...in a funny kinda way, the reason we're all here is...*because* of you...You see, Tommy, we're in a spot of bother, as it happens.'

It took considerably less time to bring Tommy up to speed than it had done to reappraise his father for the umpteenth time. Felix, feeling somewhat isolated sat at the aerodrome in his gurgling microlight, temporarily robbed of a telephone signal, could only speculate the level of drivel that was being exchanged. But he instinctively knew he was right about Tommy: his surname and canoeing background fitted perfectly, even though the guy had probably never even set foot near the Emerald Isle, or would know a Leprechaun from a Cornish leper. Luckily, winning over Tommy's cooperation proved as easy as falling out of a low flying microlight; the teenage firebrand jumped at the chance of an adventure with his two favourite Sicilian misfits. It wasn't until Tommy was safely in position, crouching in the hedgerow alongside his canoe–guru, Salvatore, white–knuckling his antediluvian rifle, that it occurred to him he might ask how his name had been implicated in the first place.

'Mm, eet eesa very stranga, my frienda...buta, I theenka eet eesa my photographa alboom...don't tella the boysa...but I just noteece, hee is...*gonna*.'

The time was nudging 8:00 when Felix finally re–established a mobile hook–up with the others. He was anxious to get going; the engine had been fizzing behind him for half an hour, yet he daren't turn it off in case it refused to start again. It felt like countdown to meltdown. He continued to listen in on the idle tittle–tattle taking place between the three water–bores – Giuseppe, sat in his new position in the second Volvo, and Salvatore and Tommy, squatting in the hedge, not far away.

PC Dring had the squits. This rendered riding his motorcycle inadvisable, and occasionally, messy. Even when driving in a straight line he was obliged to shift his weight constantly from one buttock to the other in order to sustain his colonic tourniquet in a delicate state of equilibrium. He was prone to these unannounced attacks of encopresis, although he knew exactly what had brought on this particularly petulant buttock–clencher: a saag paneer, care of his local curry house, the Rampant Raj; the cheese had been strangely unruly under the tongue while the spinach had exhibited peculiar seaweed–like tendencies. He could still taste it now, a full twenty–four hours after its imprudent consumption. At least the discomfort served to distract him from the calamity he was heading for. He'd travelled light – a pair of powerful collapsible binoculars, a posh torch and his mobile phone on which he'd taken the trouble to confirm he'd entered the mobile numbers of DI Toogood and DS Chanter. A roll of toilet paper was never far from reach; there didn't seem much call for anything else, not this evening anyway. Tomorrow, when things were far more likely to kick off, he'd be fully kitted out.

By 7:00 he'd arrived at the point he'd previously selected to stash his bike, by a fulvous metal gate a couple of minutes walk from the long hedge that encased about one third of the entire field. He'd have to roost for an hour, maybe longer, a good distance away from the roadside from where the canoes lay redundant, directing his torch in their general direction at regular intervals. He could be confident that any movement would betray Pirelli's own reconnaissance – surely no soul would come near this godforsaken place for lesser incentive than to head off a twenty–year stretch in Derbyshire's hotel for bad boys. He'd not detected any furtive rustlings, so distracted had he become by his bilious bowel.

LIFE ON MARS? A CATINEL'S CHANCE

Felix received the go ahead from Giuseppe at 8:14. By 8:19 he'd bumped his way cautiously around the apron – a small patch of tarmac normally given over to aircraft waiting in the queue for a departure window – not in itself considered sufficient space to execute a take–off. Especially at night. And Felix wasn't merely throwing caution to the wind, he was flinging himself manfully at it, hurling his flimsy plane into a vast galactic pit while wholly dependent upon broken flecks of stellar illumination for guidance; the constellation of Orion seemed to throb anaemically above him like defective fairy lights. He'd taken care of his aeronautical map, velcroed to his knee, with the main landmarks of the vicinity still marked up from his previous sorties. Not that he could expect to see anything but the vaguest outlines of hazardous landmarks as he rode roughshod across the skyline. He sat observing the oddly jerking windsock and pondered the wind strength up there.

But weather is imponderable. Paradoxically, he mused, it's always nice weather when you're sufficiently higher than the clouds. Even the grimmest day in Wolverhampton metamorphoses miraculously in seconds when you're in a jumbo jet leaving the first few thousand feet of space behind you. Microlight pilots are aware of this in a purely theoretical sense, since their insubstantial machines would self–destruct much higher than about four thousand feet, and in any case, by this point either the pilot's nose would have morphed into a phallic ice lolly or he'd have collided with half a dozen military aircraft. Cloud–base has a habit of not having a habit – at least in terms of its precise point above sea level, which is fine if you're in a helicopter and not relying on sight alone for orientation. Local weather patterns are alarmingly fickle, too; rain descending on one side of a street in Coventry can leave the other completely arid. Felix knew he'd have his work cut out in these conditions; Unnervin' Mervyn would himself have been unnerved at such a prospect – and *he* could assimilate the terrain upside down.

A diagonal sliver of rain was firming up away to the west and a crop of maverick clouds was flexing its muscles straight ahead. The ground was dry, yet his wings smelt damp from the journey up. Despite the crisper air, the heat pumping into his back from the exuberant two–stroke engine was making his helmet itch furiously. Felix hurled two words into the phone strapped to the cockpit and left this earth for another place, a wraithlike hinterland too high for all but the bravest window cleaner and too low for even the most hell–bent base–jumper. The air tasted bitter as Felix pulled the bar into his chest; he was surprised at the lack of resistance it offered. Within fifteen seconds he was incarcerated in a plume of sallow cloud, jetting its spiteful potions into his eyes as he blinked madly and struggled to hold a course at three hundred feet. The rocky terrain appeared as a subtle batik beneath him, with the road he recognised as the B5053 dozing like a replete tapeworm along the broad belly of Chrome hill. Alongside it, washed in heavy shadow, nuzzled the inconsequential farming town of Hollinsclough. No sooner he'd escaped the cloud's clutches he was dry again, stressed but still in possession of a little courage.

While Salvatore and Tommy nattered nervously in the designated shrubbery, Dring, only a few hundred feet away in the hedge opposite, nursed his volatile stomach. His semi seating position increased the downward force on his already flimsy bowel, which periodically gave up the struggle to hold back the tide of thin brown mucilage that churned horribly, deep in his gut. For, like Felix, he had more than a sneaking suspicion he was well and truly in the shit already. His vantage point was perfect from every respect other than the fact that he couldn't see a damned thing. While his torch might have served adequately from one end of a domestic garage to the other, out here its rays barely wandered as far as he could flick a rolled up bogey. He felt drained. Staring upwards at the low–wattage stars pulsating behind castellated clouds, he contemplated for the first time how this self–induced wretchedness might unfurl.

Salvatore couldn't make himself comfortable either. He was beginning to make Tommy twitchy as the pair fidgeted and fumbled about in the bedraggled greenery, retrieving twigs from their backsides and foliage from their ears. Nor was Salvatore showing much flair for the flares he'd been entrusted with; for they resembled fireworks in all respects except those they didn't. And his experience with the ugly blunderbuss he was grasping was limited to four errant shots discharged in 1986, while out shooting rabbit with his brothers Angelo and Toni. There would be no rabbit stew on that occasion, but only a fool would discount the possibility tonight.

The pair began to detect the buzz of a far off plane. Salvatore's neck stiffened a little. The plan was underway. He knew exactly what he must do: carefully he extricated himself from the bush and began to crawl furtively along the sodden grass on his elbows and knees, heading for the centre of the field. Felix was still a little way off, maybe half a mile or more, although the peculiar acoustics of the hillocky terrain made it difficult to detect the sound source, and he knew not to expect any light from the crappy little craft. Panting uncontrollably, he lay flat on his back, for in this position he felt he'd maximise the efficacy of his dispatch. There were stars up there, but they weren't shining for his benefit, just winking knowingly at each other as if sharing some pantheist in–joke. The cautious cosmographer rolled his head in a slow, smooth arc to check all was as dead as it had been, and fired his weapon directly at the moon, wincing as if it were about to fall onto his head. It issued the flare as effectively as if designed for the purpose; the amber quill etched its florid signature onto the dark canvas for ten seconds, branded for a further thirty behind his eyelids.

But Felix was still nowhere to be seen as he ran

329

amok along the uneven terrain of clouds that wept as he sliced through them at a face–contorting fifty MPH. He'd spotted the flare as it skipped gaily past him to meet the end of its short life somewhere betwixt twill and twilight. He smiled briefly and initiated a miniscule weight–shift to his left, the commencement of a circuit that would take several minutes to perform.

Dring might have reacted quicker had he not at precisely the same moment been scorching the turf with his own demonic moniker. The soiled soil at his feet reeked like a silage farm. It could have been lightning that he'd glimpsed as he crouched inelegantly with one arm clasping at a spindly branch. And there was more movement to be noticed if only he could free himself from more pressing lavatorial concerns – for Salvatore was still scuffling his way back to Tommy, whose earnest owl hoots he hadn't yet realised were for his orientation. From Dring's perspective the ground had merely quivered momentarily, as if in resonance with his latest turbocharged discharge, the diffused torchlight exaggerating the impression. But then, as he mauled at his crumpled toilet roll he saw something move – a human leg extended upwards from the ground. The foot was booted and definitely belonged to a male; presumably the other limb was somewhere close by, too. With one hand wrestling to re–engage his collapsed trousers he lost no time in reaching for his mobile phone. It rang three times before triggering an abrupt voicemail massage:

'I'm not talking to you, because I'm not here, and that's why it would make more sense to be speaking with someone who is.'

Detective Inspector Toogood's dysfunctional message proceeded to pass the buck to DS Chanter's mobile number, the one already in his possession. He rang it and when Chanter answered after a single ring, Dring stammered hopelessly. The call had interrupted the early stages of a ten–pin bowling session, as was evident from the yelps and noises–off from adjoining rinks.

'Dring...what on earth do *you* want...can't a chap swing his balls about of an evening without being hassled by the law?'

'Sor...sorry Serg, I need you to help me close the Spencer Day case...that's all' Dring replied, failing pitifully to come across as laidback. Naturally, Chanter was taking no prisoners, particularly since his entourage were already baying for a straightforward execution.

'I've heard of chicken soup for the soul, but what's this...chicken shit for the roses? Okay, so what will you be requiring, Dring' he shouted, playing to whatever crowd he imagined was still interested, 'mounted police proficient in the medieval sport of jousting...or perhaps you'd prefer a few helicopters?'

'One should do it, Serg...helicopter, that is, not jouster.'

Whatever it was Chanter blurted to his audience solicited laughter raucous enough to nearly dislodge Dring's

331

earpiece, not to mention his sphincter.

'Serg, I'm serious...look, I'm here now, at the scene of the crime.'

Chanter stemmed his sarcasm a little and indulged the man for a second. Dring changed tack too, instantaneously recognising the need to win over his surrogate boss's enthusiasm without irretrievably aligning himself to some loose–knotted story. He couldn't possibly have anticipated how his next sentence would alter the course of events.

'I received a call two days ago' he heard himself begin, using a mealy–mouthed tone, 'from a woman called Andrea Watkiss...she's a psychic, Serg...she claims to have had a vision concerning the dead man, and that other lives are in danger, *here...today*!..I didn't think it would interest Detective Inspector Toogood, so I went ahead and cased the joint myself. Serg, I wouldn't want you to think I'm...'

'Never mind all that, what's happened, Dring?...Tell me, man!'

Chanter had already exited the bowling rink and was heading hurriedly for the car park.

'Well, funnily enough, Watkiss reckoned the thing that galvanised it, her vision I mean, was...*an old canoe*, Serg.'

As he hurtled towards the first roundabout, still connected to Dring, Chanter began to dredge up two random and unrelated fragments from his alcohol–tainted memory. One involved the bizarre discovery of canoes at the field near to where Day's cremated cadaver had been dumped. The other stemmed from a recent television programme, which had documented a psychic's impressive assistance in a stagnant murder case. The two thoughts instantaneously fused together to form a powerfully compelling lead. The trouble was, PC Dring seemed in imminent danger of scooping the honours.

'Now, this Watkiss bird, Dring, I don't suppose she mentioned anything about...about *lightning strikes*...did she?'

'Well, no, Serg' answered Dring, but sensing a potential angle of attack, continued, 'strangely enough though, Serg, I think I've just witnessed a freak lightning strike, right above where I'm standing now – and there's no sign of a storm...weird...just a man's leg, sticking out of the ground, and...'

For Chanter the centrepiece of the puzzle had been tucked into place. Lightning, canoes – it all made perfect sense. His final utterance would have profound laxative properties for Dring.

'Right, stay put, I'll have a 'copter out there in ten. Don't get all heroic...that's my job.'

The line went dead.

Giuseppe was becoming restless. He'd witnessed his father's miniature comet pirouette overhead and thought he'd heard Wagtail II's approach, but had observed no air traffic from his position in the driver's seat. The phone link with Felix had long since withered and he wasn't sure whether he ought to have gone back to the car he'd left unmanned and unlocked half a mile away. Reluctantly he alighted the vehicle and dawdled down the road in the direction of the other, eyes turned to the skies in anticipation of Felix's second lap.

But Felix was irrecoverably lost. Not only that, his fate lay at the whim of each successively damaging deluge. The rain he'd been experiencing hadn't yet reached the others, but for him it had become unbearable as he bolted in and out of the clotting clouds. He mustn't land, not just yet, even though he'd received Salvatore's go–ahead; if he took a slight detour he might manage to escape a fatal drenching. He glanced at his current bearing and veered twenty degrees east, cranked open the throttle and gritted his teeth.

Chanter's head was on fire. He dialled Toogood's number and reached the same cynical recorded message as Dring had done. But he'd need the highest level of authority, with a fair amount of spin on the story, to send a police helicopter into the heavens. He'd have to ring the Chief Super in person – if it all went thumbs up he'd be in clover, but if it went tits up, he'd make certain Dring copped a fast track to Pizza Express. The Station routed his call after a few minutes, shortly after which CS Flemming, himself attending a less than salubrious function involving the random tossing about of large balls in a confined space, arrived at a judgment not dissimilar to that of his DS: if Chanter had opened a hideous tin of worms, he'd be left carrying the can for his poxy career. Besides, one of his PCs had 'gone commando', and the last thing this madcap case needed was a graphically epic balls–up in that confounded field. If Chanter was right, there'd be no time to organise anything on the ground – he could have his chopper, but he'd better take care it didn't shave him too close, or his smooth finish might just end in a bloodbath.

Salvatore and Tommy caught their breath back in the Volvo, hardly registering that Giuseppe had sloped off. The trampled grass, smelling strangely of lapsang souchong, pumped out from Salvatore's sweatshirt and the million silvery slug tracks on his jeans glistened under the courtesy light. Tommy lit a cigarette and used it as an excuse to wind down the window a fraction. The mobile on the dashboard rang hesitantly and flashed up Felix's name. Tommy snatched it, since it was clear Salvatore was not up to discussing the finer points of airborne reconnaissance with a besieged megalomaniac sat six inches away from a bleating lawnmower engine. But Felix's hectoring would smother Tommy's chance of a decorous greeting.

'Salvatore! Salvatore you Latin cretin!...I'm not landing yet 'cos the rain's too fierce. If you can hear me, I'll be around again in a few minutes...fire off another flare if it's still okay...'

The line crackled to nothing again.

The conspicuous non–appearance of heavy rain at ground zero made it hard for the others to grasp Felix's tone of anxiety, but Salvatore did as he was bid and recharged his rustic rifle with one of the three remaining flares. He sat upright in the passenger seat, uncommonly edgy and sharp–eared, as if about to lead the 'big push' from a bombarded trench. But after a further ten minutes jittering, with no sign of the portentous pilot, Salvatore mustered a rare crumb of initiative. Cautiously he made his way back to the gap in the hedge, Tommy obediently on tow, and resumed the position, his gun threatening the firmament with another feeble firework display. Clearly the moon had survived his last assault; it sneered at him with renewed contempt – for the rain that Felix had warned of had arrived, suddenly and assuredly.

◉

THE WRONG DAY–VIEW FOR A RENDEZVOUS

An engine noise unexpectedly broke the excruciating hiatus – but it was a good deal gutsier than they'd been expecting. It sounded more like a migrating flock of Wagtail IIs, not one meagre specimen. In fact, the volume level was so high it was impossible to detect where it was coming from, let alone what was causing it. Two angst–ridden faces peeked cautiously from the hedge and saw a red light winking beneath the craft like a bloodshot iguana; the entire field began to glow as if simmering above a low heat and the trees started to quake at their upper branches, unsure of what had broken their sleep.

Dring knew immediately from which planet the alien craft hailed, although he too couldn't be sure of its precise trajectory as the vegetation swayed frantically all about him. As if in resonance his phone buzzed, but Chanter had begun bellowing into his ear before he'd cued up an appropriate rebuke.

'The 'copter should be overhead now, Dring, and we've got squad cars in transit – they'll fork off into two directions, to cover the exits, but I doubt they'll arrive for a little while yet.'

'So, what should I do now, Serg…fork off myself?' Dring screamed, barely making himself heard above the manic commotion, 'I've only got my Honda here and it's

337

not so quick off the mark.'

A new optimism coloured Chanter's tone.

'There must be at least one other vehicle there for fuck sake…get after it! Get on yer bike and ride, man, like the *wind*.'

At the very thought, Dring's bowels suffered a sudden catastrophic downdraught, the resultant racket competing commendably with the helicopter.

'What the shit was that, Dring? I only ordered *one* 'copter.'

'A touch of dribble–bum, er, gastroenteritis, Serg…could be a dodgy lime pickle. I'll do my best, but…oooh!…'

Somewhat inconveniently, a second doom–laden dose of acid dung hijacked his sentence; he scurried from his cesspit, losing both his signal and his trousers as he did so. But he'd caught Chanter's gist anyway – get the measure of the enemy before the cavalry arrives. At least Pirelli wouldn't be looking out for a lobotomised muppet on a moped.

Felix's personal perdition showed little sign of lightening up either. For Wagtail II was as unsuited to amphibious exploits as her pilot, whose cheeks had bloated like a bulldog's in the pugnacious rain. Beneath his superfluous sunglasses were raw, nocturnal eyes, rooted and distended like wild radishes, and his lips had all but evacuated his warred chin. His wrists were locked in a hopeless arm–wrestle with the muscle–bound wind as the bar buried itself repeatedly into his chest; for some reason his troubles had significantly worsened in the last few seconds. But he hadn't quite given up the will to live, yet – there was just one thing keeping him from dropping like a snipped kite: his unaccountably buoyant pride. Moreover, it seemed the change to his bearing had miraculously paid off; by a bamboozling process of compensating errors the constantly altering wind dynamic had turned him through the large arc he'd planned for. But now, as he glanced above him momentarily he faced a new nemesis, far more vivid and uncompromising; for when the conditions are right, it can all go horribly wrong.

It is a rarely observed yet undeniable aphorism that a microlight is to a helicopter as an aardvark is to a senior geneticist. Except that your average woolly mammal would probably have the sense to avoid meddling in the complexities of DNA encryption. It wasn't that Felix fancied his chances head to head with this ginormous gyrating giro, merely that for a man who has flirted with the equally unctuous elements for fifteen minutes in the chilling darkness, commanding a machine only fit to potter about on a summer's day pointing out mother–in–law's vegetable patch, there is no choice, no plausible alternative. Besides, he'd just witnessed Salvatore's second flare dash randomly past his toes, ostensibly an invitation to land. But proceeding at fifty MPH over a distance of two hundred yards towards a hovering helicopter, Felix was about to discover one could make up a shocking amount of ground. The turbulence was unimaginably riotous, each seismic wave sufficient to skittle out a team of wrinkled bowlers and disperse their toupees across the adjacent rink. The affronted machine put up a courageous and honourable resistance, and yet Felix's efforts were about to succumb to the unyielding clamour of the elements.

Chaos in the cosmos reigned, while rain from the cantankerous canopy continued to pound them all, from every angle. Dring now stood prone in the middle of the field, an ominously disjointed light from above sliding down his gaunt face to give the impression of a Kurt Weil opera about to get under way. His attempt at semaphore using a hand held torch was supremely irrelevant to the needs of the baffled pilot, from whose parallactic viewpoint he still couldn't be sure why he'd been dispatched to the Quatermass Pit. The pilot hedged his bets, performing miniscule circuits over the centre of the field.

While madness in its various manifestations was being inflicted upon this random and unassuming postage stamp of countryside, a more mundane mania characterised the behaviour of the fourth member of Felix's truculent troop. Frankie's road surveillance had started off well, but following the first few circuits he'd allowed himself to become distracted at a most inopportune moment; he now found himself hopelessly lost, with dirt tracks leading off in all directions. The cause of this momentary geographical aberration had been a call from a man he'd only met once, Gideon Pee – he'd been trying to reach Giuseppe, but due to the maddeningly erratic four–way conference line they'd rigged up, the incoming call had unaccountably diverted itself to Frankie's mobile.

At this precise moment Frankie's fleeting acquaintance with Pee was not one he felt much inclination to firm up; after all, it had been upon Pee's solicitation that Spencer Day's illegal activities had first come to light – indirectly, *Pee* was the catalyst of the mayhem threatening to choke their liberty now. But it was clear the weasley wally had something important on his mind. Frankie did his best to swat the pest, anxious to resume his menial mission.

'Oh, Pee! I expect you're trying to get hold of Giuseppe...he's a little, um, preoccupied right now – but I'll be sure to let him know you...'

'No no, Frank, it's really important...this can't wait

341

another moment...'

But whatever Pee had been so eager to tell him would have to wait a good deal longer than a moment. For Frankie's brief spell of terra incognita had collided with someone else's; and so had his vehicle.

In the time it had taken to scream three expletives of increasing obscenity into the phone trapped under his chin, Frankie's van had been royally shafted. His vehicle had become an integral piece in an impressive mêlées of metal Mechano that had bulldozed its way into the space once occupied by a group of cedar trees that might have considered themselves safe, huddled together on such a rarely traversed corner. The rear of his vehicle had docked with the front section of a somewhat more brutish one; in the measly moonlight it might have been a stegosaurus humping a baby elephant, for the tearing of steel flesh and the woeful whining of wild animals would be enough to convince the most ardent anti–evolutionist he'd got it all wrong. The concertina effect had been immediate and total – five vehicles melded into one; a veritable demolition derby. To add to the mounting misery, an odour of burning rubber issued ominously from around the tiny caravan crumpled at the rear of the group. In less than twenty seconds the flames had accelerated into a full–blown blaze.

As Frankie scuttled from the ghastly scene, physically unscathed but mentally in tatters, he glanced behind him and realised the scale of the awesome spectacle – bronze flames danced more than six feet from the carnage of cars, and the noise of humans succumbing to inevitable panic was perhaps more harrowing than that coming from

342

the animals as they charged at their cages. Cries of '*Dumnezeu*! *Dumnezeu*!' carried far into the wooded area leading to the road, and were it not for the untamed enthusiasm of the rain, this too would surely have been swiftly consumed. Frankie ran blindly, unaware of the liberty Zoltán Farkas was about to bestow upon his imperilled livestock; he didn't think twice, or even once, about where he was headed, but jumped hedges, scaled gates, leapfrogged walls and galloped at a pace no smoker's lungs should be able to contemplate. If he was becoming aware of the cacophony raging above him this was, at least for the time being, subliminal. But after a further minute of painful panting he dropped to the ground under cover of a sinuous pine tree, its pleached branches showering his face with thick strips of rainwater.

Having dared to relax for a full five seconds he became aware of a voice somewhere close by. A thin, simpering tone. He looked down at his hand and saw his phone, still illuminated, and pulled it to his ear, still snorting hideously.

'...Frank? *Frank*! Are you all right? What the hell's happening?'

It was that damned fool, Pee. Frankie's impatience soared to its apotheosis.

'Gideon Pee, you *psychopathic psychic*, you nearly killed me! They should serve an ASBO on you. How dare you inflict this alchemy on me...on *us*? I'd like to poach your bollocks over a bowl of boiling rats' eyes.'

Pee's voice took on a sickeningly contemptuous timbre.

'You don't understand. You're part of it all, but you *don't* understand. I've had a *vision*...no, don't even *think* of mocking me...it's the only *real* vision I've ever had, and here's the best part...you, Giuseppe and two other numbskulls are living it out for me, as we speak. You're all in great danger. *I simply must tell you what I've foreseen.*'

Frankie had no appetite for any more of this self–congratulatory bullshit. He'd taken it from Felix and now he was getting it from Pee, a psychic whose paranormal powers had hitherto proved to be boringly subnormal. He could hardly believe he'd allowed himself to become irretrievably embroiled in this escalating calamity – what he'd give now for the uncomplicated life of a Rwandan mine detector.

'Huh, you're as useless as a pubic wig, you Pee–Wit! What are you, a weather forecaster? Half of what you predict has already happened, and the rest is a wild guess. Don't treat me like one of your pathetic punters, I know it's all a barrel of bollocks. I've had it up to my *ears*.'

Frankie's ears were about to experience rather more than he'd bargained for, but the kowtowing persisted, undiminished.

'You needn't worry, Frank...I've already contacted the police...oh, and I've phoned the press, too...'

◎

Perhaps, in the final assessment, Felix's ostrich

tactic had been the best policy. It was unfortunate that the helicopter pilot hadn't approached the impasse as passively – alas, he would pay the ultimate price for his quick–wittedness – for in manoeuvring himself away from an inevitable air collision the traumatised machine had slipped sadly into a crop of convulsing trees. Ironically the helicopter had fanned the flames of its own decrepitation, its pilot desperately in need of a safe place to land, plummeting tragically a matter of yards from the maelstrom already in full swing.

Two men stood transfixed in the field like soldiers from the Terracotta Army, the combined heat of two adjacent infernos apparently not sufficient to thaw them, let alone make each aware of the other's presence. One still pointed his apologetic torch up to the brooding sky, his body drained of every drop of duodenal juice; the other, eyes clasped shut, pointed his rifle at roughly the same spot. As if the two massive explosions had not been sufficient deterrent from landing for his barely airborne comrade, Salvatore pumped off three final flares. They forked and faded high in the darkness, quickly snuffed out by the swelling tsunami, leaving a flaccid 'V' sign to herald the beginning of what must surely be the end.

LIFE ON MARS? A CATINEL'S CHANCE

The four police vehicles dispatched to the imbroglio might have imagined themselves commissioned as extras on an 'X Files' shoot, such was the peculiar presence of impending doom and prevailing pandemonium. DS Chanter's exuberance in coordinating them bellied his sketchy memory of the terrain, the OS map on his lap frustratingly at variance with the SatNav directions he was busy doling out. The first police car to get within five miles of the trouble zone was an unmarked Sierra, hotly pursued by two ambulances that had been summoned by at least a dozen bedazzled motorists rubber–necking their way down the A52. Simultaneously a call had come in from an awe–stricken, barely comprehensible gentleman wishing to retain his anonymity. The reason for this was plain enough – he'd just released into the wild two chimpanzees, a family of toy dogs – and a fully–grown female cheetah answering to the name 'Chimera'. Bizarrely, the man, an Eastern European, had reported a multiple pile–up at the same improbable site the helicopter had been dispatched to only minutes earlier. Despite the felicitous flames, news of the assumed downfall of the said machine was at this stage still subject to confirmation. The airwaves had quickly become bottlenecked with officers of all ranks, few with anything useful to contribute; Toogood was among the most incandescent in the queue to bite Chanter's head off. He'd been ousted from his watering hole by a barrage of harried callers and was still in the early stages of playing catch–up.

Another vehicle, driven by a woman pursuing an altogether dissimilar agenda, was calmly and systematically making her way to the unlikely hotspot; heading from nearby Ashborne, hers would be the first land vehicle to make its final approach. The softly spoken gentleman who'd made contact with her an hour earlier had withheld his identity. Suffice it to say, his insight had supposedly come from "the *other* side" – by which she'd assumed he wasn't referring to Halifax – although his motive for disturbing her had been regaled in a chillingly matter of fact fashion – a vision of Armageddon with an almost practiced ring to it. She spat bullet points into her dictaphone as she travelled, tuning in simultaneously to the news on the radio, which was already rich with speculation and contrastingly light on facts. But the patchy coverage fed her imagination; she wrestled with a provisional headline: "Psychic's Sidekicks stave off Rustic Ruckus".

LIFE ON MARS? A CATINEL'S CHANCE

If Felix had been pressed to find a suitable epithet for his current predicament it might have been: 'Dissolute Desperado Emulsified by Cavalier Cavalry' – not that in his enfeebled state he could cope with anything less abstract than overcoming the wake of the hell–bound helicopter. Wagtail II was not a happy songbird either; her wings were scorched and her frame was close to buckling from the stress of an involuntary aerobatic display, the like of which the surliest RAF jump jet would have balked at. But what her pilot had cost himself in bad judgment he'd made up for in good fortune; the helicopter's mushroom cloud had pumped shockwaves towards him, filling the space with an atomic fart from the bionic bowels of Satan. Gaining distance from the malevolent force, by whatever means, could only improve his prospects for survival. But, far from flying, the little plane was being propelled backwards, its wings disintegrating like a blowtorched damselfly's, while the indomitable rain pursued its cynical impulse to crush all in its path. The aftermath would prove to be appropriately cataclysmic, the downward leg of the thermal cycle every bit as violent as the upsurge had been. Not that Felix had actually seen the helicopter's fall from grace. He'd lost his grip on the control bar, yet ironically the machine's inbuilt capacity to right itself had saved his skin – or at least some of it. His nose had relinquished its top layer and his eyebrows were now as pink as a party–bound drag–queen's.

Having descended to an altitude of below one hundred feet, Felix resigned himself to an inescapable truth: there *was* no escape, unless he could clear the area immediately. He grappled with the bar and pushed it out as far is it could go, feeling himself swing away radically. He was still losing precious height and praying for air speed, with his foot eking out what little thrust the engine could still rally. The air was ragged and enraged, his position as tenuous as a snowboarder in an avalanche. Felix closed his eyes, for they were doing him little good open, and waited for his future to clarify itself, either in this life or the next. Suddenly his prayers were answered, the Holy Grail sensed – a smidgen of lift; the wing had begun flying again, albeit following a decidedly eccentric path. Only ten seconds later did he begin to believe he'd escaped a gritty grave as he shaved the tops of the more statuesque trees. The last thing he could care about now was where he might be heading, and it would be several minutes before any vaguely recognisable structure was glimpsed beneath the squally cloud line. At least the rain was less punishing here, and at last his heart began to recover an even pace.

Salvatore's survival instincts kicked in a fraction quicker than his young acolyte's. They'd returned to their vehicle by the time the two explosions pierced the filiform sky, leaving beneath them a crimson crematorium, a ghostly vestige of the helicopter that had hovered there, just a few hundred yards away from where they now sat, speechless and expressionless. Tommy nudged Salvatore's arm gently and they exited the road, their route assisted solely by the intermittent courtesy light, just as the sagging eyes of Andrea Balentine's antique MR2 began to illuminate the opposite side of the knotted little road. She proceeded distractedly, barely noticing the two silhouetted figures cowering in the Volvo as it moved away; it might have occurred to her that this was no lover's tryst she'd disturbed, especially given the backdrop to her awakening story.

In no particular hurry she settled her rusty relic over the dry patch of uneven tarmac that had just been vacated, wound down the window and inhaled her first sample of the night air: it tasted of raw, unmitigated death. Intoxicated by its creative tang, she pulled in her headlights, picked up her pen and waited for the story to fall into her lap. Had she still been able–bodied she'd have been in the midst of it all by now, sleeves rolled up, tape recorder rolling; but her days of sketching diffident defendants on–the–fly, and waiting by dustcarts in the freezing fog for drunken ex–footballers to come home and beat up their soon–to–be–ex–wives, had long gone. Balentine's Toyota succinctly symbolised her past life and the buoyant decade she'd enjoyed working with the News of the World, during which she'd proved to herself more than should have needed proving and thus qualified herself for a new rôle three hundred miles north tackling trivia of a rather more parochial stature, recent features on ransacked allotments and prize–winning courgettes epitomising the vein. But, once in a while, a call comes in even a decrepit disillusioned hack has to respond to, a story that's so farcical it might just have a particle of credibility to it, and given suitable nourishment can be whipped up into a sandstorm of fantastic fiction.

Balentine couldn't believe her luck. The Derbyshire Chronicle had arrived ahead of the Derbyshire Constabulary. And now that she'd staked her pitch there'd be no shifting her, not if she got her wheelchair out, anyway. But that could take her ten minutes in the punishing flood, and in any case, she'd learned the hard way – don't play the handicapped card unless the plane's leaving or the ship's sinking; otherwise the story will become about *you*, not the craziness handed to you on a plate by a strangely plausible, faintly familiar sounding psychic. Thinking of which, what was it exactly that her mysterious informant had told her as she'd struggled with one arm to extricate herself from the bathtub? It had definitely implicated an old work acquaintance of his, some kind of freelance researcher, and a preposterous juxtaposition of fearsome creatures and hell–raising humans. He'd been so particular about the inconsequential details of his premonition – she recalled a certain Italian/Hispanic connotation – and yet so hopelessly vague about the factors that might *matter* – a tangential connection with a highly publicised murder case, she recalled – that she knew this was some kind of set up; it had to be. But what did it matter? If the guy cared so much about being proved right that he'd made *sure* he was, the story would be just as compelling, just as easily finessed into a riveting read. So, was the fire raging across the field the cause of his restrained hysteria, or its effect? Perhaps it had nothing to do with the demonic premonition at all? For she hadn't

351

actually *seen* the aircraft fall to earth, or *witnessed* a microlight getting swatted off as effortlessly as a horsefly. And the commotion of emergency service vehicles losing themselves down cul–de–sacs two miles away hadn't yet had a chance to shed their flashing lights on the situation.

Before they could, her position would become a good deal more precarious than she could have anticipated, sat in solitary silence behind a slowly approaching wall of incensed, whistling fire. Indeed the screeching of tyres from around the corner came as more of a surprise than a shock. A large red car reversed at speed towards her, the only clue to its make coming from the sporadically dabbed brake lights. The driver's decision to bring the thing to a halt must have been fortuitous rather than a response to her dappled presence, but either way, the Volvo slammed its way forward just in time and made off in the direction it had come from at high speed. Balentine peered through the tiny gap in her steering wheel and was about to turn over her engine when a motorcycle appeared, ridden by a callow looking man wearing no helmet, no trousers, and with what appeared to be charcoal marks smeared all over his rapt face. The broken surface of the road undermined his braking, and even on this lightweight machine he wouldn't be able to stop in time. He landed at the driver's door, or at least his body did, while the bike continued for some yards, careering and skittling its way into the hedge. It finished up nose down, a pathetic wisp of exhaust tumbling out of the mangled pipe and the whirr of a spinning wheel audible above the groans of the disorientated biker.

PC Dring peered up at the woman. Her head

352

protruded from the window sufficiently to reveal her hooknose and take–no–prisoners eyes, this despite a pair of disarmingly youthful spectacles, red and wiry, with no lassoes over the ears.

'I expect you're in a hurry then' she piped at last, augustly. She pointed accusingly to his bare legs. 'And you appear to have overlooked your obligations in the galligaskins department, young man.'

Dring rubbed his neck and grimaced as he brought his right foot up to meet his left knee, frowning at it intently, as if a clue to its state could be discerned through the thick black leather boot. He spoke without looking up to take whatever blend of sympathy and admonishment was coming his way, adjusting what he hoped might be the vestiges of his galligaskins.

'Madam, I am a police officer: PC Perry Dring. I'm here on official business and, although you may consider my appearance to be a *little* unorthodox, rest assured...I *am* in control of this situation...ooh...'

Balentine didn't feel inclined to contest his assertion, despite the blatant ignominy of his position, tangled around the sill of her car door. He continued, in case she changed her mind, a telltale waft of flatulence reaching her nose as he struggled to sequester a little dignity.

'I have requested backup, madam...it's on its way...you will of course be required to give a full statement, since...'

His own statement was rendered incomplete by the unsubtle arrival of half of Derbyshire's emergency services, while the other half continued to chew up miscellaneous hedgerows and foreshorten the retirement of many an ageing rabbit in the surrounding landscape. The area quickly jammed up with billowing uniforms fanning an air of self–importance and paraphernalia of every description unravelling across the field amid clipped orders from distinguished looking extinguishers. DS Chanter would eventually emerge, harassed and on foot, accompanied by several other breathless civilian clad gendarmerie. He made a beeline for the subdued Dring, whose position he quickly realised bordered haplessness and hopelessness.

As Frankie emerged from a sinuous wooded area abutting an oppressively light–starved lane, he became aware he was sharing a small clearing with some other living thing. He couldn't be sure this wasn't one of the convoy of drivers that had emerged from nowhere to shunt him, and yet something about the litheness and elegance of its motion, the intangibility of its aura, suggested an animal, not a fellow accident victim escaping the flames. If the creature was breathing it was managing to be quieter about it than he was. The instinct for self–preservation marginally triumphed over his capacity for rational thought; he now found himself climbing a tree, the lower limbs of which seemed even less robust than his own. It hadn't occurred to him that virtually any jungle dweller could scale four branches as quickly as

354

he, or that his options would become more limited by entrapping himself there. But here he waited, in shock, and as he did so two large eyes crystallised in his gaze, unblinking, unerring, unutterably immutable.

Wagtail II's homeward impulse had been unfalteringly impressive. She had steered herself in the dark, thwarted constantly by a pilot whose ability to gauge height and distance was little better by day than by night. She had faced unconscionable weather conditions, suffered debilitating burns and endured handling skills more commonly employed by glue–sniffing teenagers in dodgem cars. But she too knew her limits, and they'd been wildly exceeded; the oval shaped runway of Mervyn's aerodrome gradually appeared as a gaping zero beneath Felix's left boot, a vague digit symbolic of the chances remaining on his scoreboard of life. Setting her down would be an arbitrary procedure, made all the more so by the unpredictable jets of horizontal rain splintering his weather–slapped face. But somehow he'd rediscovered the crosswind runway he'd used earlier, and the un–mown grass quickly attached itself to the metal cords tensioning the base of the machine, the piquant aroma of homecoming returning a little life to his eyes.

355

LIFE ON MARS? A CATINEL'S CHANCE

Dring would have traded places with Frankie unflinchingly, even though it would have involved fending off a hypersensitive big cat, for this must surely be preferable to explaining himself to his boss, whose teeth were drawn in readiness to crack open his feeble defence. The field had dramatically been restored to a state of relative tranquillity, if tranquillity could ever realistically be resumed in a place tainted by the deaths of two men, one spilled from a toy flying–machine a matter of days earlier, the other corkscrewed by his rather more hi–tech death–trap just a few minutes ago. And anyway, emancipated big–tooths can only scare people aware of their predicament, which ruled out all but two people remaining within the one mile danger zone. But it would take Zoltán Farkas a while longer to track down Chimera than his animal had taken to home in on Frankie's appetisingly nervous scent; his position half way up a tree had turned out to be surprisingly judicious. For the animal had cultivated indefatigable patience from years of confinement, weighing up the pros and cons of titbits versus banquets, fingers versus torsos. At least the respite had granted Frankie a chance to call Giuseppe, capitalising upon the marginally improved phone signal of his elevated position. Giuseppe had taken up his former position in his Volvo, and although his eardrums had been pushed to perforation point by the strain of frustrated service vehicles flashing past him in both directions, curiously enough he'd either been unnoticed or else ignored, presumably as a result of lying low in his reclined driver's seat. Had he been on the move at the point the squad cars whizzed by him he'd surely have been clocked and clinkered. He wasn't sure what emotion to reveal in his tone when the call from Frankie came through. But on hearing of his friend's arboretum aberration he would have to suppress a modicum of relief; from a damage limitation perspective Frankie would be at his least harmful up a tree, salivated over by his furry, four–pinned foe. If only the same could be said of his father whom, for all he knew, was by now cuffed in the rear of a Morahia, claiming he was from Sicily, or worse still, Barcelona.

As the nonsensical exchange between them continued, two further incoming calls miraculously registered on the conference line that had eluded them earlier. Felix would be the first to articulate his displeasure.

'So much for the helpful flares, Salvatore...I'd rather have relied on a five year–old to wave sparklers for guidance!'

'Pop's not connected at the moment, Felix' said Giuseppe, quietly fretting over his father's whereabouts.

'*Not connected*?' Felix yelled, 'the man's got more loose screws than a new Lada! And what the buggery was that helicopter doing? For a moment, I thought one of us would cop it!'

Giuseppe paused before bringing the matter of the helicopter's calamitous kismet to Felix's attention.

'One of you *did*, mate...the other guy bit the dust just as you appeared...he must have panicked, or something.

Where the hell are you anyway, Felix? We managed to get out in the nick of time, but only just...I've never heard so many sirens...it was like Nine–Eleven out there.'

Felix checked his watch and couldn't resist a fatuous correction.

'It's nine–*twelve*, actually...Um, I'm at the aerodrome, nursing my barbequed bird and peeling dead skin from my face...thanks for the concern!...Holy camoly, guys, does that count as murder, accident or negligence? We need to get the bleedin' hell out of here, before a war starts!'

Frankie's interjection called upon an unfamiliar huskiness of tone, chosen so as not to fluster the cheetah, whose jungle instincts were showing signs of returning.

'Mate, forget it...the war's nearly over – we're into extra time, but I'm confident it's a whitewash. If it's any consolation, I've got a rapacious cougar nibbling at my goolies...some crazy chain of wagons ploughed into me while I was doing my circuits; must have been a zoo–keepers outing, or some other weird shit. You might be up the creek, but count yourself lucky – I'm up a friggin' tree!'

'By the way, Felix' interrupted Giuseppe, 'that wanker Gideon Pee's just been on the line to me. He must be orbiting some kind of parallel universe, by the sound of it...he started mumbling some crap about having had a *real* vision involving us lot, but then I heard an 'orrible scream and the line went dead. The man's barking like a herd of friggin' sea lions.'

'Huh! Tell me about it! Who's side is that wazzock on, anyway?' snapped Frankie. 'He's about as much use a chocolate codpiece...it was *his* phone call that made me lose my way in the first place. Why couldn't the man keep his pratish premonitions to himself? He's got no business getting conscientious after all these years of bullshitting!'

'Quite' asserted Felix, his composure partly restored from five minutes down–time, 'so, guys, first off, we'll go our separate ways and meet up back at the boat, later...*much* later. Second, I've figured out a way forward – we're gonna take control of this fiasco. *Someone's* about to pay, big time!'

A stomach–sapping baritone growl in the background reminded them of Frankie's unenviable retreat and that his immediate prospects lay at the paws of his maddened minder. But, still abraded by his latest debacle, Felix could raise little sympathy.

'Face it Frankie, this is as close to pussy as you're likely to get tonight...just be grateful she's not chewed your nuts off already. Stay put. Play piquet with her. You're our man on the ground, well, up the tree...stop complaining and keep your eye on what's occurring.'

'Oh *thanks*, *mate*, I'm your piggy in the middle, more like...as if I've got any choice! Anyway, when should I notify you, before or after my foot becomes this frigging feline's *food–line?*'

14

The Prophet and Loss Account

By 11:50 PM, back at the Nick, Toogood, Chanter and Dring had exchanged insults and threats worthy of any borstal gymnasium. And yet, if Andrea Balentine (whose innocence had been among the few unanimous decisions they'd been able to reach) were to be believed, the key to the events of the evening had been gallingly obvious upon receiving a phone call at 6:40. Now, sat together in the uncompelling surroundings of the Station Canteen (Balentine quietly flattered to have gatecrashed the cheerless duo's kiss 'n make up party) she addressed Toogood as if he were her recurrently unsuccessful nephew.

'You see, young man, you, as a policeman – can I call you *Sam*?…no?…okay – you will doubtless search for the dastardly regisseur capable of bringing down a helicopter and simultaneously telescoping six vehicles in

361

Derbyshire's equivalent to the Australian outback. It's not enough, for you, that some people need to make a living, while others need to feel good about themselves, or that at the heart of this Fortean affair is a sad individual whose determination to come out on top for once in his sad little life might drive him to set up a spot of al fresco theatre...*is it?*'

Toogood shrugged off the expression that had matured on his face, which was indeed that of a scalded adolescent. He reached over to her brimming cup, brandishing a milk jug procured from somewhere backstage. Balentine recoiled as if he'd been threatening her drink with anthrax.

'Milk goes in *first*, Detective Inspector...who dragged you up?'

'Ah, another pre–lactarian' grovelled Chanter, 'quite right.'

Toogood wasn't about to let him milk it any further.

'Ms Balentine – can I call you *Andrea*?...no?...okay – I thank you for your interest and cooperation in what has been, beyond a shadow of doubt, the oddest and most fractious evening of my professional career. But I might tell you, without *actually* telling you, of course, that there is a chain of inscrutable events that has been the preoccupation of my colleague and I for the past couple of weeks. The overture to this theatrical episode, as you seem to want to frame it, is *quite* monstrous, *quite* diabolical, madam. Indeed, not to put too fine a point on it, of one thing we can be absolutely certain, and that is, that if this *is* theatre, it is a play *within* a play...'

Chanter couldn't resist filling in the alluring vacuum. He turned with a smile to face the matriarch.

'Like the Taming of the Shrew, within Sweet Charity...Ms Balentine?'

'Forty–Second Street, actually, Mr Chancer' she said, flattening the officer's wistful intermezzo. 'Pray continue, Detective Inspector Toogood...flesh out the history for me, just a little.'

'Suffice it to say that the well publicised discovery of a dead ex–criminal in precisely the same spot gives rise to ramifications that you won't have failed to detect – given your journalistic perspective, I mean, Ms Balentine.'

'Well, I'll leave *you* to make whatever tenuous links you feel moved to – I, on the other hand, would not countenance too many associations at this juncture. We...*you*, are dealing with an impotent megalomaniac – a person whose will to achieve equipollence colossally out–measures his true potential.'

Her irrebuttable expression kept the two officers at bay for a moment. They turned and frowned at each other, unsure of whether they were dealing with a harmless local hack or a frustrated criminal psychologist.

'So you've not covered the Spencer Day case then, Ms Valentine?' provoked Chanter.

'Naturally, we ran a three day exclusive: *the local paper with the wider view*', she responded unscathed. 'We uncovered nothing your department wanted to bother itself with, although you might have shown a more open mind to what we learned from the airfield up the road, in Matlock' she continued.

'Ah, that'll be...Melvyn's um...' stumbled Chanter.

'*Mervyn's* Microlights, Mr Chunter.'

'Yes, yes...What's the gossip from up there then, Ms Valentine?'

'Well, one or two odd comings and goings had been reported to staff in the days leading up to Mr Day's distressing incarnation. The aerodrome manager, a Mervyn Dreyfus, suspected local youths of cavorting on his premises, after hours.'

'There's nothing unusual in that is there?' reflected Chanter, 'I mean, aerodromes make great motorcycle circuits, and in my younger days I may have been guilty of...'

'Yes, well *thank you*, Chanter' reprimanded Toogood, 'I think we're all familiar with the abuse of private property by dim–witted hooligans...what were the clues, Ms Balentine?'

'Well, as I said, it's a pity the police weren't sufficiently interested in these details a little earlier; they *might* have helped. Essentially, kit, my boy, needed to fly a microlight. A pair of gauntlets and an adjustable spanner for micro–tightening various parts of the wing mechanism were discovered early one morning, not near to the hangar or car park area where one might expect things to get dropped, but some distance away from the sites given over to pre–flight checks. It's odd that they'd been squandered like that' she added, tilting her head a little and gazing into the middle distance.

'You seem remarkably well informed in these matters, madam' commended Toogood.

'I...I used to fly one myself...some years back,

Detective Inspector. These days I derive a little vicarious satisfaction from watching others bob about over the hills of a summer's evening.'

Her eyes flicked down towards her lifeless limbs; she swallowed hard and continued.

'One of my reporters, nice lad – Tyrone, bloody silly name – questioned Dreyfus on the matter. More to the point, he suspected a spot of night flying may well have been taking place – damned dangerous, not to say illegal.'

'I'm not sure I'm catching the full significance of some random bush–mechanic's neglected tool, sir' interrupted Chanter, looking nowhere in particular. 'Shouldn't we be concerning ourselves with more pertinent issues...like...'

Toogood lifted his hand slightly, all that was needed to derail his cohort's annoying nose for recondite mundanities. But he too wanted to change the topic.

'I want to know more about your mystery caller, Ms Balentine' said Toogood, 'the man who you claim put together a self–fulfilling prophecy in order to gain his five minutes of fame. Where is he now, do you suppose? When is he likely to achieve the adulation he craved enough to kill three men, and...'

'*Three* men?' interjected Balentine impiously, an uneven smile exposing what might once have been acceptable teeth. 'I can see how, if you stretch a point, you might blame him for the poor helicopter pilot's demise, but you can't be thinking he was responsible for murder! No, I maintain the guy's *exploiting* Day's murder. He's not the culprit.'

Chanter scoffed at the martinet's quaint employment of the word 'culprit', a term hardly befitting a person complicit in a trilogy of tragedies. He picked up Toogood's thread.

'Madam, we'll need all the details you can remember about the man who called you: was he young, old, with an accent or lisp...?'

'Oh, that's easy, young man. I've got the whole forty–five second conversation on tape! My machine does that as a matter of course; you see, I'm not as mobile these days, and it saves me the trouble of making endless notes of what'll commonly turn out to be unimportant details.'

'Excellent, Ms Valentine, your impeccable journalistic acumen would serve you well as a copper!' beamed Chanter sycophantically. Toogood sent him a disapproving glance, mindful of the woman's urge to steal the show.

'You did say *three* deaths, Detective Inspector...'

'Oh, I blame this god–awful coffee – just a slip of the unruly tongue Ms Balentine, nothing to exercise yourself with.'

'Now now, Detective Inspector' Balentine adjudicated, sliding her red spectacles down her beak, 'ending a sentence with a preposition is something *up* with which I will not *put!*'

Having taken her statement, Chanter assisted Balentine to her car. She thanked him proprietarily as though he might get a tip for his trouble, and promised to send in the aforementioned telephone recording first thing the next morning. Her return journey to Ashborne, languishing unremarkably at the southern tip of the Peaks, offered scope to review what she'd gleaned from the two squabbling police officers. A half smile threatened to crack her haggard face; she'd quite enjoyed their unguarded skirmish. She might be working for a third rate rag as a second rate hack, but this was a first rate story. She would of course oblige with the tape. But not before permitting her pet hounds a brief sniff – and armed with that little titbit they'd be as stoppable as rutting weasels.

PC Dring hadn't slept a wink. All night long he'd fought off the impulse to capitulate his undercover investigation, yet at the same time couldn't face the consequences of admitting he'd frittered away one innocent soul and sold his own to the devil. How bizarrely things had unfolded; it seemed too real to have been a dream, but too fantastic to have actually happened the way he remembered it. Curiously, the bogus information he'd concocted on the spur of the moment in order to keep Chanter on side, while squatting in the hedge performing his abominable abdominal ablutions, turned out to have had a firm element of truth to it. From what he'd been able to sieve out of Chanter's abusive tirade, his fictitious psychic, Andrea Watkiss, had acquired a physical incarnation in the form of an anonymous man, who'd chosen the very same evening to expound a remarkably similar premonition of his own. The recipient of this profane prophecy had been the journalist he'd crashed into while chasing after Pirelli's Volvo following the catastrophic explosion; furthermore, her name turned out to be Andrea something, too – a bony–faced battleaxe with hard eyes and a harder heart.

He massaged his bruised ankle and sat up in bed with a cup of milky tea, a lengthy sigh changing to a moan and tapering off as a whimper. It was all too abstract, too formless – and yet his future depended on finessing a story that tied in with the events as they'd been understood by his two boneheaded bosses. Might he conceivably kick his Watkiss fantasy into the long grass now? – at the moment of its impromptu creation that's exactly what he'd intended doing. Ironically, it now turned out to be the only bit of his unilateral investigation that might still bear scrutiny. Yes, Pirelli had turned up in response to his blackmail letter, albeit a day early, but in the event the helicopter's presence at the scene had fatally scuppered his plans to expose Spencer Day's murderer. In any case, Pirelli had manifestly escaped – and without Toogood ever knowing he'd even been there. What did his case amount to anyway? A bunch of old canoes, some congealed chocolate and a snail struggling with a perverse sugar–addiction. His hypothesis consisting of Tommy McGuire's criminal association with the Pirellis didn't seem so compelling now either, and by pressing for Salvatore's arrest he'd have to explain away his decidedly dodgy blackmail letter.

Had he known of the miscreant videotapes purporting to link the deaths of the Day brothers Dring might have been tempted to concoct a fiendish new plan, but as things stood, his activities as dilettante vigilante had come to an abrupt full–stop. He groaned again and limped off to the bathroom, yawning noisily; at least he still had his self–parody of a life, his pantomime of a job, his dreams.

The bedraggled company had begun to converge on Wagtail at around 2:30 AM following the decision to travel separately. It had only taken Felix twenty minutes to dissemble the parts of Wagtail II that hadn't already fallen off or been clawed back by the ghost of Icarus, and yet, finally, Felix's get up and go had got up and gone. It hadn't helped that the aerodrome had become a temporary base for three additional police helicopters and two military aircraft. But luckily he'd had the foresight to park his Landrover behind a dilapidated hangar, some distance away from Mervyn's swish new one, thus screening himself from the traffic. Given the circumstances, he'd reluctantly elected to shed the shredded wing as collateral damage; it hadn't looked out of place shoved in among Mervyn's pitiful graveyard of aeronautical esoterica. He'd taken the long route back, concerned about possible roadblocks, but had encountered nothing out of the ordinary, despite the news already scatter–bombing the local radio station. Salvatore and Tommy had arrived home half an hour ahead of him, a stench of charred toast greeting him as he collapsed into the frail wicker sofa, his yelp of bottled–up fretfulness spontaneously orchestrated by the others.

After the initial exuberance had calmed a little, their thoughts turned to Frankie, presumably still pining in his pine tree, and Giuseppe, vulnerable in his Volvo.

'I hava spok–ed to Giuseppe...yes, hee eesa ona heesa way nowa...I cooka heema the toast already' blurted Salvatore, excitedly.

'Mm, apparently Giuseppe's given up trying to get hold of Frankie...the plonker's probably jungle–rapping the cougar into submission as we speak' continued Felix, plunging his incisors into a crust resembling corrugated cardboard. Suddenly he rose to his feet, jam dripping from his spoon.

'Boys, I'd like to propose a toast...to us...and to the sweet, sweet taste of liberty at last.'

The Department of the Environment was not impressed. The deployment of five of their officers to the task of rounding up a mobile menagerie in the wee small hours had outstretched their public–spiritedness. With the assistance of Zoltán (and the other poor little Farkas's) they'd succeeded in herding together the more innocuous members of the animal troop, Clara the chimpanzee caught flirting with Franz, whose opportunities in 'that' direction had been churlishly neutered following unfortunate irregularities with a bunch of bananas the previous year. Chimera, the wily cheetah, had been determined to stretch her moment of freedom a little further, even if it meant eventually enduring a more protracted period of solitary confinement. Strangely, the fire had only partly succeeded in scattering the creatures, and Chimera's unaccountable preoccupation with a tree, less than a quarter of a mile away, had greatly simplified matters for the rescue team. Presumably she was claiming this as her new territory, they thought, or else had lost her former enthusiasm for playing hide and seek and fancied her supper. And if Frankie's narcolepsy had not finally rendered him comatose, wedged in his tree den, he too might well have been in for a spell of incarceration. His father had often joked that his son could fall asleep anywhere, even in a tree; in this regard at least, Frankie felt proud to have measured up. Forced to wait until the main wave of human activity had desisted, Frankie had resigned himself to the watching brief Felix had assigned him; he'd have nothing much to report, except the worst dose of leg cramp he'd ever suffered and a hankering for a warm, well appointed toilet.

By the time he'd managed to slip away unnoticed from the field that morning, the first wave of police action at ground–zero had all but ceased, but he'd nevertheless chosen the most circuitous exit route possible. His industrious night watchman must have found some other soul to supervise, thank god, although his paranoiac predisposition continued to be ruffled by imaginary

371

shadows and spontaneously quivering bushes. He glanced at his watch; it was just after 6:00 AM. The air was crisp, and the shock of the morning was taking time to subside. He'd been wandering for perhaps an hour before he felt calm enough to sit and imbibe the brittle beauty of his surroundings. He stared at the sky, almost fractal with syllabub cloud, and traced the ebb and flow of the prehistoric massif forming a sleeping dinosaur's back. He sighed as he felt the first tentative drop of rain and muttered to himself 'bleedin' typical...when you can see the hills, it's about to rain; when you can't, it already is.'

The warm moisture that found Frankie's trailing hand felt almost sensual for a few seconds, until it occurred to him he might investigate what was causing it. He glanced down slowly. If the thing were much smaller it could be a rat, much larger and it mightn't resemble a poodle; his reaction to shrink away unnerved the comical specimen. It scampered off behind a small tuft of overgrown grass and peered at him cagily, half beckoning him to play, half wishing he'd leave it in peace.

'What the buggery are *you*, then?' Frankie enquired of the rapscallion in a derisory tone. The feeling was mutual, and yet the diminutive creature feigned disappointment, awaiting a more personable tactic, which was taking some time to evidence itself. The miniscule mongrel, faintly pink in the imperfect light, suddenly trotted forward, bowed its head, performed a perfect backward summersault and awaited applause. Frankie relented, eventually, and having short–circuited the courtship ritual, the two incongruous creatures quickly bonded, fellow pilgrims venturing into a hostile new world. The little thing hopped gleefully at Frankie's toes, its foolishly pert tail inscribing tiny circles in the air as it struggled to keep apace with its lanky–legged companion.

'What shall I call you, then, you little scamp?...I know...*Wagtail III.*'

It emitted a single noise, like a tooting flageolet, and accepted its new title unquestioningly, quickly blotting from its miniature memory the six years it had spent fulfilling the 'aah' rôle in the Farkas's inoffensively pathetic stage act.

An incoming call halted the pair in their tracks.

'Felix, don't disturb me now, I'm taking the dog for a walk.'

Three yaps punctuated Frankie's random opener.

'Frankie! Last I heard, you had your head up a tree with a dribbling panther sizing you up for supper. And now you've got a piffling pooch at your heels – what are you like!'

'Yeah, well, no thanks to you guys, I beat the thing off last night with a large stick and showed it who's boss.'

'Good for you, mate' responded Felix, avoiding any unwarranted hint of irony. 'Now look, Giuseppe ran out of juice on the way back to the boat last night. He's the nearest to you, so he'll be back to get you in an hour or so. Get yourself into a good reception area and sit there, for goodness sake – I've been trying to reach you for half an hour.'

'I'm not sure they have transmitters in Outer Mongolia, Felix, but I'll do my best. Nice and cosy is it, warming your tootsies on the stove?'

LIFE ON MARS? A CATINEL'S CHANCE

Two more yaps underpinned the sarcasm.

'That was the scariest night of life, Felix. I'm still not sure I didn't just dream it all – what's the score?'

'You *did* dream most of it, mate, I'll wager. Well, Wagtail II's had her wings clipped, you've pranged your van and Salvatore's burnt the toast. All in a day's work, eh? With a bit of luck the canoes will have been trashed in the fire.'

'So, now what?'

'This is where things get tasty, mate. You've had it far too easy, pissing about with big cats and small dogs, strolling in the country and kipping in tree houses. By lunchtime our problems will be over. Trust me.'

A single yap was the only fitting response.

Indeed, Felix's optimism had a habit of negating recent experience and circumnavigating conventional wisdom. And since his confidence was rarely steered by either facet of the human condition he wasn't about to curb his enthusiasm now. The team sat around him in eager anticipation of the Chamberlainesque strategy that was poised to trip from his lips. They watched as he fired up his pipe, tapped it authoritatively on the table and demolished an entire Cadbury's Creme Egg in a single manoeuvre. Producing that morning's edition of The News of the World, he slammed it ceremoniously in front of them,

374

pointing to an article sporting a somewhat inflammatory headline.

'Boys, we've reached that most precarious of moments in the proceedings – our "Events Horizon", or point of no return – alas, the valuable ground we have thus far gained remains as provisional as a pink poodle's virginity.'

A triplet of coquettish pips from Wagtail III attracted a judgmental scowl from Frankie. The bloviator held his ground, and continued.

'What last night proves is that our *real* enemy, our *real* Moriarty, isn't Detective Inspector Toogood, who himself only rallied his troops in response to a certain act of fantastical fiendishness...but the *instigator* of the said act, none other than...'

Frankie stole the moment, his acidic sotto voce timbre and absent gaze contributing to a palpable air of discomfort.

'Gideon Pee, whose life has already been snuffed out...in my mind, if not in reality.'

Felix stole back the conch.

'It is entirely possible that Pee, an indubitably reproachable character whom I have never met, nor would recognise in the street, set up this entire bonanza of bamboozling bollocks. Let us assume for a moment that Pee, lying awake one night, busily contriving another of his tawdry psychic scams, hit upon an idea that could accelerate overnight his inconspicuous position in the hierarchy of spiritualist spoofers. He's not forgotten Giuseppe's recent harrowing encounter with Spencer Day, and he begins to see that a brilliant, lucrative opportunity lies within reach. But first he must turn over the entire scenario in his mind, to ensure he understands its every ramification.'

Frankie looked at Giuseppe and the pair groaned on cue. The wordsmith drew breath sufficient to nourish his next garrulous tautology.

'I'll just recap for you. For some time, Pee had been enlisting Giuseppe's professional assistance, a man whose demonstrable research skills had enlivened many a lacklustre show that would have otherwise depended on pure showmanship. On this latest occasion, faced with the bunch of humdrum characters his sharp–eyed researcher had stumped up at short notice, Pee had been drawn to one fractionally more interesting specimen: Spencer Day. Day's chief attraction turned out to be his outrageous duplicity – the man was but a thief in sheep's clothing, as it were, doling out advice on going straight, while in reality holding firm to his pre–eminent pilfering predilections. But even when Giuseppe's life became threatened face to face with the crook, having traced the man's activities to his secret lockup, Pee isn't so easily deflected from his potentially potent prognostications. He *wants* this one. By deftly diverting his attention to Mrs Bronte at the eleventh hour Giuseppe is able to sidestep a potentially more horrific encounter with Day than the one he'd already suffered. But in doing so he scuppers Pee's plan to publicly besmirch the man by exposing his on–going criminal activities. And yet this, as we have seen all too plainly, will prove to be a story far, far from over.'

Salvatore looked at Tommy; the pair whimpered on

cue. Felix drew an even larger breath.

'Though no dialogue has been entered into between Pee and Giuseppe subsequent to the pulling of Spencer Day from the show, Pee must surely have read in the papers of the odious man's grizzly reappearance in the heart of the Derbyshire countryside – and speculated how this might tie in with Giuseppe's close shave on his own doorstep.'

Felix paused, sighed and dropped his voice.

'And yet, has no one here ever asked himself *why has Gideon Pee remained as silent as one of Frankie's famous cack–attacks?*'

The hound–dog expression on Wagtail III's face testified to her ownership of the steaming stench that had suddenly beset the tiny living area. But at least it served to pierce the hiatus.

'You see, I contend that Pee, armed with these seemingly unrelated snippets of information, has been busily buffing up a story ready for liquidation the next rainy day. And, my god...how it rained last night! Just suppose, guys, for a reckless moment, that Pee, prompted by the coverage of the Spencer Day story, travelled to the site in the hope of finding *something*, some fragment of a clue that would irrefutably tie Day's death to Giuseppe. He scours every blade...and uncovers, to his astonishment, not a blowtorch or tarpaulin covered in gore as he might have anticipated, but...'

'A pile of crappy old canoes' interrupted Giuseppe, riding joyously roughshod over Felix's sanctimonious sermon. Frankie's eyes automatically moved towards Salvatore, expecting a familiar shrug of chagrin; but for once the Sicilian's bite was venomous.

'Ah...you, you theenka I know *fack naatheeng*! But...I know *fack all!*'

Wagtail III promptly farted again, a poignant expulsion appositely timed to perforate the bubble of Shadenfreude. Windows were flung open without comment or reprisal, not that Felix, now in full flight, even seemed to notice.

'At first, Pee fails to read any significance into his discovery. But he persists with his nit–picking, his mite–sifting and tooth–combing, and is eventually rewarded by coming across...oh, I don't know, some semi–tangible means of attributing ownership of the canoes to Giuseppe or Salvatore. So, he decides to compose an anonymous letter designed to force Giuseppe's appearance at the scene. But rather than pitch it directly, he chooses to harass Salvatore instead – presumably he feels this diversionary tactic best serves his purpose? Acquiring Salvatore's address requires a little sleuthing of his own, but he's onto something now; Giuseppe's camaraderie amounts to zilch when placed alongside this once in a career opportunity – for he will predict *the unpredictable*! Remember guys, that your *enemies* never betray you...only your *friends* can do that. Pee might have missed out on his piffling exposé of Day's ongoing criminal activities, but now that the man is dead he will go one better! He will pluck Day's killer's name from thin air and broadcast it to the nation by whatever means he can...not only that, he'll predict that the killer will soon revisit the macabre scene in order to glean one final moment of satisfaction! Sure enough, his letter succeeds in scaring the living crap out of Salvatore. And, just for good measure, he draws Tommy into the frame, too – he simply can't resist a double–whammy!'

Felix turned to Tommy, who was fiddling absentmindedly with his cigarette lighter. 'Now, Tommy, Giuseppe tells me you're no stranger to a box of matches…for all I know, Swan Vesta once sponsored your oboe lessons, or perhaps Guy Fawkes was a distant relation of yours? For, either way, it seems your reputation earned you a backhanded reference in Salvatore's letter!'

Tommy's face went crimson. He sniffed and carried on wasting flint.

'You see, even though I haven't yet figured out how Pee knows about your former matchbox mischief, there can be little doubt that *you* are the impudently dubbed 'Paddy Paddler' – despite, I suspect, being far better acquainted with the viscosity of Guinness than with the current whereabouts of Shergar. Anyway, the letter summons Salvatore to the site at an appointed time and demands from him a box of cash; but it's merely a ruse of course, another diversion…he's not interested in the fifty thousand – that's chicken feed compared to the reputation he'll have after this goes public! – No, he'll make damn sure the world watches in awe when he lays claim to this magnum opus. Next he contacts a journalist – nobody too highbrow who'll think it's all claptrap, but a local reporter who'll be more willing to run with the story; in the same breath he contacts the police, confident they'll be grateful for anything they can hang their helmets on. And so, gentlemen, conjurors, canoeists…pooches, the stage is set for Pee's meteoric rise to fame.'

'But how about our videos, Felix, *our fucking videos?*' demanded Giuseppe, once the uneasy shuffling had calmed.

'Well, they've not amounted to much, so far, I'll grant you that, but of course Pee isn't *aware* of the bogus tape we've sent in to the police, is he?...and we can't assume he necessarily knows that Spencer's brother also died in mysterious circumstances, let alone the fact that the man's murderer, Paula Day, is on camera doing it!'

'But hang on a minute Felix, what's the tape Pee is referring to in his shitty little letter then?' enquired Tommy, breaking the silence he'd maintained since his arrival at the boat.

'A bluff mate...well, why not, after all, *our* tape's a bluff isn't it? Since when did we have a monopoly on bullshit?'

'So, you're saying today's newspaper article is a direct result of some lightweight reporter's efforts to drum things up last night?' Frankie stammered.

Felix gave an affirmative nod.

'Salvatore and Tommy damn near drove into her actually...some handicapped woman by the name of Balentine sold her story to them; she used to write for the rag in her former life...it says so, here.'

Wagtail III discovered a little shelter wrapped around Frankie's neck, but shivered exaggeratedly in the hope of persuading someone to shut the windows, now that the worst effects of the gas attack had waned.

'So what the hell were those bloody wild animals doing cluttering up the scene?' Frankie demanded, ignoring the little ball of fluff peering down at him affectionately. 'I suppose you're going to tell me they accidentally turned up...at the wrong premonition!'

'Something like that, yeah.' Felix replied, reigniting his pipe. 'Now, this is important, mate. Was your van registered in your name, 'cos if it was, we'd better sort out an alibi for you, pronto.'

Frankie began tapping his knees madly, causing the dog's tiny head to vibrate like a gooseberry in a liquidiser. He yawned, as if the question couldn't possibly have any bearing, but then turned on his best impersonation of Felix, striking a supercilious pose.

'Fortuitously, Felix, I've never been overly sympathetic to the bureaucratic preoccupations of the Government's highways and byways legislative bodies. Vehicle registration and taxation are but uncouth expletives from the mouths of malcontent officials determined to piss on our chips.'

'I'll take that as a no, then.'

'But does Pee really *believe* Giuseppe killed Spencer Day?' enquired Tommy, relieved at last to discover what on earth this all had to do with him.

'Absolutely, mate...and let's face it, *he did*. The slime–ball's probably got half of Giuseppe's neck under his nails 'n all!'

Giuseppe began examining himself with the back of a finger.

'Ah!...Felix, I think I know what Pee might have stumbled across in the canoe!' Tommy grinned ebulliently, as if leaving documentary evidence of himself in an otherwise unidentifiable hunk of fibreglass was something to be proud of.

'I always used to velcro my sea–scout record book to the inside of my canoe; it lived there in its laminated pouch for donkey's years…endless practice rolls, rapid descents, you name it. It's just conceivable I left it in there…Shit, it must be nearly four years since I clapped eyes on that thing…'

'There you go, another piece of the mystery demystified' Felix congratulated himself.

Salvatore looked as if he had something to confess also.

'I hava the worry, Felixa. The psycho mana, hee follow me, yes? If he eesa your mana, Mr Peese, he knows we ara heera!'

Felix considered the point carefully, appointing his pipe with an air of self–importance.

'I suppose it's possible Pee was sharp enough off the mark to have been onto you as early as that. But your crap photography put paid to any hope of corroboration. Frankly, who cares if it *was* him, anyway? It's not what he suspects of *our* movements that's important, ultimately – it's what we're able to prove about *him*, right? A psychic's currency is *prediction* – that's Pee's angle here. Merely shopping us to the police doesn't do anything for the creep's crapulous career, does it?'

'Okay, Felix, let's say for argument's sake you've got Pee's number…what are we gonna do about it? Everything we've got is *circum–bleedin'–stantial*' Frankie shouted, his persistent origami with Wagtail III's lower limbs causing a droplet of white vomit to appear on her tiny white lips.

'Simple' answered Felix nonchalantly, spittle tumbling from his pipe onto his trousers, 'we set down our evidence as clearly as we can and send it in to Toogood, before the scent cools.'

'Oh, goda, notta mora fuckinga *veedeos*!' whimpered Salvatore.

'No, no, a succinct, dispassionate letter...Smile guys, all that matters is that while Pee's in his pod, we're not having to explain *ourselves*.'

Corporate body language suggested that this part of Felix's thesis had come under the radar, but a spontaneous triple back–flip from Wagtail III soon had them guffawing like hyenas on nitrous oxide.

'You're babbling like an autistic wombat…Just how twisted can your mind be, Felix?' glowered Frankie. 'It just meanders on endlessly, like a friggin' mangrove swamp. Get yourself checked out mate, before it's too late.'

Felix smiled, unabashed.

'Actually, I got the idea from a fish called Angler.'

'Hees *fleepeda* now, yesa!' confirmed Salvatore, shaking his head.

'You see, the Angler is an ugly, dark brute of a fish. But it's a clever son of a bitch. It's got a pink, worm–like tongue that it unravels when it's peckish, tempting smaller fish to draw closer.' He sniffed meaningfully. 'Get it? Just like us, really... fish baiting a fish.'

LIFE ON MARS? A CATINEL'S CHANCE

Detective Inspector Toogood wrestled with his third capsule of half–fat milk and poured it over his stewed, tepid coffee. Pouring over Andrea Balentine's written statement would demand rather less concentration, sitting alone at the same table the four of them had occupied less than twelve hours earlier. Balentine's statement amounted to a predictably perspicacious commentary. She'd remembered the detail of the short exchange captured on the answer–machine tape rather accurately, as he'd expected; it had arrived by courier earlier that morning. The first job he'd given Chanter was to review the first of the two videotapes alongside it, on the remote chance the caller's timbre or rhythmic syntax correlated with the hysterical female voice. Toogood, now surrounded by coffee cups and the fallout from a colossal Chelsea bun, immersed himself in the events as he understood them, Balentine's bullet–point commentary aiding a succinct overview:

She'd made her way calmly to the scene, arriving at around nine, during which time she'd mentally dredged up her newspaper's puffed–up coverage of the Spencer Day story and begun to consider some of the patent connections – the location, the contrived theatricality of her anonymous caller's delivery; naturally, she'd not conveyed her instinctive suspicions to the man lest he became provoked into acting out an even more maniacal scenario than the one he'd

384

outlined. Nor had she felt the onus was on her to notify the police. On arriving, two neighbouring fires, very much in evidence a short distance away from where she'd chosen to stop, had at that time no obvious cause; she hadn't been in a position to investigate for herself.

She'd arrived marginally ahead of the police, fire–fighters and ambulances, and in the intervening period had narrowly avoided getting rammed by an old Volvo; oddly though, this vehicle had seemed in no urgency to move off upon her arrival, just a minute or two earlier; she couldn't describe the figure/figures that occupied the vehicle, due to the lack of light. Next, a motorcyclist who it later transpired had been a plain–clothed policeman, PC Dring, presumably in pursuit of the aforementioned vehicle (and unquestionably in pursuit of his chinos) came to grief at the foot of her handicapped–converted MR2, the damage estimated at six hundred pounds. (She'd lost no time in getting a quote, enclosed).

Balentine's potted statement added little to Toogood's understanding, although it had been intriguing to learn of the Volvo driver's inconsistent behaviour – unperturbed one minute, twitchy to the point of beating a hasty retreat the next. He'd need to cross–refer Balentine's account of that particular episode with PC Dring's personal statement, just as soon as it appeared. Now that he'd had time to reflect upon it, Dring's reference to the aforementioned Volvo – or, as he'd insisted at the scene, a Passat – had been conspicuously vague and at variance with Balentine's confident assertion. Neither party had been in a position to recall more than two registration characters;

furthermore, somewhat frustratingly, these did not tally.

Toogood tackled a fourth milk capsule in the hope of arousing a little life in his drink. What had this imponderable event really been about, anyway? A house–to–house mission would be unlikely to yield much, especially since there were only three registered residencies in the entire vicinity, each inhabited by reclusive cat–obsessed ex–farmers for whom an Omnibus edition of the Archers would constitute high drama. Had Balentine been off–beam with her theory of a limpet no–mark grabbing a piece of the action? And should he now be pursuing a killer who'd systematically expedited two deaths and cavalierly shrugged off the third as an occupational hazard? It was proving hard to resist the notion that he was being personally targeted: after all, the videotaped murder–diaries had been marked for his special attention and this latest instalment had a vindictive whiff to it, too. And what of the resoundingly untimely pile–up of beast–bearing vehicles, just a monkey's foreskin from the site of the helicopter's downfall? Fire–frenzied animals had been released into the open countryside by their catatonic owner, Zoltán Farkas, whose eagerness to assist in their recapture resolutely underlined his innocence. This hitherto overlooked scrap of land had been subjected to unwarranted solicitude in the past fortnight, the presence of a free–roaming cheetah surely the ultimate sacrilege. The gutter–press would have a field day; he could see it now:

Toogood to be true? The jungle drums of Derbyshire claim second victim as daredevil cop crashes among the big–cats!

THE PROPHET AND LOSS ACCOUNT

At least he'd succeeded in muzzling Balentine –
after all, she was as near to being an eyewitness as they were
likely to find, and he'd sensed what a loose cannon she
could be, armed with a loaded tongue, let alone a loaded
pen. On the other hand, perhaps a PR stunt on his behalf
might shake things up a bit? His thoughts became thwarted
by a call; his mobile phone lit up with the words 'Fat
Bastard' emblazoned across it. It was the Chief
Superintendent.

'Toogood, what's that head of yours filled with, eh?
In–growing nasal hair's my best guess! Now, get your lardy
backside on Crimewatch tomorrow night *and get this bloody
mess sorted*. I can't decide who to feed to the cheetah first,
Chanter or Dring – which one's borrowed the family grey
cell *this* week? I've got a flame–grilled, centrifuged copper
on my hands, and I'll have another one soon if you don't
wake up! We're getting some hardcore publicity
already...have you seen the papers? That bitch Balentine's
squealed to the Fleet Street shitehawks: *Crippled reporter sees
off wild animals to bail out redneck plods.'*

The slap of a newspaper striking the table assaulted
Toogood's ears. The headline was even worse than he'd
feared.

'I swear, Toogood, the next paper I read's gonna
have a picture of *me* smiling in it, or you can toss up for
spud–scraping duty with Chanter...Now, what are you
playing at with the Day murders? Why haven't you arrested
that woeful wife of Spencer's yet? Chanter tells me she's as
guilty as a dog that's puked up the cat's dinner. I've a good
mind to come and check out that frigging videotape myself.'

Unsure of which question to answer first, or which insult warranted deflection, Toogood opted for a conciliatory approach.

'Good morning, sir. I apologise for the apparent news leak, but Ms Balentine did receive unequivocal orders from me not to print *anything* pertinent to the case, as she's a material witness.'

'Well, *she* didn't...the big London boys *did*. All of a sudden it seems everyone around here's tuned in their extra–sensory perception with the conniving cow.'

'Ah, well, not necessarily, sir. You see, our mystery psychic indicated to Balentine that *he'd* notified the press, and I can't be held resp...'

'Don't give me that stack of crap, Toogood, just apply the thumbscrews on her, or she'll have you just where *I* would have put you myself – with your balls in a vice.' He groaned a Chief Superintendent–sized groan. 'My squib is damp Toogood, *decidedly* damp.'

Toogood had clearly been on the right track with his idea for a proactive publicity campaign. But appearing on a frontline TV show the following day wasn't quite what he'd had in mind. The phone rang again and shook him from his delinquent deliberations.

'Sir, it's DC Proctor.'

'Progesterex, what do you want? I'm busy extracting my nose from the Chief Super's anus.'

'Very diligent of you sir, I'm sure. I thought you should see this, sir...it's an anonymous email from someone called *The Pigeon*.'

'How can a pigeon remain anonymous, man? Aren't

all pigeons anonymous anyway? Clarify or clear off.'

'I've forwarded it to you, sir. For some reason it had found its way into three of our inboxes – mine, Bruiser's, and Gre...'

'What are you bumbling on about? Get on with it!'

'Well, it's better you read it, sir.'

Toogood's internet firewall was damn near impenetrable from the outside world, and pretty near untouchable even by him. The most benign attachment from his mum would routinely get spam–zapped – hardly the IT equivalent to the bubonic plague. Chanter's slothful arrival was, for once, a welcome sight. He soon had the thing up on the screen. The document was warped indeed, purple prose bordering on amethyst bullshit:

It is with some trepidation and yet, paradoxically, confidence, that I share with you a premonition of grotesque importance. At around nine o clock this evening an event will take place at a point to be found herein [grid reference given]. Its significance is greater than can be immediately apparent to you; indeed, it is only just beginning to settle on my own consciousness. Be assured. This is not some preposterous parody, but the manifest misery of the real in conflict with the <u>unreal</u> – a cynical clash of elements. Three men will attempt to placate nature's screaming obscenities – but their purpose will be hindered by another's: lost creatures, used to warmer climes; mangled death–cradles cast out of the heavens and two souls lost. I speak as one who knows of such matters. See if I don't.

THE PIGEON.

By 6:00 AM the following day Toogood had reached a decision of such magnitude it would warrant stirring his DS. In any case, Chanter was relieved to be distracted from a half–dream already on its fifteenth loop.

'Chanter, I'm appearing on Grimewash tonight and I don't want to look a complete *burk* in front of what's–his–name with the silly parting.'

'I think you'll find it's not Burke any more…he's parted, it's *Toss*, sir.'

'Whatever. Now, I'd rather get pilloried for proclaiming a daring hypothesis that turns out to be slightly flawed than mocked for a cautious one that's partly right, if you catch my drift. There's no point in having a pedigree dog and barking yourself, eh? So, it's time to play our trump card, Chanter: Paula Day. Go and arrest the murderous mare for the unlawful killing of her brother–in–law, just as soon as you've put your pants on and scrubbed your name off tonight's babysitting roster. Flemming won't let me hold off any longer, and besides, her arrest constitutes the central plank of our plan. And don't forget to ply her with PACE, will you.'

'So, what *does* our master plan comprise exactly, sir?' indulged Chanter, pleased at last to have been given a job worthy of his sorely underestimated resources.

Toogood let out a mighty sneeze and promptly descended to a chest voice.

THE PROPHET AND LOSS ACCOUNT

'I'm going with Balentine's phoney psychic, or should that be demented mentalist? Anyhow, the way I look at it, Paula's not guilty of Spencer's murder, only his brother's, but our necromantic Nostradamus – whose recording we'll play on air – is indubitably a key player in *both* slayings. And only a person capable of stage–managing the audacious bunch of 'coincidences' that occurred two nights ago could conceive of 'predicting' such an event publicly. The fact that he chose the same godforsaken spot as he'd used to tip Spencer's body shows he's enjoying rubbing our noses in it. Well, if he wants publicity, he can have it, with bells, knobs and whistles. What's more, I'm banking on him being responsible for cooking up both videotapes – whether Paula *knew* a second copy of hers ever existed is anybody's guess – I suspect not. But anyway, there's got to be some discernible link between those two slime–balls. That'll be something we have to drag out of her, assuming tonight's programme doesn't flag up anything. I'll put the feelers out for the whereabouts of the mysterious maroon car – why couldn't that fool Dring have been a bit more compos mentis, particularly since it was on his say so the whole damn fiasco kicked off?'

'Yeah, I've got to say I'm intrigued by young Dring's rôle in all this, sir. I mean, when he called me up at the ten–pin bowling he rattled on about an Andrea...Andrea...um'

'Watkiss. You know, the precocious twat wrote in his statement that he didn't want to "presuppose my support", and that's why he went it alone! Can you believe it! – as if I wouldn't have listened to one of my own men on something as important as that.'

Chanter smothered a chortle.

'I've a good mind to reprimand him formally when this is all done and dusted; the man's about as much use as an ashtray on a motorbike, and a bloody liability besides' Toogood continued. 'And having him larking about in the countryside showing off his polka–dot boxers isn't exactly strengthening my prospects for promotion either. Yep, it's off to the Gulag for the silly sod...my flabber has been well and truly ghasted.'

'Quite. And he seems strangely coy about this Watkiss bird now, sir; he reckons she didn't leave a contact number, and he's not even got a proper record of what she said to him. Twat.'

'To think that Sean Hewitt *died* on the back of this tit–head's titbit!' bellowed Toogood. 'When we catch this tricky bastard he'll swing for Hewitt, too, as I live and...breathe.'

He coughed like a beagle and sneezed twice as loudly.

'So, you'll be requiring my suave self on the show, naturally, sir?' piped Chanter optimistically.

'Yes. You'll be on the phones, Chanter, and we'll need four or five others, too. Choose a few of our less cretinous brethren would you, *not* Progesterex, and make sure they wear suits – no lilac T–shirts, they'll play havoc with the lights. I'll be in hair and makeup from seven–thirty...*aah–tish–ooo*!'

Chanter braced himself for the arrival of a second extravagant sneeze, but it must have taken a wrong turn.

'Should I question Paula, sir, or wait for you?'

'Well…yes, all right. She might respond to a different face. She most certainly didn't fancy mine. But don't mention the video evidence unless her solicitor demands to know our M.O. I'll be making an oblique reference to it tonight of course, but she's not to know that. Remember, we know we've got *her* bang to rights; it's her psycho–psychic–sidekick we're after…or should that be pseudo–psychic–*shite*–nick?'

His lungs rattled like frozen peas scattered over a kettledrum.

'Anyway, I don't really see her coughing up anything juicy on him, but keep me informed, preferably before Swine Flu claims its first copper.'

Another succession of abysmal barks tumbled down the phone.

'I'll be in the studio on and off during the day, sorting out mug shots and aerial footage with Nick the pri…'

'*Vick* might be a smart move sir…we don't want you snuffing it on camera – I'd have to take over, eh sir!'

'Over my dead body, Chanter.'

It might have been Giuseppe's oddly crystallising powers of psychic perception that impelled him to watch television a little before 9:00 PM – that, or the fact that he'd picked up a cloaked reference to a certain phone–in 'edutainment' programme embedded in the News of the World article. Given the absence of brain–mulching beverages the team, now fully assembled, huddled around Felix's laptop. Plugged into his phone, the machine's freshly installed iPlayer began grinding and glitching away inadequately in response to the pixel–fest climaxing on the fifteen inch screen. Nick Toss tossed off his usual saccharine greeting before issuing a trailer of the upcoming features. First they'd endure a catalogue of brutal batterings, rampant rapists and feckless thieves, as well as the usual crop of crap–headed crooks holding up banks, who could hardly be shocked at having been captured on videotape, a technological advancement that narrowly predated the Pill.

Felix's phone rang in the middle of an exceptionally riveting lost 'n found section featuring, among other crimes against humanity, four recovered box–sets of Engelbert Humperdink LPs – surely better lost in someone else's collection than found languishing mischievously in one's own?

'Hi Clay, what's up?...Really? You don't say...We're all sat here watching it, as we speak. What?...*When*?...okay, speak later, mate.' He terminated the call, purposely ignoring Frankie's inquisitive eyes.

'Well?'

'He didn't say' quipped Felix, receiving a punch to the arm for his trouble and a slobbery nose, care of Wagtail III, the animal's salt deficiency having outstripped her new owner's production rate.

'Clay's been reading about the Crimewatch programme online. Our story's on it boys!...they're saving it 'til last!'

'Holy bullshit in a bagel' sighed Giuseppe, reaching for his can of Red Bull.

When at last the feature started it caught them all by surprise. For the first section comprised videotaped footage of the vehicle pile–up that had, quite by accident, coincided with the 'event proper'. Frankie's van, smacked flat at both ends, headed a train of mangled metal that stretched perhaps thirty yards in a crescent shape around a compact wooded area, racked with inferno and under siege by a team of fire–fighters. Underscoring the action, Toss's commentary emphasised the improbable setting, the convoy's wilfully bizarre choice of route and its hazardous cargo of live animals. An abrupt switch of camera revealed mayhem of altogether more cataclysmic proportions. A police helicopter, clinging impossibly by its twisted feet from a clutch of disintegrating oak trees, was discernible only by two fragments of its blade, which resembled a pair of casually parked skis, pointing in the direction of the hole in the sky the machine had once fitted into. Yet the more captivating the film became, the less excited Toss contrived to be; he evidently *didn't* give a toss until finally the remains of the enfeebled flying machine collapsed the last twenty feet to the ground, when even he felt moved to raise his voice to the level of a laryngitic croak.

Toss turned and addressed the somewhat less telegenic man at his side, grey suited and severe in appearance, the fingers of one hand nervously toying with the end of his ill–chosen tie.

'Now, Detective Inspector Toogood, of Derbyshire

Police, your first indication of, what shall we call it...*imminent misadventure?* at this rather random, remote spot, some eight miles south of Buxton, came at around eight o clock on Thursday last, I understand – when a rather curious message came in to you.'

'That's not *quite* accurate, Dick. Actually, one of our men had fielded a call from a woman claiming to be a psychic a few days before that, but the information she'd offered – and we've not subsequently been able to pin down her identity, unfortunately – was simply too sketchy to set wheels in motion. We kept a watching brief, of course.'

Toss's confusion was entirely forgivable, since Toogood had gone off script from his opening breath.

'Ah, right...so this caller *wasn't* the writer of the email you're about to tell us about then, Detective Inspector?'

'Precisely, Dick. The email you're referring to didn't materialise until *after* the traumatic events of the Thursday night. We don't get many unsolicited emails from the "outside" carbon–copied to specific officers, as you can imagine, so this was in itself a source of mild consternation for us. More interesting however, was what the author was taking such pleasure in forecasting...an episode laden with imponderables – a line–up of coincidences and incongruities to sex–up any soap drama. And yet...*very* regrettably...this led to one of our officers paying the ultimate price. Unlike our anonymous caller, the motivation of our email author now seems chillingly clear.'

At that moment, instead of switching to a heartrending screenshot of the recently deceased Sergeant Sean Hewitt in full regalia, his dog 'Tigger' drooping loyally at his side, a mackled photograph of PC Dring and Dr. Rick Aldhaus masquerading ineptly as a pantomime horse appeared on the monitor screens. Toogood didn't spot the faux pas since he was busy extricating a copy of the email from his pocket, but Chanter, buried among the telephones a few yards away, did. He couldn't stop himself.

'Shit!...Sir, that's not Hewitt, it's that boneheaded *Perry Dring!*'

The camera swung around in time to capture the exasperated Chanter, still pointing to his monitor, receive a vituperative throat–cutting gesture from the Producer. But Toss's dispassionate tone quickly restored poise to the proceedings; he motioned to Toogood to get on with it. The officer complied. In an attempt to soft–pedal his officer's outrageous gaffe, Toogood suddenly took on an inappropriately upbeat tone, managing to make the email sound more like a recipe for truffle pâté than a premonition of death and disaster. Toss raised his eyebrows, strangely moved by the policeman's perfunctory oration.

'Right, so, as a *premonition*, then, it clearly failed...since your officers weren't able to access the email until the following day...and yet, evaluated purely in terms of its *content*, the person signing himself off as "the Pigeon" seems to have rather hit the nail on the head, Detective Inspector.'

'Well, yes...I'm reliably informed by those who make it their business to know these things, that the email had indeed been sent at about eight o clock on the night in question; the sender's web address is still being tracked, but realistically, we're not too hopeful of anything in this direction.'

Toss leaned back and stroked the full length of his glorious blond hair, while striking a screen–friendly grin for the benefit of the female viewers of a certain age with a space in their hearts vacated by the mysterious disappearance of Richard Clayderman.

'Now, I should say at this point, that Crimewatch had planned to screen a re–enactment of another story tonight, the prequel to this *coup de theatre*, if you will, which caught the public's imagination a week or so ago. It concerns the strange disappearance of a flagitious criminal well–known to the police by the name of Spencer Day, and his even more perplexing reappearance – dead, burned...and *naked* – in precisely the same spot as the horrendous event we've just featured. Now, Detective Inspector, in a nutshell, perhaps you could explain for the viewers the basis for the police associating these two odious incidents?'

'Certainly not, Dick...you see, I'm afraid a *third* ongoing case is tied to the two you've just mentioned. I am, however, pleased to report some progress. We today arrested a person in connection with the brutal, unlawful killing of Spencer Day's *brother* Neil, also, eh hem, known to us. The extent to which the alleged murderer is otherwise involved in these, er, other cases, can only be ascertained in an atmosphere of calm containment – that is, in the Nick, Dick...'

'Thank you, Detective Inspector' Toss nodded, turning to camera two, teeth twinkling like fake pearls under the studio lights. Tilting his head and leaning toward the camera a little, it was clear Toss had reached the moment of nitty–gritty.

'Now, we need *your* help at home. First, to track down an old car spotted at the scene around the time of the explosion. We think it's a Passat CL, but it might be a Volvo Estate 740 GL....maroon or burgundy in colour...take a look at these images. But there's a much more significant lead we're confident someone out there can help us to reel in: we've a recording of our sinister Svengali's telephone conversation with...a certain female reporter, in which he summoned her to witness the scene, only a couple of hours or so before the incident itself began to unfold. Remember, first the police were sent a "psychic's" ominous email, and shortly after unexpectedly hit gold, capturing the man's voice on tape. And now, now we need to put a face, or better still, a *name*, to this egotistical individual – preferably *before* he gets around to predicting the collapse of Nelson's Column on New Year's Eve, eh, Detective Inspector? I take it you *are* considering the writer a key suspect in this, er, *these* cases?'

'We certainly are, Rick...premonitions or *premeditations*? – that's the question. Is our man the visionary he claims to be, acting out of magnanimity, or merely the frivolous purveyor of a self–fulfilling prophecy? And, now that he's shown us the brutal reality of his vision, *where is he*? Is he satisfied with his achievement as it stands, or will he crave applause commensurate with his perceived acceleration in stature?'

Toogood's unexpectedly erudite enunciations brought a glint of surprise in his host, who was used to bailing out stumbling constables and defective detectives.

Extracts of the telephone conversation were played, with Andrea Balentine's abrasive interjections electronically obliterated.

Ten paces away, out of shot, Chanter's men were being kept busy manning the lines while playing silly buggers, girning at each other in the hope of soliciting an incriminating laugh. Early indications were that the pseudonym 'Pigeon' was itself more enticing to the viewers than the psychic's chalumeau tones or the doom–laden prophecy he'd so carefully explicated. Pigeon–fanciers across the Isles rushed forward to register their nominations, and even before the programme had wound up, Toss had declared a pigeon embargo and reaffirmed the seriousness of tracking down a real man for his very real crimes. As the credits rolled, DC Chris Pellow, living up to his sobriquet 'Crimewatch' by achieving a prodigious second appearance on the said programme in under three months, couldn't resist a smile and a wink to his mum, a sin for which he would be disproportionately ostracised in the BBC canteen, where the gang of reprobates quaffed coffee prior to shooting the live Update programme at eleven.

They reinstalled themselves in the studio in time to relieve the 'B' team, one of whom had just dealt with an anonymous caller who was not only able to put a name to the tape–recorded voice, but also suggest an address, postcode and a mind–bogglingly comprehensive gamut of personal minutiae. Toss, propping up a monitor with his tie contrivedly loosened and hair unconvincingly dishevelled, clearly thought the call was too good to be true. But Toogood was in no mood for softly–softly.

400

'The thing is, Rick...'

'It's *Nick*, actually, Constable Slowgood' quipped Toss, not in the least bit amused that someone of his own generation didn't appear to know who the hell he was.

'The thing is, Mick, what's the point of asking the public to come forward with detailed information, if we then treat it with kid gloves? I've a good mind to coax a confession out of the tricky bastard, live on the programme!'

'Um, we *won't* be going there, Detective Inspector...we're not at home to Mr Cockup on *this* programme. This isn't the Antiques fucking Roadshow you know...besides, we haven't come so far just to fuck it all up, big style, now have we?'

Toogood appeared visibly shaken at Toss's easy descent into Saxon vernacular.

'Patience is a virtue what will not 'urt you' pontificated Chanter, nodding wisely and receiving an unguarded scowl from his boss, who was lining up a battery of reasons to whip him to within an inch of his pension.

'I recommend we say something suitably anodyne and "BBC" along the lines of "police are already following up a particularly promising lead and are hopeful of a positive outcome in the not too distant future"' Toss trotted off, himself a consummate master of fluvial flannel.

The Crimewatch Update programme, all twenty minutes of it, evinced little, aside from a robust denial from the President of the Passat Owner's Club that the CL Estate bore any resemblance to the Volvo GL, and a swipe from the editor of the News of the World who'd been anticipating reciprocation for his back–handed heads–up that morning. CS Flemming could fish for his photo now.

15

The Day-Nouement

Needless to say, the dirt on Gideon Pee had been dished by Felix, the promulgator making use of Giuseppe's ambiguously registered mobile and dampening his voice with a tea–towel. The TV programme had played right into their hands. Not only had Pee been foolish enough to attract nationwide attention to himself and his impertinent presentiment, leaving traces of himself he'd have no prospect of covering over later, but he'd done a better job of deflecting attention away from Felix's blasé posse than they could ever have accomplished by any bean–spilling letter to Toogood. Pee had quite literally queered his own pitch – and then pissed on his own parade for good measure. But a question was niggling Felix, a question not dissimilar to the one Detective Inspector Toogood had posed so eloquently, live on the TV show: *where the gibbering giblets was Gideon Pee now?* For a man keen to bring on the heat he was behaving decidedly coolly. How might the man conceivably disentangle himself from his self–inflicted impasse with the police? Felix felt little inclination to call him – why give him the satisfaction?

Felix mulled over Pee's predicament as he availed himself of a generous pipe–full, enshrouding the small space in a fragrant fog. Assuming he was right about the order of events leading from Pee's discovery of the canoes to the psychic's diabolical attempt to incriminate the Pirellis by luring them to an audience with the police, had Pee allowed himself any manoeuvrability? Surely the very paraphernalia he'd used to fabricate his premonition – his hot–headed email to the police – now served to bind him to it? But all the same, while the psychotic psychic remained at large, he continued to be a menace and threat. The sooner Pee's in the pudding the better.

But Giuseppe's solution was more pragmatic than Felix's inclination to sit it out and wait for the police to round him up: do a deal with the conniving little bastard.

'A deal!' shrieked Felix, 'you must be crazy! *Deals* you do with ordinary, reasonable human beings, like the guy who's flogging you his conked–out karaoke machine – not some maniac who's come a gnat's gonads away from screwing you over to the cops for homicide, just to boost his poxy stage career!'

'Well, you can also do deals with people who find themselves unexpectedly on the back foot, Felix' responded Giuseppe. And Gid's the kind of creep who'd happily broker his mum's false teeth if it meant he got to eat her

404

toffee–apples.'

'Yeah, but Pee doesn't know that we've just given him a dose of his own medicine and shopped him to the police, does he? No, we're not doing any deals...this Pee is about to get pulverised!'

A shocking number of serial killers are driven to revisit the scenes of their crimes. A horrifying number of arsonists are compulsive voyeurs, their handiwork all the more satisfying when observed anonymously among awe–struck, tutting bystanders. Gideon Pee was hardly likely to miss his own party, even if he couldn't be sure who else would be in attendance, or quite what mischief they'd be capable of. And if anyone had bothered to investigate a little closer the area fractionally north of where the double wall of fire had raged in that stricken field, a location Pee really *had* prophesied, down to the nearest degree in fact, something else just as ghoulish would have been discovered. But, there again, the safest place to deposit your cash is in the bank that was robbed yesterday, and the safest plane to fly in is the one nearly hijacked a month before. You look in a tree only if you expect to find something, or someone; but if you don't, well, you don't.

And for these reasons, along with others that could only flow from a mind twisted enough to conceive of them as plausible, the body of Gideon Pee rested where it had done for the past forty–eight hours. It was now but an empty sack, drained of life, sapped of its vital fluids. It was suspended in the stratospheric branches of a lonesome larch, draped over the hardier leaves that scrounged the sunlight, but strangely self–conscientious, like a besieged bat that had forgotten it couldn't see itself. As a small boy Pee hadn't seemed to notice how removed from his own viewpoint others viewed him – yet even then he'd craved the chance to proclaim to the world his unworldly visions. But the painful, inescapable truth was that he'd never predicted anything, never caught a glimpse of a ghost nor sniffed a haunting. He'd longed to tiptoe past the hallowed line, to take some fleeting communion with a compliant spirit. But Pee would have to settle for the next best thing: he would become a professional predictor of things passed, a false prophet in the truest sense. The hardest person to convince is yourself, and yet at times he'd come close to it during those sickeningly cynical performances that formed his sham of a career, staged for the stage.

But on that one occasion, for the briefest spell, he'd accidentally tuned in to the frequency that had for so long crackled intermittently at him, calling him, luring him to heed his manic mission. His vision, lasting barely the duration of a cup of tea and a soggy Hobnob, would linger long enough to enable a partial data download. Not that it had equipped him to predict his own frightful fate: to ebb away pitifully, shrugged off by the cold shoulder of a tree. There's no consoling the man who finally gets what he's prayed for, although ultimately, Pee might have considered his demonic demise a quid pro quo par excellence, a price worth paying for his tour de force – except for one tiny flaw in his scheming: it hadn't actually worked.

For Gideon Pee had never remotely contemplated framing Giuseppe. Indeed the delirious phone call to his old cohort two nights earlier had been the warning from a friend, not the omen of an enemy. He hadn't connected Spencer Day, let alone the man's ritualistic humiliation, with the pathetic con he'd once intended to vilify on stage; no thought could have been further from his mind. He had simply glimpsed at a few frames of tumult, like catching some implausible trailer for an impending disaster movie. But Pee had been swift to respond to his madly coherent vision, promptly preparing his trumped–up email for the police and picking Andrea Balentine to be his messenger, not that she'd the slightest intention of furnishing the police until the story had already played itself out, for she'd have her own selfish little agenda to finesse. Her pathetic little rag, the Derbyshire Chronicle, had indulged him in the past with its harmless little pre–performance splashes, so he'd counted on the craggy hack rising to the challenge of his story, albeit decidedly bizarre and anonymously conveyed on this occasion; and if she covered the story, there was a chance the Fleet Street boys might, too. By 6:55 he'd installed himself in his treetop hidey–hole, just ahead of the other reckless pieces playing out this surreal game of chess. For this would be the perfect vantage point to survey the unfolding mayhem. His Blackberry would take a further sixty–six minutes to puff the email up into the ether. Here he would meditate, unaware of the ulterior motives set to collide with his own. It was fitting that not one of

Toogood's apathetic team got around to checking their inboxes until the following morning, for if they had Pee might now be alive and incarcerated, a far worse humiliation than the one he'd actually suffered.

If Chimera had still been famished she'd hardly have waited so good–naturedly at Frankie's feet that night. But she'd had her fill and she'd done all the tree scaling her cooped up body was willing to countenance. Pee's scent had established itself more firmly, somehow – or perhaps naked ambition is more pungent than raw fear? The animal had stalked and aggressed her man in seconds; Pee's damp squib of a prophecy had cost him, literally, an arm and a leg, and ultimately, his sad little life. Hoisted by his own batard. The wounds had been far from pristine, the limbs scythed with crushing carnassials, not prised evenly from the sockets, and the bloodletting had been wistfully wasteful. Pee's screams had been valueless, mercy not abounding in an emancipated wildcat used to the conditional pity of circus life. The beast had taken her meal and moved on to the next putative meal – Frankie – squatting not so far away in his own tree; and here she could show patience, if not mercy.

Paula Day never did get to see herself on videotape. She had no desire to relive the inadvertent slaying of her outlawed brother–in–law; for the very mention of the misappropriated tape was sufficient to shrink her to the state of a snivelling wreck. Chanter had expedited the interview with little cunning in the absence of his boss, whose blustering over the Crimewatch appearance belied a sick–inducing passion for treading the boards. Paula's confession to Neil's murder was achieved in the form of a dismissive motion of the hand and a single resigned grunt. She'd been in no mood to flesh in details, and had no appetite for Chanter's derby of hobbyhorses. It wasn't until a further twenty–four hours had passed, by which time Toogood had put in a reluctant appearance, that she'd come to her senses and demanded to view the 'first' videotape, with regard to which Chanter still harboured hopes she'd played a pivotal rôle.

Chanter himself had forgotten quite how appalling a scene its faceless creator had sought to capture, and yet conversely, how breathtakingly ham–fisted the 'execution' itself had been executed. Paula Day watched uncomplainingly and paused, motionless, for some seconds after it had ended. She showed hardly a trace of surprise or curiosity at what was unfolding, let alone the frenzied enthusiasm that had characterised the second video. She asked politely to see it a second time, and this time took a few notes. She turned to her solicitor, grinned unattractively and garbled something incoherent, turned back to Toogood and set upon him in a tone as black and jagged as her smoke–tainted teeth. For this was a paradigm shift exposing a strikingly transformed Paula Day, reconditioned and war–ready.

'Detective Inspector whatever the fuck your name

is, a simple request...visit the lockup. Walk on to the *next* one and put your bloody specs on. There's a secret door in there, right? Find it. It'll take you into Spence's *special* place, his *third* lockup...the place he used to hide his *real* stuff. Not that pile of bollocks he left for you clowns to trip over – most of that old tosh was our wedding presents anyway – ha! To think some daft bastards paid good money for that cheap crap. You don't think *he* was that stupid, *do you*? He was smarter than the bloody lot of you!...You won't find much in there now, but that's because you're a *plod–prick*, so you'll be looking for the wrong stuff, won't you? – even though I'm handing it to you on a plate. Look in the wall, the far wall. There are two polystyrene breezeblocks, painted grey and hollowed out at chest height, near the back. Even you lot should be able to find a VCR machine tucked in there – it'll have lights on and it's got TO–SHI–BA written on it. And even *you* should be able to chase the wires from it along the roof and outside to a gap above the swing–over door. There's a camera in there...it's a tiny little bugger, but it works all right, you'll see. Spence got a bit paranoid in his old age, yeah? So he rigged up his own pretty neat surveillance system to keep track of the dozy bastards who thought they were on to him. Well, all right, sometimes they were, but Spence wanted a warning, see?'

'Why might he need a warning, Paula?' enquired Chanter pointlessly.

'Why do you think, you asshole? People thought they were onto him all the time...Spence nabbed some nosey son of a bitch just a few days before he...disappeared actually. He didn't tell me much about it, except that he'd gone up there to check on stuff and sussed that he'd been followed. He clocked the registration though – and anyway, the camera takes a shot of anything outside the lockup that stays still for more than five seconds, so he knew the little twat would be caught on it, as sure as eggs is bacon, as you feeble coppers like to say.'

Paula shuffled herself into a position from which scratching her armpit was more feasible and paused for a response that never came from the two nonplussed officers.

'Anyway, next day, Spence checked the tape and right enough, some little weasel had been poking his snout about. So he got hold of the driver's address from the reg plate...it was a synch...yeah, it ain't just you lot that can trace that shit you know. He went to the bloke's house, and there he was, the twat who'd followed him! Spence roughed him up a bit like, nothing too serious, mind – he reckoned he was going straight didn't he, ha! And my name's Winifred frigging Atwell, sure...I told him he'd never make it...a bit like me and these sodding things.'

Paula flicked open her cigarettes and set one alight, consuming nearly half of it in a single draw. She slammed her lighter down on the table unexpectedly and snarled at Chanter with acid about to drip from her bloodshot eyes.

'You need to get that frigging tape, right! Check it...and do it properly yeah, or I'll have my Brief do it again for me.'

A cocky grin settled on her plump, sweaty face. She extended her index finger and motioned a screw–loose gesture above her right ear.

'You'll be amazed how many people stop and nose

411

about outside a boring old lockup...you should get one for *your* place Sergeant, ha! – it would freak the *shit* out of you!'

She calmed herself and refocused, dividing her next comment equally between Chanter and her portly, deadpan solicitor with new capriciousness in her eyes.

'Anyone acting suspicious between then and when Spence snuffed it's got to be your man. I suppose *I'll* be on camera, too...not that I could give a toss, not much point now, is there?'

She sparked up another Silk Cut and pushed a mushroom cloud in Chanter's face.

'Look, I'm going on the level here, yeah? God's truth, I ain't got a fucking clue who knocked up this tape. It's kids' stuff – look at it, it makes mine look pro and I wasn't even *trying*. I always knew Neil had it in for Spence...the jealous bastard...I'd have killed the bugger anyway, just for being an ugly half–wit.'

Toogood leant on his forearms and scratched his head.

'So, it's a case of get your revenge in *first*, eh Paula?' he asked rhetorically, not waiting for long enough to incur the wrath of the sweating brute.

'Let's presume for a moment that your supposition – that Neil killed Spencer – is correct. Now, *you* were the one who videotaped Neil's dying moments, correct? And you told my colleague that you had no accomplice, right? I don't suppose you gave Neil advance notice of what was going to happen to him up in that god–awful lockup, did you! And *he* didn't pop it in the post to us afterwards, on his way down to Purgatory, *did he*?'

Toogood took an ostentatious slurp of his tea and continued.

'If *you* don't know who hated you enough to stitch you up, Paula, we're not likely to, are we? Help yourself out here, why don't you?'

Paula heaved her unmistakeable breasts and bellowed formidable fumes, squinting at Toogood through the mist.

'Look, I'm telling you straight, I've never seen this pile of crap before. I only ever had one copy of *my* fucking tape, and I've got that at home...I'll show you it if you don't believe me...how you've got your hands on it I...hang on, let me take a look at it...the tape, give it to me.'

Chanter caught Toogood's eye and shrugged his shoulders.

'We've got another copy of it, sir...might as well let her see it.'

He extracted the videotape and placed it in front of her. She picked it up, looked at it and turned it over, shaking her head disdainfully.

'There you are, see, I didn't eat it, *did I?*' she said, the look on her face signalling she could devour it and anything else within reach at any moment. She turned to the po–faced pot–bellied lump at her side and, using startlingly elegant language, instructed him to arrange delivery of the original videotape from her home. The man nodded leisurely and stretched open his anus–mouth for the first time.

'Since Mrs. Day would hardly have incriminated herself, it's clear the person who laid his or her hands on the *second* videotape in your possession was also responsible for *shooting* the *first* one. My client's position is thus perfectly tenable, Detective Inspector, and entirely consistent with the statement she made to your Sergeant yesterday. She admits to filming herself killing Neil Day, while acting on the assumption he'd just executed her husband – grounds which it's conceivable, incidentally, some jury members might consider extenuatory. Furthermore, she'd hardly have gone to such lengths to commit a reprisal murder if she herself had been responsible for the *first* one. Would she, Detective Inspector? The fact of the matter is…'

Toogood affected a body–swerve. 'In my experience, when a Brief confidently prefixes his assertion with the words "the fact of the matter is", he comprehends not the subtle margin separating fact from *fucked*, and would do well to reserve his fucked facts for an audience of comparably enfeebled intellect. At this stage, *I'll* do the supposing, guessing and conjecturing, Mr Ponsford, although I'd accept there are reasons for taking in a wider perspective, at this stage.'

◎

The prospect of two new videotapes strained even Chanter's capacity for techno–detail. Alone, sat late in the inhospitable Audio–Visual Aids chamber he reviewed Paula's copy first, retrieved from her home just as she'd indicated. The videotape was identical in dimensions and vintage to the version they'd been couriered, with one salient exception: it was blank. He wound it through to each end, just to be sure. Completely blank. Next, he slipped the VHS tape that had just been recovered from Spencer Day's third lockup into the carriage and began a mind–boggling journey through the neighbourhood's cats and dogs, vagrants and other colourful misfits. Paula had been right about its peculiar effect on the senses – it ran a close parallel to an episode of Big Brother, simultaneously compelling and yet utterly, utterly mind–numbing. There was no video footage at all, just a trillion still–shots. The lack of connectivity continually jolted Chanter from his impulse to pack up, go home and lose himself in a plate of steak and kidney pudding. It was a pity there was no time–marker on the tape, and frustrating that lengthy chunks of it had become so worn that the footage had become virtually impossible to evaluate. The miniscule camera's depth of field had been impressive, especially since it had been fixed permanently to a rotting facia. And yet the scope of the on–board flash was contrastingly limited, allowing the capture of discernible faces only when a person happened to oblige by holding his face full on, close up and still. This trimmed down the gallery to a dozen or so images worthy of following up.

One face in particular cropped up several times in the space of a few days however, the only clue to the timescale being the number of nights Chanter surmised had lapsed through the nocturnal amblings of a particularly habit–prone tabby cat. The man, in his late thirties perhaps, with vaguely Italian features despite a jutting lower jaw,

415

projected a slightly nervous character; no doubt he'd have been more nervous still had he known he'd been in the queue to meet the wrath of Spencer Day, let alone Paula. And yet, conspicuously, Paula's arrival was missing; she must have moved like lightning that stormy night, chivvying her brother–in–law along death–row with god knows what vile weapon sticking in his ribs. Three other figures, males, possibly middle–aged, would have been intelligible but for the torrential rain that had gushed unfailingly across the corrugated roof and over the lens. Chanter cast his mind back to the weather over the past couple of weeks. Mandy would know, she could always remember; the area of her brain given over to monitoring birthdays and anniversaries was also capable of storing away weather patterns with shocking reliability.

Chanter's sporadic thoughts were headed off by Toogood's desultory entrance. Two minutes worth of the lockup pictures was all he was prepared to endure.

'If the bloody camera had been facing *inwards*, perhaps we'd have something worth troubling ourselves over. As it is, we've got what amounts to a peeping tom's jigsaw puzzle, with half of the pieces missing and no flamin' image to work from. Great. What's on Paula's tape then?'

'Jack Shit, sir. As blank as a leaf–blower's bonce. Actually sir, I've a theory about that.'

'I rather suspected you might – and by the way, I happen to know one or two leaf–blowers who can play a pretty mean Bach Chaconne if push comes to shove. I've told you a million times, Chanter, don't exaggerate.'

Chanter gathered himself up for a stalwart effort,

lowering his eyes towards the petite cassette case lying open on the table.

'Sir, Paula accepts we have a pucker copy of the videotape capturing her murder of Neil Day, right? Significantly, having commanded her solicitor to retrieve the original, she's not actually insisted on reviewing it. Odd, don't you think? And, unlikely as it seems, there's bugger all on the thing! I deduce, with my head in a noose, sir, something beginning with 'L'.... *luddite.*'

Toogood stood with his arms folded and the look of a man forced to attend a Val Doonican concert on his face. Chanter continued, impervious to the consequences.

'Suppose her recording *never was* on the tape she's been holding on to? I mean, if she's not interested in checking *our* copy for authenticity, there's a good chance she's never bothered to watch the original either, sir.'

Toogood shrank.

'So, by a process of *photo–synth–osmostic–paranormality*, about which you've no doubt seen a programme on the Discovery Channel, the image *sprang* from her tape on to ours, leaving no trace of itself on the original. Is that what you're saying, Chanter?'

'Well, not quite – just look at this new gizmo we have here, sir.'

Chanter caressed the top of a sleek 'n sexy–silver Blu–ray player.

'Looks ordinary enough, yes, but it does have one rather natty feature. It'll record what's known as 'direct–to–disc', sir. In other words, films can be saved direct to a massive hard–storage device within the machine itself, thus obviating the need for any portable medium. Posh camcorders can do the same thing these days, too. So, it's possible Paula Day recorded her murder–diary on what she supposed was a tape she'd put inside it, but *inadvertently* recorded the event on the camera itself!'

Chanter tapped the cassette case in order to underline his statement, but Toogood could hardly allow himself to look impressed.

'Great. So, where's the bleedin' camera now then, Watson? And even if we found it, what would it prove about Paula's murder that we don't already know from the tape we *have* got?'

He picked up the open cassette case and balanced it between his two index fingers, then snapped it shut.

'This...*this*...is no open and shut case, Chanter.'

'But the existence of an alternative primary recording source suggests the influence of a second protagonist, does it not?...either acting with or without her knowledge, sir. And this would seem to tie in with Ponsford's point.'

Toogood rehearsed a sigh of resignation at what he knew from bitter experience would likely lapse into a futile argument over pedantic semantics.

'Chanter, for goodness sake man, you've come full circle here...*I* never claimed Paula killed Spencer in the first place – that was *your* dumb idea, based on a tape that had probably been hashed up by the local amateur dramatic society. Do the math, Sergeant – I'd like nothing more than to nail the bitch for...husband–cide, if there is such a bloody thing, but let's face it, she didn't do it! Lateral thinking's one thing, *twateral* thinking's another. I suspect that this Pee plonker is in cahoots with Paula, but I'm buggered if I can figure out what the connection is. She's not even mentioned him – I mean, wouldn't *you*, if you were in her position? I suppose the guy might be a better stalker than he is a psychic.'

'Well, he's certainly more adept at the psychic ruse than cryptic *clues*. "Pigeon" is, of course, almost metathetical…rearrange the letters and add a 'd' to produce Gideon P, that is, *Pee*, sir…thus tying in perfectly with the name our anonymous caller gave us. My idea, sir, is to pretend to Paula that we've not yet watched her tape…then, in front of her, off the cuff like, we make out we're going to do a *comparison*.'

Chanter read from Toogood's body language that he may as well have been ordering chop suey in the Guggenheim Museum.

'The real purpose, of course, would be to watch her reaction when we play an extract of *her* tape. If she knows it's blank, she'll not appear genuinely surprised when there's sweet FA on the thing…eh?'

Toogood had begun retreating inch by inch from the squalid little room just as Chanter was preparing to abandon his strained hypothesis anyway.

'Do what you bleedin' want, Chanter, just leave me out of it…I've got more important things on my mind than playing Paper Scissors Stone with the likes of you. Discovering the whereabouts of this pigeon–brained Gideon Pee character is what we should be doing. The Grimewash mystery caller seems to know more about the

419

man than *I* do about my wife, let alone *yours.*'

'Still nobody at home, sir?' enquired Chanter, sidestepping the jibe.

'No. If Pee's got any sense, he'll be lying low in some overlooked mineshaft in Merthyr Tydfil.'

'Or away with the fairies up a tree house in Glastonbury, sir, waiting for the wind to turn.'

When the wind did finally turn it wasn't just ill, it was bilious and sarcastic. Whether, as Chanter had quipped, the weather in Glastonbury, whipped up by the feverish expectation of its impending festival, had any bearing on the elements in Hollinsclough, coping less easily with its newly ascribed notoriety, was, frankly, improbable. But one thing was for certain: Les Hepleston, farmer and undeservedly put–upon landowner, would not have been anticipating yet another gruesome discovery in his field barely a fortnight after the first. And he most likely wouldn't have done so at all had his arteriosclerosis–endangered hound 'Parkin' not sharpened his nasal powers in pursuit of a dying fox that crisp morning. The blood that had gushed down the gnarled trunk of the larch had by now mostly been pecked away by undiscriminating birds. The residue, a disgusting purple gummosis, had begun to peel artistically, like a lanced silver birch repelling its elephantine skin. The only skin left on

420

Pee's body was that protected from voracious insects by his less than robust attire. He'd not fussed over storm–proof leggings, still wearing the same fashion–holed denims that he'd had on at the time of his fatalistic teatime hallucination. His host's barbarous branches had attacked his bobble hat as if it were a pincushion, and a large thorny protrusion had incised his gizzard, cleanly and impassively, immobilising him in a second, a welcome if unalterable diversion from his conference with the nimble cheetah.

The chunkier branch to his side still suspended a pair of binoculars by its thin plastic strap; it arced gently over the ground, as if still monitoring the space that had been snatched by its owner's unpitying slayer. While Parkin's ascent might not have equalled Chimera's in elegance, it was every bit as effective. A single yank of the man's vacant trouser leg was all that was needed to free the pitiable carcass from its hostile home. It crashed noisily though the blotched lower branches, its limbs barely more plastic than the tree's, and landed spread–eagled, if a man with one arm and one leg can be spread–eagled, the moist turf spattering upwards momentarily. Hepleston stood there, not in shock, as he should have been, but to ignite a cigarette he'd been crafting for some time while humouring the breathless dog in its fanciful hunt. Parkin too was perplexed and affronted, but not traumatised. Pee would win no pageantry, even in this execrable condition. The dog panted hoarsely, sending as much clouded air around him as his owner, evidently too preoccupied by his elusive fox to take notice of any dreary, half–eaten human corpse.

The pair edged away through to a cupreous clearing

and eventually made off in a rust–bucket on wheels in the direction of a favoured watering hole, from where any telephoning of the police Hepleston felt inclined to do would have to compete with the stoutest stout on tap. The time was barely 8:00 AM.

Your average canoe has much to endure: reckless bum–scraping down rocky riverbeds, relentless battering from raving nutters in pursuit of pole position, not to mention being bundled together like fibreglass sharks or reinvented as conversation–piece plant pots in nautically themed pub gardens. But few become deposited so far from their natural habitat only to succumb to chronic snail infestation, fend off an attempt at cremation and become forgotten again, all within a fortnight. Salvatore's vintage canoes had been his pride and joy, a distraction from the paralysing monotony of his job tracking fake cripples on behalf of insurance companies and exposing entrepreneurial benefit fraudsters laying carpets in amusement arcades. He would draw them back into his bosom now, however sorry their state. After all, precious little notice had been taken of them, even though they'd been present throughout this chain of bizarre trials. But Salvatore's act of emancipation would have to wait just a little longer while the police stretchered away an equally incongruous object: a split–Pee, freshly shelled from its pockmarked pod.

THE DAY–NOUEMENT

The scarred terrain would remould itself so easily following the Farkas fracas and fatalistic fire fiasco, absorbing the effect of the conflagration into its corpus as easily as sea–salt on a fisherman's tongue. But whereas the savaged landscape had been pre–programmed to convalesce, the soothsayer's impulsive promulgation could never be shrugged off. Yet Pee's fate would carry beyond his horrifying mauling; he would now endure one final insult for his act of hubris – the posthumous blame for killing Spencer Day, whose sad, charred remains had tumbled to earth as if jettisoned by the captain of an itinerant spaceship, insufficiently uninspired by his company.

Nobody had cared enough to look to the skies for the solution to the conundrum of Spencer Day's reappearance. They hadn't bothered themselves unduly with incongruous bowler hats or plastic handcuffs, canoes or chip papers. Nor indeed had anyone puzzled for a moment on that most key element in any criminal investigation: motive. But who needs a motive when the weight of circumstantial evidence, however preposterous or prefabricated in appearance, is so overwhelming, so utterly eccentric?

The halcyon life that Felix had led until a few weeks earlier had rudely imploded. Suddenly, and without fair warning, it was as though some anonymous celestial being had thrust upon him a perplexing mélange of riddles and responsibilities. It was clear his career in youth work had failed to point up a plausible strategy for coping with *real* life, let alone real death. Nonetheless, he'd risen valiantly to his challenge, facing off his Banquo's ghost of intellectual impotency once and for all. Perhaps through the stimulation of Sicilian Pops, Indian rappers, burnt–out Wagtails, constipated cobras, toy dogs and stool pigeons he could face the cast–iron prospect of tedium with greater fortitude? Even so, he'd still have to face the froideur with his boss, The Bird, this particular species not famed for its mellifluous interludes or convivial nesting instincts. The phone call would last barely thirty seconds, but bring sumptuous relief.

'Mr Bird, I expect I'll be tarred and feathered!' he tittered mawkishly, his bout of foot–in–mouth disease about to get the better of him.

'Felix, you are useless – you couldn't locate your own backside with two good hands and a mirror. Take as much vacation as you like – I hope I don't make myself opaque? Take up topiary…take up line–dancing – in fact, consider yourself *permanently* on holiday, would you? I'm your ex–boss and you're my ex–assistant. Your ex–salary will be re–allocated and your ex–tremely ex–asperating habit of ex–temporising family ex–its can ex–press itself to someone else. I'm ex–*hausted*.'

Felix opened his mouth in order to change feet, but all that came out of it was more suicidal gibberish.

'I suppose a pay rise is out of the question, then?' he

began ill–advisedly, but was intercepted by a dull dial tone. 'Ah, keep your frigging job, you vile twat' he shouted bravely to himself as a cheery shiatsu danced onto his lap, sending boiling tea onto his partly exposed wedding tackle.

...Four days later...

On the cusp of a small industrial estate in Newcastle–Under–Lyme, at around 9:00 in the evening, a fire began to take hold. It didn't need much encouragement, given the helpful breeze strolling past the arsonist's ankles. A tingling sensation worked its way up the young man's spine; he remembered it distinctly now, even after such a long hiatus. The licking sound of the virgin flames worked as cunnilingus on his ears. The fresh magic of the scent targeted his nose and winched up his precarious ego. The man closed his eyes and felt pride hurry through his arteries, for there's nothing quite like giving birth to a happy, healthy inferno. The fire seemed to share the sentiment, screaming and raging to delight the planter of its seed. For Tommy McGuire's combustion compulsion, long consigned to a gang of disaffected grey cells, had broken free, quickly signing up new hoodlums in preparation for rejuvenated attacks. The targets for his infernal infernos would have little significance for him; he was free to fantasise again –

that's all that mattered, or ever did. McGuire's pyromaniac renaissance would bring about another's premature sleep, just as it always had done, when as a small child he and his brother first tasted the tang of sulphur and watched an unstoppable string of garden sheds, caravans and chip shops tumble to powder.

McGuire hadn't set the Constipated Cobra ablaze, though he wouldn't deny it had occurred to him more than once in recent times. Ironically, he'd felt a certain outrage at being short–listed for the job before he'd had a chance to get around to it; that bloody boiler had beat him to it. But now, finally, he'd permitted himself to take the perilously small step from paranoia to pyromania...

Although it was only March there was a tip–off of summer in the air. The sun gnawed at the fidgeting clouds and persuaded them to budge from Wagtail for long enough to register its presence. The forgotten Warwickshire town of Atherstone, canoodling promiscuously with both the Coventry canal and river Anker, had been home to hatters and other mercurial madmen for four centuries. So it would continue to be the perfect spot for Felix, and for a little longer, Frankie too, perched like two old men on the sundeck with cross–stitched blankets wrapped around their knees, supping coffee and smoking cigarettes amid a newfound tranquillity. For there was something uncommonly soothing about this bonhomous existence, its attendant chapishness and prolonged juvenescence tacitly sanctioned. Given the recent demise of Wagtail II – and the prudent renaming of Wagtail I to Gypsy's Kiss – Wagtail III had achieved automatic promotion to Wagtail, and she sported this change to her status with confident aplomb.

The daft dog watched with curiosity as Felix fiddled with his left shoelace.

'You know, it's all about being flexible, mate...for we must all sway to the rubato of life. Ask Chopin, now *there's* a Frog who practised his arpeggios. When you can no longer push the envelope and think outside the box, well, you might as well be *in* the box, if you catch my meaning. I'll give you an example. When you get dressed each morning, you might contemplate defying your Pavlovian reflex of pants first, socks, then trousers and shirt, with the final adornments of tie, jacket and aftershave. Indeed, I propose an alternative to this wearisome pattern, one which embraces the possibility of sock one, aftershave, pants, shirt...with shoes and tie vying for supremacy as the options wane.'

Frankie clearly had never considered such a preposterously protean scheme, but was happy enough to lend conditional support to his friend in his anomalous bid for sartorial freedom.

'Yes, I suppose it's only by re–evaluating our priorities occasionally that we get to notice what they've *been* all the time' he said, only partly confident he'd grasped Felix's point. His hangover didn't need all this soul–

427

searching twaddle. He stood up briefly and rubbed his backside, his face warping. Wagtail wasn't entirely convinced either, tilting her little head to one side as she licked attentively at an area only Dyno–Rod might be plucky enough to probe. Frankie adopted a bemused expression.

'I'd greatly appreciate your considered responses to any of the following three troubling questions, Felix. One: why *does* the sun come up each morning? Two: why *do* hotel bog–rolls have those ridiculous bloody triangle–folds, even when there are only three sheets left on them? And three, most importantly: how come your backside's always the last bit to gain relief from painkillers? I mean, my arse is *thumping*' he winced, 'those Paracetemols are about as much use as a block of tofu in a butcher's fridge.'

'Mm, I quite agree, mate...they should put that in the small print, shouldn't they?' indulged Felix.

A parturient bird settled noisily on the roof and vigilantly made its way along to the unsightly barbecue contraption dominating centre stage, jerking its head like an Egyptian dancer suffering from sciatica. It pecked with little enthusiasm at first, but grew in self–assurance as it detected items of promise within the thing's greasy cradle. It struggled onto a three–legged stool that had been home to Frankie's drying Y–fronts and began its meal. The bird was a pigeon, lonesome and pathetic. It knew it wouldn't be welcomed, but was used to that, suddenly snatching the remaining morsels from the blackened grill and making off as fast as its podgy pigeon body would permit, as if there were any likelihood of being reprimanded for the theft. Felix picked up the empty envelope that Frankie had been using to preserve some treasured rawlplugs of jaborandi and gaped far into the intractable distance. Fillets of cloud were strewn carelessly across the sky.

'There's meaning to everything, you know. The hand you use to pick your nose with isn't necessarily the hand you use to write, or the one you'd pull the bathplug out with. These things slowly become ingrained, filed and cross–referenced in the subconscious filing–cabinet of the mind; not only have they a resonance with past judgements, they help to predetermine future ones, entrenching themselves as long, meandering grooves in the memory.'

'Yeah. History's just one fucking thing after another, innit?' posited Frankie, slightly underestimating the profound randomness of his companion's thesis.

'It's clear to me now, by way of example, that Mr Kasai, your father's one time dentist partner, is, indirectly perhaps, at the root – pardon the equivoque – of all of this; *he* is responsible for three human tragedies and very nearly the cause of *our* ruination. For without his profligate attitude to company marketing, things would not and *could* not have unfolded quite as they did.'

'The man always was a malicious, reckless bastard' confirmed Frankie, staring into the half–distance and exploring his one remaining wisdom tooth with his long, slender tongue. 'Still, we're not exactly whiter than the driven, are we, mate?'

'Well, you know what they say...every saint has a past, every sinner has a future.'

'The future, mm, the future...'

Wagtail apparently approved of the arbitrary

exchange, hopping onto Frankie's knee, smiling and farting lovingly. Frankie lifted a cheek and enriched the effect, mustering a chorus of sackbuts. Felix hardly noticed.

'Our coming together the way we did was, of course, inevitable from the moment you used the Yellow Pages cut–outs to set up your ridiculously piffling card prediction. And my involvement in the whole sad episode, Day by Day, to coin another crappy phrase, sprang logically and unpreventably from that trivial act.'

Frankie nodded dreamily. He wasn't really taking any notice; he was too busy responding to the repugnant riff of his latest Gnarls Berkeley album via earphones aptly the size of aspirins.

'Perhaps, but if you weren't such a bloody nimby, by now Spencer Day would have been semi–masticated by carps in that filthy puss you call a canal, and it might all have ended right there. But no, you had to…'

'*Nimby?*'

'Not in my back yard…'

'…At least I'm not Taps.'

'…*Taps?*'

'Thick as pig shit, mate.'

'Do try not to be so *Pee*–vish, Felix. You talk so much crap' sighed Frankie, realising he wouldn't win this particular ping–pong of invective and hunting unsuccessfully for his treasured lighter. Felix casually retrieved the thing from his pocket and began wantonly discharging it.

'Maybe I do talk garbage, but at least it's biodegradable…I've got a spare one of these, if you want it' he offered, 'they were on a buy–one–get–one–free.'

'Oh yeah…you mean *bogof*.'

Felix's mobile started attention–seeking. The conversation with his brother would be brief, but he got his oar in first.

'Where the hell have you been? *We've* been to hell and back.'

'So have I, mate. Majorca actually. Remind me *never* to go on a pub–crawl with Mum again. I thought *I* could drink. And as for that Pat…the woman's a fish. And to cap it all, Mum's had me painting the kitchen, fixing the drainpipe and god knows what el…'

'I know' smiled Felix, nodding to himself airily.

'Come again?'

'Oh, nothing, just remember to take Maggie's ladder back, yeah?'

Wagtail had been toying with an old bone for about a week. Frankie leaned down to the animal, which promptly dropped the thing at his feet. It was the festering phalange of a human index finger. Felix's eyebrows rose as it dawned on him from whose contorted claw this originated.

'How does it feel to be so popular, mate? Even your frigging dog's giving you the finger.'

The rebuffed pigeon returned briefly, clearly considering a resumption of its reckless insurgence. But the prospect of more charcoaled victuals proved insufficiently inspiring and the tubby bird sped off into nearby trees, releasing a streaming white incendiary into Felix's coffee as it did so. Felix nodded and unflinchingly sparked up another pair of cigarettes.

431

'This past few weeks has been like a freak wrinkle in the millpond of my life' he mused ironically. 'Just when I was beginning to think I'd fathomed a splinter of significance it went and morphed into something even more fucking trivial and temperamental than before...why *do* I bother?'

Frankie smiled unwearyingly and caught a glimpse of Felix's consciousness drifting aimlessly up into the expansive sky. Two wordless minutes passed, Sibelius's Fifth Symphony pumping out harmlessly from below.

'I might grow another beard', muttered Frankie capriciously.

'Mm...the timeless craft of pogonotrophy...So might I' nodded Felix.

Frankie explored his complexion and shook his head disdainfully. Felix peered at him fixedly and raised an eyebrow.

'You learn something every day, you know' he asserted, gently.

'Yeah...usually it's that what you learned yesterday was utter bollocks' muttered Frankie, burping decadently while summoning a meditative pose. 'Now, quit the crap for a minute would you, you're setting my chakras into turmoil again.'

Felix sighed laconically, arching his neck impassively, like an elderly swan. 'Wicked', he murmured, nodding forwards, eyelids quivering.

The pair slept.

THE END

Catinel Cuppediae: Mark Tanner (2009)

The Catinel's pace is chosen (just in case),
It has occasion to show its disinclination.
Mostly aloof, under its makeshift roof
This oddity nurtures an unsavoury sweet tooth.
For a creature so chaste, it's got terrible taste,
Its penchant for fudge not so easy to judge.
It's not that it's picky, more that it savours
Anything sticky, regardless of flavour.
For this little critter could gorge on a fritter
But its appetite would curb at mere mention of a herb.
Neither the sight of wholemeal nor the smell of quenelle,
Is of the slightest appeal to the Catinel...
Sluggish to shift and yet gone in a glance,
Its preference for chocolate (rather than plants)
Leaves it continually miffed that supplies are so short
And so it must steal, as a last resort.
So what of its prospects for love and romance?
For a chocoholic snail, a Catinel's Chance!

www.llamapress.co.uk

Lightning Source UK Ltd.
Milton Keynes UK
24 February 2010

150543UK00001B/77/P